No 4 Slaughter Ackill

PLATINUM

Indulge in the *Platinum* lifestyle at
www.loveplatinum.co.uk

PLATINUM

Jo Rees

BANTAM PRESS

LONDON · TORONTO · SYDNEY · AUCKLAND · JOHANNESBURG

TRANSWORLD PUBLISHERS
61–63 Uxbridge Road, London W5 5SA
A Random House Group Company
www.rbooks.co.uk

First published in Great Britain
in 2008 by Bantam Press
an imprint of Transworld Publishers

A CIP catalogue record for this book
is available from the British Library.

ISBN 9780593058992 (cased)
9780593059005 (tpb)

Addresses for Random House Group Ltd companies outside the UK
can be found at: www.randomhouse.co.uk
The Random House Group Ltd Reg. No. 954009

The Random House Group Limited supports The Forest Stewardship Council
(FSC), the leading international forest-certification organization. All our titles that
are printed on Greenpeace-approved FSC-certified paper carry the FSC logo.
Our paper procurement policy can be found at
www.rbooks.co.uk/environment

Typeset in 11/13.25 pt Palatino
by Falcon Oast Graphic Art Ltd.

Printed in the UK by Clays Ltd, Bungay, Suffolk

2 4 6 8 10 9 7 5 3 1

Mixed Sources
Product group from well-managed
forests and other controlled sources
www.fsc.org   Cert no. TT-COC-2139
© 1996 Forest Stewardship Council

For Emlyn

Hell hath no fury like three women scorned . . .

Rising out of the Arabian Gulf, the Palm Jumeirah was said to be visible from space. A stunning feat of modern engineering, the palm-shaped luxury resort housed thirty-two of the world's most exclusive beachfront hotels, including the Trump Hotel and Tower as well as an assortment of Dubai's most desirable real estate.

And now Yuri Khordinsky had snapped up a controlling interest in the whole damn lot.

It had been a long day: endless meetings with those amusingly dumbfounded American bankers and equally bemused sheikhs who hadn't seen Khordinsky's contested bid coming. But now, as the cloud of Davidoff cigar smoke cleared, the mysterious Russian oligarch allowed himself a rare smile.

'I'm so glad you could visit, my old friend,' he said to Boris Ivanovich Nazin, the effusively impressed Governor of Smolenskaya, as they sat on the starlit terrace at the heart of Yuri's new empire.

'Answer my summons' would have been more accurate than 'visit', Khordinsky thought. Not, of course, that he would ever say this out loud, as he once would have. No, his wife, Natalya, with all her aristocratic breeding, had taught him that.

No, it was sometimes better to let people like the Governor think that they still had independence. Even though Nazin, like many of Khordinsky's menagerie of 'pet' politicians, was just another soldier in his business army. But Khordinsky had learnt long ago that commands laced with charm made people much more effective.

'No, it is I who am honoured, Yuri,' Nazin said.

'So?' Khordinsky said, keen to get back to business.

'The money has been transferred to London, as agreed,' the Governor said, lowering his voice even though he and Khordinsky were alone and the apartment and terrace had been swept for electronic bugging devices. Alone, that is, except for the continual presence of the armed bodyguard by the door. But he was ex-FSB and had been trained not to listen to anything that didn't concern him.

Khordinsky nodded. 'Good.'

The Governor paused, shuffling on the sandalwood chair. 'You know, Yuri, you mustn't return. To Russia. Not even fleetingly. They are waiting for you. And they will arrest you.'

Khordinsky waved his hand dismissively. He'd been forced into exile after a recent flurry of acquisitions had finally shocked the Kremlin into action. The President had even appeared on national television and personally pledged to untangle the web of financial irregularities that had allowed Khordinsky to acquire control of over 70 per cent of Russia's oil and gas reserves and the contracts for the new pipelines to Europe.

But Khordinsky knew he was safe. The President's platitudes to the people were too little, too late. Yuri Khordinsky had outwitted them all. He'd kept his profile low whilst exploiting every loophole and opportunity that the new Russia had given him. He'd raped her assets and got away with it. If anyone was to blame, it was those in power. They were stupid. And he'd punished them for their stupidity.

And now, thanks to the Governor and other supporters like him the last of Khordinsky's money was out of Russia. Not that he would ever let the relief he felt show.

His steely, hooded gaze turned slowly to the Governor. 'I don't need to return, Boris,' he said. And the subject was closed. 'Ah, here are the ladies.'

Natalya Khordinsky, a beautiful but fragile-looking blonde woman, and Yelena Nazin, the Governor's wife, walked through the intricately carved doorway on to the magnificent terrace overlooking the moonlit Arabian sea. Khordinsky let his cigar rest in the ashtray. As he drew himself up to his full height, his imposing frame towered over the Governor's.

The two women had been at school together and were laughing comfortably. Yelena was wearing a pretty chiffon summer dress – so much more flattering than Natalya's conservative grey suit. But then Yelena with all her cleavage on show looked trashy and Khordinsky didn't want his own wife looking like a whore. Not if she was going to make them into respectable members of society.

Because that was what Natalya was going to do. That's why Khordinsky had chosen her. They were going to start over in Northern Europe and they were going to get so connected that nobody would ever dare cast doubt on the Khordinsky name again.

'What are you two gossiping about?' the Governor asked.

'Natalya moving to London, of course,' Yelena answered, a happy

lilt in her voice. She rattled the pretty charm bracelet on her wrist and the diamonds in it glinted in the light. Khordinsky noticed his wife admiring it. Natalya would get more, he decided. A bigger bracelet. More diamonds. To show he was worth more than anyone.

Khordinsky turned his head and stared at Yelena, smiling at her, his eyes twinkling with a challenge that few women had ever been able to resist. For a split second, he saw her catch her breath in the spotlight of his attention. He knew then, as Yelena flushed deeply, her eyes fluttering away from his, that if he were to see her alone, the Governor's faithful wife would be his.

Yes, they were all the same. And that was why he didn't trust women. Any woman.

'And all the shopping we'll do when I visit,' Yelena quickly continued, hooking her arm through Natalya's as if to assert her loyalty to her friend, but both she and Khordinsky knew it was too late. 'Natalya says that you're getting a house right behind Harrods. And, Yuri, a grand house in the Cotswolds as well? Is it true?'

Khordinsky raised his eyebrows and snapped his attention to his wife. Natalya looked down. She knew how much he hated her discussing any of their affairs, even with her best friend. It had taken Khordinsky half a lifetime to construct the elaborate smokescreen that had hidden his business interests for so long from the authorities. Information was power. And he never, ever wanted anyone to have any information about him that he didn't want them to.

'Yes, Yelena. I have a plan to . . . acquire a very nice stately home.' He pictured again the beautiful photographs he'd seen of Wrentham Hall. He'd checked with various sources. It was definitely the most prestigious house in that part of England. The best there was. An ideal place from which to launch himself into English society. That was, of course, once he'd modernized it, decked it out with brand-new furnishings, the finest en-suite bedrooms and landscaped the grounds into a golf course. But all in good time.

'It isn't ours yet,' Natalya said, her voice catching as she tried to cover her mistake.

'Oh?' Yelena said.

'It has some private owners at the moment,' Khordinsky clarified for her. 'An English Lady, no less. But everything is subject to change. So long as the right pressure is applied.'

Again, Khordinsky stared at Natalya and she looked away. He despised her disobedience. He would not tolerate it.

She flinched as her husband prematurely called the evening to a close.

'If you need me, you can stay in touch through Alexei,' Khordinsky said as he and Natalya walked Boris and Yelena back through to the grand entrance of the apartment. 'I've made him Managing Director of Forest Holdings, so he'll be publicly running most of my affairs from now on.'

Khordinsky saw his wife's eyes narrow. Natalya was jealous of Alexei Rodokov, the younger man Khordinsky had trained to be the perfectly respectable face of his business. Jealous of the luxury yacht Yuri had given him; jealous that Yuri spoilt and pampered him as if he were his own son. But it served Natalya right. The day she performed her proper duty as a wife and provided him with a son and heir, then he might reconsider his position.

'How is Alexei?' Yelena asked. 'He seemed such a charming young man when we met him.'

She smiled at Khordinsky, but now as he addressed her his eyes were cold. She was too easy to play. He'd lifted her up and now he let her fall. He watched her shiver of alarm.

'It's his thirtieth birthday soon. I was thinking I might plan a little surprise for him. I would invite you, but I think it will be men only.' He let the comment hang in the air, so that Natalya would be in no doubt as to the kind of entertainment he would be providing. 'And I think the Governor may be . . . indisposed at the time.'

'Yuri is so very generous,' Natalya said. Her voice was barely more than a whisper.

'And Alex is very loyal. As you know, loyalty is the most important thing in life,' Khordinsky replied. 'I prize it above all else.'

'And let me assure you, Yuri, of mine,' the Governor said quickly. 'I shall continue to support you in every way I can. From the inside it might be difficult but . . . but I shall do my best.'

Khordinsky kissed him on both cheeks. He knew, but the Governor didn't – yet – that it was for the last time.

After the Governor and his wife had gone, the bodyguard followed the Khordinskys back into their apartment at a discreet distance. Yuri Khordinsky led Natalya into the bedroom and locked the door. The bodyguard stationed himself outside, rigid and impassive. When the screaming started, he didn't even blink.

CHAPTER ONE

Peaches Gold knelt on all fours on the antique ebony bed and examined her hair for split ends as Valentin pumped her from behind. Thankfully, her trademark chestnut mane was still perfect, but a trim wouldn't hurt. She made a mental note to swing by Rodeo Drive and see Sebastian at the salon in the morning. After all, he often told her she was one of the only five women in LA who he'd waive his six-week waiting list for.

Through the slit in the handmade red silk blinds covering the floor-to-ceiling windows in the penthouse suite of Boulevard 19, Tinseltown's newest – and certainly priciest – hotel, Peaches could see that the sun was already high in the sky. It was sure turning out to be a scorcher.

And it was crazily hot in here too. Peaches wished she could stop for a moment and turn up the air-con, but if Valentin got horny for her in black silk underwear first thing in the morning, hell, she wasn't complaining.

Now that she'd beaten off the competition to become Hollywood's most exclusive madam, it wouldn't be long before Peaches could stop seeing clients herself entirely. But she'd be reluctant to give up Valentin. Thanks to him, over eight hundred and fifty thou had already found its way into Peaches' bank account. Only a few more Valentins and Peaches could retire, sooner than she had planned. Certainly before anyone found out that she was five years older than anyone thought she was.

But then her youthful appearance did seem to be fooling everyone for the time being, thanks to the genius of her best friend, Ross Heartwood, California's most celebrated plastic surgeon. But Peaches knew the score. Ross couldn't keep her young for ever. Besides, she was smart. She was going to get rich and get out. And then maybe she'd really shock everyone and grow old gracefully.

'Yeah, baby, just like that,' Peaches purred, turning her attention to the job in hand. 'Deeper, baby. Oh yeah . . . let me feel it all.'

'My God, I can see why you're called Peaches,' Valentin said, in his gravelly Russian accent. He rubbed the soft skin on her taut buttock appreciatively before giving it some firm slaps.

Peaches flicked back her hair and looked over her shoulder. Valentin stood behind her, holding on to her hips, his teeth clenched, a vein throbbing at his temple. He had shaggy dark hair and his tanned face was pock-marked with bygone acne, but there was a roughness about him that appealed to her.

'You got it, baby,' she said, winking slowly.

He smiled back at her, revealing a gold tooth that matched the thick gold chain nestling in his hairy chest. He leant forward over her, wrapping his arms around her slim waist. His breath was hot and fast through her hair and smelt of the Diaka vodka Peaches had got in especially. Valentin had been excited when he'd seen it – as he should be. It was the world's most expensive vodka, distilled through diamonds. But Peaches lived by her motto: always the best of everything.

'So what you want? You like this, huh?' he asked.

She felt his fingers reach down and graze the carefully sculpted heart-shape of pubic hair and slide down into the hot moist crevasse below. Obligingly, Peaches let out a slow moan. It was important that her clients felt that their efforts were appreciated and not just their money.

Usually, she didn't allow herself to become too aroused. She had to monitor carefully how Valentin was feeling. Make sure that she held back her own pleasure. But she'd seen him quite a few times now and she'd become accustomed to his touch.

Despite the early hour, she felt the familiar tingle spread through her abdomen.

'Oh yes, baby. I like that,' she gasped, wriggling back on to him for a while, before kneeling up and sliding her hand up behind her into his hair.

She could see their reflections in the teak-framed mirror at the end of the bed. With their heads side-by-side like this, there was something about them that looked compatible. In another life, maybe they could have had a real relationship.

'Oh . . . keep going . . . keep going. You're making me want to—'

'But I want to undress you. I want to see all of you,' he said suddenly, pulling out of her and leaning back to undo the hooks on her silk basque. 'This is so sexy, but I need to feel you.'

Bull's-eye, Peaches thought. It had worked. She'd been designing her own exclusive lingerie line with Christoph Zerelli for six months now. Peaches' old friend Monica DuCane, the famously busty soap actress, had agreed to front the whole business, which was Peaches' retirement project.

The silk basque was an experiment Peaches had insisted upon, even though Christoph had claimed it wasn't sexy enough. But Peaches had explained that underwear should be like the best wrapping paper. Peaches knew what turned men on better than almost anyone. And, judging from Valentin's reaction, she'd been right on the money.

She made another mental note to call Christoph and tell him that the basques should definitely go into production. She liked the idea of them in red. The same shade as those blinds, maybe . . .

But she'd think about that later. Right now she watched in the mirror as the basque fell away and Valentin reached around her, his hands massaging her breasts.

Peaches always liked the way her perfectly full double Ds, with their dusky pink nipples, looked in a man's hands. Especially in hands as strong and dangerous as Valentin's.

She was savvy enough to know that young Russian businessmen like Valentin – what was he? A few years older than her? Thirty-seven, thirty-eight maybe? – might not have an entirely legitimate background. In fact, she wouldn't mind betting he had links with the Bratva: the Russian mafia, or Brotherhood, she'd heard talk of. He certainly didn't look as if he'd been born into the money he flashed around. She wondered whether its source would ever dry up, like the rumoured gas pipeline from which it came. Hopefully not in the near future.

Valentin knelt behind her out of sight and, starting in the crease of her bottom, began kissing up her spine. She could feel herself responding to him and began caressing her own breasts now, catching a glimpse in the mirror of her thighs starting to tremble above the lace tops of her hold-ups.

She felt behind her for Valentin's cock, but he ducked out of the way and stopped kissing her. For a moment he examined her back and then, stretching her skin, pressed his tongue hard on to the scar just below her left shoulder blade.

It felt like an electric bolt to her spine. Her whole body seemed to lock.

'It's like a sickle,' Valentin said, intrigued. He ran his finger over the scar. 'Same shape.'

Peaches felt the hot sexual energy that had been seeping through her evaporating. She hated being touched there. She knew that some girls were turned off by their belly-button being touched, or their feet. For her, it was that small scar. It triggered a nauseous feeling in her and the shadow of a dark and terrible memory, just a whisper, a flicker that left her feeling unsettled and confused.

She closed her eyes for a second, beating down the nausea, desperate to focus on the shard of memory. But nothing was clear except the feeling that the scar was connected to her being very young, in an unrecognizable, strange place, surrounded by people shouting in unfamiliar voices. And that whatever had happened there had left her vulnerable and violated. She wished she could remember more. But as always, further details were elusive, and the feeling was gone in an instant.

Was it because her subconscious wouldn't *let* her remember? she wondered. Or had she imagined something sinister when there wasn't anything sinister at all? But still the scar remained. The proof that somewhere, somehow, someone had branded her like a piece of meat.

4

She couldn't stand Valentin touching it any more. 'Don't,' she said, more harshly than she meant to, and jerking away.

'Ah!' Valentin grabbed a handful of her hair. A knowing smile played on his lips as her eyes flashed at his in the mirror. 'You know, if you weren't American, I could swear you have Russian blood in you.'

She quickly pulled away from his grip and turned around to face him, away from their reflection in the mirror. He didn't frighten her, or intimidate her. There wasn't a man in the world who frightened her. Or a man she didn't reckon she could control.

'Where *are* you from, Peaches, huh?'

She didn't answer him. He didn't get to pry for personal details. That wasn't the deal. And Valentin was a fool if he thought he could see inside her. Nobody ever had. And nobody ever would.

This was about sex. Sex he was paying her for.

Still kneeling on the bed and face to face with him, she raised her eyebrows at him and then lunged down and flicked her tongue over the end of his cock. Swiping her hair to one side, she looked up directly into his grey eyes as she held his throbbing flesh in her fist.

'I can be from wherever you want me to be. Do you want me to be Russian, Valentin, huh?' she enquired archly, pulling away from him. His cock, suddenly deprived of her, quivered in the soft lighting.

She slid quickly up the bed, still looking into his eyes. 'You vant me to be your little Russky?' she asked, her Moscow accent perfect as she dramatically spread her legs into sideways splits and touched herself with one hand. They always liked that. An early career in pole-dancing had ensured that Peaches was as supple as a gymnast.

Valentin smiled and, with a deep, lusty laugh, lunged after her. Peaches clenched her perfectly manicured nails into his buttocks, the way he liked it, as they rolled together on the bed.

But then, just as he was about to come, his cell phone bleeped. He growled with frustration as he scrambled off her. He grabbed the phone from on top of the pile of clothes on the velvet sedan.

Peaches hated cell phones and she usually insisted that her

clients turned them off. After all, she cost a hell of a lot more per hour than the best seats at Madison Square Garden. She should be treated with at least as much courtesy and respect. But somehow she'd forgotten with Valentin.

Valentin looked at the number and took the call. He gabbled something in Russian, which she didn't understand, then he waited a moment, and when he spoke again his manner had changed, his voice had become smooth and subservient, as if he were trying to impress someone.

But no one was more important than Peaches. She grabbed the ice-cold vodka from next to the bed and, making sure he was watching, trickled some over her erect nipples. She didn't care about the sheets. That's what maids were for.

Valentin winked at Peaches and said something else. This time, she understood one word, because he wasn't the only Russian client she had. And that word was 'whore'.

That was it, Peaches thought. This guy was toast. After today, she would be giving Valentin up for good, no matter how much he was willing to pay her. He hadn't been respectful enough for her liking. And Peaches required respect.

'*Da. Pushkin,*' Valentin continued, then snapped the phone shut. 'I'm sorry, baby,' he said.

'Who was that?' she asked automatically, even though she knew it was none of her business.

'Yuri.'

'Who the hell is Yuri?'

'Yuri Khordinsky.'

'Oh?' Peaches raised her eyebrows at him. She knew perfectly well who the billionaire Russian was. 'You work with him?' she asked, suddenly realizing how lucrative such a contact could be.

'I work *for* him,' Valentin said, making it clear there was a big difference. He started towards her, clearly anxious to carry on where they'd left off. 'But forget it, I'm all yours now.'

Yet as he slid between her legs and started licking the vodka from her cleavage, Peaches knew the pleasure had gone and she was on auto-pilot.

But even though she was still annoyed, pondering it now, she thought perhaps she *wouldn't* give Valentin up. The guy clearly had good contacts. And contacts were the most

6

valuable currency in Peaches' business because, in one way at least, they made her more powerful than Valentin could possibly imagine.

CHAPTER TWO

Like an untouchable celebrity, the mega-yacht *Pushkin* towered over its competitors. It reeked of class. This evening, moored up alongside the harbour wall in St Tropez, it looked vast, but sleek too. An undeniable statement of power and wealth.

Rumours abounded concerning the sumptuous luxury on board and the amazing parties attended by the world's super-rich élite, even though as yet there'd been no glossy magazine spreads featuring the ten guest state rooms, the lavish saloons and bars, or the sun-decks bursting with jet skis, scuba gear, water-skis and wake boards. Or even the helicopter landing pad on the top deck with its bespoke helicopter in the same stylish midnight-blue livery as the rest of the yacht.

But whilst everyone sipping sundowners in the exclusive club above the Café de Paris on the front admired the elegant spectacle of *Pushkin* and dreamt about being invited on board, they had no idea that on the other side of the sparkling blue hull, deep in the bowels of the yacht, twenty-five-year-old Frankie Willis was folding sheets in the laundry room and longing for a taste of their freedom.

A taste of their fresh air would be a start. The harbour wall might have been only a few metres away from where Frankie was standing at the ironing board, but it might as well have been on the moon.

Frankie changed the playlist on her iPod to some French hip-hop in the hope that it would lift her mood, but it was no good. She still felt like bloody Cinderella.

Would she have been any better off if she hadn't taken the job on board this stinkpot? she wondered as she picked up the hissing steam iron. No. No, she couldn't go there.

She didn't want to think about her old life. About her home back in South Africa. *Pushkin* was Frankie's fresh start. Her way out. Her ticket to a brighter, safer future. Her way to see the world. Her chance to forget all about who she once was, and to discover who she might become.

The only problem was that two months into her fresh start, Frankie was thoroughly disillusioned. It seemed that the closest she was ever going to get to anything remotely inter-esting, or glamorous for that matter, was watching beautiful harbours slip by through a porthole whilst she scrubbed out yet another toilet bowl.

She'd have been better off watching it all on TV.

There'd been guests on board *Pushkin* for a solid month, most recently a group of boring fat Russian businessmen. The first week had been fine, when they were on board with their wives. But then the wives had left and their girlfriends had come instead: a noisy, trashy set of diamond-clad party girls, who left revolting sex toys in the beds and crotchless panties littering the bathrooms.

Whilst they demanded to be taken from one shopping port to another, coming back laden down with designer carrier bags, Frankie hadn't stepped ashore in weeks. Now she truly understood the meaning of the phrase 'cabin fever'. Everything was bugging her: the petty rules, the hierarchy, the excess, the waste and, worst of all, the work. Christ, she'd never worked this hard in her life.

It was the numbing, relentless grind of it. Up at five a.m., straight into her crew polo shirt and short navy skirt for her shift in the galley with Bernard, the sous-chef, prepping the guests' breakfasts, then serving the crew's breakfast in the crew mess. And all that before each day's marathon of cleaning.

Roz, the chief stewardess and purser, a fiery, mean-faced

Scottish woman, made it her job to spy on the guests and predict their movements. The second a guest left one of their cabins, Frankie, Simone and Trudy, the stewardess SWAT team, would race in and strip the beds and manically clean the cabin and en-suite bathrooms with their sunken Jacuzzi baths and surround showers, replace all the lotions and potions and even fold the padded toilet roll into a point, so that when the guest returned, it was as if a magic fairy had waved a wand and made everything pristine.

Perfection. That was what it was all about. Perfect. Perfect. Everything had to be perfect. Which made it perfectly knackering too.

Perhaps it would get better, Frankie thought, trying to be optimistic. Perhaps they were giving her all the worst jobs just to test her out? She knew the other girls didn't appreciate her getting the coveted stewardess's position when, unlike them, she'd had no previous experience of working on yachts. She knew it was the qualification on her CV as a gym instructor and personal trainer that had swung the interview her way with Richard, the captain. And the fact that he hadn't been able to take his eyes off her legs.

But Roz had made it quite clear from the beginning that she certainly wasn't going to spare Frankie toilet-cleaning duties just because she knew how to lift weights. And Frankie was getting sick of the other girls' bitchy comments about her looks and her figure.

Smoothing down the surface of the fiftieth folded sheet and ironing over the top of the monogrammed Egyptian cotton, Frankie knew that something had to change soon, because right now she felt utterly trapped.

Suddenly, she jumped, lifted from her reverie by the sight of Jeff holding on to the door of the laundry room and shouting something. He was the second engineer on board and, like most of the male crew, had a regulation posh accent and blond hair. And, also like most of the others, he'd made a pass at Frankie, mistaking her arm-wrestling skills and cast-iron drinking stomach for flirting.

Jeff was arguably the cutest guy in the crew, but Frankie knew that it was too sordid and incestuous for her even to *think* about getting it together with another crew member. She wasn't easy like the other girls on board, and she didn't want anyone to think she was.

No, if Frankie were to hook up with anyone, it would have to be an altogether more mature, private relationship, with a real man in the real world. Unfortunately, she seemed to be in just the wrong place to get it.

She quickly removed the earphones of her iPod. Her ears were once more assaulted by the tumble of the dryers and hiss of the steam iron.

Jeff had been down in the engine room. He wiped grease off his hands with a rag.

'What did you say?' she asked.

'Roz wants you,' Jeff repeated.

'What have I done now?' Frankie asked.

Jeff smiled at her. 'It's not you. It's Simone. She's spilt a bottle of bleach in the owner's bathroom and stained the hand-made Moroccan tiles.' He pulled a face. 'Big fuck-up,' he said. 'Huge. Roz is in the galley. She's crazy mad.'

Frankie followed Jeff out of the laundry room, delving in her pocket for her key card. Each member of the crew had a chipped access card which allowed them entry only to relevant areas of the yacht: the places they worked, and nowhere else.

The main galley looked like the kitchen of a big commercial restaurant, with giant stainless-steel worktops and industrial cookers, as well as a wall of shiny fridges and freezers bursting with the finest ingredients from around the world.

In the middle of the room, Roz stood, her arms akimbo, her face the colour of a ripe plum. Scrawny little Simone was in front of her sobbing, begging for forgiveness. For a moment, Frankie seriously wondered whether Roz was going to pull one of the razor-sharp Global knives from the magnet on the wall and use it on Simone, such was the level of tension in the room. Even the giant salmon which Chantelle, the head chef, had prepared for dinner, gawped from the worktop.

'I should never have given you my card,' Roz barked.

Frankie could now understand why Roz was so upset. She was the only one with access clearance to the owner's state room. But she must have delegated her duties to Simone. If Richard found out, Roz would be in as much trouble as Simone was now. It might even cost her her job. And Roz would be lost without her job. Every other female crew member Roz's age had left yachting ten years ago, to have kids and live on land, but spiky Roz had never had a partner, or a real life.

'Fuck!' Roz spat. 'Do you have any idea how much those tiles cost?'

Simone was whimpering and shaking her head. She looked miserably at Frankie, her eyes rimmed in smudged mascara. There was no love lost between them, but Frankie felt she should stick up for her. Simone was only eighteen – seven years younger than Frankie. Nothing but a kid.

'Is it really that bad?' Frankie asked.

'Yes!' Roz shouted, turning on Frankie.

'But it was an accident, right, Simone?'

Simone nodded, a faint glimmer of hope in her eyes.

'Everyone makes mistakes . . .' Frankie told Roz.

'This is a luxury yacht, Frankie,' Roz said, her words measured with fury. 'Perhaps you haven't got it yet. *There are no mistakes.* Oh God. Why did this have to happen now? Why this evening?'

Frankie was confused. 'Why? What's going on?'

'For fuck's sake, Frankie, what planet have you been on?' Roz exclaimed.

Er . . . the planet where nobody tells me anything, Frankie felt like saying.

'The boss is coming on board,' Roz continued.

Now it all made sense, Frankie thought. The mysterious boss was coming . . . at last.

'Do you need me to go and clean the tiles?' Frankie asked, assuming that was why she'd been summoned.

'No!' Roz snapped. 'I will. The last thing I need is any of you lot making it worse.' Her eyes locked on Frankie's. 'I need you to go and help Hamish in the top guest saloon. Which is where I would be if it wasn't for this idiot here,' she said, glaring back at Simone.

The top guest saloon? Frankie was astonished. She'd never been up there before. Despite living on board with the guests, scrubbing their shit out of the toilets, picking up their condoms and scraping leftovers from their plates into the bin, Frankie rarely met any of the guests. Most of what she knew about them, she gleaned from rumours in the crew mess.

Roz handed Frankie a key pass. 'Do not fuck this up. And wear your cap. Your hair looks fucking terrible,' she added.

Frankie bit her lip. She mustn't answer back. She'd quit this job in her own good time, when it suited her. She was determined never to give Roz the pleasure of firing her.

What a bitch Roz was. If she gave Frankie more than two seconds to herself each day, then she might be able to do something about her appearance, Frankie thought as she hurried to the crew mess. There she looked in the small circular mirror on the wall and quickly retied her long blond hair into a bunch behind her head. She grabbed one of *Pushkin*'s midnight-blue regulation crew baseball hats and put it on.

She didn't look so bad, she decided, checking out her reflection. Her face was heart-shaped and her skin dewy and unblemished. But she knew it was her clear blue eyes that were her best feature. She smiled at herself in the mirror, checking her teeth.

The boss was coming on board tonight. And who knew? With a bit of luck, she might finally get a glimpse of Mr Big himself, the legendary Alexei Rodokov.

She was looking forward to seeing what all the fuss was about.

CHAPTER THREE

Emma Harvey moved the outer knife on the twelve-piece place setting fractionally to the left. The centre table, like the other thirty tables spread before her in the ballroom of Wrentham Hall, was festooned with rose petals, tiny silver balloons and individually chosen gifts. The finest Wedgwood crystal glasses shimmered in the candlelight from the tall Tiffany silver candelabras and the air was filled with the scent of the vast Rob Van Helden flower arrangements.

Damien was staring at her, amusement in his eyes, as he filled a glass with vintage Cristal. 'Lady Emma, this is my job,' he gently chastised her. 'Please. Just go back in and enjoy your party.'

'Sorry,' Emma said. He was right. He was the number-one party planner in the UK. She'd fought off several fashion companies and an awards ceremony to get him for tonight and ought to trust him and his huge team, even though Emma had an in-built distrust of hired-in staff. Very few of them ever did anything perfectly – or as perfectly as Emma would do it herself.

Emma forced herself to stand back and smiled at Damien. She had to admit that it was nice to get a moment with him like this. The calm before the storm.

'I'm just a hopeless control freak. I promise you, I'll leave you to it now,' Emma said, accepting the glass he handed her. She took a sip.

'How are you feeling?' Damien asked.

'Nervous. But thanks for asking. Nearly everyone has arrived.'

'And I bet they're loving it,' Damien reassured her. 'I can't get over the lights.'

He was referring to the lanterns which lit up the driveway and the gold spotlights which swirled over the imposing white stone Regency façade of Wrentham Hall, as well as the two silver strobes shimmering across the lake and lighting up the Cotswold sky. It had been worth getting the lighting design company in. It had given the whole party much more of a theatrical feel.

'Julian says it's all a bit over the top.'

'Well, I love them. You've transformed the place. And having the acrobats in the hallway is just inspired.'

'It's all thanks to you,' she said, taking another sip of champagne before handing the glass back to him, knowing that she mustn't get too drunk. 'I'd better get back to it.'

She lifted up the skirt of her Oscar de la Renta silk ball gown and swept through the tables to the door.

'Lady Emma?' Damien called after her.

She turned and smiled.

'Thank you for tonight,' he said. 'This is truly one of the best parties I've ever done.'

Emma smiled, buoyed up with the compliment. Damien had organized all of the most important parties in recent years. He'd done all the royal weddings, and all the big film premiere parties. She felt satisfied that tonight's Platinum Ball was the hottest invite around. And even though it had nearly given her a nervous breakdown to stage it, Emma was determined that it was damn well going to be worth it.

She slipped through the giant ballroom doors and closed them behind her. Keeping her hands on the handles, she breathed in, surveying her party.

Yes, it was magnificent. The grand hallway was crowded with guests already: the men all in black tie; the women in ball gowns. Everyone looked fantastic.

Damien was right. The acrobats from Cirque du Soleil *were* inspired. They twirled on their ribbon harnesses from the high glass dome of the ceiling. On the balcony, a jazz band was playing, and below, handsome waiters in immaculate Nehru jackets served delicious cocktails in twisted silver-stemmed glasses. Mountains of sumptuous caviar and sensationally enticing canapés were being presented to the guests on silver platters by loin-clothed waiters and half-naked waitresses entirely body-sprayed silver.

The enormous front doors were open and Emma could see that the driveway was crowded with Bentleys, Ferraris, Jaguars and her own vintage silver Rolls-Royce. Beyond the ha-ha, the front lawn was lit up so that the helicopter carrying Sir Paul from his gig in London would arrive in time for him to play his set after the nine-course banquet.

Emma fingered the diamonds around her neck nervously and glanced at herself in the giant gilt mirror. She looked good for her age. But then, so she should. She'd spent enough time and money getting herself perfectly groomed for tonight's event, her bright auburn hair highlighted and cut into a flattering bob.

Several friends had suggested that she have an eye-tuck, or a mini facelift, but Emma shied away from ever having surgery. It was far too vulgar. And, in her opinion, almost certainly ruined natural good looks. Besides, once you started, where and when did you stop? She didn't want to end up looking like some wrinkleless monster by the time she was seventy. She liked her age, and was rather fond of the laughter lines on her face. She'd had a bloody good time getting them. And all the magazines said these days that fifty was the new forty, didn't they?

'Hold it there!'

Emma blinked, momentarily blinded by the flash of a camera. It was Vincent, the photographer from *Tatler*. 'Thanks, Lady Em,' he called, moving on. 'Terrific necklace.'

'Thank you,' she said, smiling. The diamonds had been a gift from Julian. He'd taken her great-grandmother's chunky Victorian heirloom and had the jewels reset at Asprey's. Emma had been astounded that he'd made such a huge effort and delighted he'd chosen such a perfect setting – he knew how fussy she was. Still, she would be taking it back next week to get the clasp altered, but otherwise, the gift was perfect.

'Why are the photographers here?' Julian asked, edging through the crowd and coming up to her.

'It's good for your profile. I know it's officially your birthday party, but with so many investors here, it's also the launch of Platinum Holdings. It should be in the press.'

He stopped and kissed her bare shoulder and Emma reached up and straightened his silk bow tie. She couldn't believe that her Julian was fifty already. But somehow it seemed that he'd always been this age. His face was tanned, his dark-brown wavy hair flecked with grey, but he still had a boyishness to him; a laugh always lurked behind those hazel eyes.

Ever since his bachelor days in Chelsea and his well-documented stint as a playboy before he'd met Emma, everyone who'd ever met Julian loved him. But that was because Julian Harvey was probably one of the most charming people in the Northern hemisphere.

They watched together as Vince moved off to photograph the other guests. Julian leant in close so that his mouth was next to Emma's ear. She breathed in his familiar scent. 'Now that nobody's looking, how about we sneak off for a birthday quickie?' he whispered.

'Cheeky,' Emma said, laughing.

'But you look edible in that dress,' Julian whispered. 'And you'll never guess what Mike gave me as a birthday present?'

Emma laughed. 'What?'

'A stack of Viagra.'

'You're the last person in this room who needs Viagra, darling,' she said, kissing him. It was true. They still had a fantastic sex life, but tonight was going to be more special than ever.

They were interrupted by a loud hoot. Vivacious and über-trendy as ever, Bunny Jenovitch was bearing down on them, her arms outstretched.

'You look just like the lovebirds you always were!' she exclaimed in her familiar American twang.

'Bunny!' Julian gasped. 'You didn't,' he mouthed to Emma. She raised her eyebrows in acknowledgement and beamed at him. He looked back at the famous opera singer. 'I thought you were doing the Carnegie?'

'And miss singing Happy Birthday to my favourite man?' Bunny said, kissing Julian's cheeks. Married to Eduard Kline-Adams, the celebrated New York designer, Bunny was wearing what was almost certainly one of his catwalk specials – a sculpted, peacock-green and gold creation, squeezed in at the waist, with spiky feathers fanning out behind her head. 'We arrived on the red-eye this morning. I can see darling Emma kept me a secret,' Bunny said, reaching out to squeeze Emma's hand.

'My God! This is wonderful. It can't get any better,' Julian said, smiling at Emma. She felt herself glowing. Julian was happy and that was all that mattered.

She knew this was his moment and she wanted him to enjoy it more than anything. Because he deserved it. The last decade had been hard enough for Julian, after the financial group he had founded and built up went bankrupt. And whilst the collapse of the company hadn't exactly been Julian's fault, more a casualty of a sudden market shift and the bubble bursting in the dot com industry, he'd done the decent thing and taken the rap for it, losing everything in the process.

Emma had seen how crushed he'd been, how much the fall-out from the bankruptcy had knocked his self-confidence, and she'd done what she knew he'd have done for her in the same situation: stuck by his side, bolstered him up and supported him as best she could until he'd got back on his feet. That was why their partnership was so strong: they both knew that whatever happened, they could weather the bad times and enjoy the good times together.

And now, all the hardship Julian had suffered was firmly in the past. Any shadow over his name, or his reputation, gone. Tonight was going to be a success. She could feel it. She felt a swell of pride as she watched Julian and Bunny laughing and knew that the last few months of planning had been worth every moment.

But then she saw Cosmo.

He was lolling halfway up the central staircase, his knee bent so that the sole of his boot was planted against the newly painted wall. As she approached him, she suspected that he was drunk. Or worse: on coke. He claimed he hadn't touched the filthy stuff for over six months, but he'd lied to Emma often enough in the past for her still to be unsure.

All she could do was hope, she supposed. And not give up on him. Because if she did, she knew she'd lose him for good. She tried not to look too hard at his bloodshot eyes, or let her face betray her disapproval at the musty odour coming from his long blondy-brown matted dreadlocks.

'Mother, how do you know this many dreadful people?' he said, his words slurring as he slugged back champagne from one of the twisted flutes.

The glass looked fragile in his dirty hands with his whale-bone ring, which had replaced the three-hundred-year-old priceless family signet ring Emma had given him when he'd turned twenty-one. He was wearing black ash-smudged tight trousers and a ripped leather coat. Emma knew that Julian would be secretly thrilled their son had graced the occasion with his presence, but she felt a familiar cocktail of nerves, love and shame as she looked at him. Cosmo's new incarnation as an eco-warrior infuriated Julian and baffled Emma. Not to mention the embarrassment he'd caused the family when he appeared on the news chained to a rotten oak tree in protest about the extension of the new bypass.

'My God. There's that awful wanker off that TV show. Why is he here?' Cosmo asked.

'Laurie is a friend from way back,' Emma started, then stopped herself. She didn't have to justify any of her guests to Cosmo. 'There's no need to be so judgemental. Just . . . please. Please make an effort, darling. Don't ruin this for your father. It's his birthday. And it's lovely finally to be able to throw a proper party here.'

'It's only a fucking house, Mother.'

'Cosmo!'

'Do you know if you Google Wrentham Hall, you get directed to this poncy survey that names Wrentham as one of the top fifty most desirable places to live in the whole of England?' Cosmo sniped, adding under his breath, 'I mean, what *wank*. If only they knew the reality.'

'No, actually I didn't.'

Despite his criticism, she couldn't help feeling a sense of satisfaction. Those features in *Country Life* and *Homes & Gardens* had paid off after all.

But it made sense. Wrentham was part of the Lechley Park

estate that had been in her family for seven generations. Her brother, the Earl, known to everyone as Pim, had inherited the estate and the family seat, Lechley Hall. He'd signed over the dower house, Wrentham, to Emma after their mother had died two years ago, along with a cash fund which their mother had secretly squirrelled away for the restoration of her beloved Hall.

So Emma had embarked on her mother's dying wish, lovingly reinstating every period detail of the dilapidated, almost derelict house. She'd trawled the country to find the most skilled workmen to re-create the original décor in the huge library, billiard room and ballroom.

Every step of the way, Emma had resisted the temptation to modernize at the expense of losing the feel that only the antiquity of the place could bring. Even the kitchens had been kept mostly in their original splendour, with a working range and miles of cast-iron pipes.

And when her mother's money had run out, Emma had used her considerable initiative to raise more finance to work on the historic grounds with their rare trees, Elizabethan maze and carp lake. She hadn't stopped until the annexe, with its real tennis court and heated indoor pool had been restored, finishing with her prize-winning white-flowering kitchen garden.

So yes, given its prime location and the sheer magic of the place, Emma could see why Wrentham would end up in such a survey.

'It's nothing to gloat about,' Cosmo said, as if reading her mind. 'Being so ostentatious. And so wasteful.'

Emma rolled her eyes. 'Come on, Cosmo. Lighten up. Those surveys aren't to be taken seriously.'

'But it makes people jealous. And avaricious.'

'So what? Wrentham isn't for sale, and will never be for sale. I don't see why it's bothering you, darling.'

'But just look at all this?' Cosmo threw out his hand, gesturing to the crowd below. 'It's like the last days of the Roman fucking Empire.'

'What?' she asked, trying to be understanding. All she could see was a room full of successful, beautiful people, eating sumptuous food in her home. Her beautiful, amazing home. She'd never felt this proud of it before. During the most nerve-racking moments of the restoration, Emma had fantasized about holding parties just like this. How could Cosmo possibly understand how much tonight meant to her?

'You don't get it, do you? The penny hasn't dropped,' he said, tapping his head, as if to indicate her stupidity. 'Did it never occur to you that for every pound you spend, someone else *doesn't* have a pound? For every foie gras canapé your guests stuff down their rich throats, some kid somewhere has food denied to them . . . '

Emma had heard Cosmo's anti-capitalist rants plenty of times before. She'd had enough of him trying to make her feel guilty all the time. Why *should* she feel guilty? She'd raised nearly fifty thousand pounds for her cancer charity so far this year. If Cosmo had his way, they'd sell this place and give all the money to one of his ridiculous schemes to save the planet. He didn't seem to understand the bigger picture. It made Emma furious that he didn't see all this took hard work.

Bloody hard work.

The kind of hard work that had put him through the best public schools, so that he could have the luxury of such educated opinions. But she was determined not to lose her temper. Victoria, her best friend, had often told her that Cosmo would grow out of this angry phase and would eventually see the common ground between his upbringing and the person he wanted to become. And then, hopefully, he'd become man enough to inherit his title and the estate that had been in Emma's family for over six hundred years. But when? That was what Emma wanted to know.

'Stop it, Cosmo,' she hissed under her breath. 'If you make a scene tonight, so help me I'll . . .' She searched around for a suitable threat. The problem was if she threatened to cut Cosmo off, he'd be delighted. It would be the proof that he was looking for that their differences *were* irreconcilable after all.

Cosmo seemed amused by her outburst. Emma tried to control herself. The last thing she wanted was a fight. *Tatler* would love photographs of that: Lady Emma Harvey slapping her delinquent son. Everyone wanted to know what had happened to Cosmo. A year ago, he'd been in the tabloids every week, papped staggering out of the latest London nightclub in the early hours with a drunk blonde on each arm. But suddenly, in a typically contrary move, Cosmo had dumped his society chums and entirely dropped out of the limelight.

'Save it, Mother. I'm not going to embarrass you,' Cosmo said.

Emma let out a pent-up breath and nodded.

He was infuriating. They'd been on the brink of yet another row, and then it was gone, just like that. Emma should feel grateful to him, but instead she hated him for making her feel so out of control.

'So what's with the mafia? And the hooker?' Cosmo said, conversationally.

She followed his gaze as he nodded to the library, where an unfamiliar couple had just emerged, flanked on either side by two huge men in black suits – clearly bodyguards. Cosmo had a point. The couple themselves looked entirely out of place. He was wearing a ghastly navy blue DJ, and she . . . well, she looked like something the cat had dragged in.

Emma flushed, caught off guard. She'd personally overseen the guest list and had made an effort to memorize photos of all the guests she'd never met, and a few personal facts about them, so that she could greet each and every one of them. So who were these people?

Were they something to do with the lawyers that had set up in the library? Julian had mentioned earlier that he was going to sign some papers for the final financing for Platinum Holdings, since Pim was attending the party, and it would be a good time to pin him down to sign on the dotted line. Julian had promised it would take no more than a few moments.

Emma watched as Pim followed Julian out of the library and Julian patted her brother's arm, smiling.

'Look at them,' Cosmo continued. 'They both look so smug. I tell you, Dad's platinum mine better work out. Otherwise they're fucked.'

'Cosmo, please don't use that language. And take your boot off the wall. You know it's just been painted.'

Emma smoothed her short hair behind her ears and walked back down the steps. It took a while before she could get through the guests to Julian again.

'I see you've had a word with our son,' Julian said.

'He's promised to behave.'

'That's something at least.'

'Darling, who *are* they?' Emma gestured discreetly with her champagne glass to the couple who were now picking canapés off a tray and looking uneasily around the room.

'Dimitry Sergeyokov. You know . . .' He looked at Emma, confused. 'I've talked about him enough. He's the one who set up the whole deal. Dimitry's the one I bought the development block from. He's our main man.'

Emma was shocked. '*That's* Dimitry? But I thought. I just . . . I hadn't imagined he'd be like that.' Emma thought back to Cosmo's comment. 'He's legit, isn't he?'

Julian put his arm around her and laughed. 'Ems, don't be ridiculous. You've been reading too many thrillers. Of course he's legit.'

'I didn't realize he was coming tonight. You could have said . . .'

'Well, he was only meant to be popping in to sign the paperwork. But now he says he'd like to stay. And I told him we'd be delighted if he did.' He smiled at her.

'Oh. And what about *her*?'

'His wife . . . so he says.'

Emma looked around the shoulder of Julian's dinner jacket and glanced suspiciously at the woman. She rather stood out amid the show of elegance around her. She had shaggy dyed blond hair, a huge shiny pink pout and an obscene amount of cleavage showing above her low-cut white lace mini-dress. But the thing that annoyed Emma the most was that she was wearing red patent stilettos with the ghastly outfit. An absolute fashion no-no.

Cosmo was right. She looked like a hooker. And if there was one thing that Emma absolutely hated, it was hookers, prostitutes, call them what you will. It was manipulative sluts like that who had ruined her parents' marriage and turned her mother into an insecure, alcoholic mess. And it was hookers who stole men like Julian away from good women like her.

Julian glanced over his shoulder too. 'Try and be nice to her. She doesn't speak any English.'

'I wish I'd known. It rather mucks up the seating plan.'

Her mind was already racing. Several of the more sophisticated Russian society ladies Emma knew from her fundraising network were here tonight. Should she sit Dimitry and his companion next to one of them? It would be a hell of a risk. They certainly didn't look as if they had much in common.

'Don't worry. They can have Hugo and Victoria's places.'

Emma stiffened. 'What do you mean?'

'Now don't get all upset. I forgot to tell you—'

'Tell me what?'

'Hugo called earlier. Something's come up and they can't make it.'

Emma stared at her husband, reeling from this news and the way he'd delivered it, all thoughts of Russians, dodgy or otherwise, forgotten.

Hugo McCorquodale was their oldest friend, Cosmo's godfather and Julian's first-ever business partner. It had been through Hugo's investment bank, McCorquodale & Co, that Julian had been introduced to Dimitry in the first place. It was unthinkable that Hugo and Victoria would miss tonight. Or that Victoria hadn't spoken to Emma about it. She knew how much tonight meant to Emma.

'What's happened? Are they all right?' Emma's heart was racing with panic.

'It's nothing to worry about,' Julian said, clocking Emma's expression. 'They did apologize. Profusely. Don't worry. We'll have just as much of a good time without them.'

Before Emma could say any more, Damien appeared at the lectern outside the library and banged his gavel. It was time to get this party started.

CHAPTER FOUR

Peaches stepped out of the lift and into the hotel lobby, her Manolo Blahnik strappy sandals clicking across the chequered marble. As her red silk Gucci dress slid tantalizingly across her voluptuous yet taut curves, the slit at the front gaped intermittently, offering charged glimpses of the top of her tanned thighs.

She kept her head erect, her stride relaxed and yet purposeful, enjoying the sexual tension she left in her wake. *Walk in slow motion.* That's what Madam Suze had told her all those years ago. *Walk like you're being filmed. Like you know everyone is looking at you and wants a piece of your ass.*

By the revolving door, the young man in perfect grey livery and a top hat had his hands crossed across his crotch. 'Have a nice day, ma'am,' he said.

'I shall try, thank you, Maurice,' Peaches said, discreetly slipping a few fifty-dollar bills into his top pocket and patting it. She happened to know that Maurice was Hal Randolf's nephew. Peaches believed in looking after future investments.

Hal Randolf, the famous hotelier, owned Boulevard 19 and had an archaic, unrealistic moral issue with women of Peaches' profession. Having courted every newspaper since the hotel opened, he loved nothing more than boasting in print that, unlike some of the more famous LA hotels, *his* hotel's reputation was squeaky clean. What he hadn't worked out (unlike Maurice, his more streetwise nephew) was that thanks to his ridiculous bragging, Peaches happily charged extra if the clients wanted to meet her or any of her girls here. They always did.

It amazed Peaches that some people never realized the most fundamental rule of life: it all came down to sex. You could dress it up all you wanted, or pretend that it wasn't happening, but sex was everywhere. You couldn't stop it. It would find a way in, sure as water. And that's why business was booming.

Peaches stepped out on to the front steps of the hotel, shading her eyes to look past the giant fountain in the centre of the circular, palm-tree lined drive with its attendant queue of limousines. Taking her Marc Jacobs shades out of her vintage leather tote, she basked for a moment in the sun. It was such a goddamned shame that UV rays were so bad for you – she missed the old days of tanning to a deep brown.

A family was getting out of a yellow taxi, the father paying quickly and catching up with his two small girls. Peaches smiled at the elder one, in the blue and white dress, who was now holding her father's hand and walking past her into the hotel.

'That lady smells lovely, Daddy,' she heard her whisper.

Peaches felt a sudden pang. She couldn't have been much older than the girl herself when Albert Rockbine, the man she'd thought was her father, had made the first of his sustained assaults on her.

It had been the moment that Peaches had learnt the most important lesson of her life: she was completely on her own.

She remembered the first time. It had been one of those lazy Louisiana afternoons. Peaches had been reading an *Archie* comic on the porch, sucking an ice-pop, her legs dangling over the side of the swing, when Albert had come for her. She remembered that he'd grabbed her ankles.

At first she'd thought he was joking, that he was initiating some kind of weird game, as he'd pulled her on to the rotten porch boards. But in a second he'd rolled on top of her, squeezing the air out of her lungs. She'd struggled to push him away, but he'd grabbed her wrists, banging them down on the board above her head, laughing at her lack of strength against him.

He'd been drinking. More than usual for the time of day, and he'd stunk of whiskey and tacos. He'd lifted up her T-shirt.

'Let's see what you've got for me up here.'

Peaches hadn't cried out. She'd been too shocked. 'No. Don't, Daddy,' she'd whispered.

He'd slapped her face then. It had been the first time he'd ever hit her. 'You stupid bitch. Don't you get it yet? I ain't your daddy.'

She'd felt hot tears running into her hair. 'Don't say that.'

He'd leant in close, clearly enjoying his ability to shatter her innocence. 'You know your real mommy and daddy didn't want you no more? You know that?'

Peaches had shaken her head, unable to comprehend what he'd been saying.

''Cos when you were three years old, your mommy and your daddy sold you to me. Just like you was a dog.' He'd stroked her hair, his breath vile against her face. 'And since I paid for you, I can do what I like with you. I been waiting for you to ripen up and now I got me thinking you're ready.'

Peaches had cried out then, frantically trying to wriggle out of his grasp, as he unbuttoned his fly. She'd been aware of the net curtain moving in the window, and had twisted her neck to see Jean Rockbine, the woman she'd thought was her mother, staring blankly out in a medicated haze.

'Have a nice day, ma'am.' A smartly dressed and very pretty concierge came out of the hotel doors towards Peaches and smiled, interrupting Peaches' painful memory and snapping her back to a much more pleasant reality.

Peaches hadn't thought about Albert Rockbine for years.

She hadn't let herself.

She didn't believe Albert Rockbine's cooked-up story about her being 'sold' for one second. He'd just been trying to hurt her. But even if no one had ever told her the truth about where she was from, at least it was some comfort she wasn't genetically related to that scumbag.

Some people would have spent thousands of dollars in therapy getting over an abusive childhood like hers, but not Peaches. She was more interested in the future than the past.

She'd shed her tears about it back then and she'd never cried since. Over anything. And she was determined never to again.

Instead, she'd turned her lack of family into a positive advantage. She ran away from Louisiana to LA when she was fourteen, changing her name from Stacey-Louise Rockbine to Peaches Gold along the way. Peaches and Gold. Her two favourite things. And she'd vowed then that her life would only be filled with her favourite things. The best clothes, the fanciest cars and lots and lots of money.

And who cared how she did it? The way Peaches had seen it, having no family was a blessing. She had no one to hold her back or pass judgement on her. No one to challenge her philosophy that life was for living and for sampling as many of the finer things available to womankind as possible. In Peaches' view, then, as now, as long as you kept learning along the way you might as well reach for the stars.

She walked down the few steps to the black limo, which was now waiting for her, its back door open.

'Don't waste the air-con,' Peaches said, climbing inside and sliding back on the leather seat.

Tommy Liebermann leant across her and pulled the door shut. Tommy had been sitting here awaiting her return for exactly an hour. He'd bill her for his time too. But after what Valentin had just paid her, she'd still come out way ahead.

Peaches could tell her attorney was annoyed that she'd interrupted their meeting for the appointment with Valentin. But Tommy couldn't complain. A fabulous tax lawyer, he'd fallen on hard times when his drink problem and shady dealings with a Mafia-connected outfit had finished his career with one of the top city firms. Fortunately for him, Peaches was on very close terms with the CEO, who'd recommended Tommy, whose nickname was Loophole Liebermann. And Peaches couldn't be happier with the has-been hot shot being in charge of her affairs. So far, he'd saved her a fortune.

'The office, Paul, please,' she said, pressing the driver intercom.

Peaches never went anywhere on business unless it was in

the limo. To her, it was as much a part of her image as her underwear.

'No problem, Peaches,' Paul said. She could tell he was smiling. But then Paul was always smiling on the other side of the dark glass. Peaches paid the one-time heavyweight boxer to make sure he stayed happy and didn't talk about some of the things he heard going on in the back, or some of the places he dropped her.

'How was it for you?' Tommy asked.

Peaches laughed. 'Wouldn't you like to know.'

Tommy blushed. They both knew that he should know better than to ask. She never told him the extent of what she did. She never gave out the details of her liaisons to anyone. What went on behind closed doors stayed there. Tommy Liebermann was there to protect her legally and to acquire assets without too many questions being asked.

'As I was saying earlier, we've got a problem,' he said as the car pulled silently away from the hotel and bumped over the kerb on to the main drag.

Peaches sighed, opening her purse to find her compact and reapply her lipstick. Tommy was so serious. She glanced across at him. He was in his late fifties and his greying hair had receded, as if chased away by the frown lines on his forehead.

'What is it?'

'The DA's office. My contacts there. They say there's gonna be a crackdown.'

'I told you: I'm keeping my head down and my nose clean,' Peaches said, checking her reflection. 'I've got this thing water-tight. It's all discreet.'

'Right. Like walking out of there as if you owned the joint. And climbing into this 'mo. Come on, Peaches, the press would have a field day with you. If they ever find out about you and the Senator—'

Peaches looked up. 'Who told you that?'

'People talk.'

People like the Senator himself, Peaches thought, knowing that any leak hadn't come from her. The dumb, bragging son-of-a-bitch. Peaches made a mental note to take him to task over his indiscretion – the next time she was spanking his flabby white butt with a rolled-up copy of the United States Constitution.

'Who cares about the Senator? He'll be out next term. So quit with the doom and gloom, will you? You're making me nervous when there's no need to. Everything is just fine.'

'How do you know? You know what happened to Heidi Fleiss. There's an election coming up. Someone like you would make a fine feather in an ambitious DA's cap. It's still illegal, all this, unless you'd forgotten.'

'But my girls are loyal. I trust them all. Everyone is making too much money to rat me out.'

'And I'm telling you you're playing with fire,' Tommy said. 'Don't expand the business any more. And make sure you've checked out the new girls. One snitch jacket, honey, or one plant, and they'll slam you in the can.'

'OK, OK. I hear you.'

'Just do yourself a favour, Peaches. Get out. And soon. Before you're taken out.'

A few blocks later, Paul dropped Peaches off at the impressive atrium of Delancy Heights. The award-winning steel-and-glass tower was one of the most exclusive new apartment complexes in LA. Peaches had once lived here permanently, but now she just used it as her city base, and to hold her infamous parties.

She paid a fortune to the building manager along with the promise that she'd never openly court anyone in the building, although it boasted amongst its inhabitants A-list actors, fashion designers, interiors moguls and rock stars. It didn't matter. There were enough celebrities who'd entered the elevator and pressed the button for the nineteenth floor, as Peaches did now.

She let herself into the soundproofed hallway, with its state-of-the-art surround-sound speakers. The walls were padded with diamanté-studded midnight-blue satin. The white carpet was sumptuous and thick. Peaches kicked off her heels and let her toes sink in.

She walked through into the vast main lounge area, which she'd had modelled on her favourite private club in Miami. It was dominated on one side by a giant leather-topped bar with an impressive array of bottles and glasses stacked to the mirrored ceiling. Low curved white leather sofas were dotted around tinted glass tables. Behind them a raised area, backed by a sequined curtain, ran around the outside of the room, complete with ten silver dancing poles. Here the thick carpet gave way to a specially sprung dance floor with is own DJ booth and turntables. And finally a row of windows revealed LA stretching into the distance, block upon block of smog-covered hustle, bustle and cash.

'Babe, I'm back,' Peaches said, waggling her fingers at the discreet panel of one-way glass on the side wall. Peaches pushed the wall and the hidden door opened. Behind it was her private office.

Angela, her secretary, was standing with her back to her, making coffee at the new machine Peaches had bought.

'You want regular or cappuccino?' Angela asked. 'I think I worked out the cappuccino now.'

'Whatever's easiest,' Peaches answered, walking past the desk, which was littered with a huge array of silks and lace samples that Angela had ordered in for the new lingerie line. 'You sound cheerful.'

'Danny got off. They couldn't find enough evidence.'

Peaches smiled. Angela's kid brother was a reclusive computer geek, who spent his life in a darkened room fiddling with computers. Most recently the authorities had caught up with him for hacking into the LAPD network. The guy could probably make real money if he worked for a big organization and Peaches had suggested many times putting him in touch with someone who might give him a proper job, but Danny liked his shady nocturnal existence.

'That's great, honey,' Peaches said.

'Yeah, well, yes and no. He's moving his operation, so he says. Going undercover for a while.'

'Well, I guess that's no bad thing. You can't be responsible for him, Angie. He is a grown-up,' Peaches said, gently.

'I know.' Angela paused. 'I take it you've seen Tommy.'

'It's hard not to. He seems to be permanently installed in the limo,' Peaches said, unhooking the original artwork for *Boogie Nights* off the wall to reveal the safe. 'I think he's been watching too much TV. He was saying something about the DA's office.' Peaches pulled out the thick bundle of Valentin's

31

hundred-dollar bills from her bag and put it next to the others inside the safe, before locking it again.

She turned to face Angela, who grimaced, handing her a mug of frothy coffee.

'Talking of trouble,' Angela said, 'Marguerite's on the terrace.'

'Thanks,' Peaches said, smiling. She'd trained herself long ago never to flinch at Angela's face, half of which had been burnt with acid by the owner of the first strip joint they'd worked in together. Peaches had taken care of her ever since. And always would.

'Call Ross, will you, honey? Tell him I'll stop by at twelve tomorrow. I want an appointment and then I'll take him to lunch. And call Christoph. See whether he's got costings on those nipple tassels. Oh, and tell him the silk basques are definitely a hit.'

Angela nodded and sat back down behind the desk. 'Got anything good planned for this afternoon?'

'Oh, you know, I thought I'd turn off my phone and take the rest of the day off,' Peaches joked. They both knew that there was no such thing as a day, or even a night off, in this business. Peaches was always working: sorting out girls who'd missed their flights to Paris; finding someone for a guy in New York who'd suddenly decided he wanted a threesome at five a.m; calming down a limo driver who'd thrown some girls out in Miami; sorting out the squabble over a half-million-dollar tip between twenty girls. It was endless. And that was all on top of trying to launch the lingerie line.

'You *should* take the day off, you know,' Angela said.

'I know. One day I'll take a whole bunch of them off.'

'Oh, I forgot,' Angela said, handing Peaches a courier's package. 'This came for you.'

Peaches ripped open the package. Inside was a thick manila envelope. She turned it over in her hands. It looked official and Peaches didn't like official letters. Was some son-of-a-bitch trying to sue her?

Peaches picked up the silver letter-opener from the pot on Angela's desk and slit open the envelope. She read down the neatly typed letter inside, her face clouding with confusion.

My name is Ron Wallace and I am currently representing a prisoner called Mikhail Gorsky . . .

'Who the hell is Ron Wallace?' she asked, showing Angela the letter. 'He wants me to go to Texas, to some prison. There must be some mistake. Call him, could you, sweetheart? Tell him that he's got the wrong person. Tell him I don't care who his client is, I don't do prisons. I don't care how much money he's willing to pay.' She smiled. 'Unless, of course, it's enough to pay for a whole bunch of those days off we were talking about.'

But despite her joke, her hands were perspiring as she slid back the tinted glass doors leading to the pool terrace and stepped from the chilled air-conditioning out into the heat. If some lawyer called Ron Wallace could find her all the way from Texas, the DA shouldn't have any trouble at all.

But no – she told herself – she was just being paranoid. The DA would still need proof first, as well as people prepared to talk. And with so many people making so much money, and having their sordid fantasies so readily fulfilled, Peaches couldn't quite see that happening.

Have faith, she told herself. Keep them all rich and happy and they'd keep their mouths shut. This was LA. The city of secrets. She should relax and concentrate on what was important: her business.

On the terrace, the blare of horns from the street below and the distant sound of sirens filled the humid air. Marguerite was sitting at the far end by the black pots of pampas grass, shrinking in a chair under the grey electric sunshade, her bare feet up on the square steel rail.

She was wearing large Dior sunglasses and a floppy sun hat that hid most of her face. But even covered up, Peaches could tell that she was freaking out. Seeing Peaches, she jumped up.

'Peaches, I'm so fucking sorry.'

'What were you thinking? You can't sell that shit on my watch,' Peaches said. 'Do you want us all to get busted?'

'No, no . . .'

Everyone knew that sex and drugs went hand in hand. It was expected that there would be a free flow of cocaine and ecstasy at the parties Peaches threw here, even though she never used any herself. Not any more. And never dealt. Never had.

But Marguerite had slipped up and had tried to sell crystal

meth to a client, who'd then complained, and refused to pay up, claiming Marguerite had been too high to satisfy him. Marguerite was stupid to have thought she'd get away with it.

But she was just a kid, Peaches thought, with an exasperated sigh. And Peaches knew she needed help. Besides, Marguerite was undoubtedly one of the best in the game. She had a fragile look that drove men wild.

Marguerite took off her glasses. Her big doe eyes were red and puffy. 'Peaches, I'm begging you, please don't cut me off,' she said. 'I've got no money. Nothing. I'll end up back on the street—'

'OK, calm down,' Peaches said. 'First thing, I'm going to get you cleaned up. I've organized for you to go to Santa Fe to the clinic. Then when you're clean, you can work here for me. Answer phones. Help Angela out. And when you're better, you can start going out on jobs again.'

'You don't have to be so nice to me,' Marguerite said, her face crumpling as she started crying. 'You've done so much for me.'

'Hey, if we don't look after each other, we don't have anyone. But remember: you owe me one.'

Peaches turned, hearing the hiss of the door behind her. Angela was holding the phone out towards her.

'It's Ron Wallace,' she said. 'His letter isn't a mistake. This client of his needs to tell you something important. About your past. About where you're from.'

CHAPTER FIVE

From *Pushkin*'s top saloon, Frankie could see the shimmering lights along St Tropez harbour front way below. The sunset had been stunning, and now, as the sky started to darken and the stars come out, everything seemed to be bathed in hazy silver light. The new crescent moon hung in the sky like a smile and Frankie breathed in the scented Mediterranean air and smiled with it.

This was more like it. Looking down on the world, soft jazz coming from the floor speakers built into the teak deck, it was easy to see why the super-rich behaved as if they were gods.

The guest saloon was much more minimalist than she'd imagined. No clutter. Just big squashy leather dining chairs and an ornate mahogany table with gold inlay, polished to a glass-like finish. There was a second, higher table at the far end surrounded by white leather bar stools. Three men sat around it, playing cards.

Two of the men were Eugene and Dieter, the bodyguards who'd arrived yesterday. They were difficult to miss. Eugene was like a blond cartoon sumo wrestler, bound in a bronze body suit of muscle. Frankie had seen him pumping weights when she'd been cleaning the gym early that morning. She'd tried to tell him that if he carried on lifting them the way he was, he'd damage his back, but Eugene wasn't the kind of guy to listen to a woman. Particularly not a lowly stewardess like her.

Dieter gave her the creeps. She hadn't heard him utter a word. He had a black crew cut and sallow skin and eyes that seemed to follow you everywhere. Frankie couldn't begin to imagine what dark secrets he had in his past.

Hamish, the chief steward, was polishing glasses behind the discreet semi-circular bar tucked away at one end of the saloon. Frankie thought back to her first week on board, when Hamish had tried to kiss her late one night in the crew mess. He'd told her that she reminded him of his wife back home. He reminded her of a jerk, she'd answered back. Ever since he'd been surly and offhand with her, as if *she* were the one who'd stepped out of line.

'So who's the guy in the cream suit again?' Frankie asked Hamish, nodding towards the poker table.

'Sonny Wiseman. Big Hollywood producer. The boss financed his last film.'

There it was again. The boss. So he had his finger in the movie pie too. The more Frankie heard about him, the more intrigued she was. She imagined him to be very serious, perhaps a little frightening. After all, how exactly did you get to be this rich? And have this many associates you entertained for free on your yacht? Hardly by just being a nice guy.

Hamish nudged Frankie and nodded to the table. Taking his cue, Frankie approached Sonny Wiseman, whose glass was empty.

'May I get you another drink, sir?' she asked.

'Yes, you most certainly can.' Sonny Wiseman turned to hand her his glass and his eyes locked with Frankie's. 'Well, my oh my,' he said, his wrinkly face breaking into a charming grin, 'I cannot believe they've been hiding such a beauty downstairs.'

Frankie smiled at his compliment. 'Just a gin and tonic, then?'

He pointed a chubby finger at her. 'You're from Jo'burg, right?'

'Cape Town. Originally.'

'Ah, Cape Town. I go whale-watching there. Great place. One of the most beautiful on earth, I'd say.'

Frankie smiled again. 'I'm glad you think so.'

Sonny Wiseman lit a long, fat cigar. 'Problem with South Africa? Most of the talent leaves.'

'I guess so,' Frankie mumbled.

'You guess so? I know so. You're living proof of it.' Sonny grinned as a blush spread across Frankie's face. 'So what's your story, sugar? Why did you fly the coop?' he asked, puffing out smoke whilst Dieter shuffled the pack of cards.

Frankie was caught so off guard, that she nearly blurted out the truth. 'It's complicated. Let's just say I felt like a change. And I ended up in the Caribbean in the winter season when *Pushkin* was there and—'

Hamish coughed loudly by the bar. Frankie abruptly closed her mouth.

Sonny looked her up and down appraisingly, then nodded in approval. 'A mystery girl, huh? All the better.'

'Gin and tonic, right away,' she said, turning to go, ignoring Dieter who'd been staring at her legs, and now grunted something to Eugene that she didn't catch, but which made them both laugh.

'Make it a weak one,' Sonny Wiseman called after her.

Back at the bar, Hamish glared at her. 'Don't talk to the guests,' he hissed.

'I thought it was polite to answer when someone asks me a question. It's called manners.'

She reached for the blue Tanqueray gin bottle and a fresh glass to fix Sonny's drink. But Hamish snatched the glass from her.

'I'll do that,' he said, half filling the glass with gin.

'He said he wanted it weak,' Frankie pointed out.

'Mind your own business,' Hamish told her, topping the drink up with a splash of tonic and a hefty squeeze of lemon.

Frankie took the drink back to Sonny Wiseman and, ignoring Hamish's warning look, took a seat at the table when Sonny offered her one, insisting that she stayed a while. She knew it was a risk, but she didn't care. Why shouldn't she sit down if she was invited? Sonny Wiseman was the first human being to have a decent chat with her in two months and she wasn't going to waste the opportunity. Besides, he was interesting.

'So I hear you're in the movie business,' she said. 'I love the movies. Living downstairs turns you into an amateur buff. I've watched loads of DVDs since being on board.'

Sonny Wiseman stared at her face. 'You ever thought of acting?' he asked.

'No,' Frankie said. She shook her head, feeling flattered, but amused too. Her? An actress? He had to be kidding. 'I don't think I'd be very good.'

'You'd be surprised. I think you could have a real screen presence. You've got the face for it.'

'But I haven't had any training. I mean ... you can't just *become* an actor, surely?'

'That depends on who wants to make you one,' he said.

Before long, she'd found out that he was over in Europe for the Cannes festival in a few weeks' time and that his film, the new Todd Lands picture, would be premiering there.

'Wow,' Frankie said, awestruck. She couldn't believe she was actually talking to someone who knew possibly the most famous film star in the world. 'So, what's Todd Lands like? I think I've seen all his movies.' She knew she sounded like an infatuated schoolgirl, but she was a huge fan of Hollywood's favourite son.

Sonny sighed with satisfaction. 'That guy has it all. The chicks love him; the guys love him. He's probably the most bankable star in Hollywood. Can secure more money on an opening weekend than anyone. You'd think he'd be an arrogant shit but, between you and me, he's one of the nicest guys you could ever meet.'

'God, I'd give anything to meet him,' Frankie said, awed. 'But I guess I wouldn't know what to say, being a life-long fan.'

It seemed like only five minutes later, when Eugene told Frankie to offer Sonny another drink, that she noticed it: an imperceptible nod of Eugene's head towards Hamish.

Back at the bar, Hamish again mixed Sonny's drink – light on the tonic and hefty on the lemon and gin. It was obvious what was going on. Hamish was spiking Sonny Wiseman's drinks on Eugene's orders. Obvious to everyone, that was, apart from Sonny. The movie mogul's cheeks were already red. And, as Sonny tossed down his cards with another curse, Frankie could see that Eugene and Dieter were taking him to the cleaners on the poker table.

Frankie watched, amazed, as Eugene charmed the old guy. Then she saw him slipping a card under the table to Dieter. Did they think she was too stupid to notice?

Hamish waved a bottle at her. 'Go and get more gin up here,' he hissed. 'And be quick.'

Frankie stared at him.

'Now!'

Frankie ran down to the galley store, smarting. How dare Hamish lecture her about talking to a guest when he and Eugene and Dieter were fleecing the very same man? Well, sod Hamish, she thought, taking a gin bottle off the galley-store shelf. She checked behind her to see that no one was looking, then tipped four-fifths of the gin down the sink and topped up the bottle with water.

There, that should even up the odds, she thought. Now Hamish could spike Sonny as much as he liked and it wouldn't make a scrap of difference.

On her way back with the gin, her head was so full of the vitriolic argument she'd have with Hamish later that she almost bumped into Sonny Wiseman coming out of the bathroom at the back of the saloon.

'Don't you go running out on me now, little lady. You're my lucky charm,' he said.

Frankie couldn't look him in the eye. She felt implicated in the others' deceit. But she mustn't say anything, she told herself. She had to stay out of trouble.

'But today ain't my best day. They're creaming me out there.'

He looked directly at Frankie then, and something about his honest gaze made her blurt, 'I don't think that's *your* fault, sir.'

Shit. It was out. She felt the colour rising in her cheeks. Her and her big mouth. When would she learn?

'Eh?' Sonny looked confused.

'Just ignore me, sir, I—'

'It's OK. You can tell me.' He leant forward, his eyes amused. 'I'm a big guy. I can take it.'

'Well . . .' She hesitated, glancing over her shoulder to make sure they weren't being watched. Then she grabbed his arm and pulled him into the shadow of the doorway.

'Eugene and Dieter . . . they've told the steward to spike your drinks. And Dieter is . . . I saw him swapping cards under the table. That's why you're losing.'

Sonny looked at her. The smile faded from his face. 'You can't be serious?'

'But it's OK,' she said, unscrewing the gin bottle and holding it out for him to sniff. 'See? I've watered it right down. To give you a chance of winning your money back. I don't think you deserve to get ripped off like that. But please don't say anything, Mr Wiseman. I'm serious. If you do, it'll cost me my job.'

Sonny Wiseman nodded. 'I see. I'm glad you had the balls to say something. Hey, kiddo, what's your name again?'

'Frankie.'

He leant in close. 'Well, Frankie, I won't forget this.'

Suddenly Richard, the captain, was behind them.

'Is everything OK?' he asked. 'Mr Wiseman?'

'Just fine,' Sonny said, placing a fat hand paternalistically on Frankie's shoulder and walking her back out to the deck. Frankie could see Richard was fuming that she'd been talking to Mr Wiseman, but before he had a chance to say anything, the *thwack-thwacking* sound of a helicopter made them all look up.

'Who's that?' Sonny Wiseman asked as a helicopter swooped down towards the boat, its lights making them shade their eyes.

'The boss is coming aboard, sir,' Richard replied, before moving past them both. 'Frankie, wait at the top of the steps. Be ready to collect his bags.'

He was here. Frankie felt a ripple of excitement run through her. 'I haven't got a pass,' she said.

Richard handed her a plastic card. 'Hurry.'

Frankie ran up the steps two at a time until she was on the very top deck of the yacht. She arrived just in time to see the helicopter coming in to land on the pad, like a giant bug. She held on to her baseball cap tightly as the wind thrown off by the rotors threatened to tear it away.

Pushkin's two engineers, Paul and Jeff, were both up here too. Jeff had changed into a full fire-fighting suit, as a precaution, and was guiding the helicopter in. Dieter came up too.

Frankie jumped as Richard suddenly appeared behind her, stepping out of the elevator that ran down through the centre of the yacht. Frankie had never seen the inside of it before. It was panelled with mirrors and a thick carpet.

She turned back to watch the helicopter land carefully on the pad. The pilot took off his ear defenders, opened the door, hopped out, and, covering his head, ran towards her and Richard.

The pilot was young. A few years older than her, maybe. He was tall, with a deep golden tan. He had short black hair in a trendy messed-up style and thick dark eyebrows that almost met in the middle. His jaw was strong and he had a distinctive beauty spot just above one corner of his mouth. He was wearing a crumpled beautifully cut navy linen suit and a white T-shirt with aviator shades casually tucked in at the neck. Any formality was counteracted by the white Converse sneakers he wore on his feet.

'Hi,' he shouted. He shook hands with Richard, then smiled at Frankie. He had the nicest smile she'd ever seen. But it was his eyes that did it. Warm, blue and calm – like the ocean, Frankie thought as she drowned in his twinkling gaze.

'Hi,' she muttered back, feeling as if she'd been lifted up on a wave and placed gently back down.

Feeling herself blush, she made herself look away, back past the pilot to the silhouette of the helicopter. She watched the aircraft's rear doorway, waiting for the boss to emerge. But the pilot stayed standing in front of her, staring at her. She forced herself to concentrate on the helicopter, watching the rotors slow to a halt.

As the noise of the engine subsided, the pilot cleared his throat. 'So you're new?' he said, looking to Richard for confirmation and then back at Frankie.

'This is Frankie. The new stewardess and gym instructor. I told you about her?'

Frankie glanced at Richard uncertainly. Why would he tell the pilot about her?

'Frankie. Welcome. I'm Alexei Rodokov,' the pilot said, holding out his tanned hand for her to shake. His grip was warm and firm.

Oh my God! She couldn't believe she'd been so stupid. The pilot *was* the boss.

Frankie felt all her preconceptions crashing around her. She couldn't take her eyes off him. She'd imagined he'd be older. More Russian. An ogre, not a prince.

Richard nudged her. 'Bag,' he hissed in her ear.

'Oh, um . . . may I take your bag, sir?' Frankie asked.

'No bags,' Alexei said. 'Just as I am.' He put out his arms and shrugged.

His accent was American-English. Mid-Atlantic. It was educated and friendly and not what she'd been expecting at all. Frankie stared at him, tongue-tied.

'OK, well, good to meet you, Frankie,' he said. 'I'll see you in the gym at seven a.m. You can put me through my paces.' He smiled at her, leaving a trail of musky cologne in his wake as he strode past her into the elevator.

And there it was again. That airborne feeling.

She stayed rooted to the spot.

'Hey, Dieter,' she heard him say as Dieter followed him into the elevator. 'Where's Dimitry?'

'Still in the UK.'

'That'll be all, Frankie,' Richard told her. 'The fun's over. You can go back down now.'

Frankie turned to go back down the stairs. The elevator door was closing. The boss was inside, talking to Dieter. He didn't look at her again.

But Frankie knew at that moment that, whatever it took, she was going to get Alexei Rodokov to notice her.

CHAPTER SIX

In Wrentham Hall, the Platinum Ball was only half an hour off schedule. It was nearly eleven and Bunny had just sung Happy Birthday and a stunning rendition of '*Vissi d'arte, vissi d'amore*', Julian's favourite aria from *Tosca*, and now a happy atmosphere had descended on the ballroom as the three hundred guests digested the banquet.

Emma blushed as a peal of laughter rippled around the tables. Next to her, Julian was standing with the microphone in his hand making his after-dinner speech. So far it had all centred on her.

'Julian, stop it,' she implored, hating being the centre of attention.

But Julian waved her protestations aside. 'Seriously, ladies and gentlemen,' he continued, 'I know Emma hates me talking about her, but, darling . . .' He looked down at her. '. . . tough. I'm not going to stop.'

There was more laughter from the guests.

'Two hundred years ago,' Julian continued, 'Emma's great-great-grandparents, my distant – and, judging from their portraits on the stairs – somewhat scary in-laws, would have thrown parties like this, when Wrentham Hall was in its hey-day. It has taken Emma's enormous vision and dedication to restore the Hall to its former glory. Many of you will have seen Emma in action on the *Restoration* series on the BBC last year. Did anyone see that bit where they took the roof off?'

There were laughs of acknowledgement. Emma laughed too and covered her eyes, remembering the logistical nightmare.

'The first I heard of it was when I was in South Africa and I saw it on TV. I can tell you that I was seriously worried. But as always, Emma knew what she was doing. "You always said you wanted a courtyard effect, darling," she said. "Just think of it being like an Italian villa for a bit."' Julian smiled. 'And it was. But that is Emma all over. She's incredibly optimistic, efficient, and works harder than anyone I've ever met. And we're all sitting in the proof of that. And so I think tonight is a fitting occasion to toast Wrentham in all its refurbished glory.'

Julian raised his glass and smiled down at Emma. 'To Wrentham,' he said, and everyone joined in. Then there was a round of applause.

'But that isn't only where my wife's talents lie,' Julian went on afterwards. 'As you know, she's been very involved in her charity for the past few years. Most of you here have been dragged along to one or two of her events.'

'And the rest!' someone heckled.

'And let's not forget that she can also fly her own plane,' Julian continued. 'Even though she knows I'm scared of heights.' He smiled. 'Perhaps even *because* she knows I'm scared of heights . . .'

Emma reached out and squeezed his hand.

'No, ladies and gentleman, I am incredibly privileged to be married to such a wonderful woman. And with her help and support I have been able now to launch Platinum Holdings.'

'Here, here,' someone shouted.

'Obviously, I hate to mention business,' Julian said. 'I know it's vulgar at a party. However . . .'

Another guest heckled, but Emma didn't catch the remark.

'Recently many of you have shown your support by investing your hard-earned cash in my company.'

'So show us the money!' someone shouted. Everyone laughed.

Julian rubbed the side of his nose. 'I intend to, Harry,' he said. 'As most of you know, Platinum Holdings floated on the Alternative Investment Market this week.'

There was a smattering of applause and Julian smiled.

'Which means that the funds are now available from the AIM listing and we are ready to green light the development project on the mine in Russia.'

Emma glanced at Dimitry, but he didn't look at her. His face remained a mask.

'This is a tremendous opportunity,' Julian said. 'The geologist's report values the mine at well over a million ounces of platinum P3 reserves. I won't bore you, ladies and gentleman, but at six hundred dollars an ounce for platinum on the current market . . . I'm quietly confident that our investment is going to leap from its current value of fifty million to a great deal more than that in a mere matter of months. As we speak, the shares are rocketing, thanks to the anticipation and confidence in the City.'

There was a whoop from the crowd.

Even Julian was blushing now. 'Yes, yes. Exciting times.' He paused and looked out at the crowd intently. Emma could see how emotional he felt. 'And I want you all to know how deeply I appreciate and honour your trust in me. You won't regret it.'

He raised his glass. 'So I'd like to toast us all, my dear friends. And Platinum Holdings. And toast to success for us all. But most of all, I'd like to toast the woman who has made it all possible – my darling Emma.'

'Emma,' everyone chorused.

'Thank you for my wonderful party,' he whispered, as he leant down and kissed her.

After the speeches, as the ballroom was being cleared, Emma's brother Pim approached through the throng, with Emma's sister-in-law, Susie.

'Ems, old girl,' he shouted above the happy babble of voices, folding her into a hug. He was as massive as ever, and was wearing a flamboyant navy velvet coat and a pink cravat. She might have known that he wouldn't wear the regulation dinner jacket that the invitation had stipulated. But it didn't matter. He was Pim and everyone knew his eccentric ways.

Susie, however, her cheeks ruddy from an outdoor life running the estate, had made a supreme effort. She stooped uncomfortably in her black velvet evening gown, and her hair, which was usually scraped up in an elastic band, fell in soft brown curls around her face.

'Susie, I meant to tell you earlier, you look absolutely wonderful,' Emma said, meaning it. Susie even smelt of expensive scent, rather than her usual whiff of moth-eaten jumpers and soggy springer spaniels.

'Look at those,' Susie said, mesmerized by Emma's diamonds. 'Goodness.'

Emma blushed, feeling a pang of guilt. Pim had sold off most of his portion of the family jewellery for the upkeep of Lechley Hall. Not that he'd ever complained, or asked Emma for any help. 'Julian gave them to me earlier. Typical of him to give *me* presents on his birthday.'

'What a lovely speech,' Susie said. 'He's such a poppet. I think he's going to be so successful.'

'He better,' Pim said, catching Emma's eye.

Emma felt her stomach flip over.

Lechley Hall was one of the last few remaining privately owned stately homes of its calibre left in the world. But it was so vast and so old that it was crumbling day by day. Pim had taken the tough decision to sell a significant proportion of the land, in order to raise some precious capital to keep going.

But Emma had come up with a fabulous solution to the problem using her influence on Pim to put up the final piece of financing for Julian's deal, using the money from the sale of the estate lands to buy the shares that gave him and Julian the controlling interest in Platinum Holdings.

Pim had been reluctant. The money had been his very last chance to hold on to Lechley, but Emma had talked him into it. In six months' time, she'd argued, once the mine was up and running, Pim could sell his shares to Julian and make a fortune. A serious windfall. Enough not only to restore Lechley fully and properly to the highest spec, but to buy back the estate lands to boot. Pim hadn't been able to argue with that. And now, tonight, he'd signed the last of the papers to make it all official.

Susie leant in close. 'I just keep thinking about all the things we'll do with the money,' she confided, her voice breathless with girlie excitement. 'I can finally refurbish the stables and give some of the staff the bonuses they deserve. And the very first thing I'm going to do is get rid of the damp in the East Wing and open it up again.'

'I think you and Pim should go on holiday,' Emma suggested, smiling at her sister-in-law. 'No one deserves one more than you two.'

'But, Em, I'm not like you. I don't want to go jetting off. And neither does Pim. Lechley is the most perfect place in the world to us. If I went away, I'd just miss it.'

'You two,' Emma laughed. 'You talk about it like a lover.' Or a child, she thought to herself. It was such a shame that Pim and Susie hadn't been able to have any kids. It bothered Emma that Cosmo was the only one in the next generation who would carry on the family's heritage.

Susie shrugged, smiling apologetically; Emma squeezed her arm.

'All I know is that Julian is about to make all our dreams come true,' Susie said.

At that moment, Emma looked up and caught Dimitry's eye. He raised his glass to her and smiled. Or was it was more of a sneer? Emma felt the hairs on the back of her neck stand up. Even now she knew who he was, there was something about him that she didn't trust. And trust was the most important thing. Because if anything went wrong . . .

No, Emma thought, forcing herself to be positive. Julian had worked too hard and had put too much into this for anything to go wrong. Julian trusted this Dimitry chap implicitly, and so should she.

'Well, Susie, if you won't go away on holiday, perhaps you'll at least come up to town and I can treat you to lunch. You really should dress up more often. You look positively divine.'

'I will, I will. Now have you visited Madame Mystique?' Susie asked with a girlish giggle. 'Everyone's talking about her. But I haven't had the nerve.' She glanced at Pim.

'Poppycock,' he said.

'Oh come on, Pim. She's just a bit of fun,' Emma said.

Madame Mystique was the fortune-teller Emma had hired

for the night. She'd decorated the gazebo in the garden and made it into a bazaar.

'Everyone is raving about her,' Susie gushed. 'She's got this mad Albanian accent, apparently, and is *so dramatic.*'

Emma smiled, delighted that the fortune teller was a hit. It was all those little added touches that made a party like this a success.

'Are you going to have a go?' Susie asked Emma.

'I may do. After the music. Paul's on in a moment and we mustn't miss the dancing.'

'Well, before the evening's out, you must go, Ems. You're so fabulously lucky, she's probably going to tell you about all the marvellous things that are going to happen to you.'

Pim shook his head, keen to pooh-pooh Susie's enthusiasm, and Emma smiled after him as he led Susie away. Her brother could be pompous and eccentric, but he was family and she loved and respected him. Running Lechley was a giant labour of love and she knew how much sacrifice it involved, and how much heartbreak, as the magnificent house was sacrificed to the elements year by year.

All Emma wanted was for her brother to live out his days with the estate running as he wanted it to. If she could just repay some of the kindness and support that Pim had given her over the years, then she would be satisfied.

Her reverie was interrupted by Julian.

'The band is starting,' he said. 'Come with me, my darling.' He led her back to the ballroom, already starting to dance to the music, and Emma laughed, loving to see him being the life and soul of the party.

Emma was also delighted with the transformation that had so speedily taken place in the ballroom. The tables had been cleared and the lights now lit up the stage, where Sir Paul's back-up band had just begun their first number, Van Morrison's 'Brown-Eyed Girl', which Emma knew was one of Julian's favourites. He pulled her on to the dance floor, twirling her round. Emma sighed as he drew her in tight and clasped her hand against his chest.

'Having fun?' she asked.

'Isn't everyone?' he replied, kissing her hair. She could tell how happy he was. 'You give good party, darling,' he said.

Only a few moments later, Julian was wrenched from her arms by David Coulter, one of their oldest friends.

'Budge over, old man,' David said, cutting in and expertly prying Emma's hand out of Julian's.

Julian and Emma both laughed as David effortlessly twirled her away.

'I wondered where you'd got to,' Emma said, smiling up at him.

The years had been kind to David, she noticed, now that she had the time to study his face up close. He didn't seem any different now to the foppish, eager guy who'd picked her up in his brand-new red Porsche, a cigarette hanging out of his mouth, twenty-five years ago. He had strawberry-blond hair, a tanned freckled face and dazzling aquamarine eyes, with eyelashes so long that Emma had once told him looked like a cow's.

It had been David that Emma had dated first, before she'd ever met Julian, or realized that Julian was David's best friend. Back in those days, she'd been swept up in David's Chelsea lifestyle, more than happy to help him spend the small fortune he'd made in shrewd property investments. She'd been dazzled by his sense of humour, his crazy energy and desire for partying. He'd seemed to know everyone and every single one of his friends had assured Emma that she was *the one*. They'd all been so keen to tell her that David was crazy about her, although in the rare times she spent alone with him, David never actually confirmed that himself. In fact, he never wanted to commit to how he was feeling, only to when the next party was. And Emma had been glad. Back then, she too had been more interested in having fun than planning a future.

But then, one night, David hadn't been able to meet Emma and had sent Julian instead. And everything had changed in an instant. Emma had been smitten.

At first, it had been terrible. She'd felt so guilty about falling so hopelessly for Julian. And he'd felt the same way – not that she knew it then. They spent months skirting around the issue of their feelings, whilst making every excuse to see as much of each other as was possible. And all the while, they'd both privately agonized about hurting David's feelings.

In the end, it had been David himself who'd forced them together. He'd thrown a party and in one of his famous drunken speeches had outed them, publicly declaring that everyone knew that Julian and Emma were crazy about each other, and that they damn well better sort it out.

Of course, it hadn't stopped him ribbing Julian about stealing his girl in his best man's wedding speech – a joke he never tired of. But Emma knew how David valued Julian's happiness. And hers. And whatever he had felt back then, he'd been careful to gloss over and never mention since.

'Where have I been?' David said now, smiling down at Emma. 'Very good question. I took a visit to your psychic in the garden.'

'Oh?' Emma laughed. 'You too. What did she say?'

'Very interesting,' David said. 'Of course it's a load of old bollocks. She said I'd be paid a visit by an older woman who would come and stay with me.'

'You? Older woman? Get out of here!'

'Exactly what I thought,' David said.

'Julian says your latest girlfriend is – what? All of thirty?'

'Ex-girlfriend,' David corrected her. 'I'm working on a younger model.'

Emma laughed. The eternal bachelor and party boy, David still lived his charmed life, running his huge estate in Tortola, in the British Virgin Islands. As far as Emma could make out, he spent his entire time throwing raucous, boozy parties, getting up at midday and fishing on his yacht, in between chasing after beautiful young women. Emma and Julian had been to the Caribbean many times over the years, and each time she'd come back exhausted.

Suddenly, he twirled Emma around in his arms and leant her back with a flourish. But Emma had danced with David enough times in her life to expect this, and didn't lose her footing.

'Hey, you're still good,' he said, twisting her away and then back into his arms. 'For an old bird.'

'I swear you're nothing but a dirty old man. It's indecent. When are you going to grow up and get a proper woman? Your own age?'

'Sadly, all the good ones are taken.' He winked at her and smiled, and despite his gentle jibes, Emma felt herself won over by his easy charm.

Later, breathless from all the dancing, and thrilled that the music had been so fabulous, Emma was making her way through the guests and out to the garden to check with Damien that they were all set for the firework display over the lake, when she saw the red light in the gazebo.

She started going towards it, then stopped. She didn't need to hear what Madame Mystique had to say – even if there was any truth in it. Emma already knew what the future held. It was going to be bright and successful – just like her party. And nobody was going to tell her otherwise.

But just then Emma looked down the drive and saw Dimitry's black car sloping out of sight, silent as a snake, through the avenue of trees. How odd that they hadn't stayed for the fireworks. Or wished her goodbye, or thanked her for the party. Those Russians may be wealthy, Emma thought, but they had no bloody manners at all.

CHAPTER SEVEN

It was just before seven in the morning and Frankie felt like a new woman as she waited for the boss to arrive for his first session with her. She was out of stewardessing duties for the first time in ages, and up here, with the sunshine pouring into the ultra de-luxe glass-sided gym, she felt happy and purposeful.

Pushkin was on the move, having left St Tropez in the middle of the night, bound for the trendy Sardinian playground of Porto Cervo. As the mega-yacht sliced effortlessly through the Mediterranean waves, Frankie lay on her back on one of the pristine mats and stretched out.

Her own iPod was in the speaker dock and she'd composed a special playlist for today's session. She wondered whether Alexei Rodokov would mind that she'd brought her own music, but the familiarity of it would calm her nerves, and hopefully create some privacy.

She knew that the gym was hooked up to the yacht's monitoring system and, as if sensing her thoughts, she saw the small camera in the corner of the room rotate towards her. She wouldn't mind betting that Roz, Simone and Trudy were watching the screens on the bridge.

They had almost choked when they'd heard that Frankie would be alone with the boss in the gym this morning. But she was a professional, she'd reminded them, enjoying her sudden rise up the hierarchy. Had they forgotten that she was a trained personal instructor, that it was why she'd been employed?

But now her stomach fluttered with nerves. Would she be good enough for Alexei Rodokov? Would he like her? And what would it be like working with him one to one? She couldn't be sure who'd trained him before, or how fit he was. And if he was mega-fit, would he suss her lack of experience?

Frankie had done her gym-instructing qualification as an evening course at university, thinking it would come in handy one day. But she hadn't been a proper practising instructor for years: the only personal training she'd done had been putting together workouts for friends back home.

Of course, she'd always made it *sound* as if she was way more confident than she was, especially when Richard had employed her. But now Frankie's stomach fluttered with doubts. She would just have to bluff her way through.

She stood up and did a deep forward bend, her legs apart. It was only then that she saw Alexei standing in the doorway behind her, watching her.

Even framed as he was, upside-down, a towel flung over his shoulder, Frankie couldn't help thinking that he was even more handsome than she remembered. He looked away quickly.

Frankie stood up, feeling colour rising in her cheeks.

'Good morning, sir,' she said. 'I was just—'

'OK, before we start, can we cut the "sir" crap? In the gym it's Alex, OK?' he said, walking casually towards her as if he got a new gym instructor every day. Something that might not be so far from the truth, Frankie considered, thinking of how wealthy he was and how much travelling he did.

'OK . . . so . . . Alex. Um . . . shall we get started?'

She gestured to the bench she'd set up in front of the mirror and the stack of weights. But he didn't move. She smoothed her hair behind her ear, aware of his deep eyes boring into her. She swallowed, nervous she might have already messed up. People like Alex probably weren't used to others making decisions for them.

'So what do you want to do?' she hurriedly asked, trying to make amends.

The tiny wrinkles around his eyes appeared to relax. 'I guess some upper body work would be good, I'm feeling a bit stiff.' He tore his gaze away from her face and placed his manicured hand on his shoulder and rotated his arm. 'I've been doing quite a bit of travelling lately. And it's a bit cramped in the chopper.'

'OK. What kind of exercise are you used to?'

'Less than I should. But I've started working out with Eugene recently, you know, pumping weights,' Alex explained.

He looked at Frankie, as if he expected her to be impressed. But she frowned.

'What?' he asked.

'I don't want to interfere, but it seems to me that Eugene could be heading for some serious injuries, and you could too, if you follow his lead. Besides, you have very different physiques.'

Now, as she watched Alex sit down on the bench, in his white singlet and baggy shorts, that seemed to be a complete understatement. As far as Frankie was concerned, Alex had a perfect body. He was slim, but had impeccable pecs and his shoulders were well defined. His skin was tanned and glowing with health. She felt an almost overwhelming urge to place her hands on his shoulders and feel his muscles.

'Anyway, I don't think you need to overdo it. You're in good shape, if you don't mind me saying.'

Alex laughed, tipping his head back. Even his teeth were perfect. 'No, Frankie, I don't have a problem with a beautiful girl telling me I'm in great shape.'

She smiled, embarrassed. He'd remembered her name. And called her beautiful.

'Just lucky genes,' he explained. 'I could do with some advice, though. My hip hurts occasionally on this side.'

'One of the reasons your hip might be slightly out is if your glute med is weak,' Frankie said.

'My what?'

'Oh,' she said, smiling. 'It's a muscle group here,' she said, slapping the back of her thigh.

'Weak?'

Alex didn't sound as if he had room for weakness of any kind in his life.

'Well . . . probably not that weak,' she conceded. 'But don't worry. It's easily fixed with a few exercises. OK, let's start on the warm-up.' She walked over to the iPod and turned up the volume.

'Hey, I like this music,' he said.

'Believe me, it'll get more hardcore when I really start to work you,' she said, risking a familiar tone. 'Now get down on the mat, we've got some stretching to do.'

She'd said it before she'd even thought about it. She'd issued him with a direct order. But instead of telling her to get lost, he nodded courteously, professionally even, and did as he was told, folding his perfect frame into a sitting position.

Maybe she'd got him all wrong. Maybe he wasn't a control freak. Or maybe he'd just decided to make an exception in her case. Whichever: it didn't matter. She was being paid to teach him, and that was exactly what she was going to do.

'One thing first.' He winked at Frankie, then, taking his towel off his shoulder, aimed it at the surveillance camera and threw. It landed over the lens. 'I think gym time should be private, don't you?'

But any question in her mind that he might have an ulterior motive for cutting off the camera was immediately laid to rest by his gentle smile.

Frankie smiled back. And in that moment they seemed to form some kind of unspoken pact. For a second, Frankie felt a hot liquid feeling spreading through her, but she quickly covered it up, making Alex lie down and lifting up his leg and pressing his knee towards his chest, so that she could stretch him out. She had to be professional.

Alex groaned with pleasure.

'Just breathe,' she encouraged him.

'So do you get this intimate with all my guests?' he asked.

What did he mean? Intimate? Did he mean she was being too intimate with him? 'Is this too much? I was only—'

'Frankie, lighten up, OK? I was teasing you,' he said, smiling as she swapped over his legs. 'All I meant was that this feels great. I wondered who else you'd worked your magic on.'

Relieved that he wasn't annoyed with her, Frankie felt

buoyed up with confidence. 'I haven't had the chance. Roz has got me on a tough rota.'

Alex smiled. 'Oh yes, Roz,' he said, as if he knew exactly what she was like.

Frankie moved Alex's arm across his body and leant down on his shoulder. He groaned again with pleasure as the muscles stretched out, and Frankie felt something inside her twitch again. Something she hadn't felt for a very long time.

Something . . . sexual.

'Roz came with the yacht,' Alex whispered. 'I didn't choose her.'

He looked at her and she smiled. She felt absurdly flattered that he was confiding in her, but she knew she couldn't comment on Roz herself. Not while there was a still a chance she might be listening in.

'Just relax,' she said, concentrating. She had to get this work-out right. 'Breathe out.'

Ten minutes later, Frankie was more in her stride and had really stepped up the pressure. Alex was doing chin-ups at the bar.

'So do you have an opinion on everyone then?' Alex asked as he pulled his chin up to his hands on the bar. She'd just explained why she thought Eugene was a typical macho show-off.

'I suppose so,' she said. 'Doesn't everyone?'

'So what's your opinion of me?'

That you're possibly the most gorgeous man I've ever met and, with your butt right in front of my face like this, you're almost irresistible.

'That you can work harder,' she said instead, retreating into the relative safety of work talk once more. 'Come on, put your back into it. Five more.'

'Jesus, Frankie. You're a hard taskmaster.'

'And I get results. Now move it!'

She would get results, she thought. And the best result she could imagine would be to spend as much time as possible alone like this with Alex.

Ten minutes later, she had him on the bench, when Prince came on the iPod.

'It's a bit old school,' she said apologetically.

'I love it,' Alex said. His chest was wet with sweat. He lay on the bench looking up at her, puffing out his cheeks.

'Warmed up, then?' she asked, smiling down at him. 'Ready for these?' she asked, placing the dumbbells in his hands.

'Of course.'

She watched him press them up above his head. When he'd done his sets, she lifted them out of his hands without giving him any praise. She could tell he was showing off. She'd met men like him in the gym back home all the time: suddenly she was on familiar turf.

'Now I want you to do twenty rows with the dumbbells like this.' She half knelt on the leather bench, one knee and one hand on it, keeping her other arm straight by her side. Then she bent up her elbow and brought up the dumbbell to waist height.

She looked up suddenly. Alex was staring straight at her bum, as Prince continued singing about twenty-three positions in a one-night stand.

Oh my God, she thought. Did Alex find her attractive?

Forget it, she told herself. Alex could have any woman in the whole world. Why on earth would he be interested in her? Cinderella stories were for kids. She'd bet her life that this Prince Charming had already been bagged by someone else. Someone richer. Prettier. Better connected than she'd ever be.

Still, she felt gratified when he blushed and looked away. Boy, would she like to be proved wrong.

'On you get,' she said, making way for him on the bench. 'I think you need bigger weights. You can take them.'

He was hurting. She could tell he was. She made him do two sets of twenty.

'Now, I want you to do ten press-ups.'

'No problem,' Alex replied, dropping to the mat.

She could see his arms shaking.

'Those were easy,' she said, knowing they hadn't been. She joined him on the mat. 'So now I want you to add in an extension. A press up,' she said, demonstrating one, 'the pivot to the side, so that you're just on one arm and put your other arm up like this, so you're like a star on the side.'

It took strength and agility. Alex looked less sure of himself. After four he was flagging. At six he lost his balance.

He collapsed back on the mat, exhausted. His whole face spasmed. Oh shit, she thought. She'd pushed him too far.

But then she realized that he wasn't angry. He was laughing.

'OK, OK, I give up. You've broken me,' he admitted.

She put out her hand to help him up. 'That's just for starters,' she said. 'Time for those abs.'

He was standing now, his body close to hers, and their hands were clasped, as if they were about to dance. She couldn't help herself breathing in his aroma. She watched a trickle of sweat dripping down the dip in his neck, and, quite suddenly, an image of her licking it away flashed into her head.

She stepped quickly back from him, tripping over the large Pilates ball.

'So how come you know all this stuff?' Alex asked. If he was aware of the way she felt, he wasn't letting it show.

'I've always been interested in keeping in shape. I did the training a while ago. It just came in handy for the stewardess's job.'

'And before that?'

'Before?'

'There's always a before,' Alex said, looking into her eyes. 'The *before* that makes you so different to those other stewardesses,' he continued.

She swallowed hard, blushing at his compliment. 'It's a long story.'

But her desire to tell him everything was very strong. He seemed so easy to talk to. As if he were a friend, not the big boss. But he *was* the big boss. He owned this whole yacht, she reminded herself, and God knows what else besides. How absurd to even think that she and Alex could be friends. It was just a fantasy – yet she had to use all her concentration to get through the sets of abdominal exercises she'd planned for him.

Then his phone rang. And kept ringing.

'Shouldn't you get that?' she asked.

'It can wait,' he said. 'This is our time.'

Our time. Frankie liked the sound of that. And the fact that he was willing to ignore a potentially important call for her.

The remainder of their session flew by, Frankie joining in with his last session of cardio on the bike. They ended up sitting panting side by side on the bench in front of the mirror.

'Well done,' Frankie said, smiling at him. 'Let me stretch you out.'

She stood behind him, still facing him in the mirror. Gently, she took Alex's arm and put his elbow up by his ear and stretched his arm down his back. He groaned with pleasure.

'I feel really different from how I do after a session with Eugene,' Alex said, his eyes connecting with hers in the mirror.

'Eugene is pretty beefy, but that doesn't mean he's so strong. I'd bet you any money he couldn't do the workout you've just done.'

'Is it attractive, all that muscle?' Alex asked.

She was surprised he'd asked her such a personal question.

'I'm sure it is to you. You wouldn't want a wimp for a body-guard. But from a girl's point of view – if that's what you mean – I think he looks ridiculous.'

'So what's your type?'

You. You. You are my type. She stretched out his other arm, looking at the pattern of freckles on his shoulder.

'I haven't really got one. I suppose I'll find out when—' She stopped. She hadn't meant to say so much.

'When . . . ?' he probed.

'When I fall in love . . . I guess.'

'You've never been in love?' Alex asked. He sounded surprised.

'Not really. Not properly. I mean I've had a few long-term relationships, but I guess I've always felt there was something more waiting for me. And so I never really committed. I always let work get in the way.'

'I know exactly what you mean,' Alex said. 'Go on . . .'

'I suppose I'm holding out for the feeling of knowing that spending the rest of my life without that person would be inconceivable. That's how I *hope* it feels, anyway.'

Why was she telling him this? She never discussed her love life with anyone. Why was she discussing it with Alex Rodokov, of all people?

'What about you?' she asked. 'Have you . . . you know, ever been in love? Properly like that?' It was out before she'd even thought how intrusive it might sound.

Alex looked bashful. 'No, actually, I haven't.'

'Sorry, it's none of my business,' she said, moving away from him. Suddenly, talking like this and touching him seemed too intimate. And the session was over.

But Alex didn't move.

'What?' he asked, searching out her eyes in the mirror. 'You seem surprised?'

'I am. I mean . . . I can't believe you've never . . . I don't know. I would have thought you'd have . . .' Her voice trailed off to nothing. What could she say?

'What?' he asked.

'Don't women fall over themselves when they see all this?'

'Ah,' he said, wiping his face with a fresh towel. 'That's just the problem. I don't want someone who wants all this.'

She shook her head, confused. 'Don't you like it?'

'I shouldn't be telling you this,' Alex said, turning to her. 'In fact, I'm not quite sure why I am.'

'Go on,' Frankie said, staring into his eyes. Then she flicked her eyes to the surveillance camera. 'I mean, this is private, right?' she reminded him.

'I don't know . . .' He paused and glanced up at her, obviously deciding to trust her. 'I have this yacht for business. Yuri – he's my boss – well, he wanted this yacht for himself, until he found out that one of his rivals has a larger one. So he gave it to me and is building himself a new one that's even bigger.'

'Bigger than this?'

Alex smiled. 'A lot bigger. With a submarine.'

'Wow.'

'But if I didn't write the money off on this, I'd just be giving the money straight to the taxman. And besides, it's great for entertaining. Everyone else seems to be impressed by it.'

'But you're not?'

'It's just so fussy. I feel on show the whole time. It's all very well, but I'd prefer to do my own cooking. But you mustn't ever tell anyone,' he said, with a grin. 'Especially not Chantelle.'

'You're joking?'

He shook his head, his brow still glistening with beads of sweat. 'No. I've got this riad near Marrakech. That's much more my scene. A local woman comes in once a day and leaves me fresh ingredients. Then I can get on with it myself.'

'It sounds heavenly.'

'Maybe I'll take you there, one time.'

He seemed suddenly embarrassed, looking away. They both knew such an offer was preposterous. But Frankie's heart still thumped hard against her chest. She bit down on her lip as the silence between them lengthened.

She couldn't look at him. She wasn't sure what would happen if she did. One look might give her away. One look might acknowledge the insane sexual tension between them. And the fact that they'd just got way too intimate.

'I should . . .' he said, looking at his watch.

'Oh,' she said, jumping up and taking her cue. 'Yes, I should . . . you know . . . get along too.' She cleared her throat, focusing on sounding professional once more. 'That was a really good session. You should be proud of yourself. You did great.'

'Can we do the same again sometime?'

'Of course. Whatever you want.'

Alex nodded. 'What I actually want right now is for someone to fix my damn email, but I guess you can't help me with that?'

Frankie smiled bashfully, tucking her hair behind her ear. 'Well, it's funny you should mention that, but yes, maybe I can . . .'

CHAPTER EIGHT

Peaches liked the cool, calm atmosphere of Ross Heartwood's consulting rooms. Well, she should. She'd helped find it for him, with its exclusive location in Beverly Hills, its tinted windows and discreetly covered parking lot filled with Ferraris and Porsches. The amount of times Peaches had put people in touch with the right properties . . . she sometimes wondered whether she'd have been better off with a career in real estate.

As she pushed through the door into the waiting room, several women looked up at her, then returned to their magazines. No one spoke. No one ever did. There was a tacit agreement that they were all in Ross Heartwood's secret club.

'Ciao, honey,' Peaches said, ending the call with Marina, one of her best girls, who was in Miami on a glamour shoot, and had agreed to go to the casino later for a date with an Arab sheikh who was one of Peaches' most generous customers.

Peaches slotted the phone in her purse and took a discreet look around the other women waiting for Ross. But, as usual, it was impossible to tell what they were here for. Unlike other plastic surgeons, Ross had made his reputation by ensuring that every piece of cosmetic work he did was invisible. No ballooning, hard-ridged breasts had ever left his operating table, or any of the wide-eyed masks from the face-lift brigade.

The women who came here were mainly actresses of a certain age, who claimed in magazine articles and on chat-show couches never to have had surgery. And they got away with it. Because, of course, they didn't look remotely 'done' and never would. Ross didn't believe in making people look as if they'd been locked into suspended animation in their teens. No, Ross's philosophy was to make a woman look the best she possibly could – *for the age she was*. He was a modern miracle-maker.

'Hey, gorgeous,' he told Peaches now, coming out of his consulting room, the heavy maple door swishing shut behind him over the thick lilac carpet.

Ross Heartwood was possibly one of the most beautiful men Peaches'd ever seen. And she'd seen plenty. But Ross had an aura of charisma about him too, a magnetism which drew people towards him. And from the way the women in the waiting room almost audibly swooned, it wasn't just her who thought so.

Today he was wearing cream pants with tan handmade Italian shoes and a light blue silk shirt opened a button more than anyone else would wear it, revealing a ruffle of curly dark blond hair on his tanned chest.

He wasn't good-looking in the traditional model sense, but there was something of the twenties matinée idol about him: his carelessly coiffed forelock and easy rugged smile, boyish and yet mature too. It was the kind of smile that made teenage girls book in tit jobs, even before they had tits, so that they could claim they'd stripped off in front of him. And the kind of smile that caused old women to wear their finest jewellery and have their hair done before they kept their appointments, just as if they were going out on a date.

The mere sight of him cheered up Peaches instantly.

'Hey, yourself,' she said, taking his perfect hands in her own and kissing him on both cheeks. He smelt of Hermès cologne, Peaches thought approvingly. 'Thanks for seeing me, Ross.'

'The pleasure is all mine,' he said. 'Ladies, if you'll excuse me, I shan't be long,' he added, his voice loaded with innuendo as he held Peaches' hand and led her towards his consulting room. Peaches felt the looks of jealousy like darts in her back, but these women would wait a year for a moment of Ross's attention.

Once inside the air-conditioned consulting room, Ross winked at her, breaking the familiar flirting routine that happened every time they met. For the first time since Ron Wallace's call yesterday, Peaches felt normal.

She threw her purse on the designer couch beneath the Francis Bacon sketch – a real one, so Ross claimed – and breathed in the heady scent from the huge arrangement of pale yellow English roses.

Ross was a true anglophile, right down to his accent, which was more Yale than LA. He kept a mews house in Chelsea, London, and went there every other month. Peaches noticed that he had the miniature Paul Smith black cab she'd given him as a kitsch Christmas present on his desk.

'Was that who I thought it was going into the parking lot?' Peaches asked, glancing through the tinted window at the hot LA day outside.

Ross put his hands in his pockets and sat on the front edge of his desk, bowing his head modestly. 'If I say so myself, her nose is my finest hour. It's certainly got her the big lead in Spielberg's next movie. I told her I should get a cut of her fee.'

Peaches turned to face Ross. 'You should.' She twisted her lips and paused for a moment. 'Now then, what's all this I hear about you moving to New York?'

Ross's eyebrows shot upwards in amusement. He rubbed the side of his face. She knew that he was surprised that she knew, but Peaches was like a bloodhound when it came to rumours. Whenever she sniffed one out she pounced on it. This particular one had come from Billy Grant, the real-estate mogul, who'd told one of Peaches' girls that Ross had had his mansion valued last week. But Billy Grant had a reputation for spreading bits of gossip about people moving in order to push prices up and stimulate sales.

'Well?' Peaches demanded. 'Is it true?'

He smiled at her. 'Maybe I'm thinking about it.'

'Well, you can't go,' she said, disappointed and shocked. She hadn't expected the rumour to be true. 'I'm not letting you. Absolutely no way.'

'Oh Peaches,' he said, smiling. 'You're so sweet. But it's not a big deal, really.'

'Of course it's a big deal, Ross. Why would you ever consider moving? Your life is here.'

Ross shrugged. 'I just fancy a change. That's all. You can visit.'

She gasped. Not having Ross on hand would be terrible. Awful. Surely he couldn't honestly be considering leaving her? 'Are you up to something?' she asked.

'You'll be the first to know if I am,' he said. 'But anyway, it's only a thought. One of several options I'm thinking about. Or I might do nothing at all. So there's really no point in you getting upset.'

'But—'

Ross put up his hand to close the subject. Then he smiled at her and she knew she had to back off. Ross would tell her what was going on in his own good time. 'Now don't tell me you came here to discuss me.' She knew him well enough to know that he was scanning her features. 'Because I have to tell you, honey-bun, you don't need anything. Not after all that work we did last time. I think it's holding up fantastically well,' he continued. 'You're as lovely as ever.'

'It's not my face,' Peaches said, feeling flattered. 'It's just . . .' She decided to come straight to the point. 'I've got this scar on my back. It's bothering me, Ross. I want you to fix it.'

'OK, let's take a look.'

He nodded to the familiar leather couch and Peaches walked over to it, unbuttoning her sheer silk blouse. Ross turned to her as she unfastened her bra and held it against her breasts. His face was totally professional as he approached her.

'Here,' she said, turning her shoulder towards him. 'Just beneath my shoulder blade.'

Ross touched it, his fingers tender. This time Peaches didn't flinch.

'What is it?' she asked. 'I mean, can you tell what caused it?'

'It's difficult to say. It's certainly not a birth mark.' She felt Ross leaning in closer.

'You don't remember having any accidents do you?'

'Accidents?'

'It looks like old scar tissue from a burn. The skin here is very damaged.'

Peaches felt a shiver run through her. She searched again for the distant memory. If she'd been burnt, that might explain the feeling of fear.

'But it must be from a long time ago,' Ross continued. He straightened up in front of her. 'What's all this about? You've never been bothered by this before. Don't tell me you've only just noticed it?'

'No,' she said. 'Of course not. It's always been there.'

Peaches looked away. Ross was her best friend and she wanted to tell him about the strange snippet of memory the scar provoked, but something held her back.

She'd sound like a crank if she told him about the weird Russian connection she felt the sickle-shaped scar had. It was a feeling that had only increased after the shocking conversation she'd had with Ron Wallace yesterday. He'd told her that he represented an imprisoned Russian gangster – what was his name? Mikhail Gorsky, that was it. This Gorsky character had made Wallace track Peaches down and instructed Wallace to get her to come to Texas so that he could give her some vital information. Information about her past. Information that would affect her future. According to Wallace, Peaches had to come straight away, as Gorsky was about to be extradited back to Russia.

At first Peaches had tried to wriggle out of the whole thing, but Wallace had been insistent. He'd told her categorically: if Peaches wanted to find out any more, then this was her last chance. And so she'd agreed to go to Texas.

And now she wanted to tell Ross that she was scared. Because the past twenty-four hours had set her alarm bells ringing. First Valentin teasing her that she must have Russian blood – and on the very same day being contacted by a Russian gangster's attorney. It was all just too much. Peaches had a hunch – just a crazy hunch – that the sickle-shaped scar could mean . . .

But could mean *what*, exactly?

She knew the sickle was the Russian emblem. But her scar being that shape was surely just a fluke? It couldn't really mean that a Russian had put it there. It was more likely that Albert Rockbine or some other sick bastard from her past right here in the States had done it to her.

Either way, she'd made a decision late last night and had booked her flight to Texas for tonight. She happened to know an oil-company chief who would pay handsomely for an hour or two of her company. And then, tomorrow, she'd see this Gorsky guy and find out what the hell this was all about. But until then, she was just clutching at straws.

'It's nothing,' she told Ross, looking away from his familiar gaze. 'It's just someone commented on it. And I'd feel better if it wasn't there.'

Ross took a look at the scar again. 'It's very defined and your skin is very supple there. I'm not sure that surgery will really make it any better. I guess I could do a skin graft.'

'I don't care what you do. Just get rid of it.'

'OK. If you feel that strongly about it. But are you sure?' Ross signalled for her to get dressed again and drew away to his large desk. 'I have to tell you, I kind of like it. It's sexy.'

'It's not,' Peaches said, more harshly than she meant to. 'Besides,' she added teasingly, to make up for her tone, 'how would *you* know.'

Ross smiled at her. 'I know sexy when I see it.'

'You couldn't afford me, baby,' she said, as she buttoned up her blouse. The she raised her eyebrows at him. 'And anyway, aren't you forgetting that you're the biggest secret queer in Hollywood?'

Ross's sexuality was a constant source of banter between them. Peaches had flaunted many of her most beautiful girls under Ross's nose, but he hadn't shown even a flicker of interest, so she'd convinced herself that Ross was gay. There was no other explanation. But it wasn't something she felt she could ask him seriously, without risking offending him.

And his expression gave nothing away now – apart from the twinkle of amusement in his soft hazel eyes. Not for the first time, Peaches realized that he knew something she didn't.

'You really think I'm gay? Me?' he said. Peaches gave him a look that said she knew the idea was preposterous. 'I'm just celibate, that's all. Something *you* should try one day, Peaches. It has its rewards.'

Peaches pulled a face at him. 'Bullshit. Do yourself a favour, get laid. You could have anyone, Ross. And you know it.'

Ross shrugged. 'I know. But I'm just the way I am,' he said, his enigmatic smile making Peaches laugh. 'Besides, hasn't it occurred to you that I may be saving myself for you?'

'If only that were true,' she said.

Just why Ross Heartwood was single and celibate was a mystery to her. She wondered whether he had problems with sex. Was he impotent? Surely not. And if he was, there were a whole host of treatments that he would be aware of.

Well, she'd find out one day. Nobody could keep a secret for ever. Particularly not a man. And particularly not from her.

'So you still up for lunch?' Peaches asked, after Ross had scheduled in an appointment for her scar to be removed.

'Of course, I'll pick you up in two hours. Your place. I've got a new toy I want to show you. It's going to drive you wild.'

Exactly two hours later, Peaches was sitting on the veranda of her Santa Monica beach house, drying her last coat of nail polish, after a long and relaxing shower. She loved the secluded white and pale blue clapboard house with its minimalist interior and stunning views over the ocean. Today, the tide was way out, making the long expanse of wet sand shimmer, reflecting the blue sky and wispy white clouds above. In the distance, she could see that the surfers who came in the early morning had given way to the dog walkers and joggers.

Then came the unmistakably deep rumble of an expensive sports car coming down the private road behind her house and Peaches smiled to herself. She should have known. So *that* was Ross's surprise. She stood up, shading her eyes, as Ross drew level with the porch in a silver Aston Martin DB5. He smiled up at her and threw out his arm to the empty passenger seat next to him, beautifully upholstered in maroon leather. How typically James Bond of him, Peaches thought, grabbing her bag and running down to join him. And if she wasn't mistaken, he was wearing a brand-new Omega watch, just to complete the image.

'It's wonderful, Ross,' she said, running her hand over the immaculate paintwork.

'Get in, I'll take you for a spin,' he said.

Peaches laughed as the engine roared and they wheel-spun back out into the road and headed in the direction of the highway into town.

With Ross, Peaches felt that the world was a good place. That it was full of sunshine and possibilities and fun. Anyone watching them race by might easily have mistaken them for a happy pair of newly-weds. Peaches felt a momentary pang of regret at the sheer *otherness* of such a concept. Her and marriage: it was something she'd hoped for as a kid, the same as every little girl. But now it seemed impossible, fantastical – even absurd. She'd seen too many married men cheating on their wives ever to be able to trust one of her own.

'I booked Larry's,' Peaches shouted over the roar of the engine and the state-of-the-art sound system. Ross's musical taste, like his taste in art, was anglophile. The current MP3 selection was trippy and very louche. Peaches preferred all-American rock.

'Great.' Ross flashed her a perfect smile. With the sun glinting on the ocean between the palm trees behind him, Peaches thought he looked as if he should be on a movie poster.

Peaches knew that the restaurant was a mischievous choice – and one that Ross would love. Only someone as attuned to social nuances and body language as Peaches could have detected the frisson of scandal they caused when they were seen out together, and today was no different. As the valet sped away happily with Ross's car and Peaches and Ross walked up the steps between the manicured box hedges and entered the exclusive Hollywood haunt arm-in-arm, Peaches felt all eyes on them.

Half the women in here – mostly actresses – knew *exactly* who Ross Heartwood was, and most of them would rather die than have him acknowledge them in public. And half the men in the restaurant – studio bosses, agents and producers – knew *exactly* who Peaches Gold was and were similarly terrified of her bestowing any public attention on them. Most of their numbers were stored in her phone and in her closely guarded little black book of contacts. She held her head up and tapped her purse with her manicured hand, so they'd know she knew it. Peaches was well aware that with just one look, or a word, she could make or break a dozen reputations.

'Between us, you and I know more guilty secrets than anyone else in Hollywood,' Ross said as they were seated at the shaded corner table, the best table in the house, beneath the trellis of pink bougainvillea.

'You read my thoughts.' Peaches smiled, pretending to look at the menu, although she already knew she'd be eating the house salad. Her oil-company chief in Texas, Joel Woodrow Hawkins III, would no doubt want to feed her steak as they barbequed later on tonight by his enormous hot tub. Joel owned a dozen restaurants and casinos and had often talked about them going into business together, setting up a brothel franchise, but Peaches never would. She valued her independence way too much for that. And much as she liked the straight-talking oil baron, he was as slippery as a gallon of his finest crude.

'So let's talk about fun things. Like your party,' Ross said, a gossipy twinkle in his eyes.

Peaches had been hosting *the* party of the Hollywood calendar for three years now. Dubbed 'Depravity Night', it had started when Eddie Roland, the famous studio boss, had suggested that she throw an altogether different sort of party. Not a product launch, or a party attached to the Oscars or Grammys. Not a party where people went to be seen, or were paid to be seen, but a party where people went to have *fun*.

And not just any people. The rich and the famous. People so used to a life of utter luxury, people so bored of normal celebrity-packed parties and inured to the entertainment on offer that only a night of sheer hedonism would excite them. In other words, a party where Eddie and his friends could let down their hair (not that Eddie had much to let down) and partake of some of the finer pleasures that Peaches' girls had to offer at the same time. And Peaches, who knew a sound business suggestion when she heard it, had immediately set the wheels in motion.

The word had spread like wildfire. Everyone who was any-one had wanted a piece of the action. The élite group of men that Peaches' girls serviced had made no secret of the fact that they would pay almost any price for an invite. A-list actors, studio heads, producers and directors had all fallen over them-selves to get on to Peaches' secret guest list.

The resulting party had become the stuff of Hollywood legend. Peaches had heard vastly exaggerated stories of what had happened that night: stories that made her smile, because of their sheer sexual ludicrousness – and in some cases direct contravention of the laws of physics and biology. And yet she'd never denied them, because she was smart enough to know that such salacious word-of-mouth advertised her services better than any Madison Avenue agency ever could.

The second year – last year – had been even more outrageous, and Peaches had really splashed out on security. It seemed that the real draw of the event was its total secrecy. Everyone could party without the fear of being papped, or their names being bandied about in gossip columns. Or, most importantly, being collared by the cops.

This year would be no different. If the press had just one sniff of what she was planning, she'd be ruined. But that's why Peaches enjoyed hosting the party so much. It made her feel like she ran Hollywood. Like she was flaunting herself right underneath everyone's noses.

'So who's on the guest list?' Ross asked. 'Anyone in here?'

Peaches nodded and discreetly flicked her eyes in the direction of the table behind Ross.

'Really?' Ross said, clearly scandalized.

'Oh yes,' Peaches said, smiling and tossing her newly trimmed hair over her shoulder.

The producer sitting behind Ross was famously and happily married and his daughter was in a successful TV mini-series, but Peaches had had to buy a studded collar, a lead and a diaper especially for one session with him. She wondered what his wife, a leading socialite and Democratic candidate, would make of her husband's *real* sexual desires.

'So . . . ?' Ross asked. 'Location . . . dare I ask?'

The way she ran it, invitations to the party were sent out by courier less than an hour before with a special number for the recipient to call. Only after Peaches or Angela had vetted them for authenticity by asking them a strictly coded series of questions would the caller get the details of the party's location.

Peaches leant forward. She knew she could trust Ross. 'I'll have to whisper,' she said. 'You know everyone says this place is bugged.'

Ross smiled and half rose to lean across the table, so Peaches could whisper in his ear. She was aware of the whole restaurant watching them.

'I've got the Clover Hill mansion,' she whispered.

'You haven't!' Ross exclaimed, before clamping his hand over his mouth and sitting back down in his seat. 'That's incredible. And brilliant. Nobody would even think of it being there.'

'I know,' she said smugly. The Clover Hill Mansion was the Buckingham Palace of Beverly Hills. Since it had been built in the 1900s, only Hollywood royalty had lived there – most recently the Seagram-Cohens. Since screen legend Jessica had died last year right after her lifetime achievement award at the Oscars, old Murray Seagram-Cohen had been rattling around the vast mansion all by himself. The gossip magazines were full of talk about how Michael, Murray and Jessica's equally famous son, would be moving in with his young family to carry on the family dynasty, but Peaches had, as usual, got her timing spot on. Michael was renovating the whole building before he downgraded his father to the palatial annexe next door. For the night of the party and the few weeks either side, the entire site would be empty of Seagram-Cohens.

'It took a bit of work,' Peaches said. 'But let's just say Murray was persuadable.'

She glanced up at Ross, who hastily took a sip of mineral water.

'Don't look at me like that,' Peaches rebuffed him, adding in a whisper, 'I didn't "do it" with Murray Cohen. I *do* have standards, you know.'

Ross shrugged. 'I wouldn't blame you if you did. He was stunning in his hey-day. Some of those old films he did with Clint? Boy, he really fizzed on screen.'

'Believe me, Murray still has his charms. And I told him that it was important that he didn't get sidelined as an old guy. Not with his son moving into Clover Hill. I told him, "Murray, there're plenty of roles around for sexy older guys like you." And there are, I guess. More than for women. I told him that now Jessica's gone, it's important for him to get back to work. You know, get some credibility. And what better way to announce he's still got what it takes than if it comes out that he hosted my party? It was a simple case of appealing to his vanity.'

'You're a genius,' Ross said, smiling.

'But you know, Ross, you can't tell anyone. I mean it.'

Ross mimed zipping up his mouth.

'So how much are you charging this year?' he asked, after the waitress had poured them both a glass of the imported Hildon water Ross liked so much. 'Just in case anyone asks me.'

'Five thousand entrance, plus the usual fees for the girls.'

Ross let out an impressed whistle. 'So by my reckoning that leaves you . . . I'd say . . . two mill in the clear.'

'Two and a half. Minus some overheads.'

'My, my, Peaches,' Ross said, shaking his head. 'You are one clever girl.'

As they continued talking, Peaches forgot all about Ron Wallace and Gorsky. Laughing with Ross made her remember who she was. She was Peaches Gold, pleasure-provider, party-organizer and businesswoman. She didn't have personal problems. That wasn't part of the package. She hadn't needed a confidant before and she wasn't going to start now.

She was on her own. And that was just fine. Who cared where she'd come from? The point was that she'd made it here.

But as their lunch drew to a close, even though Peaches was laughing, the coldness returned to the pit of her belly.

All she could think about again was the Merton Correctional Institute and what tomorrow might bring.

CHAPTER NINE

On *Pushkin*, Frankie was alone with Alex in his study in the suite of rooms adjacent to the master cabin. It had a dark teak built-in desk beneath a row of oval portholes that overlooked the vast expanse of sky and ocean.

'Doesn't anyone clean up here?' Frankie asked, amazed at the state of the small room. The desk was loaded with paper. There was an open attaché case on the large swivel chair and a grey linen jacket flung over the set of wooden drawers. Several TV screens showed CNN news and various financial programmes. Beneath them, a monitor showed Reuters graphs of what Frankie assumed were stocks and shares. A fax machine spilt paper out on to the thick pile carpet with its repeated *Pushkin* monogram.

'No. I've given Richard strict instructions that this place is out of bounds,' Alex said, frantically clearing up.

Frankie picked up a mug. There was a crust of old coffee in it, probably two months old. She showed it to Alex and raised her eyebrows. 'Roz would have a fit if she could see this.'

Alex looked embarrassed and rubbed his finger up the side of his face. He was still flushed from his workout.

'To hell with Roz,' he said. 'I like stuff to be mine,

occasionally. You know – a place that has my skin cells in it.'

Frankie smiled. Who would have guessed that Alexei Rodokov could be so . . . so damned *normal*? It only served to make him a hundred times more attractive, because it suddenly made him seem attainable too.

'Take a seat,' Alex said, moving the case and offering her the swivel chair. Now that they were alone and she was in his domain, rather than in the gym, she'd expected him to be completely at ease and in control. But quite the reverse. He seemed apprehensive, nervous even. But of what? Surely not of her?

She sat down and looked at the open laptop on the desk in front of her. It was the latest Mac. She'd only read about them, never actually seen one, but to Frankie's trained eye, it was beautiful – the most powerful portable machine on the market. It would take her six months' full salary to be able to afford one for herself.

Alex leant down beside her, one arm on the chair, as he booted up the screen. Their heads were close now and, once again, Frankie had to remind herself to be professional.

It felt good being back at a computer, but it made her nervous too. She hadn't touched one for over a year, apart from to send the occasional mail to friends back home. She hadn't wanted to let herself think too much about what had happened. About how she'd been fast-tracked into a Government job as a computer technician, only to then accidentally uncover information concerning a conflict diamond scandal involving senior government officials. About how she'd blown the whistle on what she'd found and, in turn, exploded her life.

Because she was lucky to be here at all. She knew that much. Lucky to be alive. The police inspector had made that clear enough to her. Around the same time he'd told her to take a long holiday and not come back.

They could prosecute her for hacking, he'd said. Frankie had told him that she'd just been doing her job, chasing down a cyber-trail of ghost invoices that hadn't made any sense. But the inspector had made it quite clear that if she didn't leave the country and keep her mouth shut, he'd personally see to it that she ended up in prison. Or worse.

Frankie hadn't needed to think twice, because then the most

horrendous thing of all had happened. Sadie, Frankie's best friend and work companion, had been found macheted to death in the stairwell of the apartment she and Frankie shared. Her tongue had been cut out.

Even though Frankie would never be able to prove it, because the murder had been made to look like a bungled robbery, Frankie was sure it was meant to have been her who'd ended up dead.

Devastated over Sadie's death, Frankie had quickly packed up and said goodbye to her aunt and uncle. Uncle Brody had even bought her ticket. He'd always been like a father to her, since Frankie's parents had been killed in a car accident when she was only a baby. He'd made her promise to swear off politics and computers for ever.

But here she was, once again. Taking a risk. She'd hadn't told Alex anything about her run-in with the South African police, as she didn't want to alarm him. Or have to convince him of her innocence. Or have to think about what had happened to poor Sadie – and what might still happen to Frankie herself if she went shouting her mouth off.

'Are you sure about this?' Alex asked, as if sensing her apprehension.

'Of course I am. I told you, this was my old job. Whatever needs fixing, I'm your girl.'

Alex nodded and smiled.The fact that he believed her and trusted her enough to help him filled her with fresh confidence.

She couldn't blow it. Because, more than anything, she didn't want this to end. She didn't want to go back downstairs and have to face Simone and Trudy and all their prying questions, or to scrub out any more toilets. She wanted to be with Alex. With him, she felt invincible, on top of the world. Even the horrors of what had happened in South Africa seemed to fade in her mind. Alex's power and strength and her closeness to him right now were slowly rubbing them away.

'So, look,' Alex said, pointing at the screen. 'This is what happens when I try and access my account.'

She watched him type in various commands and get nowhere.

'Let me see,' Frankie said, her fingers flying over the

keyboard. Alex moved away, but Frankie hardly noticed. She tracked the problem in less than a minute.

'Bingo,' she said, gratified that she hadn't lost her touch. 'It looks like someone has been using your mail server as a relay and you've been reported for abuse, blacklisted and disconnected by your ISP. I could probably fix it for you if it's a standard server like Microsoft Exchange or a Unix Sendmail system. Then I can contact your ISP to have you reconnected. I'll need to send them a fax on headed notepaper. Why hasn't your systems administrator taken care of this?' she asked.

Alex looked taken aback for a moment. 'Fired. I'm restaffing at the moment.'

'OK, so we may as well check your firewall rules and change your administrative passwords too, just in case. Does anyone know the current passwords?'

'Sure. They're kept in an envelope in the safe at our Forest Holdings HQ.'

'OK. Well, I guess for the time being we can create a second admin account. Let me just fix the server.'

Before long, Frankie was totally absorbed in Alex's computer system.

'So do you like Italy?' he asked.

'Pardon me?' she asked, glancing across at him. He was sitting on the edge of the desk, his legs stretched out in front of him, his feet crossed. The way he was looking at her made her stomach flip over. Frankie ripped her eyes back to the computer, hoping that he couldn't see her flushing. She needed to concentrate. She wanted this to work. She wanted him to be impressed that she could help him out. She wanted him to realize that she was more than just a stewardess.

But, God, it was hard with him staring at her like this.

'I've never been there,' she said. 'But I've always wanted to go to Sardinia. The rest of the crew all say that it's awesome.'

'I love it. The Costa Smeralda, where we're heading' – he nodded out of the window – 'is an amazing bit of coastline. Do you dive?' he asked.

She nodded, looking at the screen. 'Yes, but I haven't for a while.'

'Come diving with me, then. When we get to Porto Cervo.'

'Really?'

'Yes, really. I want you to see it.'

'But . . .'

There were a dozen reasons why such an offer was ridiculous. Roz would never let her off her duties to go. And Alex requesting her presence on a trip would look so suspicious. The others would be sure to guess something was going on. When nothing was.

Was there?

She nearly blurted all this out, almost told Alex how life aboard *Pushkin* really was for her and how there was absolutely no way she could dive with him, but she didn't. She didn't want him to think less of her. She didn't want him to think that she was someone who wouldn't take risks. Because she was. She was here, wasn't she? In his study. Off limits.

'You're the boss,' she said with a smile. If Alex wanted her to go on a trip with him, then she had no choice. Richard and Roz would just have to lump it.

Maybe he sensed her acquiescence, because he suddenly grinned at her.

'Good. That's settled, then.' He paused and looked serious for a moment, now that he had her full attention. 'Listen, Frankie . . . about today. I've been thinking . . . Please don't tell the others that we've chatted like we have. I'm not usually myself like this with . . . well, anyone. Perhaps I shouldn't have told you some of the things I have . . .'

Frankie smiled. 'It's OK,' she said. 'Your secrets are safe with me. And you'll have to trust me, because now I need your passwords if I'm to fix this mess of a system of yours.'

He looked into her eyes for a second or two, before nodding decisively. 'OK,' he agreed. 'I guess I will.'

A few phone calls later, and he had the passwords ready for her. He leant down over the keyboard and she started to fix the problem. She shifted distractedly in her seat. Was he smelling her hair? She could have sworn he was. He seemed so close. She could feel his breath on her neck.

Or maybe that was just wishful thinking . . .

Alex's phone rang and he picked it up, breaking the

moment. She glanced at him as he talked in Russian. He seemed so focused. So commanding.

'OK, put me on to the financial director.' Alex suddenly switched back into English. He smiled at Frankie whilst he waited, then turned away. 'Thanks for looking into this for me, Bob,' he said. He listened for a moment. 'So they're dormant, is that right? They've been holding companies for Forest Holdings in the past, that's what I understand? . . . OK, fine then. Shut them down. I really want to tie up all these loose ends, get these finances streamlined.' Alex sighed. 'OK. You sure I have to sign? Actually go there? . . . Right. So who's the lawyer . . . Vincent Detroy . . .' He wrote the name down, then ran his hand over his hair. 'And he's in the BVIs? Tortola? Road Town? . . . Road Town? Sure. OK, I'll go. Give me his address.'

Frankie smiled absentmindedly about the address he wrote down. Heavenly House. It sounded beautiful. The kind of place she imagined Alex would fit in perfectly.

Alex flicked open another BlackBerry and consulted his diary. 'Can't it wait? I could take *Pushkin* there for the winter.' He sighed again. 'OK, if you say so. The twenty-eighth of June is the next time I can get out there,' he said firmly. 'Tell Detroy we'll have our meeting then. Thanks, Bob.' Alex rang off and flung the phone down on the desk.

'Twenty-eighth of June?' Frankie said, her fingers clattering on the keyboard. 'That's my birthday.'

Alex looked at the phone, then back at her. Was he annoyed she'd been listening in? Frankie wondered.

'I'll remember that,' he said.

His comment hung in the air as he stared at her and once again Frankie's stomach flipped over. His gaze was so intense. What was he saying? That he'd remember her birthday because he'd be celebrating it with her?

No, he wasn't saying that at all. *Stop it*, she scolded herself. She was being crazy. She forced herself to stare at the screen and concentrate. But still her mind raced. If they'd got this close in just one meeting, where on earth would they be by her birthday?

Because she couldn't deny it. There *was* something between them. Something that was almost tangible. An electricity that she'd never felt before. Even with him standing behind her, as he was now, she felt her pulse racing.

'OK. Think of a new password,' she said. 'This is just for you to access your server. No one else will know it. So it has to be something you'll remember. A phrase is better than just one word.'

'Frankie's blue eyes,' he said without missing a beat.

Turning round, Frankie realized that he hadn't stopped looking at her. She felt herself blushing. 'Seriously.'

'I am being serious. Frankie's blue eyes,' he repeated, smiling. 'The most memorable thing I can think of.'

And for a moment, she felt she couldn't breathe.

'It's an old memory trick,' he explained. 'Image association. Whenever I need to remember the password, I'll picture you here.'

Wow, she thought, weirdly thrilled at the thought of having become a permanent feature in his mind.

'OK then,' she said, her voice catching. She didn't know what to do. How should she respond to such obvious flirting? 'Whatever you want,' she said, typing in the words, putting in the numbers 3 and 5 for the Es and Ss. She couldn't look at him. 'There,' she said, a few moments later, having verified the password and returned his screen to normal. 'All fixed.'

She turned towards him on the swivel chair and then he came and leant down, and once again their heads were side by side. Closer this time. She pointed to the screen and explained how he only had to type in this new password and he could access his accounts.

And then, when she'd run out of words, there was a pause. Neither of them moved.

It was Alex's cue to move away and for her to get up and leave his study. But it was as if they were both frozen.

'Frankie, please tell me this isn't just me?' he whispered.

They were both still staring at the screen. 'What?' she asked.

But she knew. And when he rested his hand gently over her hand, she slowly turned her head towards his.

And then his lips were on hers. Softly, they barely brushed hers. But his touch set off an avalanche inside her.

'Oh,' she mumbled. 'Oh, Alex.'

He kissed her properly then and it was as if he'd ignited a

touch paper. Before she knew it, she was on her feet, her arms around him, and his hands were buried in her hair as he pressed his body against her. She stumbled backwards, still in his arms, still kissing him, as he swiped the papers off the desk behind her.

She lay down on the desk and pulled him on top of her, overtaken with an animal lust that seemed to have nothing to do with her.

She moaned softly through the frenzied kissing, the agonizing desire, as her tongue reached into his mouth, wanting him, needing him, oblivious to everything but her desire to fuse with him. She lifted her legs up behind his back and she could feel his hardness pressing down on her, just a few layers of cloth away. She felt herself melt, her hips straining against his, her whole focus zoned in on him. She wanted him deep inside her. Now.

He pulled at her top and it ripped, but she didn't care. His hand reached for her breast. It felt as if her skin was on fire.

She cried out, her head reaching back, straining, as he leant down and his tongue flicked over her erect nipple.

She'd never felt this kind of desire. This overwhelming yearning. And she realized that every moment since she'd first seen him, this had been waiting to happen. Had *needed* to happen.

'Oh Frankie, Frankie,' Alex moaned. 'Oh . . . God . . .'

But suddenly there was a loud noise. They froze. It was the buzzer on the intercom. Frankie hadn't even noticed it was there.

Entwined as they were on the desk, they stared at the small red lightbulb flashing on the wall. They were both panting. Still pressed against each other.

'Sir?' It was Richard's voice. 'Sir, are you up there?'

Alex swallowed hard, then reached up to press the button. 'Yes,' he said impatiently. 'What is it?'

'Your breakfast is ready, sir. And I was wondering? Is Frankie with you?' Richard asked.

Alex looked down at her. 'No,' he said immediately – the huge lie sounding totally plausible.

'OK. Sorry to interrupt, sir. See you in a few minutes.'

Frankie and Alex stared at each other, their faces just

centimetres apart. But the spell had been broken. There was no point in pretending they should carry on now. Richard's voice had shattered the moment, had punctured their passion like a pin popping a balloon. Frankie became suddenly aware of the warm air on her naked breast. She felt suddenly caught out, wrong-footed.

But even worse than that, she could see in Alex's eyes how he was already retreating from her. As if he'd suddenly remembered his responsibilities and the fact he was the boss.

Alex helped her to her feet and she stood up, straightening out her top, clutching the skimpy material in her fist, desperate to cover herself up. Even though every nerve, every skin cell was screaming out for him, she stepped away and smoothed her hair behind her ear. She felt crushed. A deep blush rose into her cheeks.

Was she mad? What the hell was she doing, losing control like that? What must Alex think of her?

'I should go,' she said, surreptitiously wiping her mouth on the back of her hand. She could feel her heart hammering in her chest.

'Don't.'

But Frankie shook her head. She felt as if she were being watched. 'I can't do this. Not when—' She shook her head.

'I want to see you,' he said. He sounded desperate.

'But . . . where? They watch me all the time.'

Alex pulled her towards him and lifted her chin towards his. He smiled, his eyes melting into hers.

'This is crazy, isn't it? I feel like a teenager who's just been caught.'

Relief flooded through Frankie at the admission that he was freaked out. But still, she didn't know what to say. She nodded. Whatever the next move was, she knew that it had to come from him.

'I'll find a way,' Alex said. His voice was confident, strong. He said it as a statement of fact. 'We'll be together. Just us. I don't want this to be about me being the boss. I want us to just be us, where none of this matters.'

He kissed her, gently this time, sealing their pact. And she felt as if she were floating.

'God, I want you,' he breathed.

She reached up and kissed him again, holding his face and smiling. 'I've got to go,' she said, pulling herself away from him. 'Before someone . . .'

He nodded. He looked as shocked and amazed as she felt.

She swallowed hard. There was nothing she could say. He took two steps towards her and pressed his fingertip against her lips, his eyes glittering.

'Soon,' he said. 'Really soon.'

CHAPTER TEN

In the Merton Correctional Institute in Texas, Peaches felt her hands sweating as she followed the guard along the featureless grey corridor. She'd faced plenty of tricky situations in her time – bar brawls with gun-toting drug-dealers, violent drunks, and she'd even been with a client once when his mansion was burgled by armed thieves. But nothing had ever come close to this.

This made her feel choked up with fear. Peaches loathed and detested prisons – just the thought of them, let alone actually being in one – because she was a law-breaker herself. And ending up in a place like this was just about her worst nightmare. It stank of disinfectant, but misery and death hung in the air too.

A door opened at the end of the corridor and she was ushered into a featureless grey waiting room, where a second guard stood along with another man who leapt up from the steel table and stubbed out a cigarette.

'Ron Wallace,' he said, offering her a greasy palm.

Peaches' arm stayed by her side. She drew herself up in her navy Armani trouser suit and stared down at him for a moment without speaking.

In the flesh Ron Wallace was no less annoying than he had been over the phone. He was small, with unfashionable round gold glasses and greasy black hair. His skin was grey from the amount of cigarettes he smoked. The smell of sour body odour rose up from his crumpled grey suit.

All the way here this morning, Peaches had wanted to turn around and flee back to her life in LA. And now, more than ever, she willed herself to get the hell out of jail.

Being here was crazy. Why should it matter what this Gorsky person had to say to her? Surely she was just opening a can of worms? She was fine, she reminded herself. Her life was a success. What could she possibly find out that would make a difference?

Peaches wasn't a needy person. She was all about the present and the future, not the past, so she hated herself for being needy now. And she *was* being needy. The reason she was here, the reason that she didn't leave but continued holding eye contact with Ron Wallace, was because deep down she *did* need to know what this was all about. She couldn't bear the thought of someone having information about her that she didn't know herself.

'Mr Wallace,' she said, 'this better be worth it. I'm a busy woman. I won't appreciate it if you've brought me out here on some wild goose chase.'

'I appreciate you coming, Miss Gold,' he said.

'So where is this . . . Gorsky person?' Peaches asked.

'I've arranged for us to see him in the Governor's office in a moment.'

'And he's still said nothing more to you about why he wants to see me?'

'No. He insists on speaking to you in person. I should warn you, though. He's a very religious man. He says this is something he needs to clear off his conscience.'

His *conscience*? The sick feeling in Peaches' stomach was only getting worse. What possible reason could Gorsky have to unburden himself to *her*? Was it forgiveness he was after? But forgiveness for *what*?

'The Governor will see you in his office,' one of the guards interrupted, replacing a small phone on the wall. He gestured to a set of doors on the other side of the waiting room.

There was a harsh buzzing sound and the door began to open.

Governor Judd's office was incongruously lavish, lined with law books and gilt-framed oil paintings of former governors, as well as a bank of TV screens, monitoring activity in the prison. The Governor himself was sitting in a leather swivel chair behind an absurdly large wooden desk. Behind him a window overlooked the barren exercise yard. What seemed like miles of barbed-wire fences and concrete bunkers stretched into the distance. Backlit as he was, Peaches had a chance to survey the worst hair implants she'd ever seen in her life.

'Please,' the Governor said in a twangy Southern drawl. 'Take a seat.'

Ron Wallace quickly sat on one of the two chairs in front of the desk. Peaches followed suit, but slowly, letting both men know that she hadn't come here to take orders from anyone.

'It is highly unusual for one of our more notorious prisoners to get a visit from such a beautiful and clearly sophisticated young woman,' the Governor said. 'Most of the boys in here know only whores.'

Peaches could feel Ron Wallace blushing at her side. She ignored him. He may think he knew what she did for a living, after he'd no doubt paid some two-bit private detective to track her down, but he damn well better keep his mouth shut.

'They certainly never get to see distinguished ladies such as yourself,' the Governor continued.

'It's nice to find a man who appreciates class, Governor,' Peaches said.

Governor Judd smiled, stroking the stubble on his chin, as if he wished he'd shaved. He tipped back in his chair and made a spire out of his fingers in front of his lips.

Apart from the gay guys Peaches knew, most men responded to her in one of three ways: like tongue-tied slack-jawed puppies; or like chest-beating orangutans; or, the worst kind, like leering horny teenagers who thought they stood a chance. Governor Judd was taking the latter course.

'If I may ask, Miss Gold . . . What is your connection to the prisoner?'

'I really don't know, Governor,' Peaches said, smiling, even though his slimy face made her skin crawl. 'That's what I'm here to find out.' She turned and looked down at Wallace. He was sitting next to her with his leather briefcase perched on his lap, like a little boy.

'Very well,' the Governor said. 'I was just curious, that was all.' He nodded towards a side door, which one of the guards opened.

Two further prison guards escorted in a prisoner. He was in his mid-fifties, with his prematurely white hair closely cropped and silver spectacles on his scarred face. He was wearing an orange boiler suit and his hands were cuffed in front of him. His ankles were cuffed too, with a short length of chain, forcing him to shuffle each undignified step.

So here he was at last. The mysterious Mikhail Gorsky. But any hope Peaches had entertained that she might have met him before immediately died. His face meant nothing to her. She didn't even feel a faint glimmer of recognition.

But his eyes were familiar enough. Gorsky was a thug. An ageing hood, his muscles turned to fat. She'd seen plenty of men like Gorsky standing guard outside a thousand bars and clubs. Every one of them was as ruthless and mean as a snake.

The guards pushed Gorsky down on to a shiny steel chair by the wall, which Peaches could see had been bolted to the floor.

'Cuff him to it,' Governor Judd told one of the guards. 'Mr Gorsky is a dangerous man, Miss Gold,' he went on, once the guards had done as they were told. 'I recommend that you keep well back. I'll be right outside the door if you need me.'

The prisoner stared straight ahead as the Governor left the same way he'd come in, taking the guards with him.

There was a moment of silence after the door clicked shut.

'Mr Wallace said that you wanted to see me,' Peaches said, making sure she sounded braver than she felt. Inside, her heart was racing.

'My name is Mikhail Gorsky,' the man said, his clipped English heavily accented. He sounded as if he'd rehearsed what he wanted to say. 'Tomorrow I'm going to be extradited back to Russia.'

Peaches noticed that his fingers were fiddling with a small brown rosary.

'What did you do?' she asked.

Gorsky let out a bitter laugh and looked up at the ceiling. 'Enough to know that I'll never reach the Kremlin alive.'

'I don't understand,' Peaches said, looking between Gorsky and Wallace. 'I'm still not sure what any of this has to do with me?'

Gorsky stared at her for the first time and what she saw in his eyes made her heart pound even harder. Not anger or fear over his captivity, or even amusement or triumph over whatever information he had on her. No, what she saw was shame. Shame and guilt and self-loathing. And all of it, she now knew for certain, was because of something he'd done to her. She was looking into the eyes of a man who believed himself damned in the eyes of God. Damned because of her . . .

Then he looked down at his rough hands. 'Thirty-two years ago, I worked for a bad man.' Again he worked the rosary. 'Who wanted very bad things doing.'

'Bad things?' Peaches said. She felt as if the floor was shifting away from her.

His eyes locked on Peaches'. 'Miss Gold, I was the one who took you from Russia.'

Took her from Russia? Peaches felt the sickle-shaped scar on her back twitch.

'You mean . . . You mean I'm Russian?'

Gorsky nodded. 'Yes. You are from Moscow.'

Peaches was stunned. She *was* connected to Russia. She was Russian by birth. The scar was almost burning now. That certainly explained why the memory that kept coming back to her felt so strange. It had happened in Russia. The incomprehensible voices shouting . . . all of them had been speaking Russian. Albert Rockbine had had nothing to do with it, she realized. Some other bastard had got to her first. Maybe even this bastard who was confronting her now.

She felt her fists clench. Gorsky was clearly anxious to get whatever he had to say off his chest as he was already talking again, drawing a deep breath as he hurried on with his confession.

'I was the one who took you – stole you – from your mother when you were three. And then I smuggled you into America. I sold you to Albert Rockbine in Louisiana. I supplied him with what he wanted . . . a young girl.'

His words spilt into the room and seemed to charge it with electricity.

Peaches couldn't move. There was a loud ringing in her ears. She was desperate to hear more, or to be able to say something, but she was pinioned by shock. She stared back at him, hardly able to comprehend the magnitude of what he'd told her.

Took . . . stole . . . smuggled . . . the words raced around her head.

She forced herself to focus.

Stolen from her mother. Not given up. Not abandoned. Stolen and sold.

There was another word for that: kidnapped.

Kidnapped and *deliberately sold* to a paedophile.

Peaches felt revulsion so strong, she thought she might be sick. 'Monster,' she whispered.

Gorsky stared at Peaches hard, his brown eyes boring into her. 'I'll pay for my sins, in this world and the next, Miss Gold,' he said.

Peaches was shaking. Fury coursed through her blood. 'But why? Why would someone want you to do something so terrible? Why me?'

'I don't know. I was just doing my job. Following orders.'

'And . . . what about my mother?' Peaches' voice cracked.

'I know where she is. Wallace will give you her address. Now that I've seen you, I'm truly sorry . . . for what I did to you,' he said. 'And . . . and for the terrible things I did to her. Tell your mother that when you find her.'

Before she knew what she was doing, Peaches found herself standing right in front of him. She struck Gorsky as hard as she could across his face.

'Go to hell,' she told him, before turning her back on him and walking away.

CHAPTER ELEVEN

In London in the grand hall of the Dorchester, at Cancer Cure's annual Gala Lunch, Emma was expecting to hear her name, but her hand still flew to the diamond and platinum necklace Julian had given her when Arabella Constantine, the secretary, announced that Emma had been selected as the new chair-woman of the UK's leading cancer charity.

Triumph coursed through Emma as she stood up, listening to the applause around her. As she made her way through the tables to the podium, she wished someone close could be here to see her. If only Victoria McCorquodale had been able to get away from Scotland, but Emma knew how busy she was. And there hadn't been any point in asking Susie as she was tied up with the lambing at Lechley Park.

'Emma's poise and charm made her a perfect candidate to be the international spokesperson for our charity work,' Arabella continued as Emma took to the stage. 'Her network of contacts is second to none. And she's worked tirelessly for our cause.'

Emma looked out at the sea of familiar faces. The Gala Lunch was a big event on the London social scene, but this year there were more attendees than ever. Emma took a deep breath before starting on the short speech she'd memorized, graciously thanking Lady Whiteley for all her hard work over the years, before initiating another round of polite applause for her.

Lady Whiteley was putting on a brave face, but it was no secret that she was furious she'd been ousted as chairwoman in favour of Emma. Everyone knew how much prestige the post carried, both at home and abroad. And in these circles, at least, it meant a free pass to every event on the social calendar, from Royal Ascot to Wimbledon. Now Emma and not Lady Whiteley would be at them all: something that Mabel Whiteley would miss more than Emma would appreciate.

Because Emma wasn't here just to be seen. She was here to make a difference. To get rid of the old-school thinking and really shake up this organization. She was going to grow the charity and put its research programme on the international map. She knew damn well that these days it was not good enough just to be rich. You had to be seen to be doing something worthwhile with your money. And these women had a hell of a lot of money to be worthwhile with.

And now that she'd got the post, Emma was already brimming with fundraising ideas. She'd really get to grips with breaking down the pecking order in the old hierarchy and get the staff motivated. Perhaps a fashion show to start with would be a good idea – she'd get a supermodel ambassador on board, for sure – she already had a couple in mind. And a more 'street' image was definitely required to draw in younger fundraisers and contributors. She might initiate a new symbol too. Ribbons were so last year. Not to mention a new range of Christmas cards and gift ideas. Emma's head was buzzing.

But first things first. Emma knew that the charity survived because of the people sitting in the audience. So after the speech, whilst the desserts and coffee were being served, Emma went round personally to each table to introduce herself. She headed for the front of the ballroom where the tickets for tables were most expensive.

'Ah, Emma,' her old acquaintance Yolanda De Vere Burrows said, standing up and air-kissing her on both cheeks. Emma pulled up a chair, glad that she was starting with a familiar face. Yolanda was a well-known hostess on the embassy officials' circuit and her father and Emma's had been at Harrow together. Emma was fond of her, even though several of her friends, including Victoria, found Yolanda's forthright manner too blunt, a problem that was exacerbated by Yolanda's famously excessive drinking.

Unfortunately Yolanda had been away, otherwise she'd certainly have been at the Platinum Ball. But she'd obviously heard all about it, from the way she now complimented Emma on the restoration of Wrentham and the fabled success of the party. Emma felt a frisson of satisfaction over being gossiped about in such favourable terms. She had no doubt that it was people like Yolanda that had secured Emma's position as chair-woman. It was all about image. And the recent press about Julian's imminent success in the *FT* would probably have helped, too. The Platinum Holdings shares were going through the roof.

Emma demurely batted away Yolanda's over-blown compliments, but was pleased that Yolanda had done the decent thing and had left her table of guests in absolutely no doubt as to Emma's taste and social credentials. Yolanda then expertly segued into the necessary introductions.

'Emma, I'd like you to meet Natalya Khordinsky.'

Emma shook hands with the woman to Yolanda's right. She smiled at Emma. There was something fragile-looking about her, in her fine bone structure and wary grey eyes, yet she seemed hard, too, like the diamond cluster earrings in her ears and the pearl and diamond choker around her slim neck. And now Emma noticed a similarly chunky diamond cuff bracelet, Cartier watch, and whopping set of matching engagement and wedding bands adorning her slim finger.

At events like this, in a room full of wealthy women, there were always several million pounds' worth of jewellery on dis-play, but Emma had never seen jewels like Natalya's before. And whilst they may be impressive, personally Emma thought that having so much on show was not only ostentatious, but vulgar too. Or maybe Emma was just jealous that her own diamond necklace from Julian seemed so insubstantial in com-parison.

'Natalya has moved to London recently and we're keen to get her established on the social scene,' Yolanda continued. 'Of course you will have heard of Yuri Khordinsky, Natalya's husband.'

Ah, *that* was it, Emma thought. Yuri Khordinsky. That was why Natalya's name seemed familiar. And that *certainly* explained the diamonds. Emma had read a profile about Khordinsky in the *Telegraph* a few weeks ago, but it was news to Emma that the Khordinskys were in London. She'd read that they'd settled in Dubai.

Emma's mind started to race at the implications of them being in town. Yuri Khordinsky was worth an almighty fortune, which was clearly why Natalya was Yolanda's guest of honour. As soon as it was common knowledge that Natalya was in London, everyone who was anyone would pounce, wanting her to be on this committee and that committee. Before long, she'd be completely socially booked.

Emma smiled. 'How delightful to meet you, Natalya. And welcome to London. I hope you're settling in?'

'I find it a little daunting,' Natalya said, carefully measuring her words. Her accent was Russian, but it was clear that she had a lot of class.

'I hear that you have been in Dubai?' Emma said.

'Yes, that's right.'

'We have friends there. It's so wonderful for shopping,' Emma continued, trying to make polite chit-chat.

'Especially when you're buying the Palm Jumeirah,' Yolanda chipped in, but Natalya didn't seem to find it very funny.

'Yes, I heard. That was . . . very impressive,' Emma said, making sure she didn't offend Natalya.

'Even more so when it wasn't for sale,' Yolanda added with a raucous guffaw, unaware of the quick dart-like frosty glance Natalya shot her way.

The profile Emma had read had mentioned something about dubious strong-arm tactics being used in the sale of the Palm, but now certainly wasn't the time to get into all that.

Natalya obviously agreed that this was not a suitable topic of conversation, as, for a second time, she stonewalled Yolanda's attempts at humour, choosing to stay loyal to her husband instead.

'Well, Yuri always says everything has a price,' Natalya said. 'Everything can be . . . obtained.'

Emma smiled tolerantly at this tacit declaration of

omnipotence. Natalya had a lot to learn. Maybe where she came from, money could buy everything, but not here in England. That was the difference between old money and new money. Between West and East.

But Emma kept these thoughts to herself, deciding to give Natalya Khordinsky the benefit of the doubt instead. She didn't look crass, or seem the bragging type, so perhaps her financial forthrightness was due to the language barrier, or simply that she hadn't yet learnt the art of rebuffing Yolanda De Vere Burrows's snipes subtly.

Yes, Emma thought, perhaps it would be a good idea to take Natalya under her wing, until she found her feet. She looked as if she might be quite charming, if not a little reserved. And in addition to the money and kudos she might bring to the charity, they had a lot in common – with both their husbands heavily invested in Russia . . .

For now, though, Emma had to move on. She excused herself, making a note to get Yolanda to host a lunch so that she could meet Natalya again. But despite her best efforts to get back to Yolanda's table as the afternoon progressed, Emma found herself dragged into so many other conversations that she barely caught another glimpse of the Russian beauty before the guests began to leave.

Natalya was walking towards the door of the Dorchester, looking in her snakeskin handbag. Emma extricated herself from the conversation she was having and tried to catch up with her.

She wondered whether Natalya would consider it impertinent if she were to ask her about Dimitry Sergeyokov, or his wife. The aloof look of amusement which Dimitry had shot at her at the Platinum Ball was still preying on her mind. If Emma could just get one endorsement from Natalya, then her mind would be put at ease.

But then, perhaps that wasn't how Russian society operated. There was no reason why the Sergeyokovs and the Khordinskys would even know each other, let alone be connected. They probably moved in completely different circles. And now wasn't the time to pry or risk scaring Natalya off. Not before she'd convinced her that volunteering to help the charity should be her very next step into the London scene.

Besides, Natalya was moving too fast. Emma stood by the door and saw a grim-looking bodyguard holding open the back door of a brand-new black Bentley. She watched as Natalya was swallowed into the plush interior, the door hardly making a sound as the bodyguard closed it, quickly looking around him, before walking around to the front to get into the passenger's seat next to the unseen driver. Then, silent and sleek, the car slid into the traffic heading towards Hyde Park Corner. Yes, Emma thought to herself, Natalya Khordinsky was one enigma she was determined to crack.

It was early evening by the time Emma stumbled exhausted into the flat in Chester Square. As she shut the door behind her, she felt her whole body relax. With the spotlight on her all day, this was the first moment she'd had to herself. Her feet were aching and she kicked off her new Christian Louboutin shoes, revelling in the easy shabby comfort of the long-familiar, photograph-studded hallway.

The flat was Julian's, a remnant from his bachelor days. Emma knew that it was one of the last times that she and Julian would be staying here on their own, as Julian wanted to sign over the flat to Cosmo. Emma had to admit that Chester Square was a slightly better address than Cosmo's current lodgings, in a squat somewhere south of the river. But still, she thought, running her fingers along the wall as she walked, she was going to miss the old place. It was packed with history. Hers and Julian's. A museum to their relationship. This was the first place he'd ever brought her, the first place they'd kissed, and the first place they'd feverishly torn off each other's clothes.

Julian had assured her that very soon she could buy a whole house in Chester Square – maybe even the one across the road with the basement swimming pool that Emma so admired. But somehow she already knew that all that grandeur would never be able to compete with the sheer soul of this place.

'I'm in here,' Julian called out from the bathroom.

Emma walked through to the large en suite. Julian's favourite Ella Fitzgerald CD was playing on the ancient stack sound system. Julian was humming along, naked from the waist down as he did up his dress shirt in front of the mirror. He looked so sexy, Emma thought, and despite her exhaustion she felt herself buoyed by a surge of lust rolling down her thighs.

He turned and smiled at Emma, and without a word handed her a glass of the chilled Montrachet he'd opened especially. She'd phoned him on the way over to tell him about her new post and he'd been delighted. She knew the wine was part of the special collection he'd had for years. She clinked glasses with his and he stared into her eyes; connected to him as she was, she understood he was toasting her. She could see in his eyes how proud he was and she smiled back. They had a long-standing tradition of enjoying the first sip of their best wines in silence and she knew how eager Julian was for her to savour this one. So she took a long sip, letting the cool liquid roll over her tongue.

'God, that's great,' she said eventually, leaning up to kiss him.

'Rather astonishing, I think,' Julian said, agreeing with her. 'So? How was it?'

'Hard work. I'm all talked out. Oh, I met Natalya Khordinsky. She's in London now.'

Julian looked impressed. 'Clever you. Did you manage to persuade her to get her husband to slip some money your way?'

'I'm working on it. Perhaps we should get them over to Wrentham when you're back from Russia?'

Julian pulled at the end of his bow tie and examined his jaw in the mirror, dabbing tentatively with his finger at a razor nick on his neck. 'Why not? The more Russian businessmen the merrier, as far as I'm concerned. You know, I'm still so impressed with how smoothly this deal has gone. And after everyone warned me about doing business out there. I really can't see what all the fuss is about. As I see it, if you put your money where your mouth is, these Russians are fine to work with. And this is just the start. Once this platinum mine is running, there's no reason why we can't start investing big time. There are so many other opportunities.'

'It all sounds wonderful,' she said.

'It is. And we're on a lucky streak. Just between you and me, I've got a feeling we're going to win tonight.'

Emma sighed. She wished they were having an evening in

by themselves and that she could collapse on to the four-poster in the master bedroom behind her, instead of going to Fifty, the exclusive Mayfair casino they were due at soon. But Julian had promised Zak, one of the Platinum investors, that he'd play blackjack tonight. Their old friend Graham and his new girl-friend were going, as well as Omar, Jacob and Peter from Julian's club.

Julian winked at her in the mirror. 'Come on. Don't look like that. I know you're tired, but tonight will be fun. And as Cicero said, you can sleep when you're dead.'

Emma laughed, having heard his familiar mantra hundreds of times before. He had such insatiable energy that she couldn't resist it. She wondered whether they made men like Julian any more. All of Cosmo's friends seemed to spend their whole lives sleeping and moaning. Or stoned. No one seemed to grasp life by the horns like Julian did.

'OK, OK, I'll get ready,' she said, smiling at him. She put down her wine on the antique armoire and undid the zip on her tailored black dress. Carefully she stepped out of it and put it over the arm of the chaise lounge.

Suddenly she became aware of Julian staring at her.

'What is it?' she asked, a suspicious smile on her lips. 'What are you thinking?'

'Just that you don't look like a chairwoman to me. You're not nearly austere enough. And altogether too sexy.'

Emma laughed. 'Flattery will get you everywhere.'

'I bet old Mabel Whiteley nearly swallowed her teeth.'

Emma put a foot up on the seat and rolled down one of her seamed black stockings. 'Her face was a picture.'

'If only they *really* knew how much you hate being in the limelight.'

Emma smiled. 'I don't like people saying all those nice things about me.'

'Why not? You should be celebrated, darling.'

'It all feels too much. As if I've got more than my share.'

'That's your mother in you talking. You deserve every second of it. Why can't you just accept your glory and your achievements?' Julian looked at her in the mirror. 'What is it?' he asked, concerned. 'Surely you must be happy?'

'Of course I am. I couldn't be happier. It's just I worry that . . .'

'That what?'

Emma sighed. He knew her so well. And that's why she loved him. Because he knew her inside out and wouldn't let her brood on anything. He always seemed to be able to root out any negative thoughts she was having and get her to admit them.

'I don't know. Everything seems to be changing so fast. What if anything goes wrong? What if we somehow come off the rails?'

Julian smiled and came over to her. He put his hands on her shoulders. 'We won't,' he said, 'silly.' And looking up into his face, she believed him. 'Trust me,' he promised her. 'I won't let us.'

Emma hugged him, feeling his body pressing against hers. 'I wish you weren't going away. I'm going to miss you so much,' she said.

'I haven't gone yet,' he said, nuzzling against her as he slid the straps of her silk slip off her shoulders, so that it fell in a soft pool around her feet.

'Julian,' she giggled. 'What are you doing?'

'Do you remember the first night we spent here?' he whispered.

Emma blushed. How could she forget? Julian had given her so much oral sex that when she'd had her second orgasm, she'd cried out so loudly that the neighbours had banged on the wall.

'Well, Lady Emma Harvey – or should I just call you Chairwoman Harvey?' he said, gently pushing her so that she was sitting on the chaise lounge. 'I know the way to put your mind at ease. Why don't you lie back and let me show you that some things never change at all.'

CHAPTER TWELVE

Bright golden sunlight filled the Sardinian bay of Porto Cervo as the guests on board *Pushkin* ate their breakfast on the sun-deck of the top saloon. This was where the European jet set came to start off the party season in the Med and there was a palpable buzz in the air. The Monégasque royal family was here, as well as Jason Greenburgh, the current hot name on the Formula One circuit. But for now, *Pushkin*, moored out in the bay, was the star attraction.

Below deck, Frankie was more miserable than ever as she looked out of the porthole in the galley towards the jagged Sardinian coastline and the rising promontory of land headed by a lighthouse. Dead ahead was Porto Cervo's pretty harbour, with its multicoloured buildings and jetties crammed with boats. It all looked so inviting, but the chances of Frankie ever making it ashore were nil.

Everything had changed. And yet nothing had changed. After her kiss with Alex in his study she'd hardly been able to function. And yet she hadn't even seen him since. It was as if whatever had started to blossom between them had been frozen in amber. A beautiful flower, perfectly preserved, but one that had never been given the chance to grow.

It felt like a dream. And the more time Frankie had to analyse what had happened, the crazier a dream it seemed. It didn't seem possible that she'd lost control like that, but she had. What would have happened, she'd wondered over and over again, if Richard hadn't buzzed on the intercom? Would she have had sex with Alex there and then on his desk? Well – yes – she probably *would* have done. She wouldn't have been able to stop herself.

Now that seemed unthinkable. Unimaginable. But being around Alex had made her lose all her principles. Just when she'd thought she'd overcome her impulsive streak.

What must he think of her?

Frankie shook her head. Being on *Pushkin*, knowing that Alex was with guests upstairs, was agonizing. And they weren't just any guests. They'd arrived yesterday lunchtime, an entire entourage of European royalty, including a Dutch princess and her best friend, who just happened to be the famously newly single supermodel, Thomasina Rose.

Frankie had caught a glimpse of Thomasina, her catwalk gait instantly recognizable, and she'd wanted nothing more than to push her overboard. How would Alex ever resist her, strutting around all day in her designer bikini? *And* she spoke perfect Russian.

Frankie had racked her brains, trying to think of a way of getting Alex alone, but even though he was only a few metres away, he might as well have been on a different continent. Roz had chosen Simone to help her serve last night, despite Frankie offering. She obviously didn't want Frankie thinking she had any special privileges, now that she'd had a training session with the boss.

And then late last night had come the worst blow. Alex and his guests had gone to a party on another yacht, leaving instructions that he wouldn't be needing Frankie in the gym for the forseeable future.

Simone, oblivious of how devastating this news had been for Frankie, was full of excitement about the party. When she'd been on shore provisioning, she'd bumped into several of the stewardesses from the other yachts.

'Everyone's so excited Alexei Rodokov is here. You know, I read that he's the number one most desired bachelor in the whole of

Europe. Louise on *Aurora* says that they've been overrun with guests. All the party girls from everywhere have flown in. You know, Frankie, it's really cool that right now, in the whole of Europe, this is exactly where it's at. They say that Jack Johnson is here and is doing an acoustic set tonight on the yacht. Oh, and . . .'

Frankie had made excuses and gone to bed early. She'd lain on her bunk, watching the moonlight through the tiny porthole and imagining Alex partying. She'd been able to hear the music floating across the water.

She'd felt tears prick her eyes as she'd run her finger over the photo of her family. She'd promised Uncle Brody that she wouldn't get into trouble. That she'd keep her nose clean. And what had she done? She'd blown it the very first time she'd met the boss. After all the effort she'd made not to appear 'easy' with the rest of the crew, she'd practically thrown herself at the one man who could guarantee her job security.

And now, in the bright early-morning light, as she cleared away the crew breakfast, Frankie felt even more of a fool. Alex must think that she was just some stupid little airhead. Or rewritten events. Worked it round in his mind so that she'd been the one who'd made all the moves, not him. As if she was the one who'd overstepped the mark. Why else would he have cancelled their gym sessions?

But that wasn't how it had been. *Was* it? He'd been every bit as keen as her. Hadn't he? Frankie no longer knew.

But whatever the answer to that question was, Frankie knew she'd been a total idiot. How could she ever have thought that Alex would really want her? Their lives were worlds apart.

She wondered now whether she'd even get to *see* Alex again, and if or when she did, would he be embarrassed about what had happened? Or worse . . . dismissive? As in literally. As in having Richard telling her to pack her bags and go. Maybe what had or hadn't happened between them was already yesterday's news.

'Frankie, Richard wants you on deck,' Roz said with the worst possible timing, coming into the kitchen and dumping a tray full of coffee cups and a bone-china coffee jug on the steel counter.

'Me?'

'Yes, you. Get a move on.'

For a moment, Frankie's heart lurched. Could Richard have found out about her and Alex? No, it was impossible. Alex wouldn't compromise himself like that. Would he?

But what if Alex just wanted her out of the way? What if he'd asked Richard to fire her on some other grounds? She remembered now how dismissive Alex had been of the Forest Holdings Systems Manager he'd said he'd fired. Perhaps that's what Frankie had become now: an expendable, easily replaceable resource.

On arriving up on deck, it immediately seemed that her worst fears were confirmed. Alex, dressed in shorts and a polo shirt, was there with Richard. But whereas Richard's eyes locked with Frankie's instantly, his dark gaze full of suspicion, Alex didn't even appear to notice her. He flipped down his designer shades from his head and gazed past her out to sea, as if she didn't exist.

Frankie felt her hands sweating. What if she was expected to explain herself? What if Richard wanted to know her version of what had happened in Alex's study? It was her word against Alex's and she realized now what a truly weak, humiliating position she was in.

Richard's forehead furrowed sternly. 'Ah, there you are, Frankie,' he said. 'Is it true that you're fully qualified to dive?'

Frankie was so shocked that she wasn't about to be interrogated that she felt a deep blush rising in her cheeks. Her eyes darted towards Alex, but he still didn't look at her.

It was only then that she realized what was going on. Jeff was loading the last of the scuba equipment into the Hinckley – the largest of *Pushkin*'s tenders. Alex hadn't forgotten his promise!

It took all of Frankie's willpower not to grin with relief, not to mention whoop with excitement.

'Of course. Why?' she said, smoothing her hair behind her ear.

Alex nodded at her curtly, but she noticed the trace of a smile flicker at the edge of his mouth.

That mouth.

The mouth that had kissed her. And that she hadn't been able to stop thinking about since.

'I was just explaining that my glute med is weak,' Alex deadpanned, slapping the back of his thigh. 'You know – we discussed it. I'd rather you were with me, just in case it cramps up or anything.'

Frankie nodded, keeping her face serious while still trying to suppress the urge to jump up and down on the spot. 'No problem, sir. I'll get my things.'

Richard looked exasperated. 'But I still think I should come too. Or at least Jeff, since he's an instructor. The currents around here can be treacherous.'

'Nothing I can't handle.' Alex smiled. 'Frankie and I will be fine on our own. And Dieter will look after the boat whilst we're diving.'

'But—'

'Frankie, Dieter and I will leave in five minutes,' Alex repeated. 'So kindly have the boat ready. Put the short wetsuits on board for me and Frankie. We'll change at the dive site,' Alex said, making it perfectly clear that he didn't appreciate Richard mothering him for a second more.

On board the Hinckley, Frankie watched Alex as he revved up the engine and sped away from *Pushkin* without a backwards glance. Frankie held on to the edge of her plush white leather seat as they bumped over the waves. At the wheel, Alex was completely in control of the boat, as if this was what he did every day.

Dieter sat at the prow, dressed in a black T-shirt and pants, an earpiece on. He scanned the water for other boats. He was like a figurehead. Solid. Still. Silent. He didn't turn around and glance at them once.

Frankie sat on her hands and squeezed her lips together, looking down at her legs beneath her navy crew shorts, wondering awkwardly whether Alex would notice she hadn't shaved them this morning. She wished she'd known this was coming. She wished she'd had more time so that she could have looked her best. She felt so daggy. So unprepared.

But when she looked back up, Alex was staring down at her over the top of his shades. Her heart soared as he raised his eyebrows up and down at her, his eyes shining so much that Frankie had to stifle a giggle.

Could he really be as excited as she was?

Not possible, she decided as they cut through the water,

leaving the gleaming hulk of *Pushkin* and two jets of bubbles in their wake, like a V sign. Frankie felt as if she were escaping a prison. She breathed in the fresh air, relishing the freedom, letting the breeze blow through her hair like a lover's caress.

She glanced again at Alex and saw he was grinning openly too. He held her gaze for a long moment.

All the connection she'd felt with him in the gym was back. Just as strong. Just as real.

And she was about to be alone with him again! What did it mean? What would she say to him? What would he say to *her*? And what if the same thing happened again? No, no, it couldn't. Not out here in the sea. Could it?

Alex broke eye contact, the smile still playing on his lips. Frankie's mind fizzed with questions as she looked back at *Pushkin* growing smaller and smaller as they sped away. She thought about what Roz would be saying right now. With so many important guests on board, she'd upped the workload, and not having Frankie to do all the dirty work would just about send Roz over the edge. But Frankie didn't care. She turned her face up towards the sun, grinning like a cat.

The Sardinian coastline was much more undeveloped than she'd imagined, with a mix of bays and promontories, high red rocks and white sandy beaches. Little islands rose from the clear crystal-blue water and Alex slowed down now, negotiating the tender around some rocks until they were completely out of sight of *Pushkin*.

'Here, I think,' Alex shouted, cutting the engine. He was addressing Dieter, who finally moved, dropping the anchor. Frankie could see the rocks below them. She'd never seen water so clear. Not even on the Great Barrier Reef, where she'd first learnt to dive.

The sudden silence shocked her, making the situation way more intimate. The waves lapped gently against the boat, rocking them.

'Come on, then,' Alex said, stepping towards Frankie, his balance perfect as he casually took off his T-shirt. Frankie saw the ripple of his stomach muscles as he stretched up, and something inside her flipped over with desire. Then he unzipped his shorts, revealing some tight blue swimming trunks underneath.

He was nearly naked!

And my God, what a body, Frankie thought, her eyes scanning greedily over his perfectly tanned flesh. It was all she could do not to reach out and touch him.

'Dieter, chuck us the wetsuits,' Alex said, his gaze unreadable. He caught the two wetsuits without looking up, handing one to Frankie. 'Here you go,' he said. And for the first time, his voice sounded like the Alex she remembered. Intimate and soft. And once again, she felt as if she'd been completely sucked into his world.

Frankie suddenly felt shy, but Alex must have sensed it, turning away as he pulled on his wetsuit.

Quickly, she scrambled out of her crew polo shirt and navy shorts. She was wearing her bikini underneath. It was a tatty stringy one that she'd had for ages, and she wished now that she'd splashed out on a designer one.

She yanked the wetsuit on quickly, over her hips before Alex saw her. She put her arms through the holes, wriggling the neoprene on to her shoulders.

'Here, let me help you,' Alex said. He was behind her and she felt him reach for the back zip. As he pulled it up, he let his finger gently slide up her spine and Frankie felt the whole of her body erupt into goosebumps. And there it was again: the same electricity she'd felt in his study. Like she was going to explode.

'All set,' he said. 'Let's get the tanks on and get going.'

She heaved on her diving bodice, with all its dials and weights and the oxygen tank on the back. Then they checked their air levels and went in backwards off the side of the boat.

Once they were a few metres from the boat's shimmering hull – and Dieter's watchful gaze – Alex held out his hand to her under the water. His eyes shone as he smiled at her through his mask.

As they sank deeper below the surface, Frankie watched his hair swishing in the current and the shafts of sunlight cutting through the water. She could hear her breath in a steady whoosh through her regulator, but her heart was thumping wildly as they held eye contact. Then, once they'd sunk ten metres, Alex pointed behind her and she turned and looked at the underwater scene below her.

It was stunning. The granite rocks were covered in bright yellow marine daisies and gently swaying red sea-fans, a giant shoal of Mediterranean barracudas darting in between them. A ray rose up from a sand rock pool and swam past them. Alex swam over and ran his hand through the gently swaying fronds of browny-gold seaweed. Bubbles rose above him to the surface shimmering like quicksilver.

As they swam along side by side through the warm water, their flippers kicking in unison, Frankie felt herself relax. Down here, *Pushkin* and all its petty politics and restrictions didn't matter. They were together. Alone. And she saw now that she should have kept faith. She shouldn't have doubted Alex, or her own feelings. Because here, right now, he'd proved to her that what had happened *was* special. Against all the odds, he'd achieved the impossible: he'd got her away from *Pushkin*, to a different world. And it felt amazing.

Alex squeezed her hand and pointed into the distance, towards a land mass – probably the larger island they'd seen from the boat – and she nodded.

Hand in hand again, they followed the line of the under-water granite edge. She could tell the water was getting shallower. Alex pointed to the surface and, pressing the yellow button attached to his dive jacket, increased his buoyancy so that he started rising slowly. Frankie did the same.

They both popped out into the sunshine at the same time. Sure enough, they were around the other side of the island, out of sight of Dieter.

Alex took out his regulator and lifted up his mask. Droplets of water landed on his long eyelashes, sparkling in the sun like diamonds.

For a moment, they just stared at each other. And their kiss in the office seemed as if it had happened only a moment ago. All the distance that Frankie had imagined between them simply wasn't there. It was as if they were still connected.

'I—'

'I—'

They both spoke at the same time, and then laughed.

'You first,' she said.

'Just . . .' His grin was wide and his eyes shone at her. 'At last! I finally get you to myself.' He sounded as relieved as she felt. 'I was beginning to wonder whether it was ever going to happen.'

Frankie smiled. 'Tell me about it.'

'You know . . . I didn't want you to think that the other day . . . that it didn't mean something. Because it did.'

She felt elation and relief flowing through her. And something else . . . that hot lava-flow of desire.

'You weren't offended, were you?' he asked.

'Offended?' she gasped. 'Of course I wasn't offended. I thought it was the other way around. I thought *you* thought I was—'

'I think you're gorgeous,' he said, smiling. 'Come here.' He pulled her into his arms and kissed her. He tasted of sunshine and salt water. And then he laughed and pulled her backwards into the water, hugging her.

'Oh, Frankie,' he sighed, wetting his hair and smoothing it down. 'You have no idea how nice it is to be on our own.'

'How was the party?' She'd not meant to ask. She'd have been better off seeming uninterested. Like him being with all those models hadn't mattered to her at all. But the words had just come out.

'Hell. All I could think about was diving with you today.'

Again, she felt that wash of relief. He hadn't even hesitated before answering. He must mean every word.

'It's so beautiful down there,' she said. 'Thank you for bringing me.' She reached out and held his hands. It felt so easy, so natural, and so right to be this intimate with him.

'I promised, didn't I? It just took me a while to sort things out. The last thing I want is for you to be subjected to crew gossip. I know the score, Frankie. And believe me, whatever happens between us, I want it to be about *us*, no one else.'

What did he mean? she wondered. Was he laying out rules for them? That she was his onboard squeeze? His lover? Or something more?

'And what *is* happening between us?' she asked.

Alex smiled. 'I don't know . . . yet.' He drew her towards him and kissed her again. 'But I'm itching to find out.'

She kissed him back, passionately this time, until she lost her balance in the water, and they both laughed.

'Come on,' he said, pulling her back with him. 'Let's see how you dance.'

Dance? What *did* he mean?

But she soon found out. Alex bit down on his regulator and she followed suit. Then they sank beneath the surface and Alex grabbed her, as if they were doing the tango, and led her around in a dance. She heard the squeak of her voice as she laughed into her regulator.

Then he took his regulator out of his mouth and gently did the same with hers. And he kissed her again.

It felt so strange, their mouths connecting underwater. But it was only for a second before they both put their regulators back in. She laughed again, seeing the bubbles cascade up between their faces.

They held hands, swimming side by side, pointing out the shoals of yellow and blue fish. It seemed only a moment later that their air was getting low and Alex pointed back towards the boat. Frankie wanted to scream. She wasn't ready for their time together to be snatched away again. There was so much left to say.

Back on the surface, Alex grabbed her and kissed her as they trod water. Her eyes flashed towards Dieter in the boat.

'Don't worry about Dieter. He hardly speaks any English. And anyway, I pay him not to listen to any of my conversations,' Alex said. 'Or remember anything he sees.'

Just how many secrets did Alex have? Frankie wondered. And was that what she'd just become? Another secret? Another facet of the mystery that was Alexei Rodokov?

She felt her elation waver. She'd just had one of the best hours of her entire life, and yet she hardly knew this man at all. She shouldn't be letting herself fall for him so hard, in case she got hurt.

But at the same time, she knew she couldn't help herself. She was helplessly drawn to him. She couldn't give him up, or even play hard to get. She had to know what made him tick. She had to be part of his life.

'Why do you have a bodyguard all the time?' she asked.

Alex shrugged. 'To please Yuri, I guess. It was his idea. He insists Dieter comes with me. But sometimes I manage to get away.'

'Yuri?'

'I'll tell you all about him in Marrakech. There's no time

now.'

'Marrakech?'

Alex's eyes sparkled. 'Yes, Marrakech. I've got a plan. I told you I'd think of one.'

'But . . .'

She could see Dieter standing up in the boat and waving to them.

'I'll arrange it as soon as I can, fake a phone call so you can make an excuse and leave the yacht,' Alex said, his voice urgent. 'Say you've had bad news – family problems. Dieter will take you to shore. I'll arrange a net jet to be at the airport for you and fly you to the riad. And I'll meet you there. We'll keep it a secret. Just us. No one else need know.'

Frankie was stunned at his proposal. 'But what about your guests?'

'Oh, them,' Alex said, waving his hand dismissively. 'It's nobody important. Anyway, what can they say if I get called away on urgent business?'

'It's really that simple?'

'Sure. This is supposed to be my holiday. And now I've found the person I want to spend it with.'

Frankie could hardly look at him as they mounted the steps back into the boat and took off their equipment. What Alex had just proposed . . it was beyond her wildest dreams.

She wanted to pinch herself. This was really happening. He really wanted her.

But as they approached *Pushkin*, Alex's proposal seemed more outlandish than ever. There was no *way* she could leave to fly away to some exotic riad in Marrakech on a private jet. She was destined for scrubbing out toilets, surely? Did she really have the nerve to fake a family crisis and leave *Pushkin*? Just like that?

She felt giddy with nerves at the sheer thought.

But Alex obviously thought she could do it. He seemed to know instinctively that Frankie was, at heart, hopelessly impulsive. But hadn't being impulsive got her into serious trouble before? And hadn't she vowed to learn from her past mistakes?

But then she looked at Alex and he held her gaze, his eyes sparkling with promise. He meant it, she realized. And she saw, too, that he was trusting her. If he thought she had the balls to hoodwink Richard and carry out his plan, then she'd prove him right.

As if sensing her decision, Alex winked at her as the tender drew up alongside *Pushkin*. She glanced at Dieter and then up at *Pushkin*, feeling her heart race with panic. She needed more time. There was still so much to discuss. What if their plan went wrong?

But there was no more time. Alex was already throwing up the painter to Jeff. And as they boarded *Pushkin* he instantly transformed back into the big, scary businessman. His face was emotionless and gave absolutely nothing away. Their dive together might never have happened.

In contrast, Frankie felt as if their secret was written all over her face.

Richard was striding down the deck. He was clearly furious that Alex and Frankie had been out so long, but couldn't say anything to Alex. Not unless he wanted to risk a public dressing down himself in return.

'You're back. I was starting to get worried,' he said to Alex.

'Why? There was no need,' Alex said, rubbing his wet hair with a towel and walking past him into the saloon.

Frankie watched him go. Imperious. In control. Capable of anything.

'I'll take breakfast now, thank you. Up at the top,' he said to Richard, turning in the doorway to the lower saloon, before sliding shut the tinted glass doors. He didn't so much as acknowledge Frankie's presence.

Frankie went to move past Richard, but he grabbed her arm.

'I don't know whether there's anything going on,' he hissed. 'But all I can tell you is that there better not be. If you've overstepped the line—' he threatened.

'I don't know what you mean,' Frankie said, shaking him off.

'Yes, you do. I'm watching you,' he said. 'I'm watching you very closely.'

CHAPTER THIRTEEN

In downtown Zurich, the distinctive blue trams rattled along under an even bluer sky as the chauffer-driven Mercedes Emma and Julian had picked up at the airport pulled up outside the plush private bank. It was just one of the many grand fortresses lining the wide streets in the financial district and Emma wondered how many priceless artefacts and bars of gold bullion were stored in the vaults right below her feet.

Pigeons flew up from the pavement as the car stopped, flapping into the clear air. But the pavements remained spotless in their wake, Emma noticed, as if they'd been steam cleaned. The shiny black paint of the bank's intricate cast-iron outer gates gleamed in the sunshine. She pulled out her new Dior sunglasses from her Todd's leather handbag and put them on.

'I guess Dimitry is already here,' Julian said, pointing to the black BMW parked in front of them, by the kerb, its windows blacked out. 'That's his number plate.'

'Dimitry? Why?' Emma asked. She'd been surprised when Julian had announced this morning that they would be going on a detour to the bank. He'd only told her yesterday that he was bringing her here to Switzerland for a surprise weekend break. They'd caught an obscenely early flight this morning and Emma had been looking forward to collapsing in the hotel spa and booking in a few treatments. But instead there was yet more business to be done.

'Because the cash from the AIM listing of Platinum Holdings went from the bank account in London via a clearing company in the Caribbean—'

'What clearing company? Where in the Caribbean?' Emma asked.

'In Tortola. We called the company Platinum Reach. It was more tax efficient to transfer the money via there to Russia so the mining could begin. It was quick, too. Quicker than I thought. The mine is ready to go, which means Dimitry needs his commission earlier than I thought,' he added, before telling the driver to wait, in perfect German.

Julian, who'd skied every year since he could walk, had the perfect knack of choosing the right language – French, Italian or German – whenever he was in Switzerland. Emma could tell that the chauffeur was charmed.

She watched the driver get out and walk jauntily round to the kerb in order to open the door for her. But Emma, in contrast, felt anything other than jaunty. Her mind was reeling from all this new information.

'Commission? What commission?' she asked.

'Don't be like that,' Julian said.

'Like what?'

'Disapproving. It's perfectly normal for someone who's set a deal up like ours to get a commission. He found the land and presented us with an incredible opportunity. And that's all on top of helping with the finances and the Caribbean arm of the deal. That he's done for free.'

'But . . .'

'But what?'

'I don't know. You know better than me how these things work, but isn't it all a bit irregular?'

'Well, technically, yes. But nothing that our accountants won't be able to clean up. That's what we pay them for.'

Emma really didn't like the sound of what Julian was saying, but it was clearly a fait accompli. She knew she had to back down. The last thing she wanted was a row. This was their last weekend together before Julian flew to Russia tomorrow for a month. She wanted it to be special.

But she kept picturing Dimitry Sergeyokov at her party and remembering the way he'd looked at her. The way he'd *watched* her, as if she was some kind of experiment. Or part of a puppet show with him pulling the strings. No matter how hard she tried, she couldn't shake the feeling that something was terribly wrong.

The chauffeur opened the door for Emma, and she slid along the leather seat and stood on the pavement. It was warmer than she'd thought, tugging at the neck of the cream cashmere polo-neck she'd worn under her camel trouser suit.

Julian smiled at the chauffeur, then took Emma's arm, guiding her towards the bank.

'So how much does Dimitry get?' Emma asked, pretending to sound as if it didn't matter.

'Five per cent.'

Emma stopped still on the pavement and stared at Julian. 'Five per cent?' Dimitry was getting five per cent of her brother's money? Of everyone's investment?

'He wanted seven, but I beat him down.'

Emma couldn't believe what she was hearing. 'Well, couldn't you just write him a cheque? Or transfer it from the business?'

'No. He wants it in cash.'

'*Cash?*'

Julian's face clouded. 'This isn't the time, Emma,' he said, his words measured with exasperation. He tugged her arm, guiding her past the gateway and on into the ornate stone doorway, adding, 'If I'd known you were going to be like this, I wouldn't have brought you.'

Emma smarted. How dare he talk to her as if she were a child? But, even so, she bit her lip.

The hallway of the bank was simultaneously elegant and clinical. The polished marble pillars led the eye to the grand marble staircase with its intricate wrought-iron balustrade. A huge crystal chandelier hung from the high ceiling.

A young woman in a smart black business suit approached them, smiling.

'She's the head huissière,' Julian whispered to Emma. 'Try and be nice.'

'How nice to see you again,' the huissière said, shaking Julian's hand. 'You must be Lady Emma. Welcome to Zurich,' she went on, accompanying them back to the desk and handing a keypad to Julian. He tapped in his private bank account number. Emma noticed that it was the date of their wedding anniversary.

When he'd finished, the huissière smiled. 'Please follow me.'

Emma was expecting the bank to be much more high tech, but at the top of the marble staircase, instead of a palm or fingerprint reader, there was simply another iron gate with a clunky lock.

The huissière showed them into a private consultation booth. 'Please wait here. My colleague has just gone to collect your deposit box from the safe. One moment.'

She left them alone, pulling the red curtain behind her. The wooden desk had some scissors and paper clips on it. Emma picked one of them up. She couldn't bear having an atmosphere between her and Julian. They hardly ever argued, but she guessed they were both stressed and cranky from their early start. She cleared her throat.

'I always wondered what it would be like inside one of these banks,' she said.

'Well, now you know.'

She could tell from his tone that Julian was still annoyed with her. She wished she could say something cheerful and dispel the row they'd had downstairs. The problem was she didn't know how to tell Julian what she felt about Dimitry Sergeyokov, when Julian so clearly didn't feel the same way.

But she knew how important it was to him that she supported him, and how much her disapproval hurt him. Emma tried to seek out his eyes, but he didn't look at her and she took a deep breath. She mustn't be like this. The Platinum deal had come so far, who was she to start questioning how Julian had structured the finance?

Anyway, her feelings were just that. Feelings. A hunch. Nothing solid. Why should she expect Julian to understand her paranoia when she couldn't even pin it down herself?

She took a step towards him and touched his arm.

For a moment, he looked down at her hand, then he covered it with his own. And he smiled.

There it was. Without the need for words. A truce.

They were interrupted by the huissière, who brought in Julian's deposit box and put it on the desk. Then she disappeared through the curtain and came back with a black attaché case.

'And here's the cash you requested, sir,' she said, expertly holding the case in one hand and unclipping the lid in order to flash Emma and Julian the contents. Inside were bundles of bright pink five-hundred-euro notes.

Then the huissière closed the case and handed it over, as if it was the most normal thing in the world. No questions asked. Perhaps Julian was right, Emma thought. Perhaps this was how business was done all the time.

'Thank you,' Julian said, taking it and putting it on the desk.

Then, when she'd gone, he took a key out of his pocket and opened the deposit box.

'Look in here, darling,' he said to Emma. 'There're loads of deeds and private papers. If anything happens to me, make sure you come and retrieve all of this, OK?'

He'd said it flippantly, but Emma shuddered. 'What on earth do you mean?'

'Nothing. I'm just saying . . .' He glanced up at her. 'Nothing . . . forget I mentioned it.'

Julian took a few papers out of the box and closed it again, before opening the attaché case and counting out the bundles of cash on the desk. Emma had never seen so many notes in her life.

She watched him, battling with her feelings.

'You're very quiet. What are you thinking?' he asked.

'Only that seeing it in cash . . . it seems an awful lot, that's all,' she said. Then to make sure he knew she wasn't starting an argument again, added, 'And that is the *exact* colour velvet I've been looking for to reupholster the chair in the pink room's en suite.'

Julian laughed. 'It might seem an awful lot to you, but it's nothing compared to how Dimitry is going to change our lives. This time in a month, you'll be dropping this in small change,' he joked, stacking the bundles of notes back in the case.

Downstairs, they met Dimitry Sergeyokov in the waiting room. He was wearing a long leather coat and black leather boots and was reading a Forbes business magazine. His black hair was greased back from his high pale forehead and Emma thought there was something about him that looked like a vulture, or a vampire.

He stood up from the wing-backed chair when he saw Julian and Emma, his eyes darting to the attaché case.

Julian shook hands with him, then put his hand on Emma's back, as if presenting her. 'You remember my wife Emma, of course?'

Dimitry bowed his head in silent affirmation, then looked at Emma. And in that second, as he stared down at her, before tearing his gaze away, all Emma's doubts come rushing back.

'So you have the money for me?' Dimitry said. Emma was surprised how direct he sounded and how rough his gravelly accent was in these elegant surroundings – as if he didn't – and could never – belong here.

'All here,' Julian said, handing him the attaché case.

'Good. Then I'll leave now,' Dimitry said.

'You don't want to celebrate?' Julian asked, taken aback. 'A drink? Or lunch maybe?'

'No. No. I have a plane to catch.' Dimitry lifted up his arm and glanced at his rather gaudy Rolex watch. Then he nodded at Emma. She tried to smile at him, but his dark gaze made her shudder. 'Your home is very beautiful,' he said suddenly. Somehow, he made it sound like a threat.

'It is,' she said.

'Well, good doing business with you,' Julian said. 'I'll see you in Norilsk.'

Dimitry nodded. He hesitated for just a moment, as if he was about to say something else, but obviously thought better of it. Then, without another glance at them, he walked quickly back towards the bank's reception area carrying the attaché case, his heels echoing on the marble floor.

Silence settled. Emma waited for Julian to say something. But he didn't. Like her, he was staring at the empty space where Dimitry and all that money had been just seconds before.

'I thought he was rather abrupt,' Emma said. 'Didn't you?'

'No, not really. Dimitry's not one for small talk. The Russians have a different etiquette, that's all.'

'I suppose.'

'Anyway, it's fine by me.' Julian made a show of rubbing his hands together and forced a smile. 'Now for the fun part of the day, and that surprise I promised you.' He put his arm around her. 'Come on,' he said, leading her away. 'Let's get out of here. It suddenly feels terribly cold.'

A few hours later, Emma stared down from the helicopter, watching the shadow it cast on the dazzling snow.

'Oh my God, that's Davos,' she shouted to Julian over the noise of the rotors. 'So that's where we're going!' She grinned, delighted that he'd remembered how much she loved it here.

They hadn't been to Davos for years, staying instead in Gstaad, and more recently the French Alp resorts which were more suited to Cosmo and his needs for lively après-ski.

But this place, high, high in the alpine forests, was just theirs. They'd discovered it when they'd been to Klosters on their honeymoon, more than twenty years ago. Even from this distance – a mile or two – Emma could see how much it had changed – there were many more buildings and hotels – but it still retained the charm that made it popular with celebrities and royalty. And the ice rink, the largest natural one in Europe, was still there and she could see the mountain rail tracks.

Perhaps Julian had booked into that divine little restaurant with the fondue she loved so much, Emma thought, memories flooding back.

But to her surprise, the helicopter showed no signs of landing. Instead it swooped upwards towards the summit of one of the seven high peaks surrounding the exclusive resort. Emma felt her stomach flip over.

Where the hell were they going now?

They couldn't be going skiing? Could they? Those skis in the back she thought were the pilot's. . .

'I thought you said it was too late for snow?' she said, realizing with a jolt that this was *exactly* what Julian was planning.

'It's never too late here,' he reminded her with a wicked grin.

Emma shook her head. She should have known. Julian was a skiing freak. There was no way he was going to be in Switzerland without getting on to the slopes. And Emma realized now how silly it had been of her to presume that they were going to while the day away in the hotel spa.

Now, as she watched Julian laughing at her, she rolled her eyes. He was a much better skier than Emma, with the nerves of a reckless teenager. The helicopter landed on the summit of the highest mountain peak and Emma felt her heart racing.

'But we can't,' she began.

'Why not?'

'We haven't got any ski gear,' Emma shouted.

'Oh yes we have,' Julian said, nodding over the back of their seats. Emma followed his gaze to the bag he'd brought as he leant over to get it, unloading jackets, fleeces, gloves, trousers and goggles. All brand new.

'Are these for me?' she asked, feeling the real fur around the hood of the silver Dior jacket. She'd seen the very same one photographed in a Sunday supplement and had told Julian how much she'd admired it.

'Of course.'

'But we can't just change here. And what about all our stuff? Our luggage?' Emma asked. 'I'm not skiing with my handbag.'

'Don't worry about that,' Julian said, laughing at her confusion. 'It's all sorted.'

In no time, the chopper landed on the top of the mountain, whipping up the snow, so that Emma felt as if she were in the centre of a candyfloss machine.

Once they were stationary, they hurriedly changed in the cramped conditions. Emma was amazed that Julian had even brought her favourite ski boots with him. How had he managed to arrange all this without her noticing? she wondered. Perhaps he'd been so secretive because he'd known she'd have objected.

But she had no time to worry. The pilot opened the door. The cold air hit Emma as he helped her step out of the helicopter. He held her hand and steadied her as she clicked into her ski boots. Her legs were wobbling.

She pulled down her sun visor and followed Julian's lead, skiing down a short way. Then they stopped. Julian turned and the pilot saluted before climbing back into his seat. A moment later, the rotors were stirring up the snow again, and Emma instinctively ducked as the helicopter lifted up and away.

She watched it rise into the air, like a giant bug, then the pilot expertly tipped the nose forward and a moment later, the helicopter had disappeared beneath the summit of the mountain.

A few seconds later, the noise of the departing rotors was lost and silence descended. Emma breathed in as her skis sank into the powdery crystallized snow. She couldn't believe the view. It was breathtaking. On such a clear day, it was possible to see for hundreds of miles, the mountains stretching away in all directions. The sky was an intense, unfathomable blue. The snow was glittering all around her in the sunshine, like a field of diamonds. There was something magical about it.

'Not bad, eh?' Julian said.

'Darling, it's wonderful.' Emma laughed, trying to find her balance. 'But you could have warned me.'

'But that would have ruined the surprise, silly,' he said.

'Well, I'm surprised, OK? You got me.'

Emma hadn't been skiing since last winter and now, as she peered down the steep slope, she thought it looked bloody terrifying! And she was so unfit. Usually, she took the first day of her skiing holidays gently by taking in a few easy slopes to find her feet, but this off-piste run was scary as hell.

And, despite the view and the incredible fresh air, her head filled with doubts. Was it really wise to be up here all alone? What about the risk of avalanches? The snow looked so unstable.

But Julian didn't seem worried at all. 'Follow me,' he shouted.

'Wait,' Emma shouted after him, but he was already swishing away from her, his red jacket almost obliterated by a wall of powder snow.

'Come on, Ems. It's wonderful,' he called, his voice echoing.

'Don't be a wimp,' she scolded herself as she watched Julian, his body now bending so that he made graceful arcs through the virgin snow.

If Julian could do it, then so could she. Just because she was getting older, she wasn't going to turn into a worrier like her mother. What would Julian think of her? she wondered. She couldn't back out now.

Anyway, now that the helicopter had gone, she didn't have a choice. The only way was down.

Pluck. That's what she would rely on. Good old-fashioned pluck.

She heard Julian whoop. He was getting further and further away from her. She craned her neck over the ledge of the slope and saw him take off over a snow-covered log, star-jumping in the air for her benefit.

'Oh, be careful,' she muttered.

'Come on!' he called, coming to a sudden stop and smiling up at her. 'What are you waiting for?'

'Oh God. Here goes,' Emma said, pushing off. She hurtled down the steep incline. Her teeth were rattling and she was breathless as she passed Julian. 'Oh God, oh God, oh God,' she yelled.

'That's it. It's just like riding a bike,' Julian called, laughing as he caught up with her.

Once he was next to her, she started to remember what she was doing.

'That's it. Relax. Enjoy,' Julian coaxed, overtaking her.

Emma followed in his tracks, and before long she started to get into the rhythm of the slope, her body finding its muscle memory as she swooped through the snow.

Soon, she forgot all about her fear and remembered what she loved about skiing – about skiing with Julian: the sheer exhilaration of it. He made it so much fun.

She smiled at him. And then she laughed, spitting fluffy snow out of her mouth. She felt young again, as if they were on their honeymoon, with their whole lives ahead of them. All the seriousness of the bank this morning vanished. They were back to being the people they used to be: the two of them together, living for the moment.

What felt like only minutes later, they came to a stop. Her cheeks were burning and she was out of breath.

'Wow,' Emma gasped, looking back up the mountain to the snow-covered peak from which they'd just descended, glistening against the blue of the sky. She could see their overlapping tracks on the steep slope, like the shadow of a dance. Below them, there was another long virgin slope, before the tree line.

But what was incredible was the sheer solitude of it. The fact that they were the only people for miles.

'Come on, let's keep going,' Julian said. She could tell how much he was loving this. 'My surprise is really close.'

'You mean the skiing isn't the surprise?' she asked, trying to catch her breath.

He leant over and kissed her on the cheek, and laughed. 'No. Come on.'

They skied on, fast and free, until, panting hard, Emma caught up with him near the tree line.

'Well?' Julian said, and she could see the excitement in his eyes.

'What?' she asked, confused, lifting up her goggles, her face assaulted by the glare of the sun and the cold air.

For a moment, Julian looked crestfallen.

Only now did she get back sufficient breath to realize where they were.

'You remembered!' she gasped, feeling her eyes fill with tears of an altogether different nature.

In a small clearing below them stood an old log chalet. A thin line of smoke blew straight up from the chimney.

It was the same log chalet they'd stayed in on their honeymoon all those years ago. Every detail of it was imprinted on Emma's mind and now her heart ached that Julian had remembered it too.

'This place . . . Oh, Julian. It's our cabin!'

'Come,' Julian said.

They skied through the trees to the chalet, memories exploding like fireworks in her mind. Of the first time they'd skied here and how nervous she'd been.

'But I don't understand,' Emma said. 'We can't just go in.'

'Yes we can.'

'But . . .'

'Don't you get it?' Julian said.

'Get what? Stop being so mysterious.'

'I bought it,' Julian said.

Emma stared at him. 'You did what?' she whispered.

'I vowed that if it ever came on the market, I'd buy it. I lost it once ten years ago.'

'You never said,' Emma said, stunned.

'So I put down a deposit to make sure I wouldn't lose it

again, when the owners sold. And they just have. It's yours.'

Emma clasped her gloves over her mouth and yelped. 'Oh, Julian!'

They left their skis and boots at the door. Julian smiled at her. 'I think I should carry you over the threshold, don't you?' he said, making her giggle, as he lifted her into his arms. 'For old times' sake.'

'Oh my God,' Emma gasped, still unable to take in the magnitude of his romantic gesture.

More memories. Of the orange seventies décor and pine log finish. Of how they'd made love on the shag-pile rug by the fire. And how they'd drank too much and had run out naked into the snow for dares. And how they'd played cards by candlelight and danced to cheesy records on the stereo.

But it had all changed. Emma spotted straight away that Julian had had someone in. And not just anyone. Unless the seller had exquisite taste, Emma wouldn't mind betting that Julian had hired in Rodriguez, Emma's favourite interior designer. The clues lay in the tell-tale minimalism. The way the modern fireplace had been moulded into the slate-clad walls, and the high tongue-and-groove pine ceiling painted a tasteful grey-white, so that the space had a light and airy feel. She walked over to the picture window and looked out at the hot tub on the terrace and the sauna and steam room. A bucket of iced champagne was on the table outside, with two glasses; their luggage stood in a neat pile by the door.

Emma laughed, incredulous, as she ran her hand over the fur throw on the sofa, glancing through the open door to the vast kitchen decked out with every appliance imaginable. Everything was perfect. She couldn't have done it better herself.

'What do you think?' Julian asked, taking off his gloves. He was staring at her nervously.

'I can't believe it,' Emma said. 'I love it. I love it. I absolutely love it,' she gushed, turning towards him.

'Well, it's all yours. In your name. Your hideaway.'

'But this is *our* place. I only ever want to come here with you,' she said. She ran over to him and kissed him.

He smiled down at her and she saw more wrinkles around his eyes than she'd noticed before.

'OK, if you insist,' he said. 'But it's good to know you've got a refuge. Next year we'll be entertaining so much at Wrentham – your new mate Natalya Khordinsky for starters. And all those places we'll go for the charity. I thought you deserved a present for being so fabulous.'

Emma laughed and pushed him back over the sofa, falling on top of him and kissing him. 'Come here, you gorgeous, unstoppable man, you,' she said.

Julian laughed. 'So I take it you like your surprise?'

'You are too much!' she said. 'I can't take any more.'

She kissed him again, feeling just as she had as a new bride. As if she could burst for loving him so much.

'Hey. I made sure they got a new rug for the fireplace,' Julian whispered.

Emma kissed him again, nuzzling his cold cheeks. 'Then what are we waiting for?' she said.

She wished that she could capture this moment for ever. Surely she was the luckiest woman alive.

'My darling,' she breathed. 'I love you so much.'

'I love you too, my Emma,' he said, pushing her hair back from her face. 'Do you know, you're even more beautiful now than you were when we first stayed here.'

'Oh, Julian. Whatever would I do without you?' she whispered.

CHAPTER FOURTEEN

The grimy state cab crawled along in the beeping traffic beneath the grey Moscow sky. In the back, Peaches chewed her nails and wished she still smoked. But it had been ten years since she'd cleaned up her act, cutting out nicotine and drugs in favour of health-food shakes and exercise. She'd promised herself never to turn back, and Peaches took her promises very seriously, especially the ones she made to herself.

Because she'd seen enough people do it: lapse back into old habits with disastrous consequences. Peaches knew she wouldn't let herself. In her line of business she had to look fantastic. For a while, youth made that possible. Hell, you could get away with anything when you were young. But the moment she'd hit twenty-five, Peaches realized that enough was enough and had changed her ways for good.

Yet at certain times, like now, she craved her old crutches. Because if she could just light up now, then maybe the thick cloud of acrid smoke from the Russian cab driver might stop bothering her so much. It might calm her nerves too.

High above the wide strip of rutted road, the only thing that seemed familiar was the huge cheery hoardings advertising Coca-Cola and Gap. Behind them were bleak grey Moscow apartment blocks stretching towards the white sky. The cab's radio crackled with static before giving out a loud-pitched whine. The cab driver banged the receiver roughly on the dashboard and swore in Russian.

Her mother tongue.

Mother. Everything led to her mother. Just the thought of having a mother had obsessed Peaches since her meeting with Mikhail Gorsky. And Peaches hated it.

Why did all this family shit have to happen now, just when things were going so well? What with the lingerie line and the party to organize, she really couldn't afford the time to be away from LA.

It wasn't even as if she needed a mother. Hell, she'd survived perfectly well without one all her life. So why was she here in this grim, god-forsaken suburb of Moscow? Why did it matter whether her real mother was dead or alive?

Peaches knew the answer. Because the memory of Gorsky's face had kept her awake at night. She'd met a man who'd done so many bad things he was going to be lynched even before his trial. But in this evil scumbag's own book, the worst thing he'd ever done was selling Peaches. And what he'd done to her mother.

Whatever that was . . .

Usually, Peaches loved travelling and seeing new places. She always flew first class, drinking champagne and, depending on who she was with, either chatting and watching movies, or sleeping with the help of a homeopathic cocktail cooked up by Massimo, her LA diet guru.

But the twelve-hour flight from LA to Sheremetyevo airport in Moscow had involved neither sociability nor sleep. Instead, she'd spent the whole damn journey going over and over the different scenarios in her mind, playing each one out.

There was no getting over the fact that her visit to Moscow was a huge risk. Her mother might not even want to see her. Or believe that Peaches was her daughter. And what if this woman Angela had tracked down to the nursing home Peaches was now crawling towards in the cab *wasn't* her mother at all? What if it was all a hoax of Gorsky's?

And even if this Irena Cheripaska woman *was* her mother,

then what if she was now too ill to communicate with Peaches? When Peaches had called the nursing home last week and managed to speak to her mother's nurse – a sweet woman called Yana, who mercifully spoke good English – she'd discovered that Irena was suffering from cancer and didn't have long to live.

So what was Peaches hoping to gain from a reunion with a sick old woman? Any kind of long-term relationship was out of the question. Even in the best-case scenario they would never be able to share any kind of life together.

And now she was here, Peaches worried that she was about to inflict terrible emotional pain on an ill old woman. What if raking up the past proved too much for her mother?

What exactly *had* Gorsky done to her?

Peaches couldn't imagine what could be worse for a mother than having her child stolen. But Gorsky had seemed to imply there was.

Peaches sighed. Was she doing the right thing? She'd always followed her gut instincts, but for once in her life she felt swamped with conflicting emotions. One half of her brain was telling her to get the hell away, to return to LA and forget all about it. But the other half knew she couldn't. She needed some hard facts to help her get over her anger, because no matter how much sympathy she might feel for the woman she was about to meet, it didn't alter the fact that her mother hadn't come to find her. According to Gorsky, she'd known all along that her daughter had been sold to a paedophile. So, Goddammit, why hadn't she rescued her from the Rockbines? Why hadn't she been there when Peaches needed her most?

Peaches knew that getting out of Russia back then would have been difficult, but surely not impossible? Nothing was impossible if it mattered that much. Peaches had learnt that the hard way.

If the situation had been reversed and someone had snatched Peaches' little girl, she *would* have found a way to get her back. Whatever it took.

So maybe this Irena woman, Peaches' mother, simply hadn't cared enough. Maybe that was it. She'd moved on with her life. Forgotten all about Peaches. Remarried. Had more children.

My God! Did Peaches have *siblings*?

The cab hung a sharp left off the main drag at a set of traffic lights and pulled to a stop outside an austere grey-brick building. The cab driver turned and nodded to Peaches. They were here. She handed over a stack of dollar bills and he looked impressed.

Peaches stepped out of the back of the scruffy cab into the fresh wind. Reality bit home right away. It had been all very well to imagine a Russian nursing home and the suffering of an unknown woman from the comfort of her beach house in LA. Actually being here was entirely different.

Peaches shivered. 'Jesus,' she muttered out loud. The cold wind cut into her skin so she turned up the collar on her Burberry mac, wishing she'd worn something thicker. She pulled a strand of her long chestnut hair away from her face.

The captain on the plane had assured the passengers that it was warm by Moscow standards: ten degrees. But Peaches was used to LA. God only knew what it must be like here in the winter, when the temperature plummeted to minus twelve.

As Peaches put her hands in her pockets and stared up at the high barred windows, it suddenly occurred to her that she might be too late. Irena Cheripaska might already be dead. It looked like the kind of place where people died.

She heard a wheel spin on the road and turned to see the cab driving away, the driver's glowing cigarette butt spiralling out of the window. She had to fight the urge to run after the cab and beg the driver to wait for her, but it had been hard enough communicating with him as it was, and he wouldn't have understood.

She wished more than anything that her driver Paul was here with the limo. He always made her feel safe with him; no matter where she went, she knew that she always had back-up. But Paul was thousands of miles away. Peaches was alone. And, she suddenly realized, possibly way out of her depth.

Still, it was too late to turn back now. She took a deep breath, then exhaled, trying to force the fear from her body.

Show time, she told herself, quickly walking up the steps into the building.

It had probably once been an apartment block, or a government office building, Peaches concluded as she stepped into the cavernous lobby area. The walls were yellow and chipped with age. It was freezing in here, and the building itself seemed to be groaning with cold. The iron radiators along the wall clanked sporadically and, somewhere high above, up the stairwell, came the distant sound of an elevator grate being opened.

Peaches walked towards a perfunctory wooden reception area with a chipped Formica counter and old-fashioned beige dial phone. To her left, a door opened, giving Peaches a glimpse of a lounge area beyond, with lino flooring and old people sitting in chairs. A radio playing violin music echoed eerily. Peaches caught a waft of something that smelt of cabbage or maybe sauerkraut – something unpalatable, as far as she was concerned.

She cleared her throat and pulled the piece of paper out of her purse. It had Yana's name on it, the woman she'd talked to on the phone – her mother's carer and the person who'd agreed to translate. She realized that her hands were shaking.

Keep your shit together, she told herself. *Be cool. Don't go losing it now.*

She had to keep alert. And think clearly. This was one of those moments, she could sense it, when her life was about to change.

Down the corridor, underneath the stairs, a man with a serial number tattooed on his neck and a dirty set of blue overalls pushed a clanking metal trolley full of buckets and mops. He stopped and stared at Peaches, his mouth lolling open.

Peaches somehow doubted that it was her scarf that was magnetizing his attention, and she hurriedly fastened another button of her coat to conceal her cleavage. She wished she'd looked up the translation for 'Get lost, creep!' from her Russian phrase book, but it was too late now. She had to settle for glaring at the goon instead, unblinking. Like whenever she told a client it was time to pay up. It did the trick now. The janitor, or house psycho, or whoever the hell he was, trundled off down a corridor, mumbling.

As tiny a triumph as it was, it gave Peaches the boost of confidence she needed. She could handle this. No matter what.

She leant over the desk to see if there was a bell to summon help. She could see herself as a grainy black and white image on the small monitor behind the desk. She looked up to see a small camera above the desk. She'd walked in here easily enough, so why the CCTV? Maybe it was just for show. It probably wasn't even set to record.

But even so, for a second, she didn't recognize herself. She felt so strange being here, so divorced from her natural environment. She'd devoted her whole life to having fun, to gratifying her – and others' – needs. And that didn't involve thinking about the consequences, or thinking too much about the future. In Peaches' world, people stayed young and lived life to the full, consuming, having sex, making life one big party. They didn't get old, or ill, or . . *real*, like this.

'You must be Miss Gold?'

Peaches jumped. She turned round quickly to see a young woman wearing a white nurse's coat, thick-soled white slip-on shoes and brown tights walking towards her, staring at Peaches as if admiring her clothes.

'Welcome to Moscow,' she said in perfect English, revealing a set of fixed braces as she extended her hand. 'We spoke on the phone. I'm Yana.'

Peaches shook the woman's hand, relieved by her smile and surprised by how young Yana was. She'd sounded so serious and old on the phone. But she was pretty, Peaches noticed, apart from her badly dyed hair; with some restyling she could be a real beauty.

'Irena will be so glad you came,' Yana said. 'She never has visitors.'

Peaches stared at the young woman, feeling an unexpected stab of guilt and something else too – shock, perhaps, that two of her questions had been so instantly answered. Firstly, she wasn't too late and Irena was still alive. And secondly, Peaches didn't have any siblings. Not ones who gave a shit. Not ones who cared to visit their mother. And, all of a sudden, she could understand the huge weight of responsibility that came with having a family.

'I haven't told her about you,' Yana continued. 'Just in case you couldn't make it.'

Peaches searched Yana's eyes for signs that the nurse reproached her for neglecting the woman in her care. For turning up like this, out of the blue.

But Yana smiled and Peaches found herself wanting to confide in her how nervous she was. She hadn't told Yana on the phone that she was possibly Irena's daughter. Just an old friend, she'd said. Someone who had some news.

Talk about an understatement.

Would Yana be shocked, she wondered, when she discovered the real reason that Peaches was here? Or had Irena told this kind young woman stories about her daughter being stolen from her all those years ago?

'Your English is very good,' Peaches heard herself saying instead. It was a reflex of hers, always to pay a compliment when she didn't know what to say. To switch the attention on to the other person, away from herself. To make them like her more.

'You think so?' Yana said, obviously pleased. 'I have a degree in English language, as well as nursing.'

Two degrees, thought Peaches, and she'd ended up working in this dump. Peaches was lucky she'd been born in the States.

But then she remembered. She hadn't been. She'd been born here in Russia. Just like Yana. And that was why Peaches had come. To find out what had happened next.

Yana smiled and laid her hand lightly on Peaches' arm. 'Come, follow me. We'll take the stairs. Only the service lift works. And trust me, you don't want to go in there.'

Having already had the dubious pleasure of meeting the janitor, Peaches didn't need any fuller explanation. But with each flight of stairs, she felt her earlier resolve to keep cool wavering. Her calf muscles tightened and began to ache. An image popped into her head of the seat on the plane. Then her bed at home. Suddenly, she felt so tired, like a child who needed cradling and comforting. She wished there was someone else who could take care of all this for her. Or make it go away.

But there was no one else. The buck stopped with her. And the only way this situation was going to be resolved was if she resolved it herself.

She forced herself onwards, listening to Yana, who was carefully explaining that Irena was very sick and that the treatment for her type of cancer hadn't stopped it spreading. But Irena was lucky to be here, Yana told Peaches, reaching the top floor and pushing open the swing doors. This was one of the best care homes in Moscow.

Thank God it's not me, thought Peaches selfishly. *Thank God I'll have other options when I'm old.* But as she followed Yana along the bleak grey corridor, Peaches thought of the woman who might be her mother. Left here to rot. Dying alone with no visitors. Cared for by strangers. It filled Peaches with pity.

And fear.

Suddenly Yana stopped and pushed open a side door. 'Irena's in here,' she said.

The room was sparse, more like a cell than a bedroom, with greyish-green lino on the floor and halfway up the walls. There was one window with dirty opaque glass. A single bed stood along one wall covered in a striped woollen blanket. A tourist poster of the Winter Palace at night hung at an angle above it.

Next to the bed, an old woman was sitting in an armchair. She was wearing a blue nylon nightgown and a pink knitted shawl over her shoulders. She was asleep, judging from the way her head lolled on to her chest, her face mostly covered by a large pair of sixties-style dark glasses. Her head was bald, except for a few straggly tufts of white hair. A drip stand was next to her, its line terminating in a needle going into the back of her hand. The door suddenly swung back, forcing Peaches into the room and sealing her in.

The stale air stank of chemicals and Peaches felt a wave of revulsion overcome her, so that she had to hold her cuff over her mouth and stifle a gag. Yana walked over, leant down and woke the woman up.

Immediately the woman snapped upright, pulling out a garish ginger wig from the side of her chair and yanking it down on her head like a hat. She kept on the dark shades and Peaches could understand why she'd need them. The bright fluorescent light overhead made everything seem brutally stark.

Yana spoke to the woman for a few moments.

'This is Irena,' Yana said eventually to Peaches, her hand on the woman's shoulder.

Peaches didn't move. Could Irena really be related to her? She felt her sense of revulsion growing. And shame, too, that she was reacting this way. But surely there must be some mistake? Irena was so old, and so far removed from anything

Peaches was used to. Her illness had stripped her totally of any feminine qualities.

'Come nearer,' Yana said.

Peaches forced herself to walk closer. Every step made her feel more and more self-conscious and more and more ashamed. Could Yana see her lack of compassion? Her Western prejudice against the elderly and sick?

Peaches stared at the old woman, trying to look as neutral as she could. Up close, she saw that Irena was much younger than she had thought: no more than sixty perhaps. Her cheeks had been made up, but beneath the cosmetics, her skin had an unnatural yellowy-greenish tint. The cancer, thought Peaches, not age.

Irena spoke quickly in Russian to Yana. Her voice was hoarse and hostile.

Peaches sat down heavily on an orange plastic chair. Again, she felt a wave of exhaustion wash over her. Again, she thought of her bed and how easy it would be, even now, to leave. To turn her back on this place and never look back.

Instead, she looked at Irena, this woman who might be the only family she had. Shouldn't there be some instant recognition? Wouldn't a genetic link spark some reaction in her? In them both?

But there was nothing. All Peaches saw was her own reflection in the giant lenses of Irena's sunglasses. No answers. Nothing but her own questioning face staring back.

Peaches looked up at Yana, who was patting the old woman's shoulder, as if soothing her. And it was only then that Peaches realized that Irena was mumbling something barely audible.

'What is she saying?' Peaches asked Yana.

'She asks . . . who are you? Who sent you?'

'My name is . . .' Peaches paused. She remembered what the lawyer Ron Wallace had told her. 'Tell her that once, a long time ago, I was called Anna. And that Mikhail Gorsky sent me.'

But Yana didn't have to translate. At the mention of Mikhail Gorsky, Irena rose from her chair, emitting a terrifying scream. Then she lashed out, her bony arms flailing towards Peaches. The needle wrenched from the vein in her hand. Blood flew in a livid spurt.

Peaches yelped. She scrambled backwards out of the way, the chair under her.

'Stand back,' Yana shouted at Peaches, who stumbled away, flattening herself against the wall by the door.

What the hell was going on? Was Irena crazy?

Peaches stared on horrified as Irena kept screaming and flailing around. Then she collapsed on the floor. She was gargling, choking. Her bare feet were kicking, as if someone were strangling her.

Yana pressed a rubber button high up on the wall and shouted something into an intercom.

Peaches wished she could disappear. Wished she'd never come. Wished she'd never spoken. Her mouth and throat felt like they'd been filled with sand. She struggled for breath as she watched Irena's fit worsen, and Yana's attempts to control her grow more panicky by the second.

Oh my God, Peaches thought. *What have I done? What if she dies?*

She watched in horror as blood trickled down Irena's chin. She'd bitten her tongue. Yana lunged forward and gripped the old woman's jaw, holding it open.

Just in time, the door burst open behind Peaches and a couple of male staff in green overalls rushed in with a trolley. They lifted Irena on to it, struggling as she thrashed, finally manhandling her so that they could secure her legs with barbaric-looking leather straps. And still Irena screamed.

Yana grabbed a syringe from one of the male nurses and plunged it into Irena's thigh.

A moment later, Irena stopped bucking against the straps and her scream lessened into more of a wail.

An agonizing, soul-ripping wail.

'What did you do?' Yana said to Peaches accusingly, her previously friendly face now clouded with anger. She was sweating, her neat hair dishevelled from her frenzied struggle to control Irena.

'I . . . I don't know . . . I'm sorry,' Peaches managed. Her heart was in her throat, her hand over her mouth as the trolley passed her. Irena's head snapped around to face Peaches. The dark glasses had fallen away.

Peaches let out a terrified whimper.

Where Irena's eyes should have been were two holes. Blackened. Mangled. Scar tissue.

As if ... Peaches couldn't even bear the thought ... as if *someone had deliberately burnt her eyeballs out.*

CHAPTER FIFTEEN

Frankie removed the black silky eye-patches, not that she had been sleeping. The air stewardess in the smart silk blouse, the same colour as the private jet's beige leather seats, leant over her, holding a silver tray with a single glass of pink champagne on it. Sunlight poured in through the windows, bathing everything in gold. Gentle jazz played softly, drowning out the soporific buzz of the engines.

'Would you like another glass before we land, Miss Willis?' she asked with a practised, glossy smile.

Frankie sat up straight in the giant squashy seat. 'Thank you,' she said, smiling back and taking the champagne.

'My pleasure.'

Frankie watched the stewardess walk away in her perfect high heels and start polishing the shiny surface in the plush galley kitchen, exchanging a discreet word with her male colleague – the only other member of the cabin crew.

Frankie took a sip of the champagne, letting the bubbles fizz in her mouth. She longed to admit that only a few hours ago she'd been a stewardess herself. And now she was the one being served. She wanted to blurt out how bizarre it felt – and how amazing!

But what was she thinking? There was no way she could tell any of this to the cabin crew. They were doing their job and being professional and Frankie knew if she said anything, she'd just look stupid. Why should they believe her? Or have any sympathy at all? She was being flown, on her own, in this private jet.

It *was* real, she thought, looking out of the window down at the blue sea and small islands off the North African coast. She was about to land in Marrakech. To be with Alex. She could barely sit still or keep a straight face.

The six-seater plane was compact and apart from the captain and two cabin crew, Frankie was the only passenger on board. But its bijou size certainly didn't mean that it skimped on luxury. Frankie couldn't believe the vast difference between flying privately and flying cattle class, as she was used to.

It was all so easy. She'd been whisked into the airport in a waiting Mercedes, straight on to the tarmac and out to the gleaming white Hawker 800 XP with its blue and red stripe. And, in no time at all, they'd taken off. No queuing, no questions. It had been easier than taking a cab.

On board, she'd been offered all sorts of goodies: a gourmet meal, fine wines if she'd wanted them, a luxury aromatherapy kit, but Frankie had refused them all, preferring instead to hide behind her eye-patches. Because she didn't *want* all this luxury. She wanted Alex. Without him, this all felt too much. Like she didn't deserve it.

'Don't worry about anything,' Alex had reassured her earlier when they'd had a brief conversation, after she'd lied to Richard about her departure from *Pushkin*. She'd had to fake deep shock and she wondered whether Richard had believed her at all. But Alex hadn't seem fazed. 'I'll be with you as soon as I can. Probably later on tonight. And in the meantime, you'll be completely looked after.'

'But—'

'Don't worry, Frankie. Trust me,' he'd said.

Easy for him to say, Frankie reflected. It was still a huge deal for her, to put herself in his hands like this. She had no idea what to expect, no idea how their time together would be. She felt as if she'd stepped off a cliff and was now freefalling. Exhilarating as it was, it was also scary as hell. Having agreed to all this, she couldn't even begin to imagine where she might land up.

But she didn't have long to mull it over. All too soon, the plane touched down at Menara airport, and once again, Frankie was amazed by how quick and easy it all was. There was a jeep waiting for her on the tarmac and Tariq, the driver, explained that Alex's riad was in the heart of Marrakech's old medina, close to the souks. Like all riads, it had once been a garden house, built around a courtyard, but this one was special. It was one of the grandest in the old town, with a Moorish mosaic dating back centuries.

But Frankie was hardly listening. Instead, she stared out of the window, marvelling at the sights around her as the jeep entered the city and inched through the noisy narrow streets.

Having spent so long at sea surrounded by modern luxury, it felt wonderful to be here in an old city, with all its hustle and bustle. Everywhere she looked, colour blazed, from the red dusty walls to the shimmering cloths hanging on the market stalls alongside piles of fruit and exotic vegetables, shiny copper pots and brightly patterned carpets. And the noise enveloped her: children laughing and playing; Moroccan music booming out from the street cafés; merchants haggling on street corners.

The jeep slowed as it turned off a side street from the market and manoeuvred through the narrow lane, past a motorbike repair shop with engine parts and wheels scattered everywhere, before stopping beside a dusty high terracotta wall with an imposing wooden gate.

An old man in a fez was sitting on a stool outside, smoking. When he saw the jeep, he jumped up, pushing his rifle on to his back.

Frankie felt a shiver of alarm. Was the armed guard here for her? she wondered. For Alex? Or for the property? She didn't know, but she didn't like it. She'd seen too many guns back home and she knew what they meant. They meant division and intimidation, and everything she'd left South Africa to escape.

What kind of world did Alex really inhabit? And was it one she belonged in, too?

Tariq got out of the jeep and spoke to the guard, who then

opened the large wooden gate, allowing Tariq to drive them through.

The guard closed the gate after them, sealing them in. Silence descended.

It was as if they'd come through a magic doorway. As if the motorbike repair shop and the bustling city on the other side of the wall didn't exist at all.

A clear fountain trickled water into an enormous marble carp pond. Yuccas and palms rose to the blue sky above. Parrots squawked as they flitted between the exotic foliage.

Frankie stepped out of the jeep and looked up. It was breathtaking. Intricately carved marble and woodwork shutters rose up around her. Through an archway at the far end of the courtyard she could see that the inner garden gave way to a stunning freshwater pool and, beyond, the dense foliage of the grounds were filled with blossoming trees and lush palms.

In a daze, Frankie followed Tariq to the entrance of the riad, with its ornate curved steps and hanging lanterns. Inside, old-fashioned wooden fans beat the humid air, casting shadows on the sparkling mosaic floor.

Tariq introduced the housekeeper: an old lady who spoke no English. She took Frankie's bags and led her through to the sitting room, with its low leather seats and billowing muslin curtains, then pointed up the stairs. Then, bowing, she retreated, gabbling something to Tariq that Frankie didn't understand.

'I'll see you later,' Tariq told her. 'You must make yourself at home. There's food in the kitchen.'

Frankie wanted to call out to him, to ask him to stay, but he seemed reluctant to be inside. She remembered what Alex had said about not having servants here, about having a place that was just his.

Wow, she thought. She felt incredibly, intensely alive.

She was really here. Free. Free from *Pushkin*. And this place! She twirled around, taking in the splendour. It was as if she'd stepped into a dream. It was grand yet homely; exotic yet modern. It oozed old-world charm and eclectic good taste. No wonder Alex loved it here. She was totally enchanted.

Nervously, she started exploring, stopping occasionally just to check she really was alone. But the only sounds she heard were the squawks of the parrots and the occasional muffled beep of a car horn from the city beyond.

She slowly walked from room to room, amazed at all the beautiful artwork and treasures that Alex had collected: old Moorish oil paintings, fine porcelain urns, antique tiles and intricate silver vases and lanterns. In one of the rooms downstairs there was a collection of what looked like antique percussion instruments: odd-looking drums and brightly painted wooden flutes. It felt so intimate to have the chance to look around his house like this.

In the main library, she stopped, awed by its vastness and the intricate woodwork of the bookshelves and the pointed mosaic arches running to the high dome above. She ran her hands over the laden shelves, poring over Alex's book collection. The expected business books on management strategies were there, but also history books, thrillers and biographies of Machiavelli and Garbo. Plus an impressive array of photography, art and cartoon books and even an instruction manual for a hot-air balloon. It seemed that his taste encompassed everything.

In another room, she leant by accident on one of the walls, which slid back, revealing an enormous plasma screen and a vast collection of DVDs and CDs. Everything was here, from romantic Russian composers like Rachmaninov through to jazz and modern stuff that Frankie loved too, like the Eels and the Killers. She picked out a CD that looked like local Moroccan music and tried to work out how to insert it into the complex system.

She looked around, wondering why there weren't more photos.There was only one – of Alex, smiling on a luxury fishing boat. She picked it up and ran her finger over his face. God, he was handsome!

Soon he would be here.

And what would happen then? she wondered, her stomach filled with butterflies. Being alone in the riad together . . . how would it be?And what about later? Would they share a room? Would they sleep separately? Suddenly, she thought about his body when they'd been scuba-diving and she felt breathless and hot with longing.

Surely it would be wrong to sleep with him right away?

Surely he would think she was too easy? Surely it would be better to keep her distance and let things take their course?

But then she couldn't exactly play hard to get now! Not after what had nearly happened in his study. And not now she was a guest in his house.

By herself in his house.

With no crew, no servants, no bodyguards. It felt thrilling . . . naughty even, to be so alone. Frankie realized that it had been months since she'd had the luxury of her own company, with no one to scrutinize or criticize her. It felt wonderful.

She showered and dressed, selecting her best set of pretty silk and lace underwear. Would Alex be seeing it tonight? Would he like it? Was it classy enough for him? Her mind whirred with questions.

Downstairs, in the hexagonally shaped kitchen, she found the fridge and opened it to find it well stocked, including a jug of freshly made pink lemonade. She looked through the cupboards until she found a glass and poured herself some. Then she opened a screen door in the corner, which led to a set of stone steps. Holding the lemonade, Frankie climbed up the stairs until she was out on the top of a tower on the rooftop.

She gasped, stunned by the view. The sun was setting, casting a deep pinky-red hue over the sky. The old city, with its palm trees and mosques, its tall buildings with their haphazard television aerials, was all slowly dissolving into dusky dream-like silhouette.

She sipped her drink, captivated by the sounds coming to her on the warm breeze, the beep of the traffic horns, the whine of motorbikes, music on a far-off radio. And the smells too, of stewing meat and warming spices, of orange and lemon blossom.

Beyond the city, she could see the mountains falling into deep purple and grey relief.

She sighed and stared south. The fact that she was on the same continent as her home, even though she was thousands of miles away, somehow made her feel grounded. It made her miss her parents too. She didn't think about them often, but now she wished they could see her. She bit her lip, smiling to herself. She was here as Alexei Rodokov's guest. She wondered where it might all lead.

Hearing a beep, she leant over the parapet to see Tariq's jeep speeding through the gates into the dusty courtyard. And even before it had fully stopped, Alex was jumping out of the passenger's seat.

'Alex!' she cried out. 'Oh my God!'

She ran inside and down the stairs and found herself in another corridor. She hurried along it, behind the beautifully carved sandalwood screens, which threw patterned shadows on to the wall.

'Frankie! Frankie!' Alex was calling, bounding up the stairs.

'I'm here,' she said, reaching the door at the end of the screens and bursting through into his arms.

All she saw was his smile. He picked her up and twirled her around. She squealed with delight.

'So?' he said, his eyes shining. 'What do you think? Do you like the old place?'

'I love it,' she said.

He tenderly clasped her face in his hands and pulled her tightly to him. When his lips touched hers, she felt as she had done in his office on *Pushkin*, as if her insides had turned molten.

For a brief second, she thought again about perhaps taking this all a little slower. About pulling away. About telling him to stop. That they should wait.

But when he kissed her more deeply, she knew that she was lost.

'Oh Frankie,' Alex breathed, pressing against her. 'I want you so much. I haven't been able to stop thinking about you.'

There was no point in fighting it. She wanted him too.

Right now.

More than she'd ever wanted anything.

A second later, she was ripping open Alex's shirt and he was pulling her loose top over her head. And then her silk and lace bra was against his bare chest and he leant down, kissing her neck.

'You're so beautiful,' he murmured. 'Come!' He grabbed her hand. 'I'm being a very rude host. Let's go somewhere more comfortable.'

He pulled her after him, and she laughed as he sped up the stairs and through another doorway. She could feel his desperation as strongly as her own. But she stopped, stunned, as Alex flung open the door of the most astonishing room she'd ever seen.

This must be the master suite, she thought. It was vast, the marble floor giving way to a beautiful wooden four-poster bed. A pink marble dome crowned the ceiling. Shafts of low red sunlight slanted through the pale sandalwood shutters. The CD Frankie had selected downstairs was playing through hidden speakers in here, the drums beating out a primeval rhythm.

Alex took her hand again and pulled her after him, sweeping aside the swathes of mosquito nets draped over the carved frame of the bed.

They knelt opposite each other and she cupped his face in her hands, staring into his eyes. They were breathless and wide-eyed, like children.

'I can't believe this is happening,' she said softly.

'Neither can I. Are you sure, Frankie? I don't want to force you into anything. It's just that I can't help myself whenever I'm near you. But we can wait, if you want . . .'

'You're right,' she said, pretending to be serious. 'We should wait.' She looked at him for a moment, putting her hand on his chest. She stared at him, not saying anything, feeling only the pounding of her heart and his below her palm. But his gaze was so open. So honest. 'OK, long enough,' she said.

Alex laughed, pulling her on top of him, 'Come here,' he said.

And once again, she felt the urgent need for him that had overtaken her in his study. Only this time, there was no one to stop them. There was no Richard buzzing on the intercom. As Alex kissed her more passionately, she reached down, feeling for the hardness beneath his trousers, pulling his zipper until she'd set him free and he was in her hand. She squeezed him, feeling the delicious hardness of his long cock, and he let out a long moan. It felt as if she'd always known his body, as if his was the body she'd been waiting for, to fit hers.

Then Alex was rolling her over on to her back, kissing down the flesh on her tummy, pulling away the fabric of her knickers, nuzzling his face into her, making her gasp with pleasure and surprise.

She strained towards him, crying out as his tongue flicked over her clitoris. And then he buried his face into her and she felt his tongue inside her.

Just as she was about to come, he looked up at her and began kissing his way back up her body.

She strained her hips towards his, guiding his hardness inside her, wrapping her legs around his back as he filled her and she heard herself crying out with joy.

Alex's eyes locked with hers. 'You're incredible.'

She felt lost. Lost in liquid desire. Feeling only the way he filled her completely.

Alex rolled her over until she was on top of him, straddling him. She ran her hands over his tanned chest, feeling the soft hair beneath her fingers. He reached for her breasts, sitting up so that he could cup them. Then he leant forwards and gently began sucking her nipples. Frankie tipped her head back, feeling as if her whole skin were on fire, shaking her hair down her back, lost in the sense of completeness.

'Here,' Alex whispered as she slowly started to gyrate on top of him, grinding his throbbing hardness deep inside her. He took her hand and lifted her fingers to his mouth, running his tongue over them until they were wet. Then he guided her hand between her legs. 'Touch yourself.'

Frankie had never felt so uninhibited as she caressed her own body, rubbing the pink nub of her clitoris beneath her fingers.

She closed her eyes, light-headed. Everything else melted away except the sensation of her and Alex moving slowly, sensuously, perfectly together. And then at last, one final time, Frankie rocked back on Alex and felt herself falling – uncontrollably, shuddering and gasping out loud – into the longest orgasm of her life.

Much, much later, they sat opposite one another in the deep bath, surrounded by candles. Soft guitar music played through the speakers. Frankie reached through the cinnamon-scented bath-foam bubbles for the glass of champagne on the small tiled table.

She was still reeling from their encounter earlier. The sex they'd had was amazing. More mind-blowing than she ever could have imagined was possible. It had been like all the best sex scenes she'd watched in movies or read in books. But she'd thought that those were only fantasies. She'd never even considered that sex *could* be like that for real. It was as if she'd discovered something incredible about herself, and she couldn't stop grinning.

It had all happened so quickly and had been so intense that she wanted to pinch herself. But it *was* real. She was here. With Alex. In this incredible place.

Yet, as she faced Alex through the bubbles, she realized she hardly knew anything about him. The discrepancy between her physical and her mental knowledge of him filled her with illicit excitement.

And fear.

Because now was the real test. Now, after she'd given herself away so easily, she could really blow it. Surely, if he wanted to, Alex could dismiss her as easily as he'd got her.

She searched for a subject to talk about. And then she remembered scuba-diving and what Alex had said about Yuri wanting him to have a bodyguard. Alex himself had told her that he'd tell her everything about him when they were in Marrakech. Well, now seemed as good a time as any.

'So tell me more about Yuri?' she said.

'Yuri? Why him?' Alex said defensively. His eyes had darkened.

Oh no, she thought. She'd clearly touched on a raw nerve. She hoped she hadn't ruined the moment. They'd both been so relaxed.

'We don't have to,' she said quickly. 'If you don't want to.'

Alex kept staring at her, as if trying to read her thoughts, until finally his face relaxed. 'No, you're right. Why shouldn't we talk about him?'

The question was rhetorical, as if he were giving himself permission to do just that.

'Where do you want me to start?' he asked. His face was lit by soft candlelight and, once again, she was overwhelmed by how handsome he was.

'Anywhere. Anywhere you like.'

Alex took a sip of champagne, then put the glass down. 'I suppose you could say that he's the father I never had.'

'You never had a father?' Frankie asked.

'I did, but my parents died when I was young. Yuri was good friends with them both. When they went, he took care of me. He sponsored me through all the best schools.'

Frankie sat up in the bath. 'You mean . . . ? You mean you're an orphan too?' she asked.

Alex looked at her quizzically. 'I don't understand?'

So she told him all about her own parents. How they'd both been killed in the car crash and how her aunt and uncle had brought her up.

'Do you think that's why we have the connection we do?' Alex asked. 'Do you think it could be because we both had similar experiences as kids?'

Frankie smiled at him. 'Maybe. Or maybe it's just because you're possibly the most attractive man I've ever met.'

Alex laughed.

'Seriously,' Frankie continued, wanting to hear more, thirsty now to know as much about him as possible, 'my circumstances were very different from yours, I guess. My family weren't rich, but Yuri sounds as if he was very generous.'

Alex sighed. 'He still is. He's given me so much. After my MBA at Harvard, he got me a management position in one of his smaller companies. He made me work hard, though. It hasn't been free. I've worked my way up. But now I'm the Managing Director of Forest Holdings, his company.'

'He must respect you a lot.'

'I guess Yuri wants to take a back seat. He's out of Russia now and he's determined to enjoy his success. He wants to leave his day-to-day business with someone he trusts.'

'So? What's he like to work for?' Frankie asked, intrigued.

'Difficult sometimes, just between you and me. He doesn't like delegating much. He's always checking up on me. But then, if I was him, I'd find it hard handing over control to a successor. If, indeed, that's what I turn out to be.'

From the way he said this, and the short, introspective pause that followed, Frankie was unsure whether he meant that this might not happen, not through his choice, but Yuri's. But before she could ask, he continued, 'Loyalty is the most important thing to him. To both of us. I'd never let him down. Or lie to him. About anything. I owe him everything.'

Frankie was surprised at the fervour with which Alex spoke these words. But just as suddenly, Alex smiled and sat up, running his hands up her legs beneath the water. 'Anyway, there's no point in me telling you about him. You'll like him. You'll see.'

'You mean I'll get to meet him?'

'Of course you will. You're my girlfriend, aren't you?'

'I am?'

Alex's face clouded. 'If you want to be?' he checked.

'Probably more than anything I've ever wanted . . . ever,' she gasped.

Alex lunged forward through the bubbles, the water splashing over the side of the bath. She laughed as he kissed her.

'Good,' he said. 'That's settled, then.'

CHAPTER SIXTEEN

It was four in the morning and Peaches couldn't sleep. Instead, she sat in the top bar of the Moscow hotel, nursing a Jack Daniel's on the rocks.

Outside, the floor-to-ceiling windows revealed the lights of Moscow twinkling into the distance against the black sky. It could have been any city in the world and this could have been any other five-star hotel bar and, not for the first time tonight, Peaches felt as if she was caught in a bubble.

Around her, with the low soft lighting and plush carpets, the scene was a familiar one. The pianist had given up for the night, but low jazz fusion played through the speakers. Ten tracks on a loop. She'd counted them. Twice.

It was still fairly crowded in here with late-night party-goers. It seemed that Moscow, like any big city in the world, never slept. In the corner, a group of guys playing cards sat smoking cigars, their ties, like their laughs, loosened. A group of hookers with rich Western bankers lolled at the far end of the bar, their arms around each other's shoulders. Their cocaine consumption was obvious from their wide eyes and incessant chatter.

Peaches glanced up. The small television behind the bar was

playing a news channel. The bartender seemed interested in the story and turned up the sound. Peaches couldn't understand what had happened, except there was a photograph of some middle-aged guy and a live outside broadcast from the crime scene, with yellow police tape flapping behind a serious-looking reporter.

'Couldn't have happened to a nicer fella,' an American voice said.

Peaches could usually suss out a man just from his voice, but this one's accent was hard to place. He was American for sure, though. His voice was deep, yet strong. An ex-smoker. Probably divorced, she thought, before looking along the bar to see if she was correct. The owner of the voice was a dishevelled-looking man with floppy salt-and-pepper hair. No wedding band.

'Oh yeah?' Peaches asked. 'Who was he?'

'Boris Nazin,' the man said knowingly, taking a slug of his drink. 'The Governor of Smolenskaya. Garrotted, Mafia style.'

'What a way to go,' Peaches mumbled, not wanting to continue the conversation. The guy looked kind of nice, but Peaches had too much on her mind to deal with a stranger. She hoped that whoever the man was, he would take the hint from her tone and go away. She didn't want to make conversation with anyone.

She fiddled with her glass. The Jack Daniel's had made her feel lightheaded, woozy. She watched the ice-cubes rattle over the golden liquid.

Since meeting Irena Cheripaska, Peaches' mobile had been ringing off the hook. For the first time ever, she'd ignored all her calls and hadn't spoken to anyone – even Angela.

She couldn't seem to focus on the usual stuff. Organizing parties and girls and thinking about the underwear line didn't seem possible when the image – *that* image, of Irena's burnt-out eye-sockets – remained imprinted in her head, along with a thousand questions.

Had Gorsky done that to her? Was his story true? Or had Irena been damaged by someone else? What could she possibly have done that could have merited such brutality? And what could Peaches do about it, even if she were to find out?

It was all so complicated and Peaches couldn't help feeling that she was getting in way too deep. It was her own fault for coming here, she knew that. But somehow she couldn't find it in her heart to book a flight back to LA, so she was stuck. A victim of her own curiosity. And now the two things that always came most easily to her – sleep and sociability – remained elusive.

Tomorrow – in fact only a few hours from now, she suddenly realized – Peaches would be returning to the nursing home. Mercifully, Irena Cheripaska had survived her fit and now, after a few days' rest, was apparently much calmer. Peaches had been calling Yana constantly to ask about Irena's condition and, after much persuasion, Yana had finally allowed Peaches visiting rights, but only on the strict condition that Peaches didn't upset Irena again. Peaches had promised, even though she knew it was a promise she might have to break. Yet the prospect of another scene like the one she'd witnessed the other day filled her with dread.

Peaches sensed the man shift up a couple of bar stools towards her. *Oh Jesus, here we go*, she thought. Couldn't this guy understand that she just wanted to be left alone? She was off duty, Goddamnit! And it wasn't as if she was dressed for male attention, in her jeans and black roll-neck jumper, her hair tied back in a ponytail, with just a slick of lip gloss and nothing else. Tonight, she wanted to remain as inconspicuous as possible. To be wallpaper. And left alone to think.

Besides, if it was female company this guy was after, he just had to open his eyes. Moscow was crammed with some of the most beautiful girls Peaches had ever seen. Even now there was a stunning blonde by the door who clearly had her sights on him. She was wearing a long shimmering green evening gown and a crystal choker necklace. As she walked down the steps towards the bar, Peaches could see her impossibly long legs. If she lived in LA, Peaches would guarantee she'd earn a fortune.

But the guy was far from interested. He studiously ignored the blonde, turning his back on her in order to face Peaches.

'So? You got jet lag too?' he persisted. 'You're American, right? I'm guessing LA?'

Peaches sighed heavily. Only now did she look up into the

man's blue-grey eyes. She saw that beneath the shadow of stubble, he was younger than she'd thought at first – only in his mid-forties. She was about to tell him to get lost, but something stopped her. He didn't look as if he was trying to make a move. There was no threat in his eyes, no lust, only a glimmer of curiosity. Perhaps he was just another soul far from home who couldn't get to sleep and only wanted to chat.

'That's right,' Peaches said warily, raising her eyebrows at the man and nodding in the direction of the blonde behind him. 'Hey, I think you've got an admirer.'

'I know,' the man said. He winced. 'I tell you, it's tempting to pay them to leave you alone.'

Peaches looked again over his shoulder at the blonde, who had now clocked that the man was talking to Peaches. Peaches had been in the business long enough to know what the blonde's look meant: *Hands off, bitch. Don't steal my thousand-dollar meal ticket . . .*

But the guy was still talking.

'Do you mind . . . ? I mean, I'm sorry about this, miss, but can we just look like we're having a conversation, and then I promise I'll leave you alone.'

The guy was serious! He was genuinely looking to Peaches for protection.

'But she's nice,' Peaches said, stifling an amused smile by taking a sip of her drink.

The man put his hands up. 'No kidding. She's gorgeous. But she keeps following me around. It's kind of freaking me out. Back home they call it sexual harassment.' He pulled a face at Peaches. 'These Russian girls? If you so much as smile at them, that's it – they tail you. Let's face it, there's only one reason she's interested in me. It's not exactly as if I'm some kind of oil painting.'

Peaches smiled. It was unusual to meet someone so self-deprecating. And he was right, he wasn't classically good-looking. But he had a friendly face and kind eyes. Dependable. And that voice. A voice like that could work magic in a softly lit room. Or between the sheets . . .

'You're not so bad,' Peaches said, shaking her head even as she did so, amazed at herself for even being capable of thinking about sex when she was this tired. Especially sex that wasn't work. But that's all it was, she reminded herself. A thought. A tired and lonely thought that she had no intention of acting on.

'I know they're just doing their job,' he went on, 'and most of them are bright too. College degrees, the works . . .'

'. . . but you disapprove of hookers?' Peaches prompted.

'Hell no. They say it's the oldest profession in the world. Why? Because of us men. Because we're just dumb-ass suckers. No, you can't blame the girls. I just want to be left alone, that's all. I need some peace. Rough day at work.'

'Well, you're safe. She's gone,' Peaches said, glancing behind the man to see the blonde turning on her high stilettos and strutting away.

Peaches ran her finger around the rim of her glass. There was a pause. She waited for him to fulfil his promise and leave her alone. But he didn't move, and Peaches realized that she didn't mind.

'You want another drink?' he asked.

Peaches thought about his offer. Maybe some company would be a good idea. And now she knew he wasn't on the lookout to get laid, she could relax.

'Another JD, thanks,' Peaches said.

'I'm Harry,' he said, extending his hand. 'Harry Rezler.'

Peaches reached out and shook his hand. 'Nice to meet you, Harry,' she said.

'So, you here for business too?' Harry asked her, after ordering drinks.

'Sort of.'

'What kind of business are you in?'

Peaches smiled to herself. She couldn't exactly tell him the truth now! And for the first time in ages, she realized that she could be whoever she wanted to be. 'Retail, mainly,' she replied. 'You?'

'Ah, it's boring,' he said dismissively as the bartender brought their drinks over.

Peaches nodded at the TV. 'So how come you know about the dead guy?'

'Who? Nazin?' Harry said. 'I follow all the politics out here. Russian politics are incendiary. War-like. And totally addictive.'

Peaches laughed.

'Nazin was one of the most corrupt – or should I say corruptible – politicians on the block,' Harry continued. 'And believe me, there're a lot of them about.'

'Oh? Sounds like you're frustrated?' Peaches had said it before she'd even meant to. It was an old leading question, the kind designed to get a man to loosen up, designed to imply that Peaches could relieve their frustration, mental or physical. She'd said it automatically and she realized how un-intentionally loaded with innuendo her voice was.

But, to her relief, the guy totally failed to notice, and Peaches made a note to be more careful. She liked him: he was gentle and she didn't want to scare him off.

'Oh yeah. They're slippery, these Russians,' the guy said. 'In my experience, if they tell you something, it's never the whole truth.'

'Really?' Again, Peaches felt the corners of her mouth twitch into a smile.

'You should mark my words. These guys . . . they dream up scams where you wouldn't imagine they would even *think* of scamming you. You do any business? They tell you something is true? Then get the proof. That's my advice.'

'I'll bear that in mind,' Peaches said.

'In fact, if you need any advice, you could call me.' He reached into his pocket and took out a card, sliding it along the bar to Peaches.

But just as she was reaching for it, her purse slipped off the bar. Harry Rezler darted forward and caught it before it had even hit the floor. As he bent down, Peaches caught a glimpse of a black pistol pouch, the type that Valentin wore.

But she must have imagined it, she thought, as Harry smiled. She picked up the card and studied it. *Harry Rezler. US Embassy.*

'Thanks,' she mumbled. US Embassy. This guy was Government? 'Just US Embassy?' she said, noticing the lack of job title. 'So you own the joint?'

'I'm a consul,' he said. 'I'm supposed to be the expert on Russian affairs.'

Something in his voice made Peaches suddenly think of Tommy Liebermann's warning in the limo. She couldn't afford anything to go wrong right now. Could there be some way he'd know who she was and why she was in Moscow? Could Harry Rezler have followed her all the way from LA? Had he been stalking her? Had he been waiting for her in the bar tonight?

He searched out her eyes and smiled at her, and, cautiously, she smiled back. She was just being paranoid, she decided. Harry Rezler looked like a trustworthy-enough guy. If he was here because of her, she'd know it.

But she still had to be careful. She couldn't tell Harry too much. It was too risky. He probably knew all about Gorsky and why he was being extradited back to Russia. She'd bet anything that Governor in Merton would be only too happy to talk about Peaches' visit to the prison. And one phone call from a clearly intelligent guy like Harry to the right department would finish her for ever.

'Hell, let's not talk about work,' he said, as if sensing her nervousness.

'OK,' she agreed.

She'd give it five more minutes, she decided. She'd finish her drink and then leave to go to bed.

But somehow Harry never gave her the chance. He was so easy to talk to that one drink led to another. Before long, Peaches found herself sitting in one of the small booths with Harry, having ordered a club sandwich. As they continued drinking, she found herself risking telling him part of the real reason she was in Moscow.

'I found out some stuff recently . . . ' she said, then took a deep breath. It was so unusual for her to confide in anyone. Even though she knew she wasn't going to tell him the whole truth, after days by herself, she realized how good it was to have someone to talk to. 'Basically, I found out that I'm . . . adopted. And that my mother is Russian. I'm here to track her down.'

Harry nodded. 'Wow. Big task.'

Peaches sighed. 'You can say that again. It's not as straight-forward as I thought it would be. In fact, it's pretty frustrating. And now I'm here . . . ' She trailed off. No, however much she liked talking to the guy, she had to keep her wits about her.

'What?' he asked. 'You got cold feet?'

'Something like that.'

'I guess I could help you out, if you wanted. I could pull a few strings and get you access to some databases. And I know some people who are translators.'

Peaches smiled. 'No, there's no need. Thanks anyway. I'm on to it.'

'Personally, I'm not big on family stuff myself,' Harry said. 'I was married once, but . . .' He shrugged. 'I guess work came first. And my parents? Hell, they just nag me.'

Peaches laughed.

Maybe she should stop being emotional and get logical, she decided. She still didn't know for sure that Irena Cheripaska *was* her mother. Peaches wondered again if maybe it was a scam. Perhaps Irena and Gorsky were connected. Perhaps Gorsky had tracked Peaches down so that the two of them could extort money out of her.

Well, one thing was for sure: Peaches wasn't leaving Moscow until she'd found out the truth. Even if it meant forcing a DNA test on the old woman.

Later, Harry accompanied Peaches to her room and they stopped outside in the corridor. Peaches held the plastic key card in her hand.

'Well, goodnight then, Peaches,' Harry said.

Peaches smiled, an unfamiliar sensation coming over her. She realized that it was nerves. She glanced up at him. And for a second . . . just a second . . . there was . . . something . . .

He leant forward and she thought he was going to kiss her on the lips. But at the last moment, he kissed her softly on the cheek.

Peaches blushed as he pulled away, feeling suddenly shy.

Harry Rezler was a decent guy. A straight guy. But, Christ, she fancied him.

She thought now how nice it would be to cuddle up to him. To nuzzle into his neck. Maybe lie side by side holding hands, looking at the shadows on the ceiling. Was that why he was so attractive? Because playing with Harry Rezler was like playing with fire?

But before she had a chance to say anything that might give away how she was feeling, his cell phone rang, breaking the moment. He turned away. And it was then that she saw his eyes dart up the corridor – a split-second information-gathering glance of a surveillance professinal.

'Yep, two minutes,' he said, ringing off abruptly. 'Just a work call. Sorry.'

Peaches knew instinctively when a man was hiding something from her. And she trusted her gut. Now, as she watched Harry Rezler smiling at her, she absolutely knew that he wasn't everything he claimed to be.

Why would an embassy employee get a call at four a.m.? Why would he be wearing a piece? Why would a so-called academic expert be so fit? Have such lightning reactions? She thought back over their evening. Had he really explained what he did at the embassy?

But as he looked down bashfully, she realized she was jumping to stupid conclusions. There was nothing suspicious about Harry Rezler. He was just a normal guy. A normal guy who maybe felt something for her too.

'It was good talking to you,' she said honestly.

'You too.' He smiled at her. 'So, I'll see you around?'

'Sure.' She knew that was her cue to make an arrangement, but she didn't.

'I'm working pretty hard over the next few days, but I'll keep an eye out for you. Maybe we could have another club sandwich?'

Peaches nodded. 'Maybe.'

'Well, bye then. Good luck with your mom.'

'Thanks.'

Peaches let herself into her hotel suite and leant back on the door. Get over it, she told herself. She was being stupid. Harry Rezler was an illusion. There was no point in even entertaining the thought of seeing him again, or taking the relationship further.

But still, she thought, a weight of sadness coming over her, he *was* cute in his own way. And decent too. The kind of guy that in another life she might have married, had kids with, settled down.

Pull yourself together, she told herself. What was she thinking? Had she taken leave of her senses? She could never marry. And she could certainly never marry a guy like Harry. Not once he found out the truth about her.

No, she should remember her goal. She was going to make a few more million and then get out and retire. Then she might see things differently.

And one day . . . just maybe . . .

No. She shook the image of Harry out of her head. Jesus Christ. What was wrong with her? She was Peaches Gold. She couldn't have romantic feelings. That wasn't part of the deal.

Besides, hadn't she learnt anything? Love sucked. And being in love was for suckers. Which was why she was glad that it would never happen to her. She was safe.

But she couldn't even think about her future until she'd sorted out this riddle of her past. And she would. As soon as possible. Then she'd get the hell out of here and back to reality.

CHAPTER SEVENTEEN

Frankie woke up in bed, the sound of the mullah wailing in the distance. The first chink of sunlight crept through the wooden shutters, illuminating the coral and silver tiles of the centuries-old intricate pink mosaic dome above the bed.

She smiled, not moving, just relishing the feeling of Alex lying naked, spooned up against her back, his hand wrapped over hers.

She remembered now, with amazement, their conversation in the gym on *Pushkin*, when she'd told him that she'd never been in love properly. It seemed as if that had happened years ago. But what she'd said then felt more true than ever. Because now she *did* know what it felt like to be in love properly.

Because *this was it*.

And she ached to tell him. Ached to blurt out that she loved him. That it was crazy, but she just knew.

She couldn't, though. Not yet. She couldn't risk putting him off or scaring him away.

But lying here in his arms, she wouldn't mind betting that Alex felt the same way. He must do. This couldn't be one-sided, could it? This amazing connection they had?

But she couldn't be sure. To anyone else it might seem that

she hardly knew Alex, that they'd spent only a few days together, and it was impossible to make such sweeping statements, but Frankie felt as if she'd known him all her life.

She squeezed his hand. She'd never imagined that she'd ever get swept up like this, leave one life behind and find a new one, with a new person – just like that. Because she knew that her life would never be the same. She could never go back. Alex *was* her future. She knew it in her soul, as surely as she knew that she would do everything in her power never to be apart from him.

Alex stirred, and she smiled, feeling him growing against her. It was as if their bodies were incapable of being separated.

'Come here,' he said sleepily, and she wriggled back so that his hardness slid against her. And once again they were making love.

Later, they both wrapped up in sarongs and went to the kitchen. Frankie revelled in the compatible silence between them. As they both prepared breakfast, Alex busying himself with the coffee machine whilst she chopped plump, ripe peaches and apricots, they kept catching each other's eyes and smiling. As if they were still in bed. Still connected.

They ate on the terrace and afterwards they both swam naked in the beautiful freshwater pool, floating side by side on their backs, their faces turned up towards the warm sun.

'So, what's the plan?' Frankie asked as he drew her towards the steps and she slid her naked body against his. With the sunlight glinting through the palm trees overhead, and only the sounds of the birds and the parrots in the lush foliage, she felt as if they were Adam and Eve.

'You,' Alex said, smiling. 'You're my plan.'

She loved his smile, the way it made his eyes crinkle. She smiled back at him. 'Good.'

He kissed her then. Deeply, hungrily, his tongue found hers and they pressed together in the water. She giggled, pushing him away. 'Enough already, you're insatiable.'

'Oh, *I'm* the one that's insatiable now?' he teased. '*You* were the one that jumped *me*.'

Frankie gasped. He'd teased her constantly about how quickly they'd slept together, knowing that she was worried about what he thought of her. But she knew that he'd been as powerless to stop their passion as she'd been. And now, thankfully, it didn't matter. Now it was part of their shared history. Something to laugh about.

Alex leant back on the steps and put his hands behind his head. Frankie rested her chin on his chest.

'Actually, I thought I'd take you to see Sylvie,' he said. 'And then I thought I'd take you to lunch. A picnic in the desert. The full works.'

It sounded amazing, but still Frankie felt a stab of disappointment.

'Who's Sylvie?' she asked.

'She's a friend. She used to be married to the French ambassador but now she owns most of the best hotels here. You'll like her.'

'Will I?' she asked.

'Sure you will. Trust me, OK?'

But Frankie felt her nerves mounting as they got ready to leave. Alex slung on a pair of navy linen trousers and a short-sleeved shirt and went off to make a phone call, whilst Frankie panicked about what to wear. Her tatty sundresses seemed far too shabby to meet this Sylvie: they looked terrible. She finally settled on her cut-off jeans, which showed her legs at their best, and a baggy white shirt with a chunky necklace, but, still unsure, was about to change again when she heard a beep outside and Alex calling her.

In the courtyard, Tariq had arrived with the jeep and was putting the back down. Alex sat with his arm around Frankie as they drove right through the baking city, the breeze fanning them and making Frankie's hair fly in all directions. Soon they were out into the suburbs, and before much longer, they were winding through lush palm groves. Then Alex patted Tariq on the shoulder and he turned off the road, up towards the exclusive hotel.

It was incredible. It looked more like a fairytale palace than a hotel, Frankie thought, with its high sandstone walls topped by golden domes.

'Wow!' she exclaimed as she jumped out of the jeep and breathed in the warm, dusty air, marvelling at the sumptuous grounds and the outlines of the coconut trees against the smoky blue of the Atlas mountains in the distance. She was glad now that they'd come.

'I think I might buy this place. As an investment,' Alex said nonchalantly. 'Sylvie's putting it up for sale. She's giving me first refusal. What do you think?'

Frankie felt absurdly flattered that he'd asked her opinion and amazed, too, that he was including her. She was suddenly awed by his wealth – not that it was ever really out of her mind, since she'd been surrounded by the trappings of it since she'd arrived.

She would have to get used to this kind of world, she thought, and quickly. The kind of world where Alex could buy anything he wanted.

'On first impressions, I think you should,' she said, trying to sound more confident than she felt. 'But I'd like to see more.'

Alex nodded, and she wondered whether she'd passed some kind of test.

Inside, Alex held her hand as they were met by a beautiful concierge in a white Nehru jacket, who led them through the stunning reception area, with its giant marble pillars and exotic plants falling into a clear blue water pool, in which pink flowers floated. The warm air was filled with the scent of jasmine. Hibiscus tumbled down a sandstone wall.

Ahead, the marble pillars gave way to another area, more colonial, with a giant wall of wooden bookcases. Frankie saw a woman standing up from some low seating behind the grand piano and wave to them. She was in her fifties and had the friendliest smile Frankie had ever seen. Her dark, exotic skin and large brown eyes were only made more beautiful by the fine lines around them. She was wearing a stunning lime-green silk caftan and expensive-looking gold jewellery.

She flung her arms around Alex, as if he were her long-lost son.

'You must be Frankie,' the woman said in her low French accent, kissing Frankie warmly on both cheeks. She smelt of musky perfume. 'I'm Sylvie Dumas,' she went on. 'I've been longing to meet you. I've heard all about you.'

Alex winked at Frankie, and she wondered what he'd been saying.

Just then, Alex's phone rang. He looked at the caller ID. 'I've got to take this. Sorry. I'll be with you in a moment,' he said, turning away.

Frankie watched as Alex walked over to the other side of the pool, into the gardens, talking into the phone. He looked so commanding.

Was he really hers? She wanted to pinch herself.

Sylvie led her over to a dark mahogany bench beneath a marble arch, where long silk curtains framed the view of the lush gardens. Frankie saw that a low mosaic-topped table had been laid for tea, with a silver plate full of sticky-looking sugared sweets and pastries.

'Please sit down,' Sylvie said with a smile. 'Have some mint tea.'

'Thank you,' Frankie said.

'So, my dear,' Sylvie said once they were both seated and she had picked up the silver teapot, 'I have known Alex long enough to know that if he's invited you here, then you must be very special to him.' She patted Frankie's knee. 'Marrakech is his private space.'

Frankie smiled back and, despite her nerves, felt a moment of relief. So Alex hadn't been making it up. This place *was* special to him. She hadn't wanted to ask, but just the thought of him bringing someone else here – of making love to them in the riad, as he'd made love to her – made her feel sick. It shocked her how possessive she'd become of him. And how quickly.

'Yes, he said,' Frankie mumbled.

'I knew his parents a long time ago,' Sylvie continued, a wistful note in her voice. 'Ah yes. They were lovely people. Such a terrible shame. But Alex has been very fortunate. He has made a nice life for himself. And done so amazingly well in business. They would be very proud of him.'

Frankie smiled. 'I'm sure.'

'I think that's why Alex is so generous with the orphan foundation here,' Sylvie continued in a confidential tone. 'He doesn't like anyone to know it, but he's single-handedly saved so many children from poverty. Maybe he told you?'

'No, he didn't,' Frankie said, feeling humble – and amazed too. There were still a million questions she was stacking up in her head to ask Alex – about his past and his future. She found it unbelievably touching that he was so generous with the orphans and was so highly regarded by Sylvie. What other qualities did he have? she wondered. What other kind and heroic deeds did he do in private?

Her heart was swelling with pride. She wished she knew Sylvie better, so that she could confide in her how she felt. She could barely contain herself. She wanted to blurt out that she hardly knew Alex at all, but she was hopelessly besotted, and everything she found out about him only made her fall for him harder.

'I know, like me, that his parents would have been so pleased if Alex were to settle down,' Sylvie said. 'It's time . . . '

Her loaded comment hung in the air and Frankie didn't know how to respond. There was a small pause and she felt herself blushing. She blew across the surface of the mint tea in her cup. 'I guess . . .' she mumbled.

'Well,' Sylvie continued, smiling, 'I've taken the liberty of gathering a few clothes together for you. Alex mentioned you might be travelling light.'

Frankie now saw that behind the bench she was sitting on was a whole stack of expensive-looking suit carriers.

'There're just a few pieces from the designer labels we carry at the hotels. And bikinis and underwear. You can try them on in your own time at the riad. I think you'll find most of them will fit. Alex described you as a perfect eight. Men are so rarely accurate in these things, but I can see that you are just as he described. So keep whatever you like, my dear.'

'Thank you,' Frankie said, astonished at how thoughtful Alex had been to set all this up for her. When had he called Sylvie to arrange it? How had he guessed, without her having to say anything, that she was feeling insecure about her wardrobe?

And he'd described her as a perfect eight! What did *that* mean? Did it mean he liked her enough to want to show her off? Now, as Sylvie opened the bags, Frankie marvelled at the fine linens and beautiful silk clothes Sylvie had chosen for her. There were trouser suits and the most exquisite evening gowns Frankie had ever seen.

Frankie hadn't even begun to register what being Alex's companion, let alone his girlfriend, might involve. But, of course, now she could see that they'd be going to dinner together and meeting people. Frankie felt her hands beginning to sweat. Would she be up to the job? Would she let him down? Would her lack of experience in the world of the super-rich shine through?

'I know that Alex likes to be very private at the riad, but I'm sure he wouldn't mind if one of my beauticians were to come and visit,' Sylvie said tactfully. 'In fact, I have possibly one of the best here at the moment. Coco Rochas?' Sylvie looked at Frankie as if the name should mean something. 'Her facials, manicures and pedicures . . . ? Well, I hope you'll allow me to let you find out.'

She smiled at Frankie, who wanted to sit on her hands: the very hands that only a few days ago had been scrubbing out toilets, and that were now being offered one of the finest manicures in the world!

Frankie had glimpsed enough of the super-rich to know that the women Alex was used to consorting with were extremely high maintenance. If Frankie were to fit in, then she'd have to look the part, but inwardly she balked at the idea. She didn't want to be like some of the guests she'd seen on *Pushkin*. She couldn't think of anything more boring than obsessing about her appearance. Those women were so vain. And looking perfect all the time took so much *effort*. Personally, Frankie would much rather be living life than constantly getting ready for it.

Besides, Alex didn't want a girl like that. He'd said so himself. He wanted Frankie just the way she was. She was determined that she would stay true to herself and be the down-to-earth girl he'd met on his yacht.

However, she knew it would be far too rude to turn down Sylvie's kind offer. A few treatments would be nice, she decided. And maybe this beautician woman could give Frankie a few tips on make-up. She'd been so much of a tomboy in her youth, she'd never really got the hang of all that girlie stuff. Now might be a good time to learn.

'Yes, I'd like that very much,' she said to Sylvie with a smile. And as Sylvie smiled back, Frankie felt as if she were on the start of a journey and there was no turning back.

'So, Sylvie, what do you think of my new girlfriend?' Alex asked, coming back as Frankie and Sylvie repacked the clothes.

'I think she's perfect,' Sylvie said.

Alex held out his hand for Frankie. 'So do I.'

CHAPTER EIGHTEEN

In the day room of the Moscow nursing home, the old-fashioned gas heaters made the glass weep with condensation. The room was filled with tatty armchairs and a large old-fashioned television was bracketed to the wall, the screen flickering with fuzzy black-and-white static. Six patients sat around a table in the weak sunlight playing cards. In the centre of the room was a birdcage housing a beady-eyed mangy-looking parrot.

In the far corner, Irena Cheripaska sat in a wheelchair, a grey acrylic blanket over her knees. She was wearing her ginger wig and dark glasses still, but it was clear that she was awake and alert. Peaches sat in front of her and Yana to one side.

So far, the meeting was going well, but Peaches could tell that Yana was wary. She'd told her that Peaches was not, under any circumstances, to upset Irena. That her heart and her mental condition were not stable.

'Irena wants to know who you are and why you mentioned Gorsky,' Yana said, translating Irena's gruff Russian. 'She says he is a terrible man.'

Peaches decided to cut to the chase. She took a deep breath. She'd promised to be as calm as possible and, so far, Irena and

Yana were cooperating, but there was no point in mincing her words. She was here to find out the truth and then get back to her life in LA.

'Tell Irena that I know Gorsky is a very bad man. Tell her that I had never heard of him, but that he contacted me in America. Through a lawyer. I went to see him in jail. He thinks . . .' She paused and looked at Yana. 'The thing is . . . Gorsky told me that Irena is my mother.'

Yana threw Peaches a startled stare.

'Please, Yana,' Peaches implored. 'It sounds just as crazy to me. But this may be my last chance to find out the truth.'

Yana searched Peaches' eyes for a moment, then she nodded. She leant down and put her hand over Irena's and started speaking.

Peaches watched Irena the whole time. *Was* she her mother? Or was it just a scam? It was impossible to tell. Finally, Irena started talking. She shook her head.

'*Nyet, nyet, nyet,*' she repeated.

Yana turned to Peaches. 'Miss Gold, Irena says that she is sorry, but that you have made a mistake. That her daughter is dead.'

Peaches felt her heart thudding. She had a lifetime's experience already of people saying 'no' when they really meant 'yes'. And even though she didn't speak Russian, there was something in Irena's tone . . .

She'd admitted to having had a daughter . . .

Peaches knew there was more.

'OK, I know this is difficult, Yana, but . . .' Again she paused for breath. 'Gorsky told me that he'd stolen me from my mother when I was three. And that he took me to America. And that . . .well . . . that he . . . he sold me.'

'*Sold* you?' Yana asked, shocked. 'I don't understand,' she said, clearly assuming her English was at fault. 'Did you say *sold*?'

Peaches stared at her hands, which she now gripped between her knees. 'Yes. Sold. If Irena is my mother, she will know all this already,' she said quietly.

She couldn't bear to watch as Yana translated what she'd said. This was the moment of truth. Either Irena would have no idea about all this . . .

Or what Gorsky had told Peaches was true.

She looked up as Irena suddenly took a sharp intake of breath. Yana glanced at Peaches and Peaches leant forward, scared that Irena was about to have another attack.

'Is she OK?' she asked Yana.

Irena reached out and grabbed Peaches' sweater with alarming force. She muttered something. Then her voice rose as she repeated it over and over again.

Yana stood up, prying Irena's hands away. The other patients were staring. 'She says . . . she says that she wants me to examine your back. She says that if you are who you say you are, you will have a scar . . .'

Peaches felt the floor shifting away from her. 'Ask her what kind of scar?'

Yana asked Irena.

'She says a small scar probably by now. Just below your left shoulder blade?'

'Like this,' Peaches said. She leant over clawing at her sweater, showing Yana her back. Yana stared open-mouthed.

'Describe it to her,' Peaches said. 'Now! Tell her.'

Yana spoke quickly to Irena, her eyes flickering between Peaches and the old woman.

Peaches wished more than anything that Irena had eyes. It was impossible to tell what she was thinking.

But then suddenly, she *could* tell. Because Irena's face crumpled like a paper bag, racked by a sudden and terrible anguish. She hissed a single word. '*Da.*'

Yana's eyes filled with tears. She put her hand over her mouth. 'Oh my . . .' she said.

Peaches swallowed hard. She felt the blood rush from her face as Irena turned to her. The elderly woman's mouth had fallen open and she was breathing very slowly. She raised her palm towards Peaches, as if reaching out in the darkness.

Gently Peaches touched Irena's palm with her own. It was the most primitive of gestures, but somehow more meaningful than anything Peaches had ever experienced before.

Then Irena pulled Peaches towards her, her bony arms enveloping her in a vice-like hug.

'Anna,' she whispered into Peaches' ear, before her whole body shook and she began to sob.

Peaches closed her eyes.

She finally knew the truth.

Irena *was* her mother.

And then Irena was touching Peaches, her eager fingers feeling her cheekbones and her hair, letting them be her eyes.

It was only when Peaches saw that her mother's fingertips were glistening that Peaches reached up to touch her own face, and realized that she'd started to cry and couldn't stop.

'Irena is asking how your life is, Anna? Do you have a family?' Yana said, her voice hushed and gentle. The three of them were huddled together now, deep in conversation.

Peaches pressed her lips together. She kept looking at Irena, hardly able to comprehend what had happened.

She had found her mother.

'No, tell my . . . my mother,' she said, testing out the words, 'tell her that no . . . not yet. I don't have any children.'

'She wants to know . . . have you been happy in America? Do you have work?'

Peaches cleared her throat. She hated it that one of the very first things she would tell the only relative she'd ever known was a lie. But there was no way she could begin to tell her the truth. Peaches wanted to make this old woman proud. After everything, all the loss and deprivation that Irena had so clearly already suffered, Peaches was determined to bring nothing but happiness into the rest of her life.

Irena would never find out what Peaches really did for a living, she decided. Or any of the sordid details of the road Peaches had travelled from Albert Rockbine's porch to being the top madam in Hollywood.

'Tell her that I'm a businesswoman. America has lots of opportunities. Tell her I am very fortunate. That I have nice friends,' Peaches told Yana.

Her mother spoke rapidly to Yana, who glanced several times at Peaches.

'What is she saying?' Peaches asked, feeling self-conscious.

'She wants to know what you look like.'

Yana spoke in Russian, glancing bashfully at Peaches. 'I told her that you are very beautiful. That you have long hair. That you have brown eyes and fair skin. That you are dressed in expensive American clothes.'

European clothes, Peaches thought, remembering the D&G store in Manhattan where she'd bought the leather boots and red sweater she was wearing today on a business trip to New York, just a few weeks ago. She marvelled how far away that seemed now.

But she kept these thoughts to herself. She hadn't come here to discuss her own life, rather to find out what her mother knew about her past. She had to keep focused.

Irena nodded and pointed at the floor and said something in Russian. Yana passed the plastic handbag to her and Irena groped around inside before pulling out a small book. It had a burgundy mock-leather binding.

She gave it to Peaches, who realized that it was the first time she'd ever held something belonging to a blood relative in her hands.

She opened it and saw straight away that it was a diary. Her heart thumped once, hard against her ribcage. She knew from her own what big secrets a little book like this could hold.

She leafed through the pages and saw some small photographs. Smaller than passport photos, but clear images nevertheless. A baby. A toddler in a fur hat, being lifted up in the sunshine, a grand river sparkling in the background.

Was this her? Peaches wondered. It was hard to tell. But whoever it was must have meant a great deal for Irena to have kept these at her side for all those years.

And then she did a double take. In her hands was a picture of a woman. A beautiful young woman glowing with vitality and happiness. Could it really be . . .?

Peaches looked closer. Yes it was! It was Irena. It was this broken woman in front of her, old before her time, pictured when she was younger than Peaches was now, her skin radiant, her brown hair glossy and shining with health. And then she saw it. In the next shot Irena was holding the small child and kissing its cheek. Irena's profile – it was exactly the same as Peaches'. Yes, the more she looked, the more striking the resemblance . . .

Peaches felt fresh tears springing to her eyes. How bitter she'd been as a teenager as she'd worked her way through those strip joints. The only way she'd been able to survive had been to accept that she was on her own. That nobody in the world loved her. That nobody ever had. And that she had no need to be loved. She could survive without it.

And yet here it was in her hands. The evidence that she'd been wrong all these years. The evidence that she'd once been a cherished little girl.

She handed the photographs back to her mother. Irena took them, holding them in her hands, rubbing them with her fingertips, like she was trying to erase the past, or reach out to it. Peaches wasn't sure which.

All she did know was that something terrible had happened between then and now. She had to find out what.

'I want to know everything,' Peaches said, never taking her eyes off her mother, as she reached out and held her frail-looking hand. Her skin felt crinkled and thin. 'Yana, ask her to tell me what happened with Gorsky. I must know. Did he do that to her eyes?'

Yana took a breath. 'Miss Gold, I'm not sure if Irena can take all this. I think maybe we should stop for the day and then—'

'But, Yana, don't you see? I have to know. I have to know what happened. And whilst I'm here, whilst she's able to talk . . . you said yourself that time is short . . .'

Yana nodded and spoke with Irena for a long time and then she turned to Peaches. She took a deep breath. 'This is very hard for her, you know,' she said, her eyes flashing with warning. 'And hearing it will be hard for you too.'

'I know, but please, Yana, she must have told you something.'

'What you know is true. Gorsky stole you away to America. And when Irena tried to save you . . . well, she was hurt. Warned like this.'

Irena had taken off her sunglasses whilst she was talking. Peaches recoiled, seeing once again the mangled flesh where her mother's eyes should have been.

Peaches couldn't imagine the pain and suffering Irena had been through. She felt fresh hatred for Gorsky surging through her.

But why? That's what she had to know. Why had he done something so unspeakable?

Yana shook her head. She took a handkerchief out of her pocket and pressed it to her mouth. 'I had no idea. I had no idea anyone could be so cruel.'

Peaches swallowed hard and reached for Yana's arm. There was so much more to find out. She couldn't risk Yana breaking down. She had to stay strong.

'Yana, tell my mother that Gorsky told me to tell her he was sorry for what he'd done,' Peaches said. 'I think he'd found God by the time I saw him.'

Yana talked to Irena and then lowered her eyes. 'She says that God can't save him. That he is pure evil.'

'I know he is. But Gorsky said he was just following orders. Whose? Who would order someone to do such terrible things?'

Yana shook her head. 'Oh, Miss Gold.'

'Please, Yana. Please. Just ask her.'

'What is she saying?' Peaches asked, desperate to know, as Yana stopped talking in Russian.

'Irena says this: "He took my baby, my health, my sight, my dignity. My life is over now. I will die soon. But at least I found you. Now I will die happy knowing you are alive . . ."'

Irena reached out and touched Peaches' face again. Peaches closed her eyes and held her mother's hand against her cheek. Right then, Peaches knew that if there was something she wanted to give her mother even more than protection, it was justice. It was getting whichever bastard had torn the two of them apart.

Once Peaches found whoever was responsible, she'd do her damnedest to find whatever was the most precious thing to them.

And then she'd rip it away.

Rip it away for ever.

Because she couldn't live with herself knowing that some bastard was out there who'd done this to them both. Sitting here, right now, Peaches knew in her heart that she wouldn't rest until she had justice.

'Who is he?' Peaches said. 'Who is she talking about? Who was Gorsky working for?'

Yana talked to Irena. Peaches could hear her voice laden with emotion.

'She says . . .'

'Yes?'

'She says . . .' Yana's expression twitched with disbelief. 'No, it can't be. I can't believe it.'

Peaches sat on the edge of her seat. 'What, Yana? Tell me? Please. Tell me now!'

'She says that Gorsky was working for your . . . for your father.'

'My *father*?'

Peaches felt sick. She hadn't even considered who her father might be. And now this. Now this revelation of cruelty beyond her wildest imaginings . . . by her father?

Her own father . . .

He was the one who'd done this to her mother. Who'd sold Peaches like a slave.

Irena gripped Peaches' hand tightly. Her voice shook as she spoke with fury and pain.

'Yana?' Peaches asked when Irena had stopped talking.

Yana took a deep breath. Her eyes closed for a second as she steeled herself for what she had to say next.

'Irena says that your father is responsible for everything. Everything evil that happened to her and to you. He is to blame. He ruined her life. And he tried to ruin yours even before it started. He was the one who burnt you, branding that scar on your back. He was the one who wanted to torture Irena by sending you away. But . . .'

'But what?' Peaches could hardly speak.

'But . . . she says that he is untouchable now.'

Peaches took a deep breath. So her father was still alive? Whoever this man – her father – was, he was still out there somewhere, when Irena was in here? Suffering like this?

Peaches felt hot anger run through her. Her mother might think it, but no man was untouchable. Not from Peaches Gold.

'Yana, tell her to tell me his name,' Peaches demanded, raising her voice for the first time. 'Tell me who my father is. And I swear – whatever it takes – I will find him and make him pay.'

Peaches didn't need Yana to translate the next two words her mother said.

She sat back in her seat. Silent. Stunned.

She'd heard her father's name before.

And Peaches realized, her resolve hardening, that she knew just how to get to him.

CHAPTER NINETEEN

Frankie could no longer imagine how her life had been as a stewardess. After just one week with Alex, feeling manicured, massaged, wearing the finest make-up and designer clothes seemed – well – normal.

But all those things hardly mattered. She was so happy, she barely had time to contemplate the immensity of what was happening to her.

They were constantly on the go. Alex was like a little boy, wanting to show off his toys. He insisted on introducing her to everyone he knew in Marrakech. They ate out in the evenings at all the restaurants he liked. And wherever they went, people fell over themselves to be charming and give them good service.

He seemed just as at home in the small family-run cafés in the medina as he was in the finest restaurants, making Frankie be guest of honour at the snake-charming and the belly-dancing shows and introducing her to all his favourite foods. Everywhere they went, Alex was the star attraction and Frankie shone too, just by being with him.

Could it really be possible that she'd filled the gap in his life? As he said himself, without anyone to share all this with, it didn't mean much. But still she didn't tell him how she felt, even though she knew it was radiating from her.

Did he feel the same way as her? She longed to find out.

He'd certainly spoilt her like she'd never been spoilt. The designer wardrobe Sylvie had donated was just the start. Alex couldn't stop buying her things. He plied her with gifts, from simple handbags and shoes to the most astonishing pale sapphire necklace and earrings, which he insisted matched her eyes.

She bought a camera and made him take photos of them both, wanting to cherish and savour every moment. Part of her was desperate to capture and record it all, in case it didn't last.

But the best parts for Frankie were when they were alone in the riad. Wandering around naked, lounging in the pool, showering together, listening to music, playing backgammon. And most of their time was spent exploring each other's bodies. It seemed that the more they made love, the more they needed to make love. It was like an addiction.

'I want you to be completely honest,' Alex had said on the first day. 'About everything. I want you to show me exactly what turns you on.'

And so she had shown him. In the process, she'd discovered things about her own body she'd never realized herself. He'd told her that no one had ever turned him on so much or satisfied him like she could.

Frankie couldn't get enough of him – his taste, his smell. He excited her in a way that she hadn't known was possible. She'd never felt more uninhibited, or free. Every time she had a climax, she wanted to run up to the top of the tower and shout out how amazing she felt, so that all the world could hear.

The only tiny thing that niggled Frankie was that every time Alex's phone rang, he jumped, breaking their dream-like intimacy. Most of the time, he just looked at the caller ID and didn't answer.

But whenever it was Yuri Khordinsky, Alex left her and took the call.

Mysterious Yuri.

Frankie burnt with questions about Alex's mentor, but somehow she didn't dare ask them. Especially not after the first enquiry she'd made and his initially over-defensive response.

She was determined to be cool. And it was OK to keep secrets from one another, wasn't it? Like her not telling him the real reason she'd left South Africa, for example. Or how she'd sneaked on Eugene and Dieter to Sonny Wiseman on Alex's yacht.

Or, at least, it had felt OK *at first* to keep these things to herself. Only the more emotionally tangled she became with Alex, the more Frankie needed to come clean. She ached to tell him everything and learn everything about him in return.

She didn't know what Alex expected of her, but she couldn't pretend to be some kind of trophy girlfriend, who looked manicured and wore nice clothes and would make polite chit-chat if required. It wasn't enough. Frankie might have Alex's body, but she wouldn't be satisfied until she had his mind too.

She longed to know what he was thinking about when those worry lines appeared on his brow – especially after calls from Yuri. She wanted him to trust her and to respect her enough to be able to talk his worries through. Or ask her for advice, like when he'd asked her about Sylvie's hotel.

But since then and that tiny glimpse into his business life, he'd kept everything separate from her. And she ached with questions.

What exactly were the companies he ran? And how involved was Yuri? Just what did Yuri want when he called Alex? She couldn't help wondering whether he even knew that she was here in Marrakech with Alex. And if he did, then why did he keep interrupting them? Did he disapprove? Or not deem the relationship of sufficient importance to merit any respect?

More worrying still was just how much influence Yuri had over Alex. And did that influence, as it did between some guys she'd known, extend to Alex's choice of partner?

She hoped that Alex had told Yuri how wonderfully happy he was. But somehow she doubted it. And as the days passed, she started to feel like one of the fish in the courtyard pond. In the shadows, protected from the sun. For Alex's eyes only. An exotic and secret pet.

She told herself she was just being paranoid. Each time Alex kissed her, every time he smiled, she told herself to quit worrying and just enjoy the moment.

But she did worry, because she so desperately wanted this to be more than a fleeting episode in her life. She wanted this to be real, ongoing, a gateway through which she and Alex could walk hand in hand into the rest of their life together.

A week after they'd first arrived, Frankie could bear this angst no more. They were in the bedroom and she'd just got changed into the fine white linen dress Sylvie had given her and the chunky silver necklace Alex had bought her, when his phone rang again.

'I'm sorry,' he said. 'It's Yuri. I think I'll be a while.'

Frankie smiled and squeezed his hand as he walked away from her. 'Do you mind if I use the computer?' she asked suddenly. 'To check my email?'

'Go ahead,' Alex said distractedly, holding his hand over the voice piece of his phone. 'Use the one in the library.'

Frankie knew that she really should contact Uncle Brody and tell him everything that had happened. What if he'd tried to contact her at *Pushkin* for any reason and found out that she wasn't there? It was only then that it occurred to her that nobody knew where she was. Which only made her feel even more like Alex's little secret than before.

She sat down at the computer in the library and quickly booted up a search engine. She checked over her shoulder, even though Alex had said he would be a while, before typing in the words 'Yuri Khordinsky'.

Immediately, she felt guilty, as if she was cheating. Betraying Alex's trust. But she had to find out more.

There were fewer references to Khordinsky than she'd imagined there would be for someone so astoundingly wealthy. Lots of them were in Russian, but there were quite a few articles listed. She clicked open the one in the *New York Times* and then the *Guardian*.

It made absorbing reading. As far as she could make out, Yuri Khordinsky had as many supporters as haters. Many of his associates had gone to jail in Russia, but Yuri himself had never been arrested, or held to account. He was just there, lurking in the background. Super wealthy. Super stealthy. There weren't even any photos of him to download.

Alex was mentioned a few times, listed as his associate, even his protégé, but his profile was low too.

The more Frankie read, the more she realized that she knew

very little of the world Alex operated in. He made it all sound so accessible, so normal, and yet some of the articles she'd seen boldly stated that Khordinsky was an out-and-out crook.

All this terrified Frankie because, while she couldn't believe that Alex was dishonest and corrupt – not after the kind things Sylvie had said about him, and what she knew in her heart of his goodness – she could believe that Khordinsky might lead him astray. Alex thought so much of Khordinsky: what if Khordinsky was taking advantage of that trust?

As she read the article in the *Guardian* by some undercover journalists, she shivered with alarm. After months secretly tracking his activities, they had concluded that Khordinsky was power-hungry and utterly ruthless. That he had spies all over Russia, corrupt politicians who would do his bidding for fear of their lives. They had a whole list of people who had gone missing, or who'd been killed, all of them somehow linked to Khordinsky. And they had interviewed Government officials who spoke of poison plots, midnight stabbings, mysterious suicides. Frankie read on. Was Khordinsky really as dangerous as they were making out? Or was this just some kind of smear campaign, orchestrated by his jealous business rivals, or the Russian authorities, angry and embarrassed by Khordinsky's enormous success?

Quickly, she hit a link to another article from only a few days ago about the suspected murder of a Russian politician and associate of Khordinsky's, one Boris Nazin. Did Khordinsky have anything to do with his death, as the article insinuated?

And if any of this *were* true, then what did that mean for Alex? Frankie couldn't imagine that Alex could be involved in anything shady. He was so open, so honest. What if Khordinsky was involving him in illegal activities? Activities that could have disastrous consequences for Alex? For her? For them both?

'What are you doing?' Alex asked, coming into the library.

She had been so absorbed that she hadn't heard him and she jumped. She quickly closed down the search screen. 'Just checking my emails,' she said, hating herself for lying as she stood up to face him.

She immediately regretted what she'd done. She felt sullied by what she'd read. And by lying to Alex, she felt she'd ruined something too. Should she just confront him? she wondered. Ask him straight out if these articles about Khordinsky were true?

But if she did that, she'd be admitting that she'd been checking up on him. And that in itself was an admission that she didn't trust him.

No, she'd keep her mouth shut. Just because something was in the newspapers didn't make it true. Why should she trust these journalists, these people she didn't know, who were all going on hearsay and speculation just to get a cheap headline?

Surely she should trust Alex, who she *did* know. Who was standing in front of her. It would be crazy to risk blowing their relationship by making accusations about his boss. If she wanted to know more about Khordinsky, if she wanted to satisfy her doubts, then she was going to need to be more subtle than that. And more mature.

'How was Yuri?' she asked.

Alex looked distracted for a second. 'Fine.'

'I was thinking . . . I'd so like to meet him. You know, don't you think it's better that we get our relationship out in the open with him?'

'What do you mean?' Alex looked confused.

'Well . . . does he know about us?'

Alex laughed. 'Frankie, Yuri knows about everything. Do you think that I wouldn't tell him something as important as this?'

'Well, I don't know,' Frankie said, feeling foolish, relief washing over her. So Alex *had* discussed her with Khordinsky. Well, that was something at least. She felt even more of a heel for lying to him about her snooping now.

'Why are you worrying about Yuri?' he asked, coming over to her and holding her shoulders. He looked into her face, and she wondered whether he could see her for the liar she was.

'I'm just . . you know . . . nervous. I know how important he is to you,' she mumbled.

'Well, don't be nervous. Listen, you two will get on perfectly. Anyway, I forgot to tell you, Yuri's throwing a party for me. He'll be there, so you'll see for yourself.'

'A party? Where?'

'On board *Pushkin*. It's gone back to Cannes for the festival.'

Just thinking about *Pushkin* . . . Richard, Roz, all those people . . . made her stomach churn. She'd hoped they'd be in her past but now she realized she'd have to face them.

'Actually, I was meaning to discuss this with you,' Alex continued. 'I think the best thing is if you hang out here for a few more days and then go back to the yacht and wait for me there.'

Frankie scanned his face. She felt panic racing through her. 'Wait for you? Why? Where are you going?'

Alex sighed. 'I wish I could stay here with you for ever but I've got loads I should have been taking care of. I've got to go to Paris, Geneva. Yuri needs me to go to some meetings. I can't put him off any longer.'

Frankie felt disappointment so overwhelming that she had to sit down on the arm of the sofa. It wasn't fair. Just when everything was perfect, it had to end.

She'd been so stupid. So caught up in her holiday romance. She hadn't even thought about how many sacrifices Alex had made to be with her, to make this week so special. There she'd been, annoyed about him taking phone calls from Yuri, when all the time he was probably putting off a million business meetings, just so that he could spend time with her.

But if Alex went, where did that leave her?

'Can't I come with you?' Frankie sounded pathetic, even to herself.

Alex smiled tenderly. 'It'll be boring. Just business.'

'But it's not boring. I want to be involved. I want to see what you do,' she blurted out. 'I don't want to go back to *Pushkin* without you.'

Alex laughed and, pulling her up from the chair, wrapped his arms around her and kissed her neck. 'Oh my darling, don't look like that! I'm not telling you to go back to your old job.'

'You're not?'

'No way! You're with me now and I want everyone to know it.'

'You do?'

'Of course. They're going to wait on *you* from now on.'

He touched the end of her nose and Frankie giggled, amazed that he'd read her thoughts. But at the same time she couldn't imagine staying in the master suite with Alex, and Roz and Simone having to clear up after *her*. It didn't feel right. In fact, it would be so awkward, the thought of it made her cringe. It was all very well her seeing the boss, but rubbing everyone else's nose in it . . . well, she knew she just wasn't the gloating kind.

'That's going to be a bit weird,' she said.

'Well, you're going to have to get used to it,' Alex said. 'We're a couple now. Together. And I don't care what *anyone* else thinks. Anyone at all. This is about you and me. Agreed?'

From the tone of his voice and his determined expression, it didn't look as if she had a choice. She didn't want him to think she was chickening out now. After all the sacrifices he'd made recently to be with her, she reasoned, maybe it was time she made a few to be with him. And who knew? Maybe it wouldn't be so bad. With a bit of effort, she might be able to handle the transition from staff to guest without upsetting anyone too much. She'd keep a low profile and be dignified about it. She'd make it work – for Alex. And for herself. To prove that she could.

'Agreed,' she said.

He kissed her again and she realized once more how stupid she was to worry about everything so much. Alex didn't seem to have a problem about their future or where all this was leading, or who might stand in their way, so neither should she. She had to be confident. And trust him.

The jeep outside beeped. 'That'll be Tariq. Come on,' Alex said. 'We're going to meet Marouk and Masha.'

'Can't we stay here?' Frankie asked. She was suddenly aware of how precious the time they had left was.

Alex smiled at her. 'It'll be worth it, I promise.'

The sun was about to set as they reached Essaouira on the western coast. They drove out of town, leaving the low buildings and tourist villas behind, until all Frankie could see was the breathtaking coastline.

Soon, they turned off the road and the jeep bumped over the rutted sand, towards the sand dunes.

'Where are we going?' Frankie asked, but Alex smiled.

'Over there, Tariq, my friend,' Alex said, patting Tariq on the shoulder.

Now Frankie could see a man waving. Alex jumped out of the jeep and kissed him on both cheeks, before introducing him to Frankie as Dev. He had smiling eyes and a handsome face and was wearing a red and white checked keffiyeh around his neck. He glanced at Frankie as Alex talked to him in French.

Alex was so wonderful, Frankie thought, the way he could fit in anywhere, put people at their ease and bring a smile to their faces. And then she remembered: tomorrow he would be gone.

Tears sprang to her eyes from nowhere. She was being ridiculous, she told herself. He hadn't gone yet. She wouldn't think about tomorrow.

Dev started walking into the dunes and Alex beckoned for Frankie to follow. There, grazing on the long grass, were two of the most beautiful Arabian horses Frankie had ever seen.

'Meet Marouk and Masha,' Alex said, turning to her.

Frankie thought back to the conversation they'd had a few days ago in bed, when she'd told him about growing up on Uncle Brody's farm and how she missed riding the horses. And now he'd arranged this.

'They're beautiful,' she gasped.

And they were. The stallion was a deep, glossy chestnut-brown, with a patch of white between his eyes. As they approached, he looked up, his eyes shining with imperious intelligence. He seemed to recognize Alex as he approached, butting his nose into Alex's chest as Alex leant in close and spoke to him, producing an apple from his pocket, which he fed to the horse.

'Miss Frankie, Masha is for you,' Dev said with a smile, leading her over to the other horse. She was lighter than Marouk, with a silky blond mane and long eyelashes. Her hooves scuffed the sand and Frankie noticed two of them were white. She smiled and walked up to her, holding out her hand for Masha to smell. The horse backed away, her long toffee-coloured tail swishing, so Frankie stopped. Soon, Masha came back to her. Her coat, when Frankie touched it, was unbelievably soft. These horses were obviously incredibly well cared for.

'She's – how you say? – shy,' Dev explained. 'She's young. I have just broken her in. But she is one of my finest. Alex bought her especially for you. I see you two will suit each other.'

Frankie gasped. She turned, open-mouthed, to Alex. 'You bought me a horse?' she asked.

He smiled. 'I thought you'd like her.'

'I adore her.'

As Dev got the horses ready, he explained that Alex had bought the stables when Dev's family had got into trouble, saving them from bankruptcy and shame. Now he ran a profitable business and he kept horses for Alex. Marouk had been Alex's horse for years and Dev told Frankie that Alex was a talented polo player and could be one of the best in the world if he gave it more time. But he hardly ever entered any of the tournaments, apart from the annual Cartier Polo in Windsor in Great Britain.

Horses? Polo? Alex's talents knew no bounds.

'Come on then,' Alex said, embarrassed by Dev's flattery. 'Let's saddle up and get going before we miss the sun.'

Once they were mounted, Frankie and Alex waved goodbye to Dev and set off, riding on the sandy paths over the dunes. Masha was spirited and it took Frankie a while to get her under control. She was determined to show Alex that she was competent. She still couldn't believe he'd bought Masha especially for her. Did that mean that Frankie would come back here to ride her? The gift implied a future, surely?

Frankie gasped as they crested the final tall dune and saw the beach beyond, the sea stretching out before them, with the low sun turning the waves to shimmering gold.

They trotted together down on to the white sandy beach and on towards the breaking surf. Then Alex set off at a gallop, and Frankie followed in hot pursuit, feeling the hot sea breeze through her hair. She whooped, digging her heels into Masha so that she caught up with Alex. She felt like a kid again, back on Uncle Brody's farm. She felt so free.

They rode on for miles, until Frankie, exhausted, begged Alex to stop.

Her legs were shaking as they both dismounted. Her thin white linen dress clung to her, splattered with sea spray, sand

and sweat, but she didn't care. The ride along the beach had been the most exhilarating of her life.

They let the horses rest and sat on a rock, watching the sun sink into the sea. Frankie rested her head back against Alex, regaining her breath.

'That was amazing,' she said with a sigh.

'Good.'

'You spoil me, you know,' she said, turning her head so that she could look up at him. She felt strangely emotional. 'No one has *ever* given me a horse. Not even a toy one.'

He kissed the top of her head. 'You deserve it.'

'Can I come back here and ride her all the time?'

Alex laughed. 'You can ride her wherever you want. She's yours.'

'I think she likes it here with Marouk, don't you?'

They watched the sun setting behind the two horses for a moment. Masha nuzzled against Marouk's long neck. Steam rose from both their coats.

'But you mean we'll come back here? Together?' she checked.

'As often as possible, I hope,' Alex said.

Frankie felt her heart soar.

'You know, I meant what I said about you being with me,' Alex said after a while. 'But I have to insist on one thing.'

'Anything.'

'I want you to trust me, Frankie. Completely.'

She thought back to her earlier resolution. 'I do.'

'And I want to trust you, too.'

She felt a jolt of panic. Had he realized she'd been digging for information about Yuri on his computer? She wished now more than ever that she hadn't meddled. She vowed to herself that she'd never, ever lie to him again. This was way too precious.

'There is one thing I haven't told you,' she said.

'Go on.'

Alex sounded so nervous. She was about to tell him about what had happened back in South Africa, but something about his tone made her realize that it wasn't the right time.

'It's nothing,' she said.

'No, tell me.'

Frankie took a deep breath. She bit her lip. 'It's about Sonny Wiseman,' she said, opting to tell him about what happened on *Pushkin*.

'Sonny? What about him?'

Frankie told him about Dieter and Eugene and the bent game of poker she'd witnessed, about topping up the gin with water and filling Sonny in on what had happened.

'It just seemed so unfair and I couldn't help myself telling him what they were doing,' she said.

Alex laughed. 'Is that it?' he asked.

'Aren't you cross?'

'Why would I be cross? It's between Dieter and Sonny. They're always stitching each other up. It's probably just one of Dieter's little jokes.' Alex stroked her hair, smiling. 'Oh, my sweet Frankie, have you been worrying about it all this time?'

She nodded. 'I wanted to tell you before, but . . .'

'You silly thing. You can tell me anything. You can trust me and I can trust you.'

'Of course you can. I promise you, Alex.'

Alex was silent for a moment. 'You see, I have to insist on trust. It's so important to me. And I can't help it, but I'm a jealous guy, Frankie. And I've been hurt before. If you're with me, you're mine. If I were to see you flirting with another guy – well, let's just say it would kill me.'

'Like I'm going to flirt with anyone else!' she said, laughing, turning to face him. His eyes were serious in the glow of the setting sun. 'Surely you know that I'm just yours?'

'I don't want you to think I'm overly possessive,' he said, stroking her hair out of her face.

'I don't. Not at all. In fact, I feel just the same way.'

'Good. Because I have to tell you, Frankie, that I've completely and totally fallen in love with you.'

CHAPTER TWENTY

In the executive car park of the Elstree air base where the Harveys kept their private plane, Emma slammed closed the boot of her black Porsche Cayenne and pointed the beeper at the lock, before turning away with her Mulberry overnight bag.

'You got everything?' she asked Cosmo as he came round from the other side to join her.

She'd been shocked when she'd called Cosmo to tell him that she was flying to Scotland to see Victoria and Hugo McCorquodale, and he'd told her that he was coming with her too. He used to come to Scotland every summer to go fishing with Hugo, a godfather privilege that Hugo had tried to make a tradition. But Cosmo hadn't been last year, or the year before. And lately, he'd stopped flying anywhere altogether, on account of it being bad for his carbon footprint. Admirable as that was, it irked Emma that all his principles and actions seemed to imply a criticism of her. But today was obviously different.

'Here, let me take that, Mum,' he said, grabbing her bag.

'Are you sure?' Emma asked. He was already carrying a heavy laptop case. Cosmo took it from her by way of an answer and Emma smiled. Despite all his evasiveness and surliness, underneath it all he was a gentleman. Those years of drumming in good manners had paid off after all.

'What have you got in there, anyway?' Emma asked, nodding to his laptop case.

'Just . . . stuff,' he said, slipping down a pair of vintage Ray-Ban Aviator shades from the top of his head.

He was looking healthier than normal, she noticed, and older too. And since Julian's party, he'd cut off his dreadlocks, so that his coppery brown hair now curled attractively down to his shoulders. My God, she thought suddenly. Cosmo had turned into a man. A handsome man at that.

She smiled at him, pleased to have the company. She didn't like flying alone. And she hated the fact that she couldn't get hold of Julian. She always talked to him before take-off. They always told each other that they loved each other.

But wherever he was his phone didn't seem to work, and she hadn't been able to speak to him for over a week. That was the longest time ever that she hadn't heard his voice. She'd left lots of messages for him, asking him to call her when he could. But she supposed there couldn't be any signal in Norilsk.

She was desperate to know how it was all going. Had they found as much platinum as he'd hoped? She was worried for him, working out there in the cold in the middle of nowhere. And the thought of Dimitry Sergeyokov still haunted her.

But if the mine was up and running, then she needn't worry any more. It would mean that the deal had come off. She was puzzled that Julian hadn't found a way to contact her to set her mind at rest.

It had been ten days since the magical weekend skiing in Switzerland with Julian, and Emma had distracted herself by working non-stop ever since. There'd been the charity auction of the late Lady Sacks-Forsyth's wardrobe at Christie's in the week. It had been a lavish affair, with couture outfits dating back to the thirties. Emma had been pleased to see so many collectors in the audience, as well as several old acquaintances, whom she'd been able to have a good gossip with.

Despite being so busy, she still missed Julian like crazy. There was so much to tell him. But she would just have to take her mind off it by spending some quality time with Victoria and Hugo instead.

She needed to get things back on track with Victoria in particular. Emma had asked her to come to the auction and she'd agreed, but once again, just as at the Platinum Ball, Victoria had made an excuse at the last minute, claiming she'd been unable to leave Scotland. Emma had tried to cajole her friend on the phone, but she'd just been friendly and charmingly dismissive, cutting off Emma's line of questioning.

It was so unlike Victoria that Emma was now sure that something serious was wrong. There was something Victoria couldn't – or wouldn't – speak to Emma about, despite the fact that the two women had been fast and firm best friends since they'd lived together in their twenties. Was there some horrible illness that they weren't telling her about? Or was Victoria having problems with Hugo? Lately, every time Emma had mentioned him, Victoria had changed the subject. Well, she'd find out soon enough.

Gerald Summers waved and came out of the office to greet Emma and Cosmo, and they walked together to the hangar.

'Going anywhere nice, Lady Em?' Gerald asked. He now coordinated all the planes, but he'd trained Emma years ago and she'd always had a soft spot for him. He was in his late sixties, but had a craggy friendly face and a sharp sense of humour.

'Up to Grampian, to see the McCorquodales.'

'Lovely day for a flight.'

'Isn't it? You know Cosmo, my son,' she said, pulling Cosmo forward.

Gerald shook Cosmo's hand.

'How's your dad?' Gerald asked. 'You look just like him.'

Cosmo shrugged. 'Who knows?'

'Julian's fine, as far as we know,' Emma said, annoyed that Cosmo had shown so little grace. Maybe she was wrong about those manners. 'He's in Russia. On business.'

'Ah, those Russians are taking us over,' Gerald said. 'But I'm not complaining. The net jet business is booming, which is great for us. And they seem like a nice lot. Look at that beauty over there.'

Emma looked to where he was pointing over the other side of the wide runway and saw the brand-new Gulfstream 550 sitting on the tarmac. It was the latest in luxury private jets and was flanked on either side by two matching black helicopters.

Emma whistled.

'I know. You don't see those that often over here, only in the States,' Gerald said. 'Lovely piece of kit. You know it can stay in the air for sixteen hours? The pilot who brought it in said that he'd never seen equipment so advanced. He could see the runway through twenty miles of cloud and thick fog. Incredible. Owned by a Russian.'

'Oh?' Emma asked.

'Fella called Khordinsky.'

Emma looked back at the plane. 'Really? I've met his wife.'

'I only deal with his agents,' Gerald continued. 'They're keeping it here with his helicopters. He's getting a new place down in the Cotswolds.'

'Any idea where?' Emma asked, intrigued.

Gerald shrugged. 'I don't know.'

How strange, Emma thought. She always had her ear to the ground when it came to the Cotswold property scene, especially the kind of property the Khordinskys would be interested in buying. She knew for a fact that there were no stately homes coming on the market in the near future. So where on earth could the Khordinskys be moving to?

Well, wherever it was, Emma felt sure that their paths would cross soon. And if Natalya Khordinsky was living nearby, Emma would certainly be able to secure her as a patron for the charity.

'Hang on,' Gerald said, listening to his walkie-talkie. 'I've got to do some clearing before I can get the plane out. You two wait here. Help yourself to a coffee.'

Five minutes later, Emma sat outside the cafeteria with Cosmo. She couldn't remember the last time she'd sat in the sun with him, just chatting. The thought that they'd grown so far apart suddenly made her incredibly sad.

'So, why do you want to come up to Scotland, exactly?' she asked, deciding to risk asking him a direct question. He'd been so evasive about his reasons so far.

'Why shouldn't I?' he answered, his tone as usual defensive.

Emma sighed. 'I just wondered, that's all.'

'If you must know, it's business.'

Emma laughed. 'Business?'

His eyes flickered with anger. 'Don't laugh at me.'

'OK, I'm sorry. I won't, I promise,' she said, feeling awful, and annoyed with herself for having mocked him. After all, why shouldn't Cosmo take up an interest in business? She was always nagging him to make something of his life.

'What kind of business? Can you tell me about it?'

Cosmo gazed out at the planes taxiing to the runway. 'You know I told you that I wanted to set up an eco-community, and that we've been looking for a suitable property?'

Emma nodded, biting her tongue. She knew that Cosmo had already broached the subject with Julian, who had pooh-poohed the whole idea.

'Well, I've been in touch with Hugo.'

'Hugo?' Emma asked, surprised. 'Why Hugo?'

'Because he's got that big place on his land. The one that was destroyed by fire.'

Emma shook her head, confused.

'It's the other side of the river. It's derelict. Anyway, we've been discussing it as the site for the eco-project.'

'Cosmo, I really don't think—'

Cosmo rolled his eyes and let out an exasperated sigh. 'I knew you'd be like this.'

Emma bit her lip. She needed to backtrack. She felt a sudden pang of affection towards Hugo. He must have been encouraging Cosmo without involving Emma and Julian.

Suddenly, a huge feeling of relief came over her. That was it! There wasn't a problem, after all. *That* was the reason that Victoria had been so evasive. It had to be. They'd been protecting Cosmo and this new project of his.

Well, it was very sweet of Hugo, but Emma really didn't want him feeling obliged to indulge Cosmo. He probably didn't have any idea what Cosmo's associates were like. And, quite frankly, Emma doubted Hugo wanted a bunch of travellers and free-loaders up on his land, interfering with his beloved shoot.

'I'm not being like anything,' she said carefully. 'I'm just surprised you want to involve Hugo and Victoria. I mean, Hugo is running a successful business with the shoot up there. I'm not sure he's going to be so thrilled at the prospect of a . . . you know, whatever it is . . .'

'An eco-community, Mum,' Cosmo said. 'And for your information, Hugo thinks it's a great idea.'

'He does?'

'I've shown him the plans and the budgets and outlined how we'd restore the building.'

Emma shook her head. 'You've drawn up plans? You mean for the actual building?'

'Of course I have. For the whole site,' Cosmo said, as if she was stupid. He unzipped the laptop bag and quickly booted up his laptop.

Emma was amazed by what she saw next. Cosmo had downloaded pictures of the old house that Emma only vaguely remembered and now he was showing her a professional-looking restoration plan and a slide-show presentation of the planned eco-community. As he went through it, she could tell he was bubbling with enthusiasm about how it was all going to work. But Emma could hardly take it in. How on earth did Cosmo know how to operate spreadsheets and complex presentation software? Who on earth had done these detailed architectural drawings?

Emma felt momentarily lost. Of course she was incredibly proud, but stung, too, that he'd cut her out, that he hadn't thought to consult her during the crucial planning stage of his project – because this was exactly the same type of project she'd undertaken with Wrentham. In fact, if anything, it was even more ambitious. She'd thought he'd been sneering at her the whole time, criticizing all the choices she'd made . . . now it looked as if he'd actually been paying serious attention, all the while readying himself for tackling his own grand project. And as he briefly went through the presentation, she was dazzled by his vision. If only Julian were here! He'd be even more amazed than she was.

'Anyway, I want to see Hugo to discuss all the details,' Cosmo said. 'We're nearly at the green-light stage.'

'I wish you'd discussed this with me and your father.' She couldn't help the peeved tone in her voice.

'Why? What's the point? I tried. But Dad thinks it's a load of old bollocks. He's got his head so firmly buried in that stupid mine, intent on polluting the planet for profit, that he doesn't care about the future.'

'That's not true,' Emma said, leaping to Julian's defence. 'Most of the platinum he's mining will be used for catalytic converters.'

'So why's he mining in a city that's already one of the ten most polluted cities in the world?'

'But Norilsk is above the Arctic Circle,' Emma said, surprised by Cosmo's statistic.

'Which is all the more reason why it should be protected from further development. Did you know that where Dad is right now is so damaged by the mining industry that there isn't one single tree within a fifty-kilometre radius?'

Emma swallowed hard, horrified by what Cosmo was saying. And confused too. Julian had always made it sound as if the mine was such a good idea, that the platinum would help save huge amounts of carbon emissions, but Cosmo had put a very different slant on it all. And now she couldn't help worrying about Julian being out there somewhere so grim.

'I'm sorry you feel like that, darling. Dad is only doing what he thinks is best.'

'Then he's a fool.' Cosmo glanced at her, well aware of how much he'd stung her. 'But fortunately Hugo *can* see that what I want to do with this project would do a lot of good for the land,' he continued.

Emma cleared her throat. She knew that she had to leave the issue of the mine for now. She could see that Cosmo wanted to too. She mustn't waste this opportunity of talking about what was important to him by arguing about Julian. 'You're obviously very serious about it.'

'I am. And the beauty of Scotland is that the costs would be so low. We can use sustainable wood from Hugo's pine forests and Marcus – he's the engineer – he's worked out a project for solar and wind power.'

'Really?' Emma asked, stunned.

'There's sixteen of us who are completely committed to it. Most of them have a skill – carpentry, plumbing. We'd be completely self-sufficient and we could use our template for other communities around the country.'

'And Hugo knows all this?' she asked.

'Yes. And this weekend I'm going to discuss it with him – alone. OK? I don't need you to mother me through this one.'

Emma nodded, standing up as Gerald came back. 'OK, it's your deal, darling, but just for the record, if you want any help, you can count me in.'

'I'm fine,' he said, making it clear he wouldn't be coming to her.

She didn't say anything as Cosmo closed the laptop. Once again, Emma battled with her feelings. It was her fault that Cosmo felt defensive and she realized too that she would have to be the one to repair the damage she'd done by not taking him seriously. She'd certainly make sure she backed him in front of Hugo. After all this prep work, Cosmo really did deserve a chance to realize his vision.

Cosmo stood up and picked up his bag. Emma laid her hand on his arm.

'I understand that you want to do this on your own, OK? I would feel just the same if I were you. But I have to tell you, I'm very, very proud of you. Stunned, in fact.'

Cosmo stiffened for a moment, then he grinned. 'Good,' he said. 'I hoped you would be. If I can impress a wily old pro like you, then I guess I'm in with a chance.'

Emma was still smiling to herself as she taxied her plane to the short runway and took off into blue sky. She couldn't wait to tell Julian about Cosmo. Perhaps he'd ring her when she was at Hugo and Victoria's. She radioed down to Gerald, then settled back for the flight.

When she'd reached cruising altitude, she glanced over at Cosmo. He'd fallen asleep, his head resting on his hand. She had to quell the urge to take her hands off the controls and stroke his head. He looked so much like he had done when he was a baby and her heart swelled with love.

She was so proud of him. Maybe now that he'd confided in her, this was the dawning of a new age of her relationship with him. And now that he had a proper direction and a solid ambition, Julian would find it easier to give him the support he needed.

How had all this happened without her realizing? Why hadn't she known about Cosmo's business relationship with Hugo? She was dying to know what Hugo made of it all. Was he just humouring his godson, or did he really see potential where Julian saw none?

Emma sighed, looking down at the ground way below her. She loved the feeling of flying. It relaxed her in a way that nothing else could, taking her head away from all the arrangements and details that usually clogged her mind. It left her feeling light and refreshed.

Nearly two hours later, they were past Aberdeen and soon they were looking down on the McCorquodales' estate and the yellow and purple heather-strewn mountains which stretched into the distance in every direction.

From the air, Hugo's ancestral castle was vast, standing on a raised hill, surrounded by ancient forests. Emma had always thought the grey stone rather austere, but on a day like today, with the wide river sparkling in the sunshine, she could see the romance of the turrets and towers and crenellations.

Cosmo, awake once more, pointed out of the window. 'Down there! That's the place,' he said.

Emma spotted the derelict manor house on the other side of the river. It was much bigger than she remembered. Most of its walls seemed to have collapsed into rubble, and for a moment, she had to fight the urge to blurt out all the pitfalls that were immediately obvious from up here. Access issues, soaring costs, re-roofing – that would be a nightmare. Not to mention all the other reasons why his eco-community would be hard to establish in such a remote spot.

And then she realized. Cosmo was like *her*. What he was proposing was preposterously ambitious. But Cosmo was clearly no quitter. And hadn't she faced all these problems with Wrentham? And hadn't she overcome them all, despite everyone saying it couldn't be done?

Well, maybe Cosmo would pull it off too. She'd certainly do everything in her power to help him. Every step of the way.

'It looks wonderful,' she said with a smile, forcing down her motherly urge to tell him how much she'd hate it if he moved this far away from her and Julian. 'I think you should go for it, darling.'

They touched down on the small landing strip. Eddy, Victoria and Hugo's butler, was in a blue Land-Rover waiting for them. He greeted them warmly and Emma realized how wonderful it was to be here. How much she needed the break.

Soon they were at the gravel drive below the castle and Emma noticed how lovely the gardens were at this time of year, with their banks of rhododendrons in bloom against the dark green ancient yew trees in the background. The lavender hedges on the terrace outside the drawing room, which Emma had planned with Victoria years ago, were fully mature now and formed a wonderful boundary for the outside eating area.

The giant oak front doors were open. Victoria stood in the doorway, shading her eyes against the sun. Emma waved to her, and she waved back. As usual, she was impeccably dressed, today in a yellow cashmere twinset and dog-tooth checked trousers. As Emma bounded out of the Land-Rover and started up the great flint-topped stone steps, she saw Victoria turn in the doorway and heard her shouting for Hugo.

'What a gorgeous day,' Emma called, running up the remaining steps and giving her oldest friend a hug. 'I'm so glad we're here.'

But then Emma felt Victoria shaking against her. She pulled back and looked at Victoria. Her usually perfectly made-up face was haggard and drawn.

'Oh, Ems,' Victoria said. Her voice caught in her throat and her eyes were brimming with tears.

'My God, what is it?' Emma asked. She'd never seen Victoria upset. Not like this.

'And Cosmo, darling,' Victoria said, pulling Cosmo towards her. Cosmo glanced at Emma over his shoulder. Emma could tell that he was as alarmed and bemused as she was.

Hugo appeared from the hallway inside. He was wearing tweed trousers and a button-down cotton shirt. He was tall, but his usual jaunty manner seemed subdued, his bushy eyebrows knitting with concern. Without any form of greeting, he took Emma's arm, pulling her away from Victoria. 'Come inside. I think you should both sit down. Let's go to the library.'

Sit down? The words rang inside Emma's head. People only asked you to sit down if they had very bad news.

'What is it?' Emma asked, but Hugo only shook his head, leading her and Cosmo through the lofty entrance hall with its ancient heraldic banners and through to the sofas by the fire in the library.

Hugo looked as pale as Victoria. Emma racked her brains, wondering what devastating news they could possibly have to make them so visibly upset. A tea tray was laid out by the fireplace.

'Tell me! Hugo, what is it? What the hell's going on?' Emma persisted.

'Oh, Emma,' Victoria said, covering her mouth.

Hugo laid his hand on his wife's. 'We've just had a phone call from Pim.'

Emma felt her heart jolt. 'Pim? But—'

'Emma, Cosmo, there's been some terrible news,' Hugo continued.

'What? Is Uncle Pim OK?, Cosmo asked.

Hugo shook his head. 'No. No it's not Pim . . . it's your . . . I'm afraid it's Julian.'

'Julian?' Emma gasped.

Hugo bit his lip, clearly fighting back emotion.

'What's happened?' Cosmo asked. Emma could hear the fear in his voice.

'They found him in Russia,' Victoria said.

'*Found him?*' Emma whispered.

'He's . . .' Victoria began, but couldn't continue.

No . . . No! A voice started screaming inside Emma's head. She felt a numbness creeping over her skin. Nausea rose in her throat. *No. Don't let them say it. Not what I think. Don't let that ever be true . . .*

But Hugo kept talking.

'Emma, Cosmo, I'm so terribly sorry to have to tell you this,' he said, 'but Julian has committed suicide.'

'What?' Emma whispered.

'Oh darling,' Victoria said, bursting into fresh tears. 'Your poor poor Julian is dead.'

CHAPTER TWENTY-ONE

Dressed in a floor-length, slit-to-the-thigh purple velvet halter dress, with long satin gloves and her hair piled into a dramatic chignon, Peaches parted the crowd as she sashayed up the grand staircase to the white foyer on the first floor of Moscow's Bolshoi Theatre.

It felt good to be out, surrounded by strangers. She'd had the most insane week of her life. Her phone was filled with messages, from LA, New York, London and Paris, but she couldn't leave Moscow. She'd moved her mother and Yana into her hotel suite, quadrupling Yana's wages and buying in special drugs from a private clinic that Yana had told her about. She wanted her mother to be as comfortable as possible.

And she wanted to be close to her too. To listen – when her mother had enough strength to talk – to the stories which Yana patiently translated. With everything she heard, Peaches felt as if her life was pulling into focus. She sifted the information her mother gave her over and over, searching for links, however tenuous, that would connect her to her past, and hard facts that would determine her actions in the future.

The dreamy way in which Irena spoke about her youth fascinated Peaches. Her mother, like her, had once been a performer: a celebrated dancer, and then a cabaret singer, drawing men from all over Moscow to see her late-night performances.

One young man came more than any other. A rookie who came from the back streets; a hustler with nothing to lose. He courted Irena and eventually she succumbed to his relentless advances. Within a year, she'd given up performing and was living in a small apartment with him, helping him get enough money together to enrol in the Institute of Oil and Gas. They married one Saturday in the cold of winter.

For a while they were happy. He was making money in those early days, thanks to her. Irena helped grow his illegal factories, making clothes at night for the black market. But as soon as he realized he was depending on her, jealous of her natural business acumen, he stopped being interested.

Soon, Irena was left running the factory whilst he siphoned off the profits and left her to live in squalor. When she threatened to leave him, he beat her up.

She soon discovered that he had other lovers in apartments all over town and she didn't dare tell him that she was pregnant with his child.

By now, Irena had fallen in love with Tomin, the foreman of the factory. He loved her back, promising to look after her and her child. But Irena couldn't leave for fear of what her husband would do. She knew she was being watched all the time.

Then her child was born and Irena called her Anna, after her mother. Her husband beat her for not having a boy, but Irena loved her child and took her everywhere.

After three years, Irena could stand her life of hardship no more. Tomin had been left some money and they planned to escape. But her husband found out. He came in the night when they were leaving. He made Tomin lie on top of Irena, then shot him in the head, leaving Irena to clean up his remains.

He then told Irena that he didn't believe the child was his. Irena protested, but he said he was going to kill Anna. Irena begged him to stop, that she would do anything for him as long as he didn't harm Anna. He agreed to let the child live, but not before he'd branded her back with the sickle-shaped poker they used to mark the cartons of clothes in the factory.

Peaches had wept when she'd heard this. She'd told Irena

and Yana how she'd been haunted by a memory of that awful day: voices, screaming, the feeling of fear.

But there was no relief for her in solving the mystery of how she'd got her scar. No closure. No feeling that everything slotted into place.

Not when she heard the next, terrible part of Irena's story.

Weeks had passed. Irena tended her traumatized child, using old gypsy potions to heal the sickle-shaped burn mark on her back. And all the while she grieved deeply for Tomin, gathering a secret collection from the workers to pay for a headstone for him in the cemetery.

Once again, her husband found out. He came to her, drunk and violent. She stood up to him, so angry at what he had done to Tomin that she was convinced he couldn't hurt her any more. But she was wrong.

Seeing he hadn't crushed Irena's spirit, he thought of an even worse punishment. He took Anna, taunting Irena, telling her that she'd never see her child again. Irena told him that she would scour the globe until she found her daughter. That he would never, never stop her from seeing Anna, no matter what he did. And that was when he ordered his henchman Gorsky to burn Irena's eyes out with a poker.

Peaches shuddered every time she thought about how her mother had spoken these words in agony and how Yana had broken down after translating them. Peaches had never felt so helpless. She'd known cruelty before, but this ... this was something quite new. She realized now how easy it had been not to have formed any attachments in her life, how pain-free life was when you didn't care. But for the first time, Peaches *did* care. She cared deeply and passionately. She ached for Irena and the life she'd spent longing and praying in loneliness.

Peaches had gone back over her entire life. All the bad things that had happened – the abuse at the hands of Albert Rockbine, then the cheap, undignified way she'd sold herself in those early days – had all been because of one man.

Now, after her stay in Russia, she could see that because of him, she'd been condemned to a life of isolation. A life without a family. A life without the possibility of a decent guy or children of her own. And all this time, a sweet, intelligent woman had also been condemned: to a life of heartache and blindness.

And now she was about to die – all because of that evil son-of-a-bitch.

Who just happened to be Peaches' father.

Peaches knew that whatever it took, she would make things right. She would seek vengeance for her mother.

At first, Valentin had been surprised to hear from Peaches, as usually he contacted her. But it had only taken a few compliments and an expressed desire to do some sightseeing in Moscow before he'd agreed to take her to the ballet.

Now Peaches felt her heart flutter with excitement as she stood below the glittering chandelier. Yes, tonight, she felt as if she were recapturing some of her heritage.

It wasn't long before she spotted Valentin. He was wearing a tuxedo, which made him look more handsome than she remembered, but he seemed to be more anxious than she'd seen him before, hurrying her towards the royal box in the dress circle.

He stopped outside in the corridor and introduced Peaches to a swarthy man in a leather coat. 'This is my friend, Dimitry Sergeyokov,' Valentin said.

The man in the coat, Sergeyokov, reached out and kissed Peaches' hand and she inwardly recoiled. Peaches trusted her instincts, and her instincts told her that this one was no good.

'It is a shame I am going away,' Dimitry said. He turned to his friend, teasing, 'I would like to get to know her better.' He added to Peaches, 'Valentin always says that you're the best. Perhaps you have friends in town we could call?'

From the way he flicked his eyes towards Valentin, Peaches was in no doubt what he was suggesting. Peaches smiled, despite the hardness behind Dimitry's eyes.

Much to Peaches' relief, however, it seemed that Valentin didn't like the idea. He had a rapid conversation with Dimitry in Russian. Then Dimitry looked around nervously, as if he were worried that they were being watched.

Wordlessly, he hugged Valentin. When the men withdrew from one another, Peaches noticed that they both had tears in their eyes. Then Dimitry slapped Valentin on the shoulder before giving him a bundle of banknotes. He nodded at Peaches and quickly walked away.

'How long is he going away for?' Peaches asked Valentin as he opened the door of the private box, surprised by the emotion she'd just witnessed.

'Let's just say . . . he is disappearing for a while,' Valentin said.

'Disappearing?'

But Valentin didn't answer. He led Peaches to the box with its plush red velvet seats and thick curtain. Peaches walked to the front and peered down over the balcony to the theatre below, and gasped. It was vast, with ornate gilt plasterwork covering the ceiling and the walls. A safety curtain was drawn over the enormous stage. It was like stepping back in time and Peaches felt a thrill of anticipation. There was a happy hubbub of voices as the stalls below them filled up. The sound of the orchestra starting to tune up added to the excitement.

Peaches turned as Valentin handed her a glass of champagne. 'You look very beautiful tonight,' he said.

'Thank you.'

'So what brings you to Moscow?' he asked.

'Oh, just some business.'

'And what about this?' he asked. 'Is this business?'

'Not tonight. I think tonight is about pleasure, don't you?' she said, smiling at him. 'I'm so glad you could meet me.'

'It was not easy getting this box, but I thought you would like it.'

'I do. Very much.'

Valentin came towards her and suddenly he kissed her. She felt herself twitch with unexpected pleasure and she kissed him back. She could feel him stiffening against her thigh and she wrapped her hands around his buttocks and squeezed them.

'Let me have you now,' he said, gently easing her down towards the floor. 'No one can see us in here. Doesn't it turn you on that we're surrounded by so many people?'

She laughed and pulled away. 'Shhh. Wait. I want to see the ballet.'

She sat demurely in one of the plush chairs at the front of the box. She felt like royalty, sitting up here with her uninterrupted view of the stage. The stalls were filling up fast, and she saw people reach for their opera glasses and look in her direction.

'So you like Moscow, huh?' Valentin said, clearly searching for small talk. It was odd for them to be having a conversation fully clothed. She could tell he was desperate for her.

'I like the girls you have here. I'm surprised you come to America for pleasure.'

Valentin smiled. 'Russian women are very beautiful, but they're not the same as you American girls.'

Peaches decided to cut to the chase. She turned in her chair and leant forward towards him. She let the front of her dress fall open. 'Oh? In what way?'

'They don't know how to talk to a man like you do.'

Peaches smiled as the lights were lowered and the orchestra started up. 'You know, you make my nipples so hard,' she whispered, sensually licking her forefinger. She could see his cock twitching against the fabric of his trousers. She uncrossed her legs, watching him watching her.

She could see how aroused he was, but she wouldn't let him touch her. As the sheath of fabric fell away, she gave him a full view of her silk crotch-less knickers – samples from her underwear collection.

Valentin went to lunge towards her, but Peaches smiled and shifted further back in her seat, crossing her smooth long legs. 'Wait,' she told him imperiously, flicking her eyes back to the stage.

The lights had gone down fully now and the curtain lifted. She could feel Valentin's brooding presence in the semi-darkness next to her, waiting to pounce. But for a moment, as the ballerinas came on to the stage and the music from the orchestra soared to the ceiling, Peaches was totally caught up in the beauty of the scene before her. The ballerinas, dressed as white swans, glided on to the stage, pirouetting and jumping in the soft lighting. There was something so serene about them, and mesmerizing too.

But then she remembered why she was here.

Slowly, she reached out and let her hand slide up Valentin's thigh towards his throbbing erection. He moaned softly, as she squeezed him hard and her fingers reached for his zip in the dark. She teased him for ages, never taking her eyes off the ballet as she freed him, letting her fingertips brush over his balls. When she knew he could stand it no more, she grabbed his hard cock in her fist. She could hear his breath, ragged and horny, and, slipping off her chair, she knelt in front of him.

Slowly she began licking up his length, again and again, up and down, before finally giving him what he wanted and taking him deep in her mouth. She could feel the veins throbbing beneath his smooth flesh as she rhythmically moved her lips and tongue up and down his long shaft until, suddenly, he came, jerking his hips towards her, hot liquid bursting into her mouth.

But that, she whispered to him, was just the warm-up. They moved to the red velvet sofa at the back of the box, where she lay him down and slid on top of him and slowly fucked him until he climaxed again. She had to put her hand over his mouth to stop his gasps of pleasure drawing any attention from the rest of the audience.

Afterwards, as they sat whispering, he affectionately rubbed her neck before feeding her a chocolate from the tray next to the champagne, his earlier bad mood now having mysteriously vanished.

When he put his arm around her, Peaches suddenly felt as if they were on a date. For a fleeting moment, she imagined that she wasn't here with Valentin, but with Harry Rezler. What would he be like to kiss? she wondered. And where was he now? Somewhere on his own? Maybe even thinking about her?

She forced the thought of him from her mind. Tonight was about Valentin. About work. Not Harry Rezler and whatever childish romantic fantasy her subconscious had been busy cooking up about him.

She must have been craving male company more than she realized. Or perhaps it was just stress relief. Either way, it felt good to be working, even on a freebie like this. To be doing what came naturally. All the powerlessness she'd felt over the past week caring for her mother had gone. She was back to being Peaches Gold. Back to being the woman who could manipulate a player like Valentin with the flick of her tongue or a squeeze of her thighs.

'So? What kind of business are you here for?' he asked, pouring her more champagne.

'Just looking for opportunities. I need some more work.'

Valentin laughed. 'I thought you said this was pleasure.'

'It is. I'm not talking about this. I'm talking about real work. For me and my girls. I've got the party coming up in LA – I told you about it. I need a big stake.'

'You want money? I can give you money,' Valentin said, a lazy smile on his face.

Men, thought Peaches. They could turn from a thug to a teddy bear, just by having their cocks sucked.

'You are so sweet, baby,' Peaches said, snuggling up against him. 'But I want a big gig. Hey, maybe you know some people who might be able to help. What about your contacts? Didn't you mention once the . . . ' She pretended to grope around for the memory. '*Pushkin*? Wasn't that it? Isn't that some kind of big yacht in the Med?'

Valentin looked confused and then annoyed that she'd listened to and remembered one of his conversations. But it passed in a moment.

'Sure,' he said with a shrug. 'So what?'

'So . . .' she pried, 'I've been in this business long enough to know that this time of year is party time, what with Cannes and everything being on. I supply loads of girls for those big yachts. *Pushkin* – does it belong to your boss? What did you say his name was again?'

'Yuri,' Valentin said. 'Yuri Khordinsky.'

'That's right. So is *Pushkin* his?'

Valentin snorted. 'No. It belongs to Alexei. It's Alexei who throws his money around in the Med.'

She watched him slug back the champagne in his glass. She was getting somewhere . . . 'Oh? So who's Alexei?' she asked.

'Alexei Rodokov. He is Yuri's favourite. And he is stupid. He does not see that he is just Yuri's puppet.' There was no mistaking the scorn in Valentin's voice.

'Oh? You don't like him?'

'I never see him. People like me and Dimitry do all the dirty work, but Alexei, he just gets spoilt . . .'

'Uh-huh? How?' she asked.

'Yuri wants to throw a party for Alexei at the weekend, for his birthday. '

Peaches smiled. She was right on the money, once again. She still had what it took to sniff out business.

'The best Russian girls he wants. It is a headache for me. And then I'm not invited to the party,' Valentin continued. She could tell he was sulking about it.

'Oh, poor baby,' she said, smiling and leaning forward to kiss his neck. 'You silly boy. You should have come to me first.'

'But I've arranged it all. It's too late.'

'But will the girls be able to talk to him? Excite him? Like this?' She slid her hand inside his fly and grabbed his cock. He looked surprised, and pleased too. 'Well?'

'I don't know. It's what Yuri wants. And what Yuri wants, he always gets.'

Peaches was right against him, whispering in his ear. 'But I've got better girls. American girls. Girls that look innocent, but go like crazy.' She licked his earlobe, then sensually sucked it before continuing, 'Girls that will fuck each other in the best floor show you've ever seen.'

Valentin's eyelids fluttered as she expertly massaged his cock, feeling it grow once more in her hand. 'You think?' he sighed.

'I *know*. Why don't you cancel what you've planned and let me take care of it?'

'I don't know . . .'

'Will Yuri be at Alexei's party?'

'Sure.'

'So I'll make sure that they both know that you've brought the best girls in the world. Your present.'

'You will?'

'It's what I do best.'

'I know what you do best,' Valentin said.

Peaches raised an eyebrow and smiled. She leant back against the side of the sofa, letting the fabric of her dress fall away. Slowly, she lifted one leg up, hooking it over the back of the sofa, and let her other foot rest on the floor. Then, looking Valentin in the eye, she licked her finger, taking it deep in her mouth, just as she'd taken his cock. She touched herself, then ran her wet finger across her pussy. Then she slid her finger inside her ass.

Valentin drew a breath in through his teeth, watching her as he unleashed his cock. It sprang to attention.

'So you'll let me take care of it?' she asked, looking up at him. 'We have a deal?'

'Oh yes,' he murmured. 'Yes, yes . . .' He leant down on top of her. 'But . . .'

'But what, baby?' Peaches purred, sensually closing her eyes as he entered her.

Valentin breathed heavily, pulling her off the seat and holding her buttocks firmly so that he could penetrate her more deeply.

'You won't be there, will you? On *Pushkin*?' he suddenly hissed.

'Why?'

'Well, because . . . because you're mine,' he said.

'Don't you worry, honey,' she whispered in his ear. 'I have no intention of going. I'm in charge, remember? I don't do the gigs, I just collect all the money from my lovely girls when they come home.' Already her plan was whirring in her mind. 'Now fuck me hard, you gorgeous Russian stud. Fuck me hard, like you know I want it.'

CHAPTER TWENTY-TWO

On the bridge of *Pushkin*, Richard, the captain, nodded to Roz, who closed the door. Frankie faced them both. So much for the welcoming committee. Everyone had been acting very strangely since she'd arrived back on board, clearly preoccupied with the preparations for Alex's birthday party. She'd been hustled up here as soon as she'd put down her bag.

'So . . .' Frankie started, clasping her hands together. She suddenly felt nervous and shy. She wished she didn't have to do this alone. She wished she'd come with Alex. 'So I'm back . . .'

'Yes. Well, you're fired,' Richard said without preamble.

'What?' So much for her plan of making a dignified return and trying not to put people's noses out of joint. She'd been expecting the 'little chat' he'd proposed when she'd come on board to be about the fact that the crew now knew she was having a relationship with Alex. 'You're firing me?' she said, and then she laughed. 'I don't think you understand, Richard. I'm not even working here any more—'

'We know where you've been. With Alexei Rodokov,' Roz said, not hiding the smug tone in her voice.

Were they serious? What was this? Frankie stared at Richard, dumbfounded. She'd thought he'd know all about her and Alex. Surely Alex had called him? Hadn't he?

'Er . . . yes. So? Alex and I . . . we—'

'Yeah, yeah, I'm sure it's all very beautiful and wonderful,' Roz interrupted sarcastically, 'but it's still a sackable offence.'

Frankie had to fight down her urge to tell Roz to go fuck herself. Jealous cow. Be mature, she told herself again, and wait and see where all this is leading before you go shooting your mouth off.

'Richard,' Frankie said reasonably, ignoring Roz, 'you really don't understand. I thought all this was sorted out. If you'd just call Alex, then he'd tell you—'

'What? That he's managed to bone one of my stewardesses? Big deal. Do you think you're the first?'

Frankie felt blood rushing to her cheeks. 'How dare you! I'm waiting here for Alex. Until he gets here for his birthday party.'

'No you're not.'

Frankie felt her hackles rising. Richard was staring at her, exasperated now, like a teacher trying to explain a simple problem to a thick kid in school.

'Richard, for God's sake, just call Alex,' she said.

'Frankie, you're the one that doesn't understand. You're to leave immediately. These are orders *from the boss*,' he said.

They couldn't be serious! Frankie looked between Richard and Roz.

Apparently, they *were* serious.

Her brain was racing. There must be a perfectly plausible explanation, but she had to remain calm. She was determined not to lose it in front of them. They clearly had no idea what had happened between her and Alex. She must maintain her dignity at all costs. They were *her* staff – they just didn't know it yet.

'Fine. OK,' she said, holding up her hands. She wasn't going to give them the satisfaction of seeing her upset. 'Whatever you say. I'll go. And once Alex hears about this, then we'll soon see who else is being fired on the boss's orders.'

Richard and Roz exchanged a look.

'Eugene will take you ashore,' Richard said. 'I wouldn't bother asking for a reference in future. Just in case you thought—'

'I didn't.'

All she'd done was fall in love, but Frankie felt as if she'd committed a murder, the way that Richard escorted her to the deck and marched her to the waiting tender.

'Don't I even get to say goodbye?'

'No one wants to talk to you,' Roz said.

The words stung, but Frankie ignored them. She and Alex were in love and Richard and Roz were making a very, very big mistake.

Huge.

'You'll regret this, Richard,' Frankie said as she started down the ladder towards the speedboat.

'Maybe not as much as you will, Frankie. You're a very foolish girl.'

He was enjoying this. She could see it in his eyes. He spent so much time being subservient to the guests that the only thing that made him feel important was playing God with his crew. It sucked. Well, he'd be sorry when she was back in a few hours with Alex.

Eugene didn't even look at her. Jeff pulled the speedboat away fast and Frankie had to grab hold of the rail as they sped across the bay of Cannes. The water was crowded with yachts of all sizes. Everyone was here, trying to get the best position.

It wasn't long before Frankie lost sight of *Pushkin* as Jeff negotiated the RIB around the other boats. Only when they entered the channel that led to the nearest part of the dock did Frankie catch a final glimpse of *Pushkin*. Now that she was approaching the shore, it looked like a model. A toy. Something pretend and not real at all. Frankie felt her stomach lurch, feeling suddenly small and insignificant herself. Her old doubts assailed her once more. Was that what this had been right from the start? Nothing but pretend and make-believe?

No. She pushed the thought from her mind. She had to concentrate on what was real. What she knew in her heart.

Why were they all treating her like this? Was it really such a crime to fall in love with the boss?

'Eugene? What's going on?' she asked.

Eugene ignored her question and refused to look at her as they sped towards the dock, whizzing through the water at breakneck speed. It was as if they couldn't wait to get rid of her.

'Guys, come on,' Frankie said, as the boat neared the docks. 'At least drop me in town. It would make no difference. Surely?' And besides, she felt like adding, it wouldn't be long before they were coming back to fetch her. And then how stupid would they feel?

The speedboat slowed, pulled around and idled next to the steps up to the harbour. Frankie couldn't believe it. They were dropping her off miles away from anywhere.

She looked up at the metal steps up to the rough concrete. 'Come on,' she said. 'Eugene? This is crazy.'

'You must go,' he said, gruffly.

Frankie sighed. 'OK, OK.' She put out her hand for her bag, but Eugene refused to let it go.

'You can't take that. It's got my passport . . .' Frankie stared at him, angry tears rising up in her. It had all her clothes from Marrakech. All the presents Alex had given her, not to mention her make-up, money and camera . . . 'Give it back, Eugene. Please. It's got everything—'

'Boss's orders,' Eugene said. 'You're to leave with nothing.'

Fear gripped Frankie. There it was again. *Boss's orders*.

Surely it couldn't be true. It was impossible.

Unthinkable.

She felt her eyes prickle with tears, but rubbed at them furiously, still determined not to let the others witness her dismay.

If Jeff was sorry, he didn't show it. He watched as Eugene talked briefly into the microphone on the lapel of his black suit jacket. Then he revved the engine.

Frankie tried one last time, lunging for her bag. It had the camera in it. Proof. Pictures of her and Alex. Precious memories. 'Give it to me!' she snapped.

'Get off,' Eugene shouted, pushing her backwards so that she stumbled on to the edge of the boat.

'My bag!'

But Eugene wasn't listening. In a second Jeff had revved the engine and Frankie had toppled into the water, landing with a huge splash in the dirty cold sea.

Frankie surfaced to watch the boat swooping around, an arc of water cascading towards her, pushing her over towards the harbour wall. Treading water furiously, she reached out, coughing and choking, desperately clamping hold of the metal ladder rungs in the wall and clinging on. She watched the boat tear away back towards *Pushkin*. She saw Eugene throw her bag out. She watched it land in the water and sink.

'You bastard,' she said, tears catching in her throat. She slapped the water hard. 'Fuck!' she screamed.

What the hell was she supposed to do now?

Frankie hugged her arms around her wet T-shirt. The thin fabric of her skirt was clinging unpleasantly around her thighs as she walked with difficulty along the quayside. She'd lost one of her leather flip-flops in the water and she was hobbling, the rough tarmac hurting her feet.

Goddamnit! How had this happened? Roz and Richard's faces loomed large in her mind. Not to mention that jerk-off Jeff and Eugene too. *Boss's orders. You're to leave with nothing.*

She shook her head, refusing to believe it. It had to be some kind of terrible mix-up, a disastrous mistake. Alex loved her. He'd told her so on the phone only this morning.

Richard must have got the wrong end of the stick and was just flexing his muscles, wanting her gone so that he didn't have to deal with the others' jealousy. As for Eugene getting so heavy . . . well, he must have been misinformed too. Alex would be furious when he found out how she'd been treated. And how she'd lost all her stuff. Her photos . . . the necklace Alex had given her . . . all her money . . .

Tears fogged her vision and she sat down for a moment on an iron mooring post to try and calm down. Angrily, she brushed some glass from the bottom of her foot. If only she had a phone. If only she had some way of contacting Alex. He'd sort all of this out. And she'd make sure he fired Richard and Roz. And Eugene. Immediately. And Jeff too. She'd thought he'd been her friend, but he'd turned against her with the others.

Those *bastards*.

Her instincts about returning alone to *Pushkin* had been right. She'd known it would be a disaster – but she hadn't expected *anything* like that.

She had to get hold of Alex, whatever it took.

She started walking again, trying to ignore the pain in her

foot. Further along the quayside crammed with boats, she could see the town of Cannes in the distance. It still looked miles away.

She spotted a luxury yacht mooring just up the jetty and, for a second, she wondered whether she should go and ask if she could borrow their phone.

But then, miraculously, she heard a car approaching behind her: a sleek black limousine. She felt herself go limp with relief. Thank God, Alex was here! Come to rescue her. She waved at the limo as it drew level with her. The tinted black window in the back slid down and a familiar face peered out through a haze of cigar smoke.

Only it wasn't the face she was expecting.

It wasn't Alex at all. It was Sonny Wiseman: the movie producer she'd met on *Pushkin*.

'Well, hey there! If it isn't my pretty Cape Town friend . . .'

'Oh, it's you. Oh, Mr Wiseman, thank God,' she said, wanting to cry. She felt absolutely pitiful. She'd been so convinced it was Alex. The disappointment was crushing. But maybe Alex had sent Sonny to fetch her . . .

'It's Frankie, right? What the hell happened, kiddo?' he asked. 'Can I help at all? Can I give you a lift?'

Frankie nodded, her teeth still chattering. The driver jumped out and opened the limo door for her.

Inside, Sonny Wiseman shook out a picnic blanket from the back shelf and held it out to her.

'Thanks,' she said, wrapping herself in it and sitting on the seat. 'I'm so glad to see you.'

'If I'm remembering correctly, I owe you a favour. By the looks of you, I guess this would be a good time for you to call it in, eh?'

'Just take me to him,' Frankie said, wiping her face on the blanket.

'Who?'

'Alex. He sent you, right? That's why you're here?'

Sonny Wiseman drew his eyebrows together. 'Sent me? Alex didn't send me anywhere, honey. What do you mean?'

Frankie's heart sank but her mind started racing. 'Listen, Mr Wiseman, I'll explain everything, but really all I need is to get hold of Alex. And I need to get some clothes. And . . . and . . .

my passport. Those bastards have my passport and all my money and cards and—' She felt tears threatening to choke her again.

'OK. Slow down. Let's get you dried out. One thing at a time.'

Frankie grabbed his arm, desperately. 'But you'll help me?'

'Sure I'll help you. Alex is flying in for the film premiere tonight at the festival. He must have told you about it. *Blue Zero*: the new Todd Lands picture? It's one of his best. Might even be in with a shout for a gong. You must come too.'

Frankie felt an icicle drop into her stomach. Alex hadn't mentioned the premiere, or that he'd be flying in for it. But, of course, it made sense that was why *Pushkin* was here.

She'd thought tonight was Alex's own party. His birthday party. She'd thought she would be with him on the yacht . . .

But now, it seemed, Alex would be at a film premiere.

It was all so confusing.

There must be an explanation, she reasoned. Trust. Alex had told her time and time again it was the most important thing. She had to have faith. And she would.

In the presidential suite of the Carlton hotel in Cannes, Frankie emerged from the deep bubble bath, feeling as if she'd woken up in a dream. And to think that only a few hours ago, she'd been walking along that seedy quayside. Here in these luxurious surroundings, the way she'd been treated seemed more outrageous than ever. She could have been killed by the tender, or caught any number of horrible bugs from the dirty water. Or still be abandoned at the side of the road.

Thank God she felt more back to normal. Alex would be here soon to clear up all this mess. She longed to be in his arms again, to hug him, and to have him tell her that everything was OK.

As she wrapped herself in a sumptuous thick white robe, she heard a discreet knock.

'Hair and make-up is here,' Debbie called.

Frankie opened the bathroom door. Debbie, one of the many assistants Sonny had magicked up on their arrival at the hotel, slipped into the bathroom and handed Frankie a glass of champagne. She had a large gap between her front teeth and a friendly smile and Frankie had liked her the moment Sonny had introduced her when they'd arrived at the grand suite. Sonny had explained that the film company had hired the suite for its meetings in Cannes. Life-size cardboard cut-outs of Todd Lands were everywhere, as well as posters and promotional flyers for the movie.

Debbie was carrying a clipboard under her arm and had a walkie-talkie strapped to the belt of her jeans. Her afro hair was bound up in a green silk scarf and bracelets jangled on her arm.

Frankie smiled. 'Debbie, honestly, you're like an angel.'

'Hey, well, you've got your bit to do, girl,' Debbie replied in her sassy American accent, her cheerful face serious for a moment.

Bit to do? What could Debbie mean? But before Frankie had a chance to ask, Debbie was already chattering away again.

'Sonny wants you to be ready by seven. That doesn't give us much time. I had some sushi brought up. Don't eat too much, or else you'll bloat out and won't get into your dress. But you'll feel better once you've eaten. And, hey, smile. Don't be nervous. This is going to be fun!'

Debbie threw open the bathroom door and Frankie's jaw dropped in amazement. The suite was filled with people scurrying everywhere. In one corner, a whole booth had been set up with a chair in front of a giant mirror, surrounded by lightbulbs. An absurdly trendy guy with a blue Mohican and tight black trousers was plugging in a hairdryer and laying out combs and brushes. Next to him, a girl with magenta-red hair tied up into two knots so that they looked like Minnie-Mouse ears was laying out the contents of a giant plastic case full of make-up.

In the centre of the room, a white sheet was laid out on the thick carpet. Rising up from it was a mannequin stand housing the most exquisite long ball dress Frankie had ever seen. It was a sheer white sheath covered in rhinestones and crystals. The plunging neckline with its diamanté clasps was stunning. A row of high, strappy, to-die-for shoes were lined up next to it.

Debbie clapped her hands. 'Guys! Everyone! This is Frankie.'

Everyone turned to look at Frankie in the doorway at the

exact moment her towel turban fell off her head and she spilt champagne all down her front.

Everyone laughed and Frankie shrugged. 'Hi.'

Someone hit a sound system and the suite was filled with James Brown singing 'I Feel Good'.

Debbie escorted Frankie to the mirror in the corner and introduced her to the hair stylist, Marc, the guy with the Mohican, and Vic, the redhead who was going to do her make-up.

First it was Marc's turn, smoothing serum into Frankie's hair before straightening it with a giant barrel brush, then blow drying it with an enormous dryer. Then came clouds of hair spray and more drying, before he rolled up sections of her hair into curlers. Whilst he was doing that, two of Vic's assistants took a hand each and manicured Frankie's nails. But in spite of all the work they were doing, the more time that passed, the more they seemed to be getting into a frenzied rush.

Frankie couldn't believe what a fuss all this was. Sure, it was lovely of Sonny to lay all of this on so that she'd be ready in time for the premiere, but she was just one of the guests. She couldn't imagine what absurd levels of pampering the real film stars must be subjected to, the actors and actresses and all the other people who'd actually made the film. If a lowly last-minute invitee like her was getting all this, then what must they be going through?

She was glad this was just a one-off: she could never live like this for real. It was absurd, and not to mention slightly embarrassing, spending all this time and money just for the sake of looking good.

'You been doing lots of skincare in preparation for the big night? Yes?' Vic asked in a heavy French accent once Marc was satisfied to leave Frankie in rollers. Vic held Frankie's chin between her thumb and forefinger and inspected her face in the light.

'Well . . . er . . . I did have a facial in Marrakech a few days ago.'

'Oh yes? Where?'

'A friend of mine Sylvie organized it. The beautician was called Coco?'

'You don't mean Coco Rochas?'

'Yes, that's her.'

Vic whistled, impressed. 'Just as well. You lucky girl. Do you know how long the waiting list for her was? Universal begged her to come over to Cannes, but she stayed in Marrakech.'

Frankie was astounded at Vic's reaction. She'd had no idea that Coco was so famous. She'd thought that Sylvie was exaggerating when she'd said that Coco was one of the best beauticians in the world. Frankie felt retrospectively guilty about being so blasé about all those free treatments.

'Now, what do you usually wear?' Vic asked.

'Nothing. Well, some lip gloss maybe. I—'

Vic frowned. 'For these parties, I mean? What you want me to do? Come on, honey, we don't have much time.'

Frankie pressed her lips together, feeling at a loss. This all seemed so *professional*. 'Er . . . you know, why don't you do what you think will look best?'

Vic wobbled her head as if in shock. 'If only everyone could be like you. I can do anything, yes?'

'Whatever looks good. I'll leave it up to you.'

She twirled Frankie round so that she was facing the mirror and leant her head down next to hers. 'OK. You mind if I pluck your eyebrows a bit?'

'You know, do you mind if I just . . .?' Frankie desperately wanted to find Sonny, to find out whether he'd contacted Alex, but Vic scowled at her.

'Zip,' she said. 'Don't say a word. Don't move a muscle until I say so.'

'But—'

'OK, you guys,' Debbie said, her walkie-talkie going crazy. 'Come on. Step it up. We have to get out of here in half an hour, tops. We *cannot miss the slot*, OK?'

Twenty minutes later, Vic had worked her magic and Frankie's face was made up, her skin glowing with vitality, her eyes outlined, the lids expertly shaded in frosted lilacs and silvers. Her lips had been lined into a generous pout. Her cheekbones shimmered. A stranger looked back at her from the mirror. She wondered what Alex would say when he saw her. He might not even recognize her any more, she thought in dismay.

Debbie came over and smiled. 'You look lovely,' she said. 'Ready to try on the dress?'

'What about underwear?'

Debbie shook her head. 'Valentino sculpted this one inside for support. I suppose you could wear a thong, but I think you'll find it more comfortable and less risky without. Let's just hope it fits.'

Frankie gasped. The dress was an original Valentino? 'Isn't there something . . .?' she began. 'I mean, it's lovely . . . but can't I wear something a little more low key?' She felt horribly nervous all of a sudden. Now she was up close, she could see that it was just as much a work of art as it was a dress. Not even the beautiful clothes Sylvie had given her could compare with this. What if she spilt something on it? What if it tore? Frankie knew that you needed serious balls to pull off a dress like this. What if she didn't look good in it? What if she looked as awkward, uncomfortable and out of her depth as she felt?

Debbie glanced at one of the other dressers. 'This is Cannes, darling. You can't wear anything low key!' She screwed up her nose. 'Anyway, you wanna give up the chance of wearing couture?'

'But . . . I've never worn anything so expensive before.'

'No buts. If I were you and I got to wear one of the most beautiful dresses in the world, then I'd darn-well jump at the chance. Do you have any idea how many girls would bite your hand off just to be *near* this dress? To be doing what you're doing?'

Frankie took a deep breath. 'OK.'

'Good, because the top designer from Valentino is coming to check out his creation.'

Whatever misgivings Frankie had been feeling now promptly doubled. 'The actual designer? Is coming here? To the hotel? But . . .' Frankie groaned. Could this get any worse?

'Shhh. Now arms up. We got to concentrate to make sure it goes on right.'

Frankie's head was reeling as she was escorted down in the lift to the front of the hotel to meet Sonny. She was surrounded by five bodyguards all carrying black sheets, so that she was completely shielded. This was crazy, she thought, beginning to panic. They'd appeared from nowhere as she'd stepped out of the suite and none of them spoke a word of English. None of them could explain what was going on.

'You don't want to be photographed yet,' Debbie warned, poking her head through the sheets before disappearing again. Or at least that's what Frankie *thought* she said, but she was already being hustled into the lift.

Photographed? What did she mean? Frankie could hardly think.

The lift pinged open and they were moving at breakneck speed across the hotel lobby. The noise was unbelievable. Frankie could hear the shouting as she looked at her shoes and continued to be shuffled by the bodyguards through the glass doors to the kerb outside.

Then, suddenly, she was at the door of another limousine. One of the bodyguards pushed her head down and she fell inside, opposite Sonny Wiseman and another man.

'Good luck,' she heard Debbie call.

The door closed, sealing off the noise. Frankie caught her breath.

The car was already moving, gliding away from the entrance of the hotel. Frankie stared back and saw a bank of photographers scrabbling against the bodyguards to get a shot of the car.

'Wow!' Sonny Wiseman said. 'You scrub up pretty well, kiddo.' He smiled at her.

'But I thought you said it was just a party. I never thought—'

The man next to him was slowly taking off his shades. Frankie's sentence remained unfinished. She gasped.

Todd Lands was sitting opposite her.

The Todd Lands.

'There's no time to explain,' Sonny said. 'Frankie, this is Todd. Todd, Frankie.' He waved his fat hand between them.

'She's perfect, Sonny,' Todd said. 'Just right. You OK, sweetheart?' he asked Frankie.

His voice was so familiar, his smile, his face, so recognizable from all the films she'd seen him star in, that she must have gawped even further at him. His teeth were a dazzling white.

But no, she wasn't OK, Goddamnit. She was going to be sick. This was way too scary. She was sitting opposite the biggest star in Hollywood. In the world, even.

And why? That's what she now desperately wanted to know. And what did he mean *perfect*? And *just right*? Just right for *wha*t?

'Has she signed the contract?' Todd asked Sonny.

Sonny Wiseman picked up a sheaf of papers beside him and handed Frankie a pen.

'OK, kiddo, just put your name here,' he said, putting the pen into her hand and the finely typed sheets on her lap. 'It's nothing at all. Just a confidentiality agreement. We get everyone to sign them to protect Todd. Go on, hon, there's no time. Just put your squiggle on it. We can go over the details later.'

Stunned, her stomach churning, Frankie signed the paper and handed it back to Sonny Wiseman.

'Good girl. OK. It's Todd's big night. My big night, too,' Sonny Wiseman continued. 'We've just heard our film's tipped to win the Palme d'Or. So listen up. There's nothing to it. It's an easy gig. Just step out on to the red carpet with Todd here and walk up to the Palais entrance.'

Oh my God! Frankie thought. *He can't be serious.*

'But, Mr Wiseman,' she said, 'I couldn't! I've never—'

Sonny Wiseman waved his hand. 'All you gotta do is make sure you don't trip over,' he continued. 'But Todd will keep hold of you. Then you'll stop with Todd on the steps whilst he talks to the press. There's nothing to it. It's a walk-on, walk-off part. Just make sure you don't say anything, OK? OK? Anything at all. Let Todd do all the talking. Just smile and look your radiant self.'

'But where's Alex? I thought—' Frankie glanced around for somewhere to run to but she was trapped. And already the limo had started to slow.

'Don't worry about Alex for now,' Sonny said.

Frankie looked outside, horrified. The limo was in the centre of a press swarm. Cameras flashed. Muffled voices yelled.

'But when will I see him? Mr Wiseman, I'm really not sure I—'

'You know the drill, honey?' Todd interrupted. She could hear the nervous energy in his voice. She watched him shake himself, stretching his face muscles. 'Just do as Sonny says and don't let me down.'

If he was nervous, how the hell was she meant to feel? Her

legs wouldn't move. She was petrified. How had she let herself get sucked into this? She didn't want to escort anyone anywhere. Not even if it *was* Todd Lands. She only wanted Alex.

But Alex was nowhere to be seen.

The car stopped. Now the noise from the crowd outside was growing louder.

'Make sure you talk to CNN first, Todd, OK?' Sonny called.

CNN!

But Frankie didn't have time to ask any questions, because the limo door was suddenly opening and the crowd's screams were deafening.

'Smile,' whispered Todd, leaning in as close as he could to her ear as he took her hand and helped her out of the limousine. 'Like you mean it.'

This was terrifying. She wanted to run. There were so many people . . .

Todd was much smaller than she'd imagined. In her heels she was a few inches taller than him, but what he lacked in stature, he made up for in sheer star quality. He held her hand in a vice-like grip as the crowd behind the photographers went wild. And there it was – his film-star grin – as he held up her hand in his and acknowledged his adoring fans.

Frankie felt his hand on the small of her back, guiding her, and she was walking next to him, slowly up the red carpet. She sensed a million eyes on her. There were so many cameras she felt dizzy, as if she were in front of a relentless strobe.

And then they were standing in front of a bank of black TV cameras like a plague of overgrown bugs. She could just about make out the CNN logo of the one nearest her.

'Hey, Todd, is this your new leading lady?' someone shouted out.

Todd Lands grinned. 'Well, guys, since you ask, this is Frankie, the new love of my life,' he said, and before Frankie could protest, he held her firmly and tipped her backwards. And then he kissed her fully on the lips.

The crowd went wild as the assembled members of the world's press burst into an overwhelming and delighted round of applause and the sky lit up with camera flashes.

CHAPTER TWENTY-THREE

In Lechley Hall the rain hammered on the lead-pane kitchen windows. Emma slugged back the whisky shot and slammed the glass down on the table. Above the Aga, on a hinge on the wall, the small television was tuned into the news and Emma watched as the perfunctory report of Julian's death was replaced by showbiz news and a sunny report about Todd Lands kissing a pretty girl at the Cannes film festival. Emma couldn't bear it. She pointed the zapper at the small TV and put her head in her hands.

How could the newsreader do that? Move from something so serious to something so flippant and inconsequential?

Didn't they realize that Julian's death meant *everything*?

'I don't know how they got hold of the story,' Susie said to Emma apologetically.

Emma rubbed her face. Of course the news channels were going to pick the story up. The table was strewn with the day's papers, all detailing Julian's suicide and the financial disaster he'd left in his wake. She couldn't help resent the gloating tone that some of the papers had taken, delighting in the downfall of many of Julian's investors.

'Those bastards,' Emma said, wiping her eyes, which

seemed to leak continual tears. 'Can't they leave anyone alone?'

'There's a Lady Whiteley for you,' Pim said, coming into the kitchen. 'I left the phone on the bureau in the hall.'

Since they'd heard the news of Julian's death, five days ago, Pim and Susie had been amazing, but Emma could tell from the strain on her brother's face that he too was reeling from the financial consequences of the platinum mine being a hoax.

Because that's what it had been: a hoax.

The worst part was that deep down, on a very subconscious level, Emma realized that she'd known. She'd known from the moment she'd first seen Dimitry Sergeyokov's evil face. Yet she'd allowed Julian to go ahead with it. She'd ignored her intuition and looked the other way. And now he was dead.

Poor Julian had arrived in Russia to find panicked engineers at the mine site telling him that the mine he'd purchased was full of sand. The geologist's report that Sergeyokov had given him was totally fraudulent.

The next discovery was even worse. Sergeyokov had been offloading his own shareholding secretly and steadily at the top of the market. When Julian tried to contact him, he discovered that Sergeyokov had vanished into thin air.

The shambles that had followed had been inevitable. When word got out about the mine, the shares went into freefall. Within twenty-four hours of Julian's arrival at the site, the shares were as worthless as the mine itself.

In addition came the catastrophic news that most of the money that was supposed to have been transferred from Platinum Reach in the BVIs to the bank in Norilsk had never arrived.

Julian hadn't been able to bear it – or so Emma assumed because of what he'd done next.

He'd jumped. After midnight. From the twentieth floor of his hotel. A kitchen porter had found his bloodied body frozen in the gutter the next day.

Hugo had been distraught at the news of Julian's suicide, explaining to Emma that he felt partly responsible.

He'd told Emma about a terrible row he'd had with Julian about the platinum mine and the whole financial deal surrounding Platinum Holdings and more specifically Platinum Reach in the BVIs. A row that had ended so bitterly that Hugo and Victoria hadn't felt able to come to the ball.

Emma still couldn't believe that Julian hadn't told her he'd fallen out with Hugo. Hugo was his best friend, his most trusted business partner. And Victoria had kept quiet too. She hadn't said a word to Emma because Julian had made them swear not to. He'd told them not to interfere or to upset Emma.

'He wouldn't listen,' Hugo had told Emma as she'd sat on the McCorquodales' sofa and tried to take in the magnitude of what he was saying. 'I tried. Believe me, I tried. I told him that the mine was too risky. That the facts in the geologist's report didn't stack up. That he should have got it double-checked, no matter how much it cost.'

'But Sergeyokov? What about him?' Emma had asked.

'I contacted all my associates in Russia and he simply wasn't connected to anyone reputable. All his credentials were bogus. I begged Julian to pull out, but he refused. He had other city backers who said I was talking rot. He decided to trust them instead of me.'

'But why?' Emma had asked. 'Why would he do such a thing? How could he be so reckless?'

'For the oldest reason in the world,' Hugo had said sadly. 'Because he wanted to be right. And because he had so much money invested in the scheme by then, and so much at stake, he couldn't afford to be wrong.'

But Emma had felt – and still felt now – that *she* was to blame. She'd let Julian go alone to Russia. She'd let herself be blinded by his enthusiasm.

And now he was gone. For ever.

His body had been flown back from Russia and driven in an unmarked black van to Lechley Park, where the funeral would take place tomorrow. Emma didn't care how many people would come. She just wanted to disappear into a hole herself and never come out.

Now, wearily, Emma shuffled into the draughty hallway and picked up the phone. She already knew what was coming. Lady Whiteley sounded genuinely sorry, but Emma was hardly listening.

'So you do understand, Emma, I hope. I know you're always

the first to defend the reputation of the charity. Owing to the recent adverse publicity . . . we no longer think it's suitable to have you as a chairwoman when so many of our members have lost their investments—'

Emma put down the phone, cutting her off. For a moment, she stared at the dusty oil portraits in the shadowy stairwell. They stared back at her with betrayal in their unseeing eyes. After all she'd tried to do – Julian had hoped to do – to protect their ancient home and their descendants who lived here now, everything would have to go. Pim and Susie would almost certainly lose Lechley Hall and the park. They'd be left with nothing. Nothing at all.

A door slammed, making her flinch. Cosmo was marching down the black and white tiles of the corridor, leaving muddy footprints in his wake. Emma's heart leapt. She'd been worried sick about him all day. Poor Cosmo. He was devastated by Julian's death. Emma wished she could support him, but he seemed too distant and her own grief was too great.

'Darling, where have you been?' Emma said, going to him, but he shook her off.

'They found this, in with the body,' Comso said. She could see that his face was strained with fury. 'The undertaker gave it to me.'

'What?' Emma asked, taking the note from him. Her hands were shaking.

'From Dad. Read it.'

Emma sat with a thump on the small Queen Anne chair in the hallway. How could she have let Cosmo get hold of this? She was so shocked at seeing Julian's handwriting that she hardly had time to register that Cosmo had opened a letter addressed to her.

I'm sorry, she read, *for letting you down . . .*

Cosmo was standing above her, watching her read. Emma felt a wail inside her. She bit down on her lip, determined to stay strong in front of her son.

I've made a fool of myself. And of you. I've lost everything and I cannot expect you to stand by me. I cannot live with the shame. You married a coward, Emma. I'm sorry for your pain, but you are better off without me.

She shook her head, rereading the short note. It couldn't be.

223

It went against everything she knew about Julian. He wasn't a coward. He embraced life. He *loved* life. How could he throw it away over a business deal that had gone wrong?

It didn't make *sense*.

She stared in mortification down the dark corridor, as if it were the barrel of a gun.

So he'd been conned? So what? It wasn't the first time it had happened to a British businessman and wouldn't be the last. Julian had said himself at the outset that business dealings in Russia for Westerners like himself were notoriously tricky. And if anyone could bounce back from a bad business deal, Julian could.

He'd been bankrupt before, for God's sake. He'd lost everything and built it all again from scratch. And they'd done it together. Side by side.

So to do this? Her Julian?

Yet here it was, in front of her own eyes: the evidence of what he'd done. It was Julian's handwriting. Unmistakably. Handwriting that she recognized from a thousand cards and gift tags and love letters, from the Post-It notes he left around the house, from the stories he'd written Cosmo when he was little . . .

Emma felt as if her heart was breaking all over again.

How could her Julian have done such an unspeakable thing?

Helpless anger overtook her. Did he know her so little that he would think for a moment she wouldn't have stuck by him? That her financial discomfort or social embarrassment mattered compared to losing him?

'You see, Mother . . .' Cosmo said. Emma looked up at him, surprised to see him standing above her still. His voice was strong, but tears brimmed in his eyes. 'It's your fault.'

Emma felt as if she'd been stabbed. 'My *what*?'

'He couldn't let you down. Dad decided to take the coward's way out because he couldn't face your disapproval. Because you're so fucking materialistic.'

'No,' Emma gasped.

Cosmo's eyes darkened. 'It's true. You just don't want to admit it because all you care about is money. And how it makes you look.'

Emma couldn't breathe. She staggered to her feet. She

wanted to hit him. Claw out at him. Punish him for saying something so cruel.

'No, no,' she sobbed. Anger flooded her again. 'Take it back. Take it back,' she shouted.

'No, I won't!'

Emma reached out and struck him hard across the face.

Cosmo barely flinched. She stared at him, reeling, watching the red mark appear on his cheek. She couldn't believe she'd hit him, but she hadn't been able to stop herself. He really believed what he'd just said. He really thought this was her fault.

His face was bereft of pity; only anger and hurt remained. He didn't so much as blink. 'Well, just so that you know, I'm not going to stick around and pick up the pieces,' he said, holding his hands out and backing away from her. 'You did this to him, Mother. You did it.'

'Where are you going?' she asked as he turned to leave. It was no more than a whisper.

'Away.'

'But you can't. Cosmo, please—'

'I swear, as long as I live, I'll never forgive you.'

Emma reached out to him, but he turned on his heel and strode away from her. Outside. Beyond her reach. He slammed the front door behind him, shutting her back in the gloom. Emma lifted her shaking hand to her mouth and the silent wail inside her was silent no more.

'He'll calm down,' she heard Susie say as she lifted her from the seat. But Emma couldn't stop crying.

'I want to go home,' she gasped. 'I want to be alone. Please, Susie. Just let me go home.'

'You'll have to talk to Sebastian first, I'm afraid,' Susie said, 'Pim's with him. They're in the drawing room.'

Sebastian Gatsworth had been the family lawyer for as long as Emma could remember. She'd never liked him.

He stood up as she entered with Susie. He was dressed in a dark-navy pin-striped suit and a striped tie. As if this was just another day. How could everyone else's world keep turning when hers had smashed to a bloody stop in a gutter in an unknown street in Russia?

The drawing room was vast and under-furnished, with an

oppressive ceiling of low beams. Shabby blue wallpaper was peeling off, revealing plaster dotted with mould. Without the normally roaring fire in the large hearth, it was chilly.

Emma had spent most of her childhood in this room, family Christmases and long evenings playing cards with Julian, Susie and Pim. And yet now these familiar surroundings seemed alien, as if any attachment or sense of belonging had slipped from her grasp.

'I'm terribly sorry about all this,' Sebastian said once Emma had composed herself. Emma nodded, sitting down on the sofa, which was covered in dog hair.

Sebastian paced by the fire for a moment.

'I can't tell you how difficult what I have to say is, Emma, and I know this isn't the best time, but it really can't wait.'

'What can't?' Emma looked between Pim and Susie, but they both looked at the floor. Suddenly, she felt a shadow of foreboding like she'd never felt before.

Sebastian took a deep breath. 'I've been going through the paperwork and I'm afraid your assets have been frozen.'

'But—'

'And Wrentham is no longer yours. Your late husband used the house as collateral for the deal. I'm not sure if you realized, but there was an immediate forfeit clause.'

'But Wrentham . . . ? It's . . . it's mine . . . it's—'

'No, Lady Emma, I'm afraid it's not. The house has gone. And the contents. In fact today we received news from the bank that there's already been a purchaser.'

'A what?'

'A Russian,' Pim said. His voice was grim. 'He's going to be in by the end of the week.'

'A Russian?' Emma said.

'Quite a well-known chap, actually, if not exactly above board,' Sebastian Gatsworth said. 'His name is Yuri Khordinsky.'

CHAPTER TWENTY-FOUR

In the reflection of the dark window of the stretch limo, Peaches carefully adjusted her Marilyn Monroe-style blond wig. She'd done a good job with the disguise. She hardly recognized herself. She chewed her gum and took a swig of the champagne, counselling herself to keep up with the Southern accent.

Did she look as nervous as she felt? she wondered. Peaches was usually on the phone organizing this kind of gig, not taking part in one. Especially undercover. Oh yes, in more ways than one this was definitely a first.

But so far so good. It felt so weird to be in the gang of strange girls, drinking champagne as the driver wound through the back streets of Nice, where the plane had landed. With the drive along the coast, it was a long time to keep up the act.

Tonight she was posing as Tammy, one of Peaches Gold's top girls. One of her own employees, no less. As far as everyone else (apart from Angela) knew, Peaches was still in Russia. And none of the other girls here had ever met Peaches face to face before. So none of them would ever suspect that she was Peaches Gold.

Peaches still didn't know whether Valentin would be at the

party on *Pushkin*. Hence the cover story and disguise. Besides, she didn't know how tonight would pan out. She couldn't take the risk of compromising her true identity.

She took another swig of champagne, hardly tasting it. She wished it was something stronger. Something that would calm her nerves. But she had to stay level-headed and focused. Even so, when Mallory nudged her and pointed at the lines of cocaine she'd laid out on the small table, she was sorely tempted. Peaches hadn't done coke for ten years. But then, she hadn't been this stressed for ten years either.

'You want some, Tammy?' Mallory asked her.

Peaches shook her head. 'I'm doing NA,' she lied.

Mallory shrugged and snorted a line of coke and giggled, passing the silver tube on to Daisy.

'It's good shit,' Mallory said, nodding. 'But then everything's so much better in France.'

'You know, you don't want to do too much,' Peaches said. 'I heard Peaches Gold doesn't approve of drugs. And one of her girls just got busted.'

'So, you worked for Peaches before?' Mandy asked from the seat opposite. Peaches had only ever spoken to Mandy on the phone before and she was surprised at how good-looking she was in the flesh. Glammed up in evening dresses as they were, all the girls looked stunning, but Mandy looked amazing in an electric-blue number. She had smooth tanned skin and amazing small but pert breasts. The plunging neckline showed just the tiniest sliver of her pale nipples. She had what it took to drive men wild: Peaches could recognize it in an instant.

'Sure. Loads of times,' Peaches said.

'What's she like?'

'I've never met her in person, but I know girls who have. They say she's real nice . . .'

'Nice? Hah!' Heather piped up. 'I heard she's the most mean, hard-nosed businesswoman in LA.'

Heather was part of a double act Peaches had hired in through her contact in the high-end skin trade. Heather and Hailey were a well-known west coast lesbian couple and had done several successful porn movies together, which in escort terms was like having a degree from Harvard on your CV.

Peaches could pretty much charge what she liked for these two, especially for after-show work. She was delighted to have them on her books after Tommy Liebermann had brokered the deal for her with their film producer.

They were working a Barbie doll look tonight, with matching sequined hot-pants and high T-bar shoes, their silver halter-neck tops stretched tight across their amply filled bikini tops. They both had very long blonde hair swept tight into a high ponytail which curled down their backs.

Peaches was looking forward to seeing them in action. If they were as hot as they said they were, she'd be signing them up to work at her party. But, boy, did the party in LA seem like a long way off right now. Peaches' radar switched back to the matter in hand. So many things could go wrong at the party on *Pushkin* but mustn't be allowed to. Not if she wanted to live to see LA again.

'She may be,' Peaches said, freaked out to hear the girls speaking about her like this. 'But Peaches is always good to her girls. And fair. They all compete to get on jobs like this.'

'Yeah . . . you want to stay in with her,' piped up Daisy, coming up for air from the cocaine. 'Peaches Gold hosts this incredible party every year, like the party at the Playboy Mansion in Bel-Air used to be. Last year, these girls I knew made wild tips.'

Another girl – Nicki, was it? – was quiet. Peaches knew nothing about her. She'd come along with Mandy when one of the girls had dropped out. Usually she had time to vet the girls for a job like this: there was something about Nicki that unnerved her.

She thought back again to Tommy Liebermann's warning about the Feds. That was all she needed, today of all days: someone trying to bust one of her parties on top of everything else. It was time to sound this girl out and, if necessary, weed her out – before they got on board *Pushkin* and it was too late for them all.

'So what about you, Nicki?' Peaches asked. 'You done these gigs before?'

'One or two. Nothing heavy though.'

Which makes you a liar, Peaches thought, knowing that Nikki had never worked for her before.

'So what will happen tonight?' Nikki asked nervously.

'Don't worry, honey,' Peaches said, figuring it was smarter to keep her close. 'You just stick with me. It'll be the usual. A bit of stripping, a bit of teasing.'

'What if they want to – you know – do it?' Nikki asked, shyly this time.

The others laughed and Nicki blushed.

'Listen,' Peaches said, deciding to test this girl out, guessing that a real Fed agent wouldn't want to actually screw anyone, not unless her life depended on it. 'The more you can turn these guys on, the bigger the tip. And if you fuck them, all the better. That's what they want. And these are rich guys. Charming rich guys. Not sleaze balls.'

'Peaches told me that it's a birthday party for this Russian guy. His thirtieth. He's seriously rich,' Mandy said.

'That's right,' Peaches said, still watching Nicki for a reaction, a tell that would give her away. 'His name's Alexei Rodokov. And Peaches says we're there to show him the best time. Whichever one of us he likes the best, we've got to make sure he can't stand up by tomorrow morning. You know what I mean?'

The other girls laughed. Nicki smiled nervously.

'You know these Russian guys?' Heather said. 'I heard they love girl-on-girl action. Watching at first.'

'Really?' Nicki asked.

'You leave that to me and Heather,' Hailey said. 'We've got a routine that'll drive them all wild. Guaranteed.'

'And I love eating your pussy,' Heather said, leaning over and kissing Hailey, their tongues lapping at each other. The other girls laughed.

'Yeah,' Peaches said, watching Nicki biting her nails and looking out of the window. 'We're gonna give this Alex guy a birthday he'll never forget.'

CHAPTER TWENTY-FIVE

Frankie had never experienced anything remotely like being with Todd Lands. His sheer star quality was so intense, it seemed to charge the air around him and she felt totally dazzled in his presence.

Frankie hadn't seen a moment of the screening of *Blue Zero*. Todd had talked the entire way through it, introducing her in whispers to a succession of well-wishers who made their pilgrimage to their party on the front row. She'd been completely hemmed in, not least of all by Todd, but by Sonny Wiseman too, who had watched her like a hawk, and Todd's entourage – his agent, his PA, his stylist and his co-stars. Not to mention the countless other hangers-on who drooled off Todd's every word.

Now, as they stepped out of the Palais, the whole circus was back on show. It was insane.

Frankie found herself back at the centre of a scrummage of press and fans, moving slowly along the roped red carpet to the after-screening party, hustled through the crush of the crowd by six giant bouncers. The brightness of the TV camera's lights picked them out; the noise was deafening. Yet Todd remained relaxed all the while, waving to his fans and stopping to sign numerous autographs.

Blue Zero was without a doubt this year's biggest party in Cannes. An entire stretch of the Croisette had been cordoned off on the approach to the beach. Enormous screens showing Todd and images from the film hid the queue of guests from the swarm of fans trying to get a glimpse of the action. Blue lasers lit up the clear night sky above the Killers performing their set; the music echoed out across the bay.

Inside the VIP entrance tunnel leading from the pavement, swirls of bright lights lit up giant holograms of Todd's face. Huge, serious-looking security men and scantily dressed chaperones bearing designer gifts led them to the party on the beach.

Everyone who was on the A-list in Cannes was here, drinking vintage champagne cocktails. All of them wanted a piece of Todd. And, by default, Frankie. He kept her right by his side. Hand in hand. Like lovers.

Frankie's hands were sweating, her feet cramping in her high heels, but there was no way she could leave Todd, let alone go and see if she could find Alex. Everything was happening too fast. Quick-fire questions from a *Time* magazine journalist. Then an MTV VJ. Then the BBC.

Frankie still couldn't believe this was happening. She was with Todd Lands. *Todd Lands*. And he was behaving as if they'd known each other for ages – intimately. Cheek-to-cheek now for a *Vogue* photographer. Arm draped over her shoulder for French *Marie Claire*. The sheer audacity of it!

And he'd kissed her like that in front of all those people! She was still reeling from the shock of it. Terrified, too, in case he did it again.

But much as Frankie wanted to, she didn't have the nerve to contradict him. Every time he insinuated that they were a serious item, instead of exposing it for the outrageous charade it was, she smiled and kept her mouth shut.

If she made a fuss now, she knew it would only make matters worse. It would lead to more questions. Even if she just ran, she knew the cameras would follow her. And anyway, where would she run to? It was Alex she wanted and she knew he was somewhere here. She'd just have to bite her lip and smile for the cameras and wait for an opportunity to slip back into the anonymity and safety of the crowd.

All the same, she couldn't help wondering how come no one else could see how uncomfortable she was. Wasn't it obvious this was all a lie?

Apparently not.

Such was Todd's skill that so far nobody had mentioned that Frankie was a mute and hadn't backed up one of his claims. But it wasn't as if Todd gave her a second to speak up for herself: he answered every question with a charming throwaway line, a cheeky wink, or a simple 'no comment' which of course implied so much.

'Smile,' he whispered in her ear as yet another camera flashed in their face. 'You're doing good. Not long now. We've just got to show our faces here, then we're going back to the Hotel du Cap for Bruce's party.'

'Bruce?'

'The director. Now, smile!'

'But . . .' Frankie began to protest. She didn't want to go to another party. She wanted one thing: to find Alex and be rescued from all of this. But once again Todd gripped her elbow.

'Todd! Todd! Over here!' Frankie heard someone else yell. Todd turned around to face another camera, his perfect smile unwavering.

Frankie scanned the crowd again. She had to find Alex and explain that this was all a crazy set-up. Because if he thought for one second that she'd *wanted* any of this, then . . .

Even here, under the barrage of camera flashes, Alex's face in Marrakech kept coming back to her and, despite being a hapless bystander in all of tonight's mad proceedings, her skin crept with guilt. His words kept coming back to haunt her, like he was whispering them in her ear. *I can't help it, but I'm a jealous guy, Frankie . . .*

Alex. She kept repeating his name in her head, like a mantra. She stood on tiptoe, straining to look through the mass of tuxedos, hoping to catch a glimpse of him.

'Time, Todd,' Sonny said, leaning in between them. 'The limo's here in two.'

Todd smiled. 'We'll be right there.'

Sonny winked at Frankie. 'Having fun?' he asked.

Fun! Frankie wanted to punch him. How could he have done this to her?

But just as she was about to give him a piece of her mind, she felt her stomach dissolving. It was Alex. There he was. Heading for the exit. She shoved Sonny aside and elbowed through the crowd, ducking between people, keeping her head down until finally she was near the tunnel that led back up to the street.

'Alex,' she called. 'Alex! Wait! I'm here!'

He turned at the sound of her voice. He looked so handsome in his tuxedo. She'd missed him, *needed* him so much since she'd last seen him. Her eyes filled with tears of relief.

'Oh Alex, thank God you're here,' she said, breathless as she finally managed to battle to his side. She'd been longing for nothing more than to throw herself into his arms and for him to tell her that everything was going to be OK. She wanted him to tell her that what had happened on *Pushkin* was all a huge mistake and that it was unforgivable for Richard and Eugene and Jeff to have treated her like that. But Alex's look was anything but compassionate.

'Get away from me,' he hissed. His voice was brutal and harsh. 'Before I do something in public I'll regret.'

'Alex?' The look of loathing in his eyes stopped her in her tracks, like a punch to the face.

'I saw you, Frankie. I was right behind you on that red carpet. Didn't you see me?' He stared at her, his eyes hard. 'No? I supposed that was because you were too busy kissing Lands.'

Frankie let out an aghast laugh, but her legs were trembling. 'But it's not what you think! Todd kissed *me*! I didn't know—'

'Todd now, is it?' he said, impersonating her voice. 'Fuck you, Frankie,' Alex snarled at her suddenly, leaning in close. 'The *whole world* saw you. Boy, you really know how to stab a guy in the guts.'

'But—' Frankie started to protest, but Alex wasn't listening.

'Did someone set you up for this? Is this Sonny Wiseman's way of getting back at me for having been ripped off at poker on my yacht? How long have you been planning this, huh?'

Planning?

Frankie thought she was going to faint.

He didn't believe her.

Her heart hammered inside her chest.

'Planning . . . what? No . . . I—'

'Don't try and deny it, or make some pathetic excuse. I've spoken to Richard, Dieter . . . even Hamish. They all told me how you flirted with Sonny Wiseman, trying to get an invitation to Cannes. How you were trying to meet Todd Lands all along. That you were a *life-long* fan. That you'd *give anything* to meet him.'

Frankie felt her cheeks burning. 'No, that's not true. I wasn't, I—'

'I told them that they'd got it all wrong and you weren't like that,' Alex continued. 'I was furious that they'd thrown you off the yacht. I came here to bring you back. But now I see they were right all along.'

She was shaking now. 'No, Alex, no—'

'You know, I was expecting to have to apologize to you for the way my staff treated you, but it seems to me that they did exactly the right thing. Because what do I find? I find that you're here, dressed up like this . . .' He gestured to her dress, as if she was in her underwear. Like she was some kind of whore. 'Todd Land's *leading lady*, no less. You've been using me all along, haven't you? Just like Richard said.'

'No!' Frankie cried, unable to bear him treating her like this. How could he believe such lies? 'Alex. No. You mustn't listen to them. You've got it all wrong. You can't really think that—'

'What I think is no longer any of your concern.' There was no mistaking the pain in his voice. Or the finality. 'I have nothing more to say to you.' The cold look in his eyes froze the words in her mouth. 'I was willing to give you everything, Frankie. And you betrayed me.'

Frankie let out a sob. She grabbed his arm, wanting to drag him over to Todd. To prove how wrong he was. 'Just come with me. Talk to Todd and then you'll see—'

'No. Forget it, Frankie. It's over.'

'But I love you,' she implored.

He looked down at her hand on his arm. 'No, you don't. You don't even know what the word means.'

'But I do.'

He shook her from him like dirt. Then he stared through her. As if she was invisible. As if she didn't exist to him any more. His dark eyes registered nothing as the tears ran down her face.

'Eugene,' he called out, clicking his fingers.

Out of nowhere, the bodyguard appeared. He stepped between Frankie and Alex and stood there like a wall.

Alex strode into the crowd.

Eugene gazed unblinkingly down at Frankie. His tongue flicked across his lips in anticipation. Like a lizard contemplating its next meal. 'Keep away from him, bitch,' he told her, a malicious smile crossing his face. 'Or next time it will be more than your bag that ends up at the bottom of the sea.'

Back at Todd's palatial suite in the Hotel du Cap, Sonny Wiseman walked to the antique drinks cabinet, picked up a cut-glass decanter, sniffed the clear amber liquid inside and poured himself a large glass.

The hotel was possibly the best and most famous along the whole stretch of coast and the room was the height of luxury. Enormous bowls of roses perfumed the night air. Tasteful French furniture led the eye across Persian rugs and past the ancient tapestry to the vast windows with their giant drapes, framing the view down over the gardens of the hotel and the moon over the Cap Ferrat: the same view painted by Toulouse-Lautrec in 1892. Frankie should have felt privileged, thrilled even, to be here, but she didn't care about any of it. She felt sick.

Todd leant back against the door and closed his eyes for a moment.

'Nice to be away from the crowd, huh?' Sonny remarked, as if everything was OK. He chuckled. 'It was madness tonight. But trust Bruce to throw such a great party. You sure you don't want go back downstairs and join in the singing? Todd, man, you were great on the piano—'

'Sonny, you're an asshole,' Todd interrupted, snapping his eyes open. All the charming smiles had vanished. He looked between Frankie and Sonny. 'How could you do that to her?'

Frankie was still shaking. When Todd had finally noticed how upset she was downstairs at the party, he'd taken her to one side and she'd had the chance to explain what had happened with Alex.

'Have another drink, Frankie,' Sonny Wiseman said. 'Come on, it'll relax you. Make you feel better.'

'Relax me?' she gasped. She had so much to say and so much pent-up frustration, she could hardly get her words out. 'You owed me a favour. Do you realize what you've done?'

He topped up his drink and sighed. 'Sorry, kiddo. I had no choice.'

'No choice? What do you mean?' Todd asked, flinging his tuxedo jacket over the back of an ornate gilt armchair.

Suddenly Frankie saw it. No choice. Of course. How could she have been so stupid? Why had she never questioned that Sonny Wiseman just 'happened' to be on the dock when Eugene had thrown her off the tender?

Alex hadn't set it up. Alex didn't know anything about it. Someone had made sure Sonny was there waiting to pick her up. And *set* her up.

Sonny smiled sadly at Frankie. 'Look, I've no doubt you love the guy,' he said. 'Who wouldn't love Alex? He's smart and charming and rich. But you see, he's not yours to love.'

'That's not true. He's . . . he's the boss. He can do whatever he likes.'

Sonny Wiseman shook his head. 'He's not the boss, Frankie. He never was the boss.'

Frankie thought back to all her conversations with Alex in Morocco. And suddenly, everything slotted into place. She slumped on to the peppermint silk sofa. 'Yuri Khordinsky?'

'Khordinsky the billionaire?' Todd asked.

'You betcha. What he says goes. And he doesn't want his protégé having anything to do with you. Which is why he contacted me.'

Frankie gasped. Of course Alex hadn't ordered her to be kicked off *Pushkin*. Boss's orders . . . Yuri Khordinsky's orders. Alex had been telling the truth when he'd said he'd stood up for her and had come to get her back.

But Yuri had thought of that possibility too. So he'd come up with some proof to go along with a rumour he'd already started about Frankie and Todd Lands . . .

The kiss. Right there on the red carpet. It had all been for Alex, not just the rest of the world to see. The fact that it had created a little extra intrigue and publicity around Todd Lands had just been incidental. A bonus. Just Sonny being efficient and killing two birds with one stone.

Jesus, Frankie thought, Khordinsky was clever. He had it all worked out. The one way they could turn Alex against her was to make it look as if she were with another man. *If I were to see you flirting with another guy – well, let's just say it would kill me.*

And the one other person who knew that about Alex was Yuri.

'But that's so unfair. Yuri Khordinsky doesn't even know me!'

'He knows about what happened back in South Africa. He knows that because of what you uncovered your friend was killed. And he's the kind of businessman that can't afford to have anyone digging around into his affairs,' Sonny said, an ominous tone in his voice.

Frankie stared at him, her chin trembling. How had Khordinsky found out about Sadie? How did Sonny Wiseman know about all of that? And how could this be happening? How could someone else eject her from Alex's life like this?

Todd stepped forward to speak, clearly confused by everything Sonny was saying, but Sonny put up his hand to stop Todd interrupting.

'Listen to me, Frankie,' Sonny said, putting his drink down on the table. 'Khordinsky could have done much worse. He might have dealt with you permanently. But I owed you a favour, so we came up with this instead.' He walked over to the desk in the corner and plucked several tissues from the silver box. He handed them to Frankie but a few tissues were useless against the tide of anguish she felt now.

She'd lost Alex. It made her feel breathless with pain, as if her heart were being ripped out.

'Look at it this way,' Sonny continued more kindly. 'You got a good dress and hair-do out of it, and a great story to tell your kids. You walked out with Todd Lands. How many girls would give everything they had to do that?'

Frankie swiped her tears away. 'Khordinsky's not going to get away with this. He's not. I'll tell Alex. And Alex will never have anything to do with him again.'

But even as she said it, she knew it was hopeless.

'You think that Alex will listen to a stewardess caught on the world's cameras kissing another man? You made him look like a fool. The proof's already splashed all over the media. Even if Alex wanted to, he couldn't take you back. Not now he's lost so much face.'

His words stung like a slap.

'Take it on the chin, Frankie. Walk away. Yuri Khordinsky is a very – and I mean *very* – powerful man.'

Frankie remembered what Eugene had said, and in the same instant she realized that Eugene didn't really work for Alex at all. Khordinsky was his real boss.

'I'm telling you, kiddo, if you get in his way again, next time you won't be so lucky.'

Frankie put her head in her hands. Lucky! This didn't feel like lucky. This felt like the worst thing in the world.

'Look, I'm going to go to my room. Get some sleep,' Sonny advised, standing up. He patted her on the shoulder. 'You'll feel better in the morning.'

After Sonny had gone, Todd sat next to Frankie on the sofa. 'Hell, Frankie,' he said, rubbing his jaw. 'About tonight. I meant what I said downstairs – I had no idea about you and Alex. I'm so sorry.'

Frankie turned towards him, her eyes full of scorn. 'What did you think? That I was just hired in?'

Todd unknotted his bow tie. 'Why wouldn't I? It happens all the time. Sonny told me that Lucy was out of the picture, which suited me fine. She's a grade-A mega-bitch, believe me. And then he told me about you. How he thought you'd have amazing screen presence. How you were a big fan and you'd be happy for everyone to think we were together. And to be honest, a beautiful, mysterious stranger on my arm is good news. It's just the kind of stunt that'll mean more column inches. More publicity for the film.'

'Stunt?'

Todd undid the top button of his dress shirt and looked at her. Frankie saw that something of the movie star about him had suddenly vanished. As if the high-voltage Todd had been switched off. Up close like this, he seemed like an ordinary guy. A *short* ordinary guy. With a big nose, at that.

Frankie's head was buzzing, still trying to process everything she'd just heard. 'I must seem like such an innocent hick to you,' she said.

'Not at all. I think you're sweet. So much better than all the others. No one can pull off coy and shy like you did.' Todd stared off into the distance for a second, as if reliving their evening. 'Girls like you make a guy look so good.'

Frankie stared at him as he stood up and plucked a grape from the glistening bunch in the fruit bowl. 'I wasn't being coy and shy, Todd,' she said. 'I was being terrified.'

'Well, you did great and you're not even a pro, which is a result. Actresses . . . phew! Who needs 'em? Amy, my last fiancée . . . Boy, did she turn out to be a nutcase. And we paid her a fortune.' Todd flicked the grape up in the air and caught it in his mouth.

Paid? Frankie was reeling from this succession of body blows. Amy-Kay Bowers and Todd Lands had been on the cover of every magazine in the world. And it was all a set-up?

'You mean you and her weren't for real?' she asked.

Todd pulled a face. 'Are you kidding me? She is *so* not my type. But people will believe anything.'

'All of this . . . tonight? It's just a charade, isn't it?'

'It might seem that way, but it's just part of the job. You have to make friends with the fame, not fight it. It's a machine and the trick is to be the driver.'

Frankie thought back to how Todd had worked the crowd and all the thousands of pictures that had been taken. 'But don't you feel . . . I don't know . . . soiled? Over-exposed? How do you know what's real?'

Todd laughed softly. 'Let's just say I have a way of keeping sane. A very well-kept secret.'

'What kind of secret?' Despite everything, Frankie couldn't help being intrigued.

'Well, it wouldn't be a very well-kept one if I told you, now would it?' He smiled at her gently: the kind of twinkly-eyed smile that Frankie had seen in a dozen of his movies. And despite her resolve to hate Todd Lands, she couldn't.

Frankie wiped her eyes. 'Oh God,' she said. 'I can't believe this is happening.'

She realized now how colossal her enemy was. Khordinsky had everyone in his pocket. He could even manipulate the biggest movie star in the world to further his own ends. She couldn't believe the lengths he'd go to protect Alex. His investment. The man he'd groomed since birth to do exactly as he was told – if what Sonny said was true.

But Alex *had* to know the truth. He was being lied to – by the very people who ought to be loyal to him.

And what was Frankie meant to do now? Take it lying down? Walk away? Let Alex go on thinking that she'd betrayed him? That their time together had meant nothing to her?

Hell no. She wouldn't.

She *couldn't*.

'What can I do?' Todd asked. 'I hate seeing you so upset. You looked incredible tonight. But now . . .' he said, pointing to her face and pulling a face himself, 'trust me, it's not a good look.'

Frankie was too exhausted to laugh. She wiped away her smudged mascara. '*Will* you help me, Todd?'

'Sure.'

She studied Todd's face. Was this all just another act? Was he only offering his assistance to ease the awkwardness of the moment? He didn't look as if he was lying. It was a chance she was going to have to take, she knew, because even the faintest glimmer of hope was better than the black hole she found her-self in right now.

'Tell Alex,' she implored, turning and grabbing his arm. 'Tell him it was just a stunt, as you put it. He might believe it if it came from you.'

'But I don't even know the guy.'

'Then talk to Sonny. Sonny will do what you tell him to.'

Todd stroked his chiselled jaw. 'Yeah, but Sonny's beholden to these Russian guys. I know. He's in deep. Loads of gambling debts . . . the works. And they launder money through the movies. It's all . . . complicated.'

'But Alex and I . . . we're *meant* to be together. I know it. Right in my soul. If I could just explain . . .' she said, trying to focus. She thumped her chest, aching for everything she'd lost tonight. For everything that had been stolen from her – by a man she'd never even met.

There was no point in staying here talking to Todd. She couldn't stand another minute knowing that Alex hated her the way he did right now. 'I've got to go to him. I've got to make him see.'

'You can't go anywhere,' Todd said. 'I'm all for crusades of the heart, but come on, Frankie. It's the middle of the night. You're tired and you're upset.'

'Alex is having a birthday party on his yacht. If I can just get there . . .'

Suddenly, she knew it was the only way. She'd been so stupid to have been awestruck by Todd. She should have fought for Alex at the party. She should never have let him walk away.

'I suppose trying to talk you out of it would be pointless?' Todd said, then sighed and rubbed his eyebrows. 'I can't believe I've got you captive in a hotel room, and all you want to do is chase after another guy. It's not very good for my ego.'

Frankie pulled a face at him. 'I think your ego can handle it.'

Todd laughed. 'OK, if you've got to do it, you've got to do it, but I can't come with you. What if we get papped together again? That's not going to help. Let me get some of my people to help you out.' He moved towards the phone.

'No. I've got to do this alone.'

Her mind was racing. She'd get to the dock. Yes . . . All those yachts she'd seen earlier this afternoon . . . Those yachts all had tenders. She'd borrow one – *take* one if she had to.

'I'll just slip away,' Frankie said. 'I've got a plan. All I need is some money. Just enough for a cab to get me back into town to the dock. I'll pay you back.'

Todd walked over to the bureau and took a wallet off the table. He handed her some notes.

'I'll give you my private cell number,' he told her. 'If anything happens, I want you to call me. But don't give this number out, OK? And *don't* get into trouble.'

Frankie picked up a pen. 'Shoot,' she said, writing on her wrist as he told her the number.

CHAPTER TWENTY-SIX

Way out in the bay, Peaches could see the whole of Cannes from the top salon of *Pushkin*. A cat's cradle of blue lasers lit up the sky above a beach party. Bursts of rock music wafted faintly on the warm breeze.

Close by, she noticed some kind of commotion kicking off. Twenty or so metres away, a coastguard vessel locked its searchlights on a small speedboat and pulled alongside it. French commands were being barked through a loudhailer.

A minute later, armed police boarded the small boat. Someone was being arrested – a woman in a long dress by the looks of things. Some bimbo trying to crash this Alexei Rodokov guy's birthday party, no doubt.

Next to her, Peaches saw the captain look out over the scene and then turn away, smiling as he spoke into his walkie-talkie. She'd met his type so many times before: officious and bossy, usually with little boy tendencies in the bedroom. And a small cock. Peaches could always tell.

She kept scanning the faces around her, her senses on red alert. She'd been on board many private yachts before, but boy, this one sure was something else. A mega-yacht for the mega-rich. Smartly dressed staff wandered through the guests, carrying trays of canapés and cocktails. Peaches scoured each and every face, still nervous in case Valentin was at the party. But so far she hadn't seen him, only a couple of Russian-looking bodyguards, one of whom was getting friendly with Daisy.

Film-industry players mingled with actors and hangers-on and a drunk crowd of Russian businessmen, who leered at the women and drank like they were at a frat party. Another crowd were dancing to the New York DJ in the top salon. The party was in full swing, but there was still no sign of the yacht's boss himself.

'Tammy, isn't it? May I have a word?' the captain said, discreetly gesturing Peaches to follow him. He drew her away towards the elevator. 'I'd like to discuss the . . . entertainment with you.'

About time.

Inside the elevator, the captain crossed his hands in front of him and looked down at the thick carpet. Peaches draped herself against the rail as the doors closed, the white silky fabric of her long halter-neck dress falling so that the plunging neckline nearly exposed her entire breast. She fiddled with the long diamond and pearl necklace she was wearing, running her fingertip over each pearl, and stared hard at him. She wasn't sure how tonight would play out, but it was always good to keep the captain on side.

'I'm not sure whether you're familiar with how these things work,' he said, clearing his throat as the elevator started to slide down gently.

'Oh yes, captain, I'm *very* familiar with how these things work.'

'But . . . um . . . technically, as the captain, I'm responsible for everything that happens on board. So if anything untoward were to go on, it would have to be out of my sight.'

Even as he read her his little riot act, Peaches could tell that he was itching to touch her. 'Whatever you say, captain,' Peaches said.

'You can call me Richard,' he said.

He reminded her of a slavering dog. Given half the chance, he would hump her leg right this minute.

The elevator pinged open.

'The master suite,' he announced, like a realtor who'd saved the most stunning room for last. 'Privacy and security guaranteed.'

'Satisfaction, too, if we girls have anything to do with it,' Peaches joked. 'It'll do just fine.'

Peaches admired the lounge room with its low sofas and plush fittings. It was classy. Understated and elegant. If she wasn't mistaken, that was a Miró on the panelled wall. Ross had one from the same series in his consulting rooms.

'I'll just wait for you to say the word, and then we'll come here. Just the girls and whoever's coming to Alexei's *real* birthday party,' she continued, with a wink.

'Good. Good.' Richard rubbed his temple, clearly finding himself compromised. He could barely look at her and she could tell from the way he now shifted that that little dick of his was hard as wood.

'So . . . why don't you introduce me to the birthday boy?' she said, her smile making it obvious that she knew exactly what was happening in his smart blue pants.

'Of course. I think he's just in here in his office.' Richard pointed to an open door a little way along the corridor. Then his walkie-talkie went and, excusing himself, he hurried away.

Peaches walked silently in her high silver stilettos over the carpet towards the door. Through it she could see a young guy standing with his profile to her. He was tall and slender, with well-defined shoulders. He was staring at a TV screen, his face serious and his eyes dark.

So *this* was Alexei Rodokov, she thought, swallowing hard.

He looked younger than she'd imagined. And less Russian. Almost preppy, as if he belonged with the rich set in the Hamptons rather than here. She stopped in the doorway, watching him, remembering what Valentin had said about him in Moscow: *He is Yuri's favourite. And he is stupid. He does not see that he is just Yuri's puppet.*

He didn't look remotely stupid to her. Or like a puppet. He looked intelligent, and handsome too. He had a small mole just above the corner of his lip, a tiny imperfection which made his classically symmetrical face all the more attractive.

She stepped closer still, until she was inside the doorway right behind him, but he didn't turn around. He was listening intently to what the CNN newscaster was saying.

The woman described by Todd Lands as his new leading lady has clearly stolen the heart of Hollywood's most desirable bachelor. The star, who is a staunch Catholic, and has spoken out about sex before marriage in the past, was keen to avoid speculation about the couple's sexual relations, but the pictures speak for themselves. Sonny Wiseman, producer of Todd Lands's latest movie, confirmed that Frankie Willis, an unknown actress, has been the focus of the star's attention for some time. He made no comment when asked if Ms Willis was the same young lady who has recently been linked to Russian multi-millionaire and the film's financier, Alexei Rodokov . . .

A taller man stepped out of the shadows of the office and clapped Alexei Rodokov on the shoulder, making him jump. He towered above Alexei, his neck thick and muscular as he pulled on his black silk jumper. He was in his sixties with grey close-cropped hair.

Peaches recognized him instantly.

It was Yuri Khordinsky. The Russian billionaire.

Peaches felt her heart thump so hard she felt dizzy.

She forced herself to focus. To remember why she was here. Yet inside, she felt a familiar fire that came with danger. It made every sense burn. Everything suddenly seemed intensely focused.

'Well, hi there, boys,' Peaches said, remembering her southern accent. She reached up the doorframe and let one foot fall behind the other, so that the slit of her dress revealed her tanned bare legs. 'I was told I could find y'all hiding down here.'

'Ah. The entertainment has arrived,' Khordinsky said. His English was rougher, less educated than Valentin's, who'd spent so much time in the US.

Now that Khordinsky was facing her, Peaches could see his sallow skin and a small straight scar on his cheek: the kind a knife left. His eyes were ice-blue. Dead. Like a shark's. He looked her up and down like meat.

'You bet it has,' Peaches said, automatically arranging her face into one of her most alluring smiles.

'Good, because, you know, my boy here needs cheering up,'

Khordinsky said, suddenly picking up a remote control and zapping the TV dead.

My boy. He said it as if he meant it.

But Alexei didn't respond to Khordinsky's tone. He didn't look like he wanted cheering up by her or anyone else. He looked annoyed that Peaches was standing inside his office.

'It'll be our pleasure,' Peaches said.

Something in Rodokov's eyes made her instantly cautious, but Peaches forced herself to remember what she was capable of. These were only men, and even the strongest and scariest of men could be undone. She knew that – because she knew how.

'Well, hey there,' she purred. 'Happy birthday, darlin'. Why don't you let me introduce the girls?'

Alexei said something in Russian to Khordinsky.

'No, Alexei,' Khordinsky said, undressing Peaches with his eyes. He put his arm around Alexei's shoulder. 'Come. It's your birthday. Valentin hired in these girls especially for you. Forget that slut and enjoy them. Do it for me. Show me you're moving on . . .'

Even Peaches could tell that was an order, not a request.

Peaches called the girls downstairs to the master suite. Then she supervised the lighting as the men came in. Yuri, Alexei, Dieter and Eugene the bodyguards, and six other guys Peaches hadn't met. All of them were Russian, well dressed and undoubtedly Bratva.

It didn't take long for the party to hot up. Soon, the glass table was covered in chopped-up lines of cocaine and empty bottles of vodka. Peaches realized that it was time to get down to business.

Khordinsky and Rodokov were standing, still chatting intently. Peaches stared at them, occasionally catching Khordinsky's eye. When she did, he held her gaze and she wondered what he was thinking. Did he desire her? Despise her? Or both?

She mustn't think about it, she told herself. Tonight, she had all the power. She was Peaches Gold. And she must do what she'd come here to do.

As the music changed, she started dancing, pulling Mandy towards her. She winked at Heather and Hailey, who joined in.

Heather and Hailey slipped seamlessly into their routine, making it look natural and instinctive, when in fact Peaches knew it was contrived and rehearsed. Heather reached for Hailey's pert, well-rounded breasts and fondled them through her sequined bikini as they pressed together, kissing lasciviously. Tongues flickering. Hips grinding. Breath shuddering. Proving to the men, who'd cut their conversations and gathered around to watch, that this was for real. Then Hailey pulled off Heather's top to reveal a matching shiny skimpy bikini. Heather stood in front of Hailey, massaging her own breasts against Heather's, their bikini tops coming away, their kissing becoming more frenzied as they flicked their erect nipples against each other's.

Peaches watched Khordinsky the whole time. He was nodding, drinking his vodka, clearly enjoying watching Hailey and Heather as Hailey knelt down in front of Heather and pulled aside the crotch of her hot-pants and started lapping at her pussy, eliciting yelps of satisfaction.

Like Peaches' girls, these Russian boys weren't shy. Peaches had expected them to lead the girls off in ones or twos to the adjoining empty cabins and rooms, but most of these men seemed perfectly comfortable getting right down to business in front of each other.

More than comfortable, in fact. Determined was a more accurate description, Peaches thought. To prove that they could. That they weren't afraid. That they had nothing to hide. Peaches had been to and had participated in many orgies in her time, but this was different. She soon saw that this wasn't just about the sex and the drugs, or even fun. It was about machismo. Strength. Daring. It was about these gangsters proving to themselves and each other who was (quite literally) the hardest man in the room.

And all of it, every last thrust, was for the coldly amused eyes of the biggest kingpin of all: Khordinsky. The puppet master. The grand controller. The boss who clearly had more fire, more power, more balls than the rest of them put together.

Soon Eugene was kissing Daisy. Hungrily. Aggressively. Rummaging his hand inside her underwear, claiming her as his in front of the other men. He led her over to the other side of the drinks cabinet in the corner of the room and set about stripping off her remaining clothes in the cool, dim light. Before long, Peaches could see his trousers around his ankles. Then he pulled Daisy down on top of him and she began crying out with either real or, more likely, feigned joy as he bounced her on his eager cock.

Meanwhile, Mallory was going down on Dieter, the bodyguard she'd met upstairs. His eyes were closed as she knelt in front of him and reached for his flies.

Peaches nodded to herself with professional pride as she continued to grind her crotch against Mandy enticingly, just beyond the reach of Khordinsky himself.

But the billionaire seemed distracted and, far from anticipation, she noticed anger flash inside his eyes. Turning, she saw why. As much fun as the rest of Khordinsky's guests might be having, the birthday boy himself, Alexei Rodokov, was heading for the door.

Peaches whispered to Mandy to follow him. Then she widened her eyes at Nicki, nodding for her to go too. If the two of them couldn't crack the young guy, then surely no one could.

Peaches prepared herself.

It was now or never.

One . . . two . . . three . . .

Time to take the plunge.

She winked at Khordinsky. And then she smiled. *That* smile. The smile that left men in no doubt that she wanted them. Slowly she sashayed into the master bedroom and held the door open for him. She wiggled her finger at him for him to follow.

He took the bait, rising from his chair and walking towards the bedroom.

She stood inside the door. Her back turned on him. She couldn't risk giving anything away with her expression. She didn't know whether she'd crack under the gaze of those blank shark's eyes.

She waited, heart pounding, hearing his muffled footsteps on the thick carpet as he entered the bedroom. The sound of the door closing firmly. The lock turning. The noise of the party next door fading like a radio dropped into a bath.

She could feel him behind her now, his hand clasping her ass, making her jump.

'Undress. Get on the bed,' he said, pushing her towards the giant bed with its lavishly embroidered midnight-blue and gold cover. She recognized the sexual urgency in his tone. 'I will be back in one minute.'

He strode towards the en-suite bathroom.

For a moment, Peaches felt panic the like of which she'd never felt before. Danger was all around. Her instinct told her to run.

But then she remembered why she was here. She must be strong.

She had Khordinsky here in this room, without his body-guards. She had to act. Now. This was her only chance.

She closed her eyes for one moment, picturing Irena's face.

I'm doing this for you, she said silently.

And then she thought about Albert Rockbine and the innocent girl she'd once been, and bile rose in her throat. Everything that had happened to Peaches and Irena was because of that brute behind the bathroom door . . .

Yuri Khordinsky.

The monster. The thief. He'd stolen Irena's eyesight. Her health.

Her child . . .

And now it was payback time.

Peaches searched the room for a suitable weapon. A heavy Lalique glass paperweight lay on the writing bureau. She snatched it up and hid it behind her back before turning to face the bathroom door.

She had no intention of getting on the bed or getting undressed. Of him seeing her naked.

She'd make sure it was all over well before that. She pictured herself lashing out, smashing the paperweight against his skull, hearing it crack. She rehearsed it in her mind: he'd fall down; she'd get him on the bed, stay a while, then make out he was sleeping after the biggest sex marathon of his life. No one would dare disturb the big boss. She'd be gone by the time they discovered he was dead. She pictured it over and over.

This was her moment. The moment she'd been waiting for. The moment she would do what she *had* to do. For herself. For her mother.

Khordinsky came out of the bathroom. He was naked, already erect. His sagging chest and belly was pock-marked and scarred. Tattoos ran the length of his powerful, hairy arms.

Again, Peaches saw the flash of anger in his eyes. 'Why are you still dressed?'

She could feel herself shaking. The concealed paperweight felt moist in her hand, covered in her sweat. At any second it might slip and clatter to the floor.

'Now!' a voice inside her screamed. But she kept her cool. He was still too far away. She tightened her grip on the paperweight. Took a step closer to him.

'Because I want to strip for you,' she said. 'I want you to watch.'

It was a line she'd used a hundred times, on a hundred guys. It had never failed to get them hot.

Until now.

'I don't give a fuck what you want,' he said. 'From now on you're going to learn to do what you're told.'

This time it was he who stepped forward, close enough that the fat tip of his penis pressed hard against her waist.

Close enough.

Peaches lunged for him. Swinging her arm around fast and hard, to smash the paperweight into the side of his skull.

But Khordinsky moved quickly for such a big man. Quicker than Peaches could ever have imagined. He reached out and grabbed her wrist and twisted down hard. The paperweight thudded to the floor.

His eyes sparkled with menace – but with something worse than that too. Amusement. As if this was all just part of a sick game that he knew he was better at than anyone else.

Peaches' throat went dry.

'Ah . . . you like to play rough, huh? Good. So do I.'

He toppled her over on the huge bed and she yelped. Khordinsky laughed, enjoying his power over her. 'Good. Good. I see you have done your homework. You know I like a fight.'

He grabbed Peaches' hair, but her wig came off in his hand.

'You don't know who I am,' she gasped, trying to struggle away from him.

He laughed, a terrifying, menacing sound. 'Yes I do. You're a filthy American whore.'

She tried desperately to scramble away from him on the bed but he pinned her down, his elbow across her throat.

He pushed his belly hard against her. 'You feel that, huh? You feel my strong Russian cock? You feel that good, little American bitch? Because now I'm going to fuck you,' he said slowly, vodka fumes overwhelming her, his spit landing on her face. 'Until you'll never be able to fuck anyone ever again.'

Peaches felt fear rip through her.

What had she been thinking? That she'd be able to over-power a man like Khordinsky? She'd been so wrapped up in just getting to *Pushkin* tonight, in finally seeing face to face the man she'd been obsessing about, that she'd been fatally unprepared.

She should have brought a knife. A gun. If only she'd done that he would already be dead.

But now it was too late. There was no time . . .

No time to think . . .

She struggled to breathe as Khordinsky continued to pin her down and tried forcing her legs apart.

Her mind focused.

She was *not* going to be raped. Not by *any* man.

But certainly not *this* man . . .

Her own father.

Think!

A memory surfaced. The one memory that might save her now. A girl she'd met once who'd killed a redneck biker in the same situation. This was her only chance – but it was a hell of a risk.

'Go on then,' she taunted, smiling and going limp beneath Khordinsky.

He laughed roughly, still groping up her dress with his filthy sweaty paw, pushing his weight down harder now, burying his face in her hair. She yelped as he tore away her thong.

Peaches bent her knee and reached for her foot. She tore off her stiletto and held it in her hand.

She could feel Khordinsky's cock against the top of her thigh.

It was now or never.

Peaches used all her might and plunged the razor-sharp stiletto heel into his neck.

Khordinsky screamed, twisting, rolling off her. Blood sprayed on to her face. She scrambled back as he fell off the bed. He checked his hand. It was drenched in blood.

Still holding the shoe in front of her, Peaches backed towards the wall. She was shaking uncontrollably. Frantically, she looked around her for another way out of the room.

'Dieter!' Khordinsky roared.

A splintering sound. The door burst open. The bodyguard rushed in holding a gun. In a second, he had one arm around Peaches' throat and the gun jammed against her temple.

Khordinsky screamed something in Russian, holding tissues against the wound in his neck. He stared at Peaches. 'You tried to kill me, bitch.'

Peaches heard the gun cock against her temple. She felt all her energy drain from her. All her plans. All her scheming. It had come to nothing. She'd failed.

Then – one thought. One flash of hope. Tell him why. So he knew that his actions did have consequences. That the past would catch up with him. One day.

'That's for Irena, pig,' she said.

Khordinsky's face clouded first with incomprehension, then with anger. He flew across the room and punched Peaches hard in the stomach. She'd never experienced pain like it. Dieter let go of her as her body crumpled. She vomited on the floor.

That's when the kicking started.

When she came around, Alexei Rodokov was in the room. 'Yuri? Yuri? Are you OK?'

She saw that Khordinsky was sitting astride her, holding a knife above his head. About to finish her off.

Alexei grabbed Khordinsky's wrist. 'No,' he cried out. He spoke rapidly in Russian. Khordinsky stared at his bloodied hands and let the knife thud to the carpet. He backed away, cursing. He collapsed on to a sofa, before starting to rant at Rodokov again, still in Russian. Peaches understood none of it. Except for the word *Irena*, which was repeated over and over again.

Rodokov flicked his eyes towards the door and Dieter lifted Peaches up and marched her through. The room was empty.

The party over. The girls gone. There was no one left to help.

Peaches felt nothing. No pain. Nothing. She shifted in and out of darkness, like someone was opening and shutting curtains. Is this it? she wondered. Am I already dead?

But then the cold sea air hit her like a slap. Her eyes snapped open. She saw stars above. The pain rushed into her, through her, making her gasp and reel.

Someone was carrying her like a butcher would carry a side of beef. Dieter's face swam into focus. Peaches craned her neck. Rodokov was marching up ahead. They were out on the deck of a boat. There was still no one else around. No guests. No staff. No witnesses.

'What are you going to do to me?' she managed.

Dieter dropped her on to the floor of the boat. She hit her head hard. He knelt down beside her and smashed her across the face with his gun.

How much time had gone by? Minutes . . . hours? All Peaches knew was that she was now lying on sand. On a beach. She could hear the hiss of waves nearby. A black wall of cliffs stretched up into the deep dark velvet sky. She could taste blood in her mouth. Her body was drenched in white pain. She tried to lift her head, but she couldn't move. One eye was sealed shut.

But with the other, she could see that Alexei Rodokov was crouched down in front of her.

'Do you think we don't get people like you all the time?' he said. 'Thieves who want to rob us? Or get revenge for something they think we did?' He was loading a pistol, snapping back the mechanism so that it was primed. Beads of sweat on his smooth suntanned brow glistened in the moonlight. 'Some birthday this is turning out to be,' he said. 'I didn't even want any fucking whores on my yacht. And now you've brought me to this.'

Peaches tried to look around for help. All she saw was the brooding hulk of Dieter, sitting on the edge of a dinghy ten yards away, just out of the reach of the surf. The red eye of his cigarette flared and glowed malevolently in the dark.

'Please . . .' Peaches said.

Rodokov's face was impassive. 'Tell me about Irena,' he said.

'Tell me everything you know and I might let you live.'

Peaches opened her mouth to speak. Then snapped it shut. *Might*. He'd said *might*. *Might* meant nothing on a night when no one else knew they were here. There was no point in trying to bargain her way out of this. She was dead. She'd been dead from the instant she'd failed to kill Khordinsky. Tell Rodokov about Irena and Khordinsky would kill her too.

'Fuck you,' she said. She knew she was going to die, but some part of her clung desperately to these last precious moments of life, like a shipwreck survivor refusing to let go of a disintegrating raft. 'I'd rather die than tell you anything.'

Rodokov's expression seemed to harden in the moonlight. 'I was afraid you'd say that.'

He aimed the pistol at her head.

Peaches heard a soft whimper. It was her own. She thought about saying her prayers, but there was only fear.

Then he fired.

CHAPTER TWENTY-SEVEN

Frankie must have dozed off, for the clank of bars jolted her awake, like a gunshot. A woman screamed in the distance. Frankie rubbed her face. Her hair was matted and tangled from all the hairspray Marc had applied last night when she'd been getting ready in the Carlton hotel. That seemed like a week ago now.

Frankie groaned. It was dawn already and she was still here. In jail. Under arrest. The small police cell she was in stank of urine. A high window let in weak daylight, showing the streaks of dirt and graffiti on the painted walls.

She stood up from the ripped plastic mattress and started pacing. The sound of the woman screaming was getting closer and she could hear footsteps approaching the cell.

Frankie's Valentino couture dress – probably worth tens of thousands – was comprehensively ruined. She was covered in grease and oil after her scuffle with the harbour master.

She'd never felt so frustrated. She'd tried to explain who she was and that she'd just been *borrowing* the tender from the luxury yacht. But the harbour master wouldn't hear of it. And when she'd admitted that she was trying to get to *Pushkin*, it had only made matters ten times worse.

The owner of the yacht whose tender she'd commandeered had been equally unforgiving. He'd told the gendarmes she'd been handed over to next that he wanted her prosecuted to the full extent of the law. The officer in charge was furious that she'd been brought in on such a busy night, and when she'd finally cracked and started shouting at them, he'd locked her in the cell.

Now Frankie leant down to rip off a whole section from the bottom of the dress, where the once gorgeous sequined silk was frayed and torn. She needed a bath, a drink of water, some food. But, most of all, she needed to get out of here.

'Oh, Todd, please . . .' she muttered, closing her eyes in silent prayer.

Earlier, the gendarmes, finally responding to her desperate cries and banging on the door, had allowed her a phone call. She'd still had Todd's mobile number written on her wrist. She'd left a desperate message on his answering service, but she'd heard nothing.

But Todd would probably still be fast asleep, she reasoned. Why would he have listened to his messages? And even if he did, would he really help her like he said he would?

It was still impossible to comprehend that the only person in the world who could help her also happened to be the most famous movie star in the world. He was *Todd Lands*, for God's sake. The very magnitude of this fact now filled her with fresh doubt. Why shouldn't he walk away and forget all about her? Especially since his last words to her had been a warning to stay out of trouble.

What if the press had got hold of the story somehow? If they found out that the same girl who'd been Todd's date earlier in the evening had stolen a boat and attempted to crash a party on *Pushkin*, that would mean a hell of a lot more than just a few column inches – it would be a major embarrassment to Todd.

But Todd *had* to come through for her and get her out of here – because there was no alternative. Apart from him, Frankie had nothing.

Absolutely nothing.

The thought terrified her. She slumped back down on to the ripped mattress and put her head in her hands, fighting back tears. This was all her own fault. She hadn't been strong enough. She'd allowed herself to be bullied, right from the second she'd arrived back from Marrakech and Richard had treated her the way he had. And, like an idiot, she'd gone along with Sonny's plan without a murmur. Why hadn't she protested more and demanded to see Alex as soon as they'd got to the Carlton? Why hadn't she fought to get out of the limo when she'd been whisked to the premiere with Todd? Why had she been so weak? So easily led?

From Alex's point of view, her actions must seem terrible. They'd made it impossible for him not to swallow the lies Khordinsky had told him.

But even here, in the cold light of dawn, Frankie still felt a flicker of hope. She loved Alex and she wouldn't give up on him, no matter what anyone else might tell her to do. Hadn't Alex told her to have faith? Hadn't he told her right from the start that trust was the most important thing?

Well, even if Alex had lost his faith in her, she wasn't going to lose hers in him. Angrily, determinedly, she wiped the tears from her face.

No more weakness. She was going to make damn sure he found out the truth. She was going to prove to him that he could trust her again. That he always could have. That he always would be able to.

She'd come this far; she wasn't going to give up. She'd lost everything once before in South Africa and she was damn sure it wasn't going to happen again – not without a fight.

Frankie flinched and sat up as a cacophony of screaming erupted in the corridor outside. The key turned in the lock and the door burst open. A gendarme – one she recognized from last night – was manhandling a skinny, sallow-faced young woman into the cell. She was hissing like a cat. Her make-up was smudged and her tight jeans were torn. Frankie didn't know much French, but she knew that the girl was swearing furiously.

She stuck her chin up, talking rapidly, then spat on the gendarme's polished black boots. She looked like a hooker, Frankie concluded, a junkie. Someone Frankie usually crossed the street to avoid.

But who was she to be so judgemental? she thought. Frankie

had stolen a boat herself last night. She was probably in a lot more trouble than this girl.

'*Monsieur*!' Frankie said, standing up and getting the gendarme's attention. She smoothed her hair behind her ear and gave him her most polite smile.

He looked her up and down wearily, then nodded, as if he'd just remembered her existence. '*Ah, oui*, come this way,' he said, in clipped English.

At this show of preferential treatment the skinny girl launched into another vicious tirade. But Frankie's stomach tipped over with hope and apprehension. She was being released from the cell – but into what? she wondered. Freedom? Had her message reached Todd? Had he managed to pull some strings? Or was she being taken somewhere worse? An interrogation room? A bus to another prison? Somewhere that was going to make this cell like a blast?

The skinny girl pounded on the door behind her as Frankie was led down the corridor, then on through two security doors and up two flights of stairs. She was shown into another cell. This one was empty and clean, with a bottle of chilled Evian on the table next to two plastic cups. A barred window overlooked the twinkling blue bay – a world away.

'Wait,' said the gendarme.

He stepped back outside, leaving her alone. No cuffs. No need, she saw. A security camera winked its red eye from the ceiling.

Be strong, Frankie reminded herself, beating down her fear as she slugged back the water from the bottle. No more fuck-ups. Do whatever it takes to get out of here in one piece.

A few minutes later, the door opened and a man with a button-down cream cotton shirt and smart chinos came in. He had a pointed beard and kind green eyes behind half-moon spectacles. He reached forward and shook Frankie's hand, before laying his smart attaché case on the table.

'Miss Willis. I am Laurent Ricard. Todd Lands sent me to get you out of this mess.'

Frankie smiled. Thank God. Todd hadn't forgotten about her after all. 'Thank you,' she said, shaking his hand gratefully.

'Why don't you tell me what happened? And then we'll see

what we can do about persuading these people that what you did wasn't so bad at all.'

An hour later, Frankie had been reprimanded, but thanks to Laurent had walked away from the whole ordeal. No fine. All charges had been magically and mysteriously dropped.

Laurent quickly ushered her into his waiting car, grabbing her arm rather than letting her savour the morning air and the unbelievable euphoria she felt at getting her freedom back. 'You can enjoy this better where we are going,' he said.

In no time, they were on their way to Nice airport, where Todd had left his helicopter and pilot at their disposal. Todd himself had left the Hotel du Cap and was now up at his residence in the hills where they were to join him.

Todd's place turned out to be a short flight but a million miles away from the madness of Cannes. It was tucked away in a beautiful valley patterned with rows of vines and surrounded by olive groves and orchards. As they flew over fields of wild poppies and along an avenue of cypress trees to touch down on the front lawn of the pretty seventeenth-century château, with its steep tiled roof and sky-blue shutters, Frankie could see the long sweep of a gravel drive and a gleaming gold Maserati parked outside the front doors.

Inside, Frankie held her shoes in her hand as she followed Laurent and a slightly officious English butler across the cool flagstones and through a maze of hallways and grand rooms, marvelling at the way the place had been done up. A grid of giant Andy Warhol-style pictures of Todd hung above the stone fireplace. Modern furniture and life-sized sculptures stood out against portcullis-style gates and ancient stone arches. The whole place had a comfortable yet stylish feel to it; it was as much of a statement as Todd himself.

Towards the back of the château, staff scuttled about, carrying vast flower arrangements and ice-buckets out to the terrace, where a long dining table was being set up.

The butler barked a few instructions to the staff as he led them past an ornate stone fountain and out to the back gardens, with their beds of scented rose bushes and lavender and neat gravel pathways. Frankie, trying to take in the splendour, shielded her eyes against the glare of the late morning sun and wished she had her shades. But they, like everything else, had been lost.

She followed the butler through a wrought-iron gate in a hedge of sculpted box trees and they all stopped. Ahead of them Todd Lands was getting out of the most incredible black slate infinity swimming pool.

The sight of him seemed oddly familiar. But then, Todd Lands half naked was an iconic image throughout the world. There were postcard stalls from Tokyo to Berlin selling this exact image of him. And here he was in the flesh.

Most girls would almost certainly swoon, but Frankie felt too tired. And too embarrassed, and too in his debt.

He was wearing a skimpy turquoise thong; it was a look Frankie thought was ridiculous, but she had to concede that his body was in incredible shape. Despite his petite stature, he was perfectly proportioned, with a toned, tanned stomach, the muscles of which positively rippled as he bent over and plucked an ochre silk dhoti from the back of a teak deckchair and languidly wrapped it round his waist and thighs. There was no doubt that he liked the fact that he had an audience.

'Glad you could make it,' he said, running up the steps to greet Frankie. His smile turned to a frown as he drew nearer. 'My God,' he said, as if he didn't know that she'd spent the night in a French prison cell. 'You're a mess!'

'Some leading lady, huh?' Frankie said, managing a weak smile.

'Lal,' Todd chastised the lawyer. 'You could at least have stopped off at a chichi shop and picked up poor Cinders some new threads.'

Laurent smiled wryly. 'Clothes shopping is not my forte. Dealing with the gendarmes is.'

Todd grinned. 'Dry as ever. I like it.' He slapped the lawyer on the back, leaving a wet handprint on Laurent's linen suit. 'Good job, though,' he said. 'Getting Frankie out. How much did it cost me?'

'Nothing you need worry about. The owner of the tender proved very amenable, once he found out your interest. It seems his wife's a big fan of yours. I've promised them tickets to the New York premiere. I said you'd say hello.'

Todd rolled his eyes. 'I'd rather have paid cash.'

'Thanks for bailing me out, Todd,' Frankie said, realizing how inconvenienced he'd be as a result.

'Is there anything else you need?' Laurent said, bowing his head.

Todd looked at Frankie. 'Well?' he said. 'Here's your chance. Laurent is the main man. He can get anything.'

'What I really need is a passport,' Frankie said, wondering whether it was too much to ask.

Laurent Ricard nodded. 'Of course. Give me your details and a couple of days and I'll have one delivered.'

A couple of days! She couldn't believe he could sort it out that quickly. But at the same time it presented another problem. What was Frankie going to do for a couple of days? She had nowhere to stay and no money; nothing but the torn, borrowed clothes on her back.

'You can bring it here, Lal. You'll stay, won't you, Frankie?' Todd said as if reading her mind. 'I'm not sure I want to let you out of my sight. You get into too much trouble. Quite an impressive stunt, though,' he said, winking at her. Frankie smiled. She was so relieved he wasn't angry. And so touched that he was prepared to be so generous.

'Ah, here's Claire,' Todd said, as a woman in a pretty sundress on a mobile phone came down from the terrace. 'You remember her from last night? My PA. She'll figure out clothes. We're having a lunch party, so you're going to have to get cleaned up.'

Frankie felt her shoulders sag. The thought of being on show at another party made her want to cry. All she wanted to do was curl up in a ball somewhere and sleep. She gazed past the sunlight twinkling on the pool, and on down the gently sloping immaculate lawn which reached into the valley below. She thought of Alex, of the two of them in the pool in Morocco, of them riding along the beach. So free. So different from now.

Todd read her expression. 'Come on,' he told her. 'Get a smile on that pretty face of yours. No more moping, OK? You're stuck with me. You might as well enjoy yourself.'

After Laurent had departed and Claire had gone to prepare a room and they were alone, Frankie sat down on one of the terrace chairs and faced Todd. A nearby table was strewn with newspapers, most of which were carrying pictures of her and Todd.

'Todd, about last night . . .' she began.

'Alex better not have read today's papers,' he said, with a whistle. 'They're sizzling hot. All over you and me.'

'I can see,' Frankie said glumly. Alex must hate her even more by now.

'They're all very flattering, though, I must say. They think you and I look great together.'

'Oh.' Frankie bit her lip and squeezed her hands between her knees.

'You know,' Todd continued, pouring two glasses of sparkling mineral water, 'I got a call from my PR people. They say you and I should keep working it. That there's still plenty of mileage left in our so-called romance. The hit rate on my website's gone astral. Jay Leno and Letterman have been on the phone. And you know, since you didn't patch things up with Alex, I thought maybe you might like to reconsider. I mean, we're cool. And it'd be fun. I know you're currently unemployed, so I could make it worth your while financially.'

Frankie stared at him. Was he serious?

Oh God. He was.

'Todd . . . I can't,' Frankie stumbled. 'I know I mucked things up with Alex this time, but next time I won't. You know how I feel about him, Todd. I love him, and I want him back. Pretending I'm your girlfriend is really *not* going to help.'

'Yes, yes,' Todd said.

'No, I mean it, Todd. I can't do it. I'm not an actress. I know you'd be able to find a thousand girls who'd walk over hot coals for an offer like that, but I can't do it.'

Todd rolled his eyes. 'I hear you. Well, I know I'm not your style, but let me tell you, before you start planning another escapade, Alexei Rodokov's yacht has left Cannes. Nobody knows where this precious boyfriend of yours is.'

'I'm still not giving up,' Frankie said. 'I'll find him.'

Todd nodded. 'But not without your passport, right?'

'Right.'

'Which makes you mine for at least the next twenty-four hours.'

Frankie nodded. 'I guess.'

'Well, it can't be *that* bad,' he said, pointing out to the view. He pulled a face at her and she laughed.

'That's better. Now then, tell you what: while you're here, why not make yourself useful?' he said, throwing a script down on the table in front of her. She picked it up and saw that it was for a play. 'I've got a great offer to do a show on Broadway and, if I'm going to do it, I have to commit today. Take a look at it. Tell me what you think. I'm up for the part of Arty.'

Frankie stared back at him blankly. He couldn't be serious. After what she'd just been through, he wanted her to *read a play*? Right now? 'But I don't know a thing about theatre,' she said.

Todd shrugged. 'You watch TV, don't you?'

'Sure.'

'Well, that's all theatre is: TV up close.'

Frankie tentatively picked up the script. 'But why me? Why not ask . . . I don't know . . . your PA, Claire? Someone else in the biz?'

'No. I need a neutral. Someone who's not on my payroll. And I like you. You're smart. I'd like to hear what you think.'

'But do you want to do theatre?' she asked. 'You must get great film offers all the time.'

He leant forward, looking around him to make sure they weren't being overheard. 'I know, but the last few reviews have slammed me for playing the same role. And none of these toadies will give me a straight answer. My agent is so scared of losing his commission, he won't give me any advice. And the press are on side right now, but who knows how long they'll let me stay at the top?' He looked at her seriously. 'You're a fan. You can tell me. Am I *really* the same in all my films?'

He stared at her. Frankie felt her throat go dry. Jesus. He was serious.

'Well,' she said tentatively, putting the script back down on the table, realizing that this wasn't about the play at all, but more about Todd's ego. She chose her words carefully. 'You always do the same *type* of movies. You know, all that action-hero stuff. And I guess it's hard for people to differentiate when you're so famous.'

Todd frowned.

'But so what if you're always Todd Lands? It seems to be working to me,' she hurried on.

'You don't have to pay me compliments. I want the truth.'

'The truth?'

He nodded, waving his fingertips at her to bring it on.

'Well . . . it seems to me that the problem is that you're now too famous for the movies you take on,' she began. She bit her lip and looked at him. She could see that he really *did* want her to be honest. 'Those critics aren't seeing what you bring to the role, just who you are. No matter what you do on screen, all they see is Todd Lands the celebrity actor. I think you're a victim of that giant PR machine you're so fond of.' Inwardly she winced. Had that been *too* honest?

Todd nodded and smiled wryly as he thought it over. 'So maybe Broadway would be a good idea. Prove to everyone that I've still got what it takes . . .'

'Todd, who cares what everyone else thinks? It's what *you* think that's important.'

And right at that moment, Frankie realized that she should follow her own advice. She would find a way of putting things right between her and Alex however long it took. Didn't he say he'd be going to Tortola? On her birthday? She remembered him writing it down in his study. Well, if Laurent could get her a passport, then Frankie would make damn sure that she'd get herself to the BVI's. Yes, that's what she'd do. Alex couldn't ignore her if she was there to meet him.

It wasn't until later on that night that Frankie had another chance to talk to Todd alone. She was dizzy with exhaustion, but despite everything on her mind, the lunch had been fun. Todd was so magnetic, it was impossible not to get drawn into his circle. Clearly buoyed up with confidence, he'd announced that he'd be taking the role in the Broadway show, much to everyone's approval.

Now, as they sat in the candlelit orangery, having a nightcap, Todd was finally relaxing.

'You were very charming at lunch. They all liked you,' he said. 'For someone who isn't my companion, you're doing a great job.'

Frankie laughed. 'I thought it was a bit over the top when you told them all that I was your muse.'

'Who cares?' Todd said. 'Half of them are jerks. They'll spread loads of rumours, I know, but it doesn't matter as long as I pull off this Broadway gig.'

'You know, I much prefer you like this,' Frankie said. 'The real you rather than that high-energy thing you do. I don't know how you can turn it on and off.'

Todd smiled and rubbed the side of his face. 'I know someone else who says exactly the same thing.' He looked away quickly, embarrassed that such a clearly intimate comment had slipped out.

'Oh . . . so you *do* have someone,' Frankie probed.

Todd was silent for a moment longer. Then he looked into her eyes. 'Maybe,' he said.

Frankie smiled. 'I'll take that as a "yes".'

She could tell he was weighing up whether or not to say more. 'Is this the very well-kept secret you told me about?' she asked, thinking she might be getting somewhere near the real Todd Lands. 'I mean, I guess it is. You can trust me. I'm not going to tell anyone anything you tell me, Todd. You saved my life this morning. Besides, according to you, I'm your muse, so I ought to know everything about you.'

'All right then. I do have someone special,' he said. 'And yes, it is very very secret.'

'OK,' Frankie said.

'And you never know,' Todd said, taking a deep breath, 'maybe you'll meet him some day.'

Him? 'You mean . . .'

Todd blushed, then he put his hand on his chest. 'Wow! It feels odd saying it.'

'You're . . . *gay*?' Frankie was staring at him, her mouth open. She was completely stunned, but she also felt relief and hope surge through her. Todd being gay . . . it changed everything.

'Surprised?' he asked.

Frankie thought for a moment. No, she wasn't surprised. The turquoise G-string . . . Suddenly, it all made sense.

'I told you it was a well-kept secret.'

'You can say that again.'

Todd looked at her. 'It has to stay a secret. You must

absolutely promise not to tell anyone. Anyone at all. Or my career is finished. I mean it, Frankie. I've trusted you and helped you out, but if I've made the biggest mistake of my life and you let me down, I swear I'll sue that gorgeous ass off you. In the limo . . . you signed the contract, remember? And let me tell you, my contracts are watertight. As in totally.'

CHAPTER TWENTY-EIGHT

Emma woke suddenly, the wooden ceiling fan blowing papers off the desk in the corner. The power must be back on. Wearily, she got up and opened the shutters, letting in light. She yawned, staring out of the window in the familiar guest suite of David Coulter's colonial mansion and saw that the storm had finally abated. The world glistened. It smelt fresh, newly washed, but the devastation was everywhere.

She could see where the tiles had been torn down from the roof and smashed on the veranda. A banana tree had been uprooted and now lay across the drive. She leant on the wide wooden windowsill, watching the grey light creep across the horizon and over the lawns to the house. Foliage from the shrubbery had blown everywhere; broken red flowers dotted the lawn, like spots of blood. Clothes lay scattered, ripped from the line. It looked like the site of an air crash.

David's house was built of stone and had withstood the unpredictable Caribbean weather for two hundred years or more. But now Emma thought of the corrugated iron shacks just down the road from the bottom of David's long drive and the smiling, waving children in their immaculate school uniforms she'd passed on the drive from the airport yesterday morning. She prayed they'd all survived last night's storm.

Emma rubbed her eyes. Between the howling of the wind and the lashing of the rain against the rattling wooden shutters, she'd slept fitfully, feverishly, her nightmares haunted by ghosts. But she knew that it was pointless crawling back into the bed behind her and trying to sleep now. She couldn't sleep. And she wondered whether she would ever be able to sleep properly again. Sleep certainly held no appeal. Or relief.

The pain seemed so much worse at night, and the cruellest blow of all came if she *did* drift off, because for a split second before she woke up she forgot what had happened. She thought that her life was as it should be, that Julian was in bed next to her, that she was inches away from his familiar sleepy embrace.

Only then she remembered – and the pain hit her all over again like a fist.

She missed him so badly, it was as if she'd lost one of her limbs. Sadness overwhelmed her so completely that she was helpless against the enormous waves of grief that washed over her, leaving her feeling capsized and weak.

And without her home, she felt more adrift than ever. She could never have imagined that something so solid – so *hers* – could be whipped from under her nose like that. But Wrentham, including all her furniture, her art and all the precious little things that had made it a home, had gone. It filled her with a sense of helpless injustice and of violation so profound that she couldn't shake it.

Now, as always with the morning light, came her focus on the one thing that fuelled her need to go on. One man. One name.

Khordinsky.

Once again, Emma cast her mind back to Natalya Khordinsky at the Gala Lunch, how she'd pronounced that her husband thought that everything could be obtained, and how Emma herself had been so dismissive of such an arrogant assumption.

How safe Emma thought she'd been. How invulnerable. How disparaging she'd felt about those newly moneyed Russians and their vulgar ways.

But she'd been so, so wrong. The Khordinskys *had* got their hands on Wrentham. She still couldn't make sense of it, no matter how many times she tried to think it through. It wasn't possible for them to know that Wrentham was going on the market unless they'd known about the details of the finances controlling the platinum deal. And Julian would never have put Wrentham up – or, more likely, been *persuaded* to put Wrentham up – as security, if he'd thought for one second that his life was in danger, or that the deal wasn't certain. It just wasn't a risk he would have taken.

Which meant that somehow Yuri Khordinsky was involved. He had to be. How else would he have been able to get hold of Wrentham so quickly?

But, as Pim and Susie had pointed out, all of that was just speculation. She had no proof. Not yet anyway. Because that's what Emma had vowed to herself as she'd stood in the rain looking at Julian's coffin. She would find proof that Julian wasn't a crook, or a fool, or a coward. She'd prove to everyone that he'd been swindled right from the start. She wouldn't have a moment's peace until she'd done everything she possibly could to uncover the truth.

Because Emma didn't believe that Julian had committed suicide. Everyone kept telling her to accept it, that it had been a spontaneous selfish act, that he'd obviously seen no alternative. But she knew Julian better than anyone else. He just wouldn't have done that. Not to himself and not to her. And certainly not for the trite, implausible reasons he'd given in his note. It went against everything she knew and loved about him.

Something didn't add up. The only reason Julian would ever have sacrificed himself was to save her and his family. Which meant that whoever had perpetrated the fraud over Julian's platinum mine was truly responsible.

That was why she was here in Tortola staying with David. She was going to start at the beginning of the paper trail. It was here that Julian had registered Platinum Reach; this was where the money had come and where the rot had set in. Emma was determined to find out who else he'd seen and who'd been involved in the company. There had to be lawyers. Accountants. Witnesses or evidence. Something to prove Julian was innocent, that he'd just been duped. That he'd been talked into something that was out of his control.

Emma went back to the bedside and picked up her iPhone. She looked at her mail, but there was nothing new. She opened her saved folder, reading for the hundredth time the last message she'd received from Cosmo.

It was the only communication she'd had from him since their terrible row. She read it now. *I'm sorry for the things I said. The less you know the better. But I am determined to clear Dad's name.*

Now her fury over him missing Julian's funeral had turned to panic. Cosmo was half the man Julian was. What chance did he have against the people who'd brought Julian's life and dreams crashing down around him?

The less you know the better. What did *that* mean? What was Cosmo up to?

She emailed him again. It was at least the twentieth reply she'd typed. She didn't expect him to answer. She'd long ago given up hope of that. He was as stubborn as a mule – even more stubborn than her when he put his mind to it. But she knew he'd read it, wherever he was. Whatever he was doing. Even if, like her, he'd come to the BVIs to trace his father's business back to the start. He'd read her mail and know she was still here for him, whenever he needed her and whatever he found out. She typed: *I'm thinking of you, Cosmo, and sending you my love. Be careful. Don't try and fix this alone. You are not alone. Call me and I'll be there.*

She took in a deep breath, steeling herself for the day ahead. Someone here must know who else was involved in the company. And she was determined to find them.

Down in Road Town harbour, flotsam marred the choppy blue Caribbean water: storm detritus, palm leaves and litter. Emma had stationed herself with her back to the harbour and its bobbing parade of gin palaces and yachts. She sat outside the front of a busy café on the quayside, assaulted by the loud reggae playing on the radio hanging from the beam above her. But she endured it for the table's almost 360-degree view of the harbour and the main street with its hotchpotch of dusty red-brick and faded pastel-coloured buildings.

Billboards clung to their sides advertising sun-creams, soft drinks and beers, resorts and strip clubs. Shops, yacht brokers, restaurants and banks jostled for space along the pavement. There were plenty of people too, leaning against walls, perching on motorbikes, sitting on slatted wooden chairs. Flicking through newspapers, puffing on cigarettes and sipping coffees. There were people from all walks of life: beach bums, yachties, gigolos and suits; all of them taking advantage of the relative cool of the morning before they were forced to flee the encroaching humidity and retreat to the cool confines of their shuttered, air-conditioned offices behind the tinted windows above the shop-fronts. Or to brave the hot stoves in the restaurants, or search the beaches for middle-aged women with dollars in their purses and a twinkle in their eyes.

This early-morning scene should have been pretty and inviting, Emma thought, like a snapshot from a tourist-board brochure. But after last night's storm, there was an unsettled air hanging over it all. Everyone looked on edge; collectively, they had one eye fixed on the horizon, searching for a gathering pall of cloud. And they had one ear listening out for a change in the tinkling of the ships' rigging in the harbour, which was chiming gently – at least for now – in the breeze.

None of the people gathered here today even dared whisper it, but you could tell they were all thinking the same thing. Hurricane.

More bad weather was forecast. It was all over the papers and websites and on the television news. Emma couldn't have chosen a worse time to come.

Yet the words of warning splashed across the headlines didn't bother Emma. She was fixated on two glimmering words on one of the several golden plaques attached to the windowless black door of a thin brick office wedged between a diving shop and a juice bar.

Heavenly House. What a joke. The place was so grim, it looked more like an adjunct of hell. It was the kind of place she would have walked right past if she hadn't already known it was there. But she did know, because she had the address. Because the two words on the plaque she was fixating on read PLATINUM REACH.

Two little words.

The beginning of Julian's end. Emma had been here for over an hour already. Watching. Waiting. But so far no one had turned up for work.

There were eighteen other companies listed on the door of Heavenly House. She'd already Googled the lot. They were all totally disconnected, ranging from pharmaceutical companies to grain-importers. None of them or the people listed as working for them meant a thing.

But still, someone had to work here. Someone who knew something about Platinum Holdings and its link to Platinum Reach. Someone Julian had flown here to see. Someone whom Emma was going to meet, no matter how long she had to wait.

Emma was just ordering her second juice smoothie when she saw a man ride up to the office on a moped smoking a cigarette. He was white and had to be in his fifties; he was wearing a scruffy green cotton suit stretched across his plump frame. Even from across the road she could see a dark V of sweat up his back. She watched him park and unlock the door of the building.

Emma quickly left some dollars on the table and hurried across the road, sprinting to catch the door before it closed.

Inside, it was stifling: no air-con. No reception either, just a single bare lightbulb and a stack of wooden crates blocking a thin corridor leading to a back door and a rickety tiled staircase leading steeply upwards. Emma heard a noise upstairs. Footsteps. She didn't give herself time to chicken out: she started climbing.

At the top, she knocked on a frosted glass door. 'Hello?' she called, pushing it open.

The man she'd seen arrive was still smoking a filterless cigarette. He had bulging eyes and a crooked nose. He looked up briefly from the mound of papers spread across his desk, then he switched on his computer and fan.

'Yes?' he said, smoothing his greasy brown hair over his balding head.

'Platinum Reach,' Emma said, trying not to choke on the acrid cigarette smoke which filled the room. The shutters were still closed, the small windows shut. 'Are these the offices?'

'Maybe.' His accent was American, hard to place, his voice gravelly and uncaring.

'There's a plaque outside. It says these are the offices.'

'I can't help you,' the man said.

Emma bristled at his lack of manners. It was time to get to the point. 'But you know *of* Platinum Reach?'

The man held up his chubby hand to stop her. He was wearing a gaudy ring on his little finger with a ruby set in gold.

'Please,' Emma persisted. 'My husband, Julian Harvey is – was – a director. It's his company.'

The man's expression altered at the mention of Julian's name. His eyes narrowed, sparking with interest. Or was it wariness? He must know Julian. They must have met. Did he know what had happened?

'I need some information,' she hurried on, keen to press home her advantage. 'You see, a lot of money came through here and I need to know where the money went. I mean to which account when it left here.'

'You got power of attorney?' he asked.

'What?'

'Because if you haven't, I can't tell you anything, lady,' he stonewalled her.

'But I'm his wife.'

'Let me tell you, you wouldn't be the first wife to come snooping round here trying to find out where the money went.'

'So you do know something? Does that mean you know the directors?' she probed.

'It makes no difference what I know. I can't tell you. Everything and everyone I deal with is confidential.' He turned back to his papers. 'Now, if you'll excuse me, I've got work to do.'

Emma felt her voice crack with desperation. 'Please,' she begged. 'I need your help. I've come here all the way from London. You *have* to tell me . . .'

The man rocked back in his chair. 'I don't have to tell you diddly squat.'

How dare he be so rude! Emma felt her patience snap. She was getting nowhere. 'Fine. I'll get a lawyer to do this, if that's what you want. I can get someone to investigate Platinum Reach, all these other companies . . . and you.'

The man shrugged, unfazed by her threat. He leant forward

and stubbed his cigarette out in the overflowing ashtray, then took his cell phone from his jacket pocket and laid it on the desk, like a gun. His fingers never left it. The implication was obvious. If she didn't clear out, he had people he could call to make her go away before she started any trouble. 'I'm going to count to ten . . .'

'I'll stay here for as long as it takes for you to tell me the truth.' She could tell her stern tone shocked him. It shocked her too. How strong she sounded. How determined.

Slowly, he leant back in his chair, looking her up and down. 'My, my,' he said, whistling through his teeth. Then he smiled – a thin, mean curling of the lips. 'Ain't you a feisty one?'

Emma opened her mouth to protest.

'Watch it there, honey. It's too early in the morning for dramatics.'

'But—'

'I'll tell you what. Seeing as how you've come such a long way, and how much this seems to mean to you, perhaps I might see my way to coming to some sort of arrangement after all.'

'You mean you *will* help me?' Emma said, taken aback by this seeming volte-face.

The man rubbed his fat hands together and looked her lingeringly up and down. Emma felt her skin flush and sudden adrenalin pump through her. She glanced quickly at the closed windows.

'What I'm suggesting . . . yes, seeing as we're *all alone* . . . is that we indulge in a little asset information. I let you in on a little information regarding Platinum Reach, then you allow me to . . . familiarize myself with your assets.'

'You've got to be joking.'

'I never joke about business.' His eyes glinted with menace.

Emma stared at him with revulsion and horror. He couldn't be serious, could he? But as she stared at the fixed smile, she knew that he was. She watched him flick his tongue over his yellow teeth, waiting for her answer. Daring her.

She had to take control, she thought, panicking, before he took control of her. She had to remember why she was here and that he had the information she desperately needed – maybe enough to solve the mystery of Julian's death. Certainly enough to send her on the next part of the trail that might lead to that solution.

She swallowed hard and stared once more into his dark, unblinking eyes. She knew what she had to do. She had no choice. And she no longer had anything left to lose.

'Very well,' she said, walking round the side of the desk. She held his eye as she slowly unbuttoned the top button of her shirt. This was all just an act, she reminded herself, but if this was the way he was going to play it, she'd set the rules. 'If a lady has to do what a lady has to do, I guess I don't mind . . .'

He laughed, as if unable to believe that she was cooperating so easily. She continued slowly, unbuttoning her shirt a little more, until her lacy black bra was showing against her pale smooth skin.

She stopped, just out of reach, leaning both hands on the desk so that he could see a tiny glimpse of her cleavage. 'But you go first,' she said.

'Kind of like strip poker,' he said. His eyes were bulging. A small white cluster of spit lodged in his lip. 'I show you mine, you show me yours.'

'Kind of like that.' She watched him unfasten his belt. 'But you know, if we're going to get . . . um . . . intimate . . . surely you should at least tell me your name?'

'Vincent. Vincent Detroy,' he said, staring at her bra.

She smiled, playing the game. She could tell he was eager. Too eager. Ready to be undone by his filthy desires.

'So, Vinny, tell me something. You're a bit of a hot shot, aren't you? Running all these companies? Or do you own them?'

He smiled, running his tongue around his filthy teeth. 'They ain't mine.'

'Oh?' Emma tiptoed her fingers across the desk towards him. She stared into his eyes.

'Most of them are subsidiaries of Matryoshka-Enterprises,' he said, unzipping his fly in a hurry, desperate to claim her before she changed her mind. 'And you're shit out of luck. The sole director of them all is coming tomorrow to shut 'em all down.' He tapped his computer screen. 'Got all the paperwork lined up to be signed.'

'Matryoshka-Enterprises? Does that have anything to do with Platinum Reach?'

'Maybe. Maybe not.'

Emma smiled. 'Oh, come on, Vinny. You can tell me. Why don't you tell me the director's name?'

'Not a chance. Until you come right over here.'

'I can find out, if you won't tell me.'

Vincent Detroy laughed. 'No you won't. Once he's signed, there'll be no trace of any companies here. There'll be nothing here but bricks. So the best advice I can give you, lady, is to get on with the rest of your life. Starting right now, right here.'

Emma was pleased she'd made her decision. It had been the right one. She hadn't trusted Detroy as far as she could throw him. There was no way this low life *would* ever or *could* ever have laid one fat finger on her.

She stood up and backed away, buttoning up her shirt.

'Hey?' Detroy said. He had his hand in his fly. 'Where you think you're going?' He stood up. He had his stubby, revolting cock in his hand and his cheap suit trousers fell around his ankles, preventing him from running after her.

'Oh, put it away,' she said, fixing him with a withering look.

'But . . . but . . . we had a deal!' he spluttered.

'Believe me, Mr Detroy, you have *absolutely nothing* of interest to me whatsoever. Good day.'

Emma walked quickly through the door and slammed it as hard as she could. She hated the fact she'd had to stoop to the tactics of a whore to get what she wanted, but they had worked. She ran down the stairs and out on to the street.

Hot rain hammered down on the ferry landing dock. Low thunder rumbled out in the bay. Rufus, David's groundsman, crouched down beside the table where Emma, David and Eli sat in the Jolly Roger bar in Sopher's Hole. Rufus's huge black biceps shone beneath his white T-shirt as he petted Louis, David's Labrador, who whined as another fork of lightning split the grey sky.

'Easy, boy,' David said to his beloved dog. Emma thought that David looked more stressed today than usual, his easy grin replaced by a worried frown. He'd certainly dropped everything to help her as soon as he'd heard the news about Julian. Emma knew that losing Julian had hit him hard. And now David couldn't be more determined for her to prove her theory right about Julian being set up.

Eli was Tortola's police chief. He'd come as a favour to David, to see if there was any way of forcing Vincent Detroy to tell them more about what he knew. Eli had got caught in the downpour on the way over from his office. He was wearing khaki long shorts and flip-flops and a soaking Hawaiian print shirt.

Emma hadn't told Eli or David about the trick she'd pulled to loosen Detroy's tongue. She was still horrified by her encounter with him. Just the thought of what he'd proposed made her skin crawl. And in retrospect she was amazed too. Amazed that someone as disgusting as Detroy could have thought she'd give herself to him, just like that. It was unbelievable. One thing was absolutely clear, Vincent Detroy had absolutely no scruples.

'So what do you know about him?' David asked.

'Detroy? Well, he describes himself as attorney-at-law,' Eli said, folding one flip-flopped foot on to his knee. 'One-man band. Specializes in offshore accounts. Holding companies.'

'Tax avoidance,' David explained to Emma. 'If American or European companies register here, they save themselves a hell of a lot of money. All they need is a plaque and an attorney with enough paperwork to show that the company is registered here.'

'But isn't that illegal?' Emma asked. 'All those millions running through here unregulated?'

Eli smiled. 'There are regulations. Just a lot fewer of them. Less red tape. But these companies still abide by the British Virgin Islands' law. That's what Detroy does. He dots the i's and crosses the t's. Files the accounts and makes it look as if it's all above board. We're subject to money-laundering laws here, the same as anywhere else. But Detroy's good at what he does. He might not break the law, but he does bend it. As far as he can.'

Emma cut to the chase. 'Surely you must be able to get a warrant or something so that we could search the offices and the accounts.'

'Not unless you've got hard evidence that the law has been

broken, by him, here on the island. Otherwise there's no way a judge is going to give a warrant.'

'But all the money that was in Platinum Reach, it was stolen.'

'So you say. And for what it's worth, I believe you. But my answer's the same. Unless you can get me proof, there's nothing I can do. I'm sorry,' he said, turning to David, 'I really am.'

'So what do we do now?' Emma asked after Eli had gone. 'I'm sure there's a link between Platinum Reach and Matryoshka-Enterprises. Think about it, it sounds Russian. And if the director of Matryoshka-Enterprises is coming tomorrow . . .'

'. . . then I think we should keep watch on the building. See who's going in and out of there,' David said.

'I'll stay in the café opposite,' Emma volunteered.

'You can't stay all day,' David said. 'Not in this weather.'

'I'll stay day and night. I don't care,' Emma replied.

'I'll do it,' Rufus said, standing up to his full height of six feet five. His voice was deep, yet soft. 'No one will notice if I'm hanging around.'

'I think it's a good idea, Emma. You're exhausted,' David reasoned. 'Let Rufus keep a lookout. As soon as anything happens, he can call us.'

'Are you sure?' Emma asked.

'I'm sure. I want you to go back to the house. You need some rest.'

Emma smiled weakly at him. He was right, of course, but she'd rather be there herself. Would someone really turn up at the offices? she wondered. Someone who could give her the information she needed? She couldn't believe she had no legal recourse to get at the information on that computer. In spite of all those millions that had been lost. The thought of poor Pim and all the other investors; a low-life toad like Detroy was getting away with murder. Literally.

Well, perhaps it was time she stopped playing by the rules, Emma thought as she stared at the distant lightning. Perhaps it was time she prepared herself to fight fire with fire.

Much later that night, Emma sat in the corner of the old snooker room on the low sofa with David, beneath a copper hanging light. A fan whirred beside them cooling the humid air. Louis lay curled up at their feet, gently snoring.

On the glass chess table beside them was a bottle of Balvenie, Julian's favourite single malt whisky, two tumblers and a pile of battered photo albums. Ella Fitzgerald played on the sound system. Emma had begged David not to play the songs that reminded her so much of Julian, but David had decided that some nostalgia would be good for them both, to banish the disappointment of their meeting with Eli and to get them back to themselves.

David poured another finger of whisky into Emma's glass.

'I'm getting pissed,' she said with a sniff.

'So am I,' David said. 'Julian would approve.'

Emma let out a weary laugh. 'I can't believe you kept these photos.' She stroked the photo of her, David and Julian, and a whole gang of other people at a yacht regatta twenty years ago. Cosmo was just a boy, laughing as David held him high on his shoulder, a trophy in his hand. 'And what's even more un-believable is that you put them into albums.'

'Why's that unbelievable?' David asked.

'I wouldn't have thought you'd have had the time. Too busy partying.'

'You may disapprove of my lifestyle, Emma, but some things are precious and worth preserving. Like pictures of all my favourite people. Good memories are what it's all about.'

'Are you telling me that underneath it all you're an old softie?'

David pulled a face at her over the rim of his glass. 'You found me out.'

Emma smiled at him, feeling a surge of affection. She knew how hard he'd taken Julian's death and how much he was looking out for her.

'I don't even know where my photo albums are any more,' Emma said. She rubbed her face. 'It's all such a mess. When I think about all the ones of Cosmo as a baby . . .'

She trailed off, tears overwhelming her again. David moved in closer next to her and put his arms around her. He kissed her hair as she cried.

'Sorry,' she said.

'Don't be.'

'Ugh. It's just so damn painful.'

'It won't be for ever,' David said.

She looked up at him sharply. 'But don't you see? I don't want the pain to stop. If it does, then it'll mean I've got used to him being gone. And I never want to do that. I never want it to be normal that he's not here any more. Or OK that I'll sleep alone every night now for the rest of my life. I can't bear it. I can't.' She buried her head back in his shoulder, shuddering as tears ran down her face.

'Shh,' David soothed, stroking her hair.

It felt so good to be held. To be comforted and protected. This was how Julian had always made her feel: safe and loved. But at the same time she knew that David wasn't Julian. They were just friends and she was too old to be relying on him like this. He had no magic wand: he couldn't bring Julian back, couldn't turn back time. She pulled away from him and took a deep breath, forcing herself to smile.

'Sorry,' she said. 'I'm ruining this. We're supposed to be thinking happy thoughts. Remembering the good times.'

'That was the plan,' David said, pouring her more whisky.

'OK,' Emma said, pulling herself together. 'So tell me what you remember about him.' Would that help? Would talking about the wonderful man Julian had been make her stop thinking about his death? Well, it was certainly worth a try.

'So many things. Mostly that he was always so much better than me at everything,' David said with a sad laugh. 'I don't think I even beat him at tennis.'

'You were always much better at chasing women,' Emma teased with a smile. It still felt good to have David's arm around her. She leant back against him and felt herself relax.

'But he was the one who always caught them and kept them. He managed to keep the best one, anyway.'

David paused. Emma took a sip of whisky, lingering as she looked at the bottom of the glass, amazed that he'd raised a subject they'd never discussed on their own before.

'You know, Ems, you could always stay here. I mean, if you wanted to. My door is always open. This could be your home too.'

Emma could hear the sincerity in his voice. 'That's very sweet of you, darling, but I wouldn't want to cramp your style.'

'You're the last person in the world who could do that.' David's voice was so tender that Emma looked up. She could see how serious he was. 'You don't have to say anything, or commit to anything,' David hurried on. 'Only I want you to know that the offer is there.'

There was a beat as they stared at one another, but David's telephone rang and he quickly got up to answer it. As he did, Emma realized how woozy the whisky had made her. She watched David talking. She was unsure of what the moment just now had meant. Was he offering her friendship? Or had he meant something more than that? Had he really been carrying a torch for her all these years? Could he still find her attractive? Even now?

He turned to face her. 'That was Rufus,' he said.

Emma felt as if she'd just been thrown into an icy lake. 'What's going on? Has anyone been in or out of there?'

'No. He rang to tell us that he thinks someone else is watching the building too.'

CHAPTER TWENTY-NINE

Frankie watched a road sign whizz past. They were speeding out of Road Town along the coast road. The huge black guy sitting beside Frankie in the front of the jeep had introduced himself as Rufus.

'It's gonna get bumpy. Hold on,' Rufus called as they shuddered over the pot-hole-ridden, mud-slicked road.

Frankie pulled at her hair, which was blowing into her carefully applied lip gloss and tucked it down the collar of her cropped combat jacket – one of Todd's PA Claire's trendy freebies. She hoped that by the time she arrived to see Alex, she didn't look too much of a state. She'd hardly slept last night, not least because of the storm, but knowing that today was the day she would finally get to see him.

She hadn't been to the Caribbean since she'd first taken the job aboard *Pushkin* and she'd forgotten just how inviting those waters were, how intoxicating the colours, the sheer vibrancy of the place.

And now as they headed inland from the coast, the road they were following grew rougher, as if the tourist dollars which funded the rest of the island hadn't quite stretched this far. Rufus wasn't kidding about the bumps. Frankie's teeth were rattling as the jeep twisted through the rutted tarmac.

The land was rougher too, less cultivated. In fewer than ten minutes they were cutting through thick jungle. Lushly vegetated hills stretched up either side of the jeep. She looked at the birds now flying down to the sparkling ocean which she glimpsed through the trees.

Rufus waved as they passed a wooden roadside shack. A pretty woman waved back, flashing them a smile. Some kids playing cricket, using a petrol can as stumps, ran a little way after them as the jeep drove past, beeping its horn.

It was good to see real people again, Frankie thought, and to be out in the open air. Ever since she'd caught the puddle-jumper down from Puerto Rico a few days ago, she'd relished her feeling fo freedom. She'd seen so much in the last few weeks: Alex's riad, the hotel in Cannes, Todd's French villa. Then Todd's Lear jet, which had flown them back to his palatial mansion in Beverly Hills. But their existence had been so enclosed, cut-off, defended. It had been like living in a series of castles, where the cost of all that opulence had been a loss of personal freedom. Frankie realized now, more than ever, why Alex loved his place in Marrakech so much.

Frankie thought of all the conversations she'd had with Todd as their friendship had developed and they'd walked through the walled gardens of his residences learning the lines for his play.

If only Alex had known that Todd was gay. If only he could see what a great person Todd was, then none of their stupid misunderstanding would have happened. And even though Todd had sworn her to secrecy, Frankie was here on a mission to get Alex back. And she *would* get him back, she'd make sure of it. With a face and a heart like hers, Todd had told her, how could she fail?

But it was one thing to be buoyed up by Todd's enthusiasm about her romantic trip to the BVIs, it was quite another to be here. As the jeep turned into the drive of a huge mansion, she felt jittery with nerves.

Since he'd stopped her outside Heavenly House (which had looked absolutely nothing like the place she'd imagined when she'd seen Alex first write it down on *Pushkin*) and asked her why she was here, Rufus had said very little. She'd said she was here to meet Alexei Rodokov, that she knew he was due at this address today. In the face of his further silence, she panicked. She'd then lied and told him she was one of Alex's colleagues.

He'd stepped away from her and made a discreet phone call. Then he'd told her that she needed to come with him. He worked for Alex and he'd take her to him.

And now Frankie was just seconds away from seeing Alex. She looked up at the stone mansion. It was typical Alex: elegant, understated; probably an old plantation property, she guessed. Rich in history, just like Alex's riad in Morocco had been.

Would he keep horses here too? she wondered. Would they end up riding through these hills together and watching the sun set over the distant horizon?

Yet it was only now as they came to a stop outside the mansion's colonnaded front door that the possibility of failure occurred to her.

What if Khordinsky was with Alex? What if he was furious that she was interrupting a business meeting? What if Khordinsky stopped her from speaking to Alex? Or Alex still flatly refused to give her an opportunity to explain herself?

She would have to deal with it, she told herself, remembering her resolution in the police cell to be brave. She was here, wasn't she? What more could she do to prove to Alex how much their relationship meant to her? And if she had to, she'd confront Khordinsky and expose him for the liar he was. She'd risk Khordinsky's wrath and his reputation for violence. Alex would have to protect her once he found out she was telling the truth.

Frankie followed Rufus through the open front door and across a large marbled entrance hall, down a short corridor with white painted floorboards and into a vast kitchen overlooking a colourful garden at the back of the house.

A man and a woman, both in their late forties, sat at an old wooden table. The woman looked up from the newspaper she'd been reading, then stood and stared hard into Frankie's eyes. She was small with stylish short copper hair swept back from her face with sunglasses and she was wearing a loose white linen smock top and trousers.

She glanced anxiously across at a man, who was talking into a cell phone. He was English, educated and wealthy. He finished his call and placed the phone on the table. He stood up. He was tall with amazing blue eyes and reddish-blond hair.

'This is her,' Rufus said to them both. He clicked at the Labrador, who followed him towards the kitchen screen door. 'I've left Eli there watching the offices. He'll call if he sees anything,' he said to the man. As Rufus went through the door with the dog, the man touched his arm and thanked him.

Frankie was confused. Where was Alex? Were these people his staff? They certainly didn't look like it. Why was some guy called Eli watching the offices? It didn't make sense.

'Um . . .' Frankie began. 'I'm not sure I'm in the right place . . .'

'I'm Emma Harvey,' the woman said. 'And this is my friend David Coulter.'

'I don't understand?'

'I'm afraid we've rather tricked you,' David said.

'You mean Alex isn't here?' Frankie said. 'But I thought—'

'Who's Alex?' Emma asked.

'Alexei Rodokov,' Frankie said. 'I thought Rufus was bringing me to meet Alex? Here?'

David and Emma exchanged a look. 'Yes,' David said. 'I'm afraid Rufus lied. My fault, not his. I told him to get you here no matter what it took. Telling you what you wanted to hear seemed like the easiest way.'

'But that's kidnapping,' Frankie said, horrified at how easily she'd been duped, the feeling of freedom she'd been so enjoying evaporating.

David grimaced. 'Um, technically, for it to be kidnapping you'd have to have been brought here against your will.'

'Call it what you will, you've still brought me here under completely false pretences.'

Emma cleared her throat. 'You said Alexei Rodokov. He's Russian, I take it?'

'What of it?' Frankie demanded, no longer in the mood to play along, not while she didn't have a clue who these people were.

'He's not anything to do with Yuri Khordinsky, is he?' Emma asked.

Frankie was getting more and more confused. 'Khordinsky is his boss. Why?'

Emma covered her face.

'Can someone please tell me what's going on?' Frankie asked.

'You'd better sit down,' David said. 'I think we've all got a lot of explaining to do.'

Frankie stared at Emma and David in astonishment, her mind spinning from everything they'd just told her about poor Emma's husband and the fake platinum mine. About all the investors who'd been fleeced, the money that had disappeared here in Tortola and about Khordinsky moving into Emma's ancestral home.

Her overriding reaction was of pity for Emma, for the loss of her husband. But Frankie felt something else equally powerful as she stared at the older woman. In Emma's eyes she saw kinship. Solidarity. She was looking at another woman whose life Khordinsky had decided to destroy.

Frankie had always worked on instinct and followed her heart. It was no different now. She trusted Emma automatically. She could sense the honesty in her. Her panic over having been tricked into coming subsided. Fate had brought her here. Emma was just after information. The same as her.

'Listen, Frankie, you seem like an intelligent girl,' David said. 'But I have to tell you, I don't like the sound of this.' He glanced at Emma. 'If this Rodokov guy is linked to Julian's companies in any way, then there's every chance that he's involved in the fraud. I mean, have you any idea what poor Julian went through? And if your boyfriend is involved then—'

'But I know Alex had nothing to do with it,' Frankie insisted. 'Well,' she added, determined not to lie, 'I don't know for sure.' She turned to Emma, appealing to her. 'But I do know that he wouldn't have wanted anything to happen to your husband.'

But Emma's face was drawn. 'How do you know? Why do you trust him so much?'

'Because I know him. Because . . .' Before Frankie could stop herself, she found herself blurting out everything about her relationship with Alex. About her time with him on the boat and in Morocco. She found herself defending him too, telling them about his work at the orphanage and his honesty and integrity.

She was desperate for them not to put Alex and Khordinsky in the same camp, because they weren't the same – were they? They couldn't be. Not in a million years.

She also told them about Alex's blind loyalty to Khordinsky. 'But I know that Khordinsky is using him,' Frankie explained. 'He went to great lengths to set me up and get me away from Alex. He's clever: Alex knew nothing about it. And Alex trusts him. So Khordinsky could say anything he wanted to Alex and he'd believe it. Which is why I think he's using him to front his companies.'

'But if he's here to shut down all those companies,' David said, 'and there is a link between Matryoshka-Enterprises and Platinum Reach, then surely that proves that Alex knows all about the missing money? Surely he's here to close down the paper trail?'

'I don't think so. Alex thinks he's coming here to sign off paperwork on dormant companies. He talked about it as if it was tedious admin.'

'You obviously care about him a great deal,' Emma said.

Frankie nodded. 'Yes I do.'

'Excuse me, David,' Rufus said, appearing in the doorway with another, shorter man. Emma immediately looked worried.

David went out of the room for a moment. When he returned he said, 'I've got to go down to the mooring. The yacht's breaking loose. But I want you both to stay here,' he went on. 'Promise me. You're not to do anything stupid.'

As soon as David had gone, Frankie turned to Emma. 'Look, Emma, it seems to me that you've borne the brunt of people thinking Julian was a coward when you know he wasn't. And I know it seems to you as if Alex could be involved with this fraud with the platinum mine, but you have to believe me on this one. Alex is a man of integrity. I know it. And I'll prove it to you.'

Emma nodded, biting her lip.

'Alex said he'd be here today: he's going to visit those offices. I've got to be there too. I've got to see if I can talk to him. This is my only chance. So I'm going back there, OK?'

'If you're going, then I'm coming with you,' Emma said. 'That other man who was with Rufus just now, he was Eli. He was meant to be watching Detroy's offices, but he obviously isn't.'

'But what about your . . .?' She nearly said 'boyfriend'. It was obvious to Frankie that David cared very deeply about Emma. 'What about David?'

'No. This is too important,' Emma said. 'If I tell him we're going back there, he'll only try and stop us. It's best not to tell him at all.'

Frankie nodded at Emma. She could see that the older woman had made a decision: she would be Frankie's ally. Frankie smiled to herself. Yes, that's what she'd got here. Someone with a common goal: to break down Khordinsky's web of lies.

She reached out her hand and Emma took it and they shook.

'To uncovering the truth,' Emma said, her bright eyes steely with determination.

'The truth,' Frankie agreed, and they both stood up and walked together, side by side, to the door.

Emma and Frankie soon made it back to Road Town, with the help of Johnnie, the local taxi driver, who hung out at the bar in Sopher's Hole'.

Johnnie was an amicable man, who drove slowly, asking Emma questions about Julian, slowing down to look in the rear-view mirror as Emma replied. Emma answered as best she could and Frankie could tell how painful it was for her. But she also knew that Emma was just as frustrated as Frankie. Emma glanced at Frankie, as if to apologize for Johnnie. As they reached the centre of Road Town, Johnnie stopped the car right in the middle of the road and started bantering with another driver, pointing to the mass of black clouds in the distance.

'Oh God,' Emma said, glancing at her watch, then back at Frankie.

They weren't far from Heavenly House. Maybe a five-minute walk. Frankie felt apprehension growing inside her. What if Alex was already there? What if she'd missed her chance?

Each second hung heavy, like a tolling bell, as Johnnie continued to chat.

'Please,' Frankie finally interrupted him. 'Can we just—'

She never finished her sentence. A shiny black SUV had just crossed the road ahead of them, coming from the direction of Heavenly House. It slowed at the entrance to the harbour, less than twenty metres from where Frankie and Emma were in the taxi.

The driver's window dropped. The SUV drove through on to the dock, where the most expensive yachts were moored.

The SUV was far too sleek to be local. Too moneyed. Too Russian. Frankie knew in her guts that Alex was inside.

She didn't waste another second.

'Where are you going?' Emma called as Frankie scrambled out of the taxi.

But Frankie had no time to reply. She ran across the road and ducked under the security barrier, ignoring the shouts of the guards in the booths to its side. At the far end of the pier, a hundred metres away, the SUV had stopped next to a silver seaplane which bobbed in the choppy harbour water.

Frankie shaded her eyes, watching as several men got out. And then she saw Alex and her heart jolted, her legs automatically moving as if a starter pistol had gone off. She called out, frantically sprinting up the jetty. But Alex didn't hear her and didn't turn to see her.

'Wait! Wait!' she shouted, frantic and breathless, running with all her might, but it was too late. The seaplane was already drifting away. As she reached the end of the jetty, she watched the seaplane speed across the water. She put her hands on her knees, her heart thumping wildly in her throat. As she looked up, panting, she saw the seaplane take off into the air.

'Shit!' she cried out. 'Shit. Shit. Shit.'

Her first thought was that it was Emma and David's fault. If they hadn't tricked her into going to David's house, then she'd have been at Detroy's offices to intercept Alex when he'd arrived. But then she remembered she and Emma were on the same side. It was just rotten timing, that was all.

Not that this made her feel any better. She wanted to scream. To have travelled all this way and to have missed him by mere seconds ... it was too cruel to be true. As if the fate she'd thought had brought her to Emma was now playing a trick on her.

She shielded her eyes as lightning momentarily illuminated the dark clouds. Already Alex's plane was just a black line, tiny as a seagull. Then it headed into the clouds and was gone, running from the storm that was heading this way.

Frankie shivered as lightning flickered again. She wondered where he was rushing off to. What task had Khordinsky lined up for him next? It could be anything. Anywhere.

A heavy hand gripped her shoulder. 'What you doing, lady?' the guard demanded.

Frankie shook herself free. 'Do you know where that plane's going?'

'No, but it's the last one allowed out. The storm's coming. And you're not supposed to be here. You'd better get going.'

Frankie saw Emma waving at her frantically from the other side of the barrier. Her hope lifted slightly. She wasn't alone. Emma could help her.

'Sorry,' Frankie said to the guard, 'I won't bother you again.'

'Was it him?' Emma asked, as Frankie reached her. 'Your Alex?'

'I'm afraid so.' Frankie bit down on her lip to stop it from trembling. She didn't want to make a fool of herself in front of this woman who'd suffered so much more than her, but who still hadn't given up hope.

'It's OK. I'm sorry,' Emma said. She laid her hand on Frankie's arm.

'Me too. And for you as well,' Frankie added. 'Because without Alex you haven't got anything either, have you? This is such a disaster.'

Emma pulled her jacket closer around her as heavy raindrops started to spit. 'That's not entirely true.'

'What is it?' Frankie asked, following Emma as she ducked against the wind and headed across the road to the safety of the bus shelter.

When they'd run in from the onslaught of the rain, Emma turned to Frankie. 'Detroy,' she said. 'He's got a computer in his office. He said all the files were on there. If we could somehow get that computer out of there ... I don't know ... then maybe we could find someone who could—'

But Frankie was already grinning.

'No need. We don't have to,' Frankie said.

'What do you mean?' Emma asked.

'We don't need to get the computer out of there. All we need is to find a way of getting *me* in.'

The back door of Heavenly House gave easily. Its rusted lock was in the same state of disrepair as the rest of the building. Frankie stepped nervously inside. After stopping by the stationery store, where Frankie had bought a USB memory stick, they'd hung out in the café watching and waiting for Detroy to leave the building. And, sure enough, ten minutes ago, they'd seen him get on his moped, heading home like just about everyone in town, running for cover before the storm closed in.

But they still couldn't be sure that he wouldn't come back, or that he didn't have someone watching the offices himself. Emma had explained what had happened when she'd been alone with Detroy; they both knew what he'd be capable of if he found them snooping around his office.

Frankie glanced back over her shoulder at Emma, silhouetted in the dusky light of the open doorway. Wind howled down the alleyway that ran along the back of the buildings. A tin can rattled past. Frankie raised her finger to her lips and Emma nodded, quickly stepping inside behind her and heaving the windowless door closed.

Darkness enveloped them; the howl of the wind was cut to a muffled moan. Frankie's ears strained, listening for signs of life, but all she could hear was Emma's soft breathing at her back.

Frankie waited another full minute before she decided it was safe to move. Weak light filtered through from somewhere up ahead. The building was dank and smelt of mould. Frankie edged forward, keeping one arm outstretched, praying that whatever she touched, it wouldn't be warm, wouldn't be flesh.

Her other arm was raised above her head, gripping the long and heavy metal flashlight Emma had bought in the ship's chandlery further along the street. It was still switched off. They'd agreed they'd only use it when they needed to: once they reached Detroy's office upstairs.

The torch had been strong enough to shatter the back door's padlock. Frankie figured it would do the same for anyone who might be hiding here, waiting to take them by surprise.

Frankie stopped. Her hand had touched something solid. A dark shape loomed ahead of her in the corridor. Her whole body tensed like a fist ready to strike. Information dripped through to her mind. Whatever she was touching was cold and hard. Not alive then, she thought with relief. She breathed out, relaxing her grip on the torch.

As Frankie's eyes slowly grew accustomed to the gloom, she saw that her path was being blocked by a stack of wooden crates wedged up against the corridor wall. Each one had the words 'JONES INTERNATIONAL REMOVALS' stamped on their sides.

Frankie stood on tiptoe and peered at the shipping date on the side of the nearest crate. The pick-up date was tomorrow. Looked like Detroy wasn't planning on hanging around . . .

Which meant Emma had been right, Frankie thought. They'd had no choice but to break the law and break in. Not that this made what they were doing any less dangerous. She wished Emma had told David what they were planning, but Emma'd insisted on keeping him out of it. He'd never have let them risk it, she'd said. Which meant no one else knew they were here.

Still, it was too late to turn back now. Frankie pressed her back up against the damp corridor wall and edged sideways, squeezing past the crates. She reached the bottom of a staircase. The front door was shut. Still no sign of anyone else inside.

She began to climb, step by step. She hardly dared breathe. It got lighter the higher she got. Noisier too. The storm's rage was rising, but not as fast as Frankie's blood pressure. The wooden stairs softly creaked: Emma was following behind. Frankie stopped again to listen when she reached the tiny landing at the top. Then she opened the door to the office and went in.

She felt herself grinning with relief. The office was empty. Detroy hadn't come back. And he hadn't left a guard.

Thin shafts of light stretched in through the slats of the closed wooden shutters. Frankie hurried over to the nearest window and peered outside. The street was deserted. Lights glowed iridescent, like a chain of pearls, behind the closed doors and windows of the buildings overlooking the harbour. Boats swayed back and forth like drunks. Palm leaves lurched against the blackening sky. A sudden spattering of rain against the windows made her jump.

'OK, let's do it,' Frankie said, running over to the desk and sitting down. 'You watch the window and I'll get digging.'

Frankie switched on the torch, keeping its beam pointed away from the windows, in case anybody of an overly curious nature happened to be passing by outside. She booted up the computer, plugged in her brand-new USB stick and got to work.

Within minutes, she'd accessed Detroy's hard drive and had started copying across recently accessed files and directories. She had no idea which ones would be useful or how easy their security would be to bypass later on; she just knew she had to get as much information as she could as quickly as she could.

'Hurry up, Frankie,' Emma said. 'This storm is getting really bad. David will be wondering where we are.'

Frankie glanced up. Emma was still at the window. There was a noise downstairs. A crashing sound. Then another.

'Shit!' Emma said, rushing to the office door.

'What's happening?' Frankie asked, eyes flickering between the computer screen and the doorway as she desperately continued to copy the rest of Detroy's hard drive files to her USB.

Another crash. Another burst of adrenalin raced through Frankie's veins.

'Frankie, stop!' Emma hissed. 'I don't think it's the storm. I think someone's down there.'

Frankie's fingers slipped on the keyboard, slick with sweat. On screen, the copy icon showed the final data transfer was almost complete. 'Two seconds,' she begged. 'I'm almost done.'

'No!' Emma shouted, running to the window. 'We've got to go. Now!'

More crashing, like packing crates being thrown angrily aside. A wave of fear swept over Frankie, but she still didn't quit her post.

The transfer icon flashed up finished.

'Yes!' Frankie hissed in triumph, tearing the memory stick

from the back of the computer. She leapt to her feet. That's when she heard the footsteps. They were pounding up the stairs like an avalanche. She grabbed for the torch but missed it, knocking it over instead. It rolled across the desk, clattering to the floor, sending a beam of light flickering across the room. Frankie rushed to join Emma who was struggling to open the window.

But it was too late. Three huge men with balaclavas over their faces burst into the office.

Frankie screamed as one of the men grabbed her, twisting her arm behind her back and slamming her down on the desk. She watched helplessly as another man grabbed Emma around the neck and pinioned her against the wall.

Frankie tried to break free but the more she struggled, the more fiercely she was crushed against the desk. Her jaw ached with pain. It felt like it was going to crack.

She watched in horror as the man holding Emma leant in close to her. A long knife appeared in his hand, glinting in the torchlight. Emma's eyes widened as he pressed its curved blade hard against her face.

'Mr Detroy says hello,' he said.

Frankie recognized the accent. It was Russian.

And these men had been sent here by Detroy. He must have known they'd been watching him all along.

The man slashed the knife downwards. Fast. Through Emma's cheek.

Frankie lunged desperately sideways. She had to help Emma. They had to get out. But it was useless. The man holding her laughed. He jerked her upright easily, as if she were a rag doll. He wrapped one arm round her throat. The other pressed something – some kind of cloth – down hard over her mouth and nose. A sickly chemical stink filled her nostrils.

Don't breathe in! a voice inside Frankie's head screamed. *Breathe in and you're dead!*

She watched helplessly as the third man threw a lighted rag in a bottle on to the desk. It burst into flames.

Frankie gagged. She couldn't hold her breath any longer. Acrid fumes filled her mouth. She started to choke.

She watched Emma fall to the floor.

Frankie's eyes filled with tears. The room shifted sideways, as if her legs had been kicked out from beneath her.

Then everything went black.

Frankie came round with a start. She was sitting on a chair, her hands tied behind her. She was naked. The lights were too bright. Startled, her eyes snapped shut. Fear swept over her. She tried to move, but she couldn't. It was as if the connection between her mind and body had been cut.

Loud rock music was playing. Too loud. But above the music there were voices too. Men's voices.

There was a flash. She winced.

Thirsty. She was so thirsty.

She felt a bottle against her lips. Water.

Then it had gone. In the light she turned her face up, groping for more liquid with her tongue.

Flash. Flash.

Then something else. Not the water now. Hot and sticky. Over her mouth and dripping on her chin.

Flash.

'Suck it, bitch,' she heard. Her hair was being grabbed. Then something was in her mouth. Something hard. Flesh.

She gagged and tried to scream, but all she heard was a muffled moan. And she realized it was her own. She couldn't move.

Flash. Flash.

She was blinded by the light now. Closer. Closer. And she was choking.

Again she tried to struggle, but it was as if she were swimming in glue.

'You getting it?' she heard a man say. 'You getting it all? Let's show Rodokov what this dirty little bitch is really like.'

CHAPTER THIRTY

In the small Road Town hospital, rain hammered against the window. Emma's cheek ached like crazy, despite all the painkillers she'd been given. She couldn't stop shaking as the doctor held her chin, pointing her face up to the light to finish the dressing.

Emma had looked at the wound once in the mirror and once was enough. It had nearly made her sick. And even though these temporary stitches were now holding her cheek together, just the memory of her cheek flapping made every nerve in her body scream.

'You're being very brave, Lady Emma. All done,' the doctor said, peeling off his surgical gloves. 'That's the best I can do for now. But I'm afraid you're going to have to get proper plastic surgery, otherwise you'll have a very bad scar. There's no one here who can do it. I suggest that you get back to the UK or the States as quickly as you can.'

Emma shook her head. There was no way she was going anywhere until she found Frankie.

Emma knew she'd been lucky to escape Detroy's building alive. The Russian thugs who'd attacked them had left her bleeding and choking on the floor. Through the swirling madness of smoke and flames, she'd watched them bundle Frankie's limp body through the doorway. Emma had struggled to her feet and staggered after them, but she'd been too slow. Locked in shock, half asphyxiated, she'd stumbled down the stairs, through the open front door and out on to the pavement. Through the howling wind and driving rain, she'd heard the screech of tyres. A blacked-out BMW raced away from her down the street into the dark.

Now Emma felt racked with guilt and furious with herself for letting them get away. She should have moved faster. Fought back. Not just sat there on the floor. So what if she'd been cut? So what if she'd been choking? She should still have done something and she hated herself for the fact that she hadn't.

Because it hadn't been the pain or the smoke that had paralysed her for those precious few moments. It had been fear. She'd played dead and waited for them to go before she'd got out herself. And if she hadn't ... if she'd been stronger, braver, she would have got out quicker. In time to see the BMW up close, get its number plate: she'd have had something to tell the police to help get Frankie back.

This was all her fault. She should never have made Frankie break into that office with her. But she'd needed answers. Needed something ... anything ... that might throw light on what had happened to Julian. And being with Frankie had made her feel for the first time since Julian's death that she might get them.

Julian. Her darling Julian. Her heart cried out for him now. For the strength and comfort that he'd always given her in times of crisis. But he'd never be able to kiss her better ever again. He'd never be there to lean on. The knowledge of this felt like a fresh wound far worse than anything a knife could do.

'Christ, you're so lucky to be alive,' David said, reaching out and squeezing her hand. Emma knew how furious he was that she'd broken into Detroy's office. She could tell that he was biting back a lecture on how stupid she'd been.

'But if those bastards did this to me, what are they doing to Frankie? And Cosmo?' she said, her voice muffled and weird from the anaesthetic in her cheek. It hurt to talk but she went on, 'Oh God, Cosmo. David, you've got to get hold of him. You've got to warn him. If they catch him sniffing around their business ... they could do much worse.' Emma's stomach churned at the thought. Her little boy. These animals would eat him alive.

'I've done all I can,' said David, soothing her. 'I've left messages for him on his UK phone and his mobile. And emailed him too. I've called Hugo and Victoria. But I've heard nothing back.'

'Oh God,' she murmured, her mind refocusing. 'Where the hell is she?'

'Frankie, you mean?' David said. 'Listen, Emma, I was thinking ... we hardly know her. And you heard it from her yourself, she's in pretty deep with this Rodokov guy. Why should you trust her? I mean, we have no idea how far she's involved. I'm not saying that it's not terrible that those guys took her, but we don't know all the facts. She could be mixed up in all sorts of stuff. And I think it's best if you just focus on yourself for now and rest—'

'No.' Emma cut David off, her eyes flashing at him, then turned back in misery to stare out of the window. It was now over three hours since she and Frankie had broken into Detroy's and it would be nightfall soon. Only hours, yet Emma's whole world had imploded. She'd felt so buoyed up with confidence with Frankie, so full of determination and hope. Frankie hadn't thought for a second she was being paranoid about Khordinsky. She'd been totally understanding of Emma's plight and Emma had been grateful. In Frankie she'd seen something of herself: her determination and total conviction about her feelings.

But everything that could go wrong had gone wrong. Frankie had been taken and the evidence of the corruption involving Platinum Holdings had disappeared with her. In addition to the injury she'd sustained, Emma was also now in trouble with the police.

When she'd called them to report the fire and Frankie's abduction, she'd also had to confess being in Detroy's office. At least she'd had the common sense to claim the back door was already open, which meant the police might not press charges. Unless, of course, Detroy chose to do so himself. Though that seemed pretty unlikely, seeing as he seemed to have vanished off the island.

The police had already searched the dives he usually frequented, as well as his house. They'd found nothing. Apart from a few items in the fridge and a camp bed, the place had been empty. Detroy had obviously been planning this little disappearing act for weeks. And with him gone, there was no way to track down the Russians who'd taken Frankie.

Even if the police did discover whatever rock Detroy was hiding under, they only had Emma's word that he'd sent the three thugs round to torch the building.

Emma jumped as the door opened and Eli came in.

'Have you found her?' Emma asked, desperately searching the policeman's eyes for a glimmer of hope.

He shook his head. 'Nothing. But we're still looking. The good news is that because of the storm, the chances are that she's still on the island. The bad news is it's a big island and with no means of identifying these men, they could be anywhere by now.'

'But what about the car?' David asked. 'And their accents?'

'My men are doing what they can, but they've got other priorities to deal with as well. The storm's brought down three apartment blocks and the power lines around the school. We're getting reports of further damage all the time.'

Emma's cheeks burnt with shame. The implication was obvious: Eli's resources were already overstretched. His people had more than enough to deal with without her having added to their load. 'It'll be easier in the morning,' he said. 'I've already notified the coastguard to be on the lookout for anything suspicious.'

'But by the morning it might be too late,' Emma said, her cheek screaming with pain.

'I'm afraid all we can do now is wait,' Eli said, his look making it clear that the subject was closed.

Emma bit her lip, all hope now extinguished. Again, Emma saw the knife blade flashing in her mind. Poor Frankie. She was just a kid with her whole life ahead of her.

If she wasn't already dead.

It wasn't until the storm had blown itself out and the dawn had broken over the wind-lashed harbour that Frankie showed up. Eli brought her over to David's house early. He'd had a call from the cab driver, Johnnie, who'd found her wandering around Sopher's Hole, he explained to Emma and David at the door, as a policewoman helped Frankie out of the police car parked on the drive.

'Oh thank God,' Emma said, starting to run to hug Frankie, but Eli held her arm.

'She was pretty disorientated when we picked her up,' he said in a low voice. 'We had a doctor check her over at the station. She seems fine. Some bruising around the neck consistent with what happened in Detroy's office.'

Frankie was walking towards them now, but Eli hadn't finished.

'But she's experiencing some memory loss. From when she last saw you. It's not unusual for cases of extreme shock to trigger localized amnesia.' Eli frowned. 'But it could be something worse.'

'What do you mean?' Emma asked.

'It's possible she's been drugged. Rohypnol, for example, or something similar. The doctor took blood tests. We'll know this afternoon.'

'OK,' Emma said, nodding to him in thanks.

'But I think she's OK now – aren't you, Frankie?' Eli said in his normal voice as Frankie reached the top of the steps.

Emma was so relieved to see her, but now she was worried too. Frankie looked pale and drawn. Emma hugged her, but Frankie seemed to stiffen at her touch and Emma drew back.

Eli looked at Emma, his eyebrows knitting together, but Emma could tell that Frankie didn't want to be crowded. She nodded to him and David to go. She watched them walk outside into the garden and light cigarettes. The low mumble of their conversation drifted in on the breeze and Emma suspected that Eli was telling David what he'd just told her. Emma focused her attention back on Frankie. She looked so fragile, like a ghost of her former self.

'Come, sweetie,' she said. 'Come in here.'

She took Frankie's hand and pulled her gently into the study off the hallway and shut the door.

'Your face,' Frankie mumbled, looking at Emma. 'I'm so sorry.'

Something was very wrong. The bubbly confident Frankie was gone. She seemed spaced-out and frightened.

'Where did they take you?' Emma asked, still holding Frankie's hand.

'I don't know,' Frankie said. She gripped Emma's hand tightly and Emma could tell how frightened she was. 'I can't remember anything. I can't seem to . . .' Her voice trailed off.

'Take your time,' Emma said, moving some magazines and helping her to sit down on the sofa. 'It'll come back. You're here now. You're safe.' She tried to sound comforting, but Frankie just looked even more confused.

Maybe it was just shock that was making Frankie act this way, Emma thought. Emma had read an article about it in the paper: how sometimes car-crash victims, even though they'd suffered no actual physical trauma, erased the entire incident from their mind.

She poured Frankie some coffee from the jug on the side and brought it back to where she was sitting.

'Tell me what you *do* remember,' Emma said, silently hoping that any memory loss was just temporary.

Frankie reached for the memory stick hanging on a cord under her T-shirt and she picked it up in her hand. 'I remember getting into Detroy's office. I'll still have the files on here,' Frankie said. 'Don't worry.'

Emma would have been lying if she'd claimed she didn't feel a jolt of excitement on seeing the stick. She couldn't believe those pigs had been stupid enough to let Frankie walk away with that around her neck. But maybe they hadn't known what it was, Emma reasoned. After all, Emma herself had only known because Cosmo had taken to wearing one at school like a necklace. She couldn't believe their luck that Frankie still had it on her.

Emma waved her hand. 'We can talk about that later. Right now, I'm worried about you. I think you should rest. Sleep. Is there anything you need. Are you hungry?'

'No, let's see what I managed to get,' Frankie said.

Emma tried to stop her, but Frankie seemed so determined. She suddenly got up off the sofa and plugged in the USB stick into the back of David's laptop.

It was good to see Frankie typing. Whatever it was that had

affected her memory, it certainly didn't seem to have affected her aptitude.

Emma watched as the information downloaded. Hope spiralled inside her. There had to be something about Platinum Reach on here, didn't there? Some definitive evidence that would prove where the money had gone? Emma bit down on the knuckle of her thumb of her right hand. It was a habit she'd made herself grow out of after her tenth birthday, but she couldn't help herself now. She kept gnawing as she watched row after row of icons spread out across the screen as if Frankie was dealing with a deck of cards.

Emma hardly knew anything about computers, but this looked like a lot of information to her. The tension was unbearable. Had Detroy really slipped up and left all this evidence for them to find? What secrets did each of those brightly coloured boxes have to share? Had all the risks they'd taken been worth it after all?

Emma watched Frankie turn to face her, but the triumphant smile she'd been expecting wasn't there. A look of strained incomprehension was in its place.

'What is it?' Emma asked. She felt herself being hijacked by a feeling of dread. It was obvious something wasn't right.

'I'm not sure. The files I copied last night aren't here. There are just dozens of jpegs instead.'

'Jpegs?'

'You know . . . picture files,' Frankie explained. 'Photos.'

'But I don't understand,' Emma said. 'Photos of what?'

Frankie's skin had drained to the colour of alabaster. 'I suppose we'd better find out.'

The two women stared into each other's eyes for a second. Although of course she had no real way of knowing, Emma somehow felt that their minds had set out upon the same horrendous logical journey.

The three Russian thugs weren't stupid at all. They hadn't simply not noticed the memory stick around Frankie's neck, or the information she'd downloaded from Detroy's hard drive. They'd known exactly what it was worth. If they'd let her keep it, it could mean only one thing. They'd corrupted the information saved on it. They'd switched it for something they wanted her to see.

Frankie turned back to the screen. Her finger hovered over the mouse button as if she was taking a deep breath. Emma found herself doing likewise as she stared on.

Then Frankie hit the button. They watched the jpeg activate, ballooning to fill the whole screen. Then both Emma and Frankie's worst fears were confirmed.

'Oh Jesus,' Emma gasped, covering her mouth.

In the image, Frankie was naked on a chair. Two men were standing over her, their erect penises above her mouth.

'No . . . no,' Frankie gasped.

She started to retch. She wrapped her arms around herself, clawing at her back. Emma tried to hold her, but Frankie violently shook herself free. Frankie tried to stand, but her legs wouldn't hold her. She lurched sideways across the desk and began to whimper.

Emma glanced at the screen, over her shoulder, horrified. She could hardly bear to look at the vile image, but she needed to check something. She looked at Frankie's face on the screen. Eyes white. Barely seeing. Eli had been right, then. Rohypnol: the date-rape drug. No wonder Frankie couldn't remember anything.

Emma thought about all the other jpegs there'd been just now on the screen. What else had those sick bastards done?

The door behind them clicked. Emma quickly turned and hurriedly waved David away. She stood guard in silence over Frankie as her moaning turned to heart-wrenching sobs. Emma felt so helpless and shocked, she wanted to cry herself for the violation Frankie had suffered. It was so horrible. And so unfair.

She searched for words of comfort and for the first time since Julian's death she truly remembered her strength. She gently placed her hands on Frankie's shoulders and took a deep breath.

'Listen. Whatever they did to you,' she said with absolute certainty, 'it doesn't change who you are. It's over now. You're alive. And you're still you. Whatever they've tried to take from you . . . we won't let them. You hear me? We won't let them.'

Frankie looked up at her and wiped her face. 'Oh Emma,' she said.

'Can you remember anything at all? Any of this?'

Frankie shook her head firmly, clearing her throat. 'Nothing. Just being in the office with you when they cut your face. And . . .'

Frankie expression switched again. Something flashed in her eyes. Anger? Fear?

'Yes?' Emma encouraged, squeezing her hand.

'I remember now, them saying something about Alex seeing pictures. They meant these.' Frankie clutched Emma's arms so hard she nearly cried out in pain. 'They're going to show Alex,' she whimpered, 'and—'

'Shhh,' Emma soothed, gently prising her hands free. 'You look exhausted. You need to rest. Then we can talk about all of this. We need time to think.'

It was true. Emma did need time to think. Her mind whirred now with all the implications of those pictures on the screen. Were they evidence against Detroy? Would Eli have to see them? How bad were the rest of the images? Who else were those thugs intending these pictures for apart from Alex?

Frankie sat in silence for a moment, as if she saw the sense in what Emma was saying. But then she quickly turned back to the computer. She stared hard at the screen. At the image of herself. The two men violating her. She continued to stare for five seconds, ten, fifteen. She didn't even blink.

'No,' she said then. She gripped the mouse and shut the jpeg. She dragged it along with all the others into the trash icon at the corner of the screen.

'No,' she said again, her voice rising.

'What?' Emma asked, panicking now, fearful she was out of her depth. Frankie probably needed a doctor, a counsellor, or a psychiatrist – someone who could help. And surely these pictures, however vile, were evidence. She couldn't just put them in the trash, could she?

But before she could tell her to stop, Frankie tore the USB stick from the computer, put it down on the desk and brought a polished paperweight smashing down on it.

'Wait—'

'No,' Frankie said as she spun around to face Emma. 'We can't stay here. They left you for dead in the fire, but they let me go for a reason: to find out who else we were working with. To find out who else knows about Platinum Holdings. That stick could have been bugged. Or someone could have followed us here. The rest of them might be on their way already. We've got to get out of here now.'

'We can't,' Emma said. Frankie was being paranoid. She was exhausted, not thinking straight. She had to stop her. 'I'll get David,' she said. 'He'll know what to do.'

Frankie grabbed her arm. 'The longer we stay here, the more danger we're putting him in. Trust me, Emma. I know about this. I used to work for the Government in South Africa. I know how quickly people can wind up dead.'

'But—'

'What you just told me,' Frankie said, 'about them having taken nothing from me, about me still being myself. Well, I am.'

Emma stared into Frankie's eyes. They were bloodshot, but calm. Far from insane.

'If we're going to make right what they did, then the first thing we need to do is get out of here alive.'

Somehow Emma knew, right then, that Frankie was telling the truth. She also knew that she had no choice but to back her up. She swallowed hard. She didn't want to leave the comfort of David's home, but if they were putting him in danger, then she'd have to leave.

'But where will we go?' she asked.

'I've got a friend. An American. He'll be able to protect us. He'll know what to do. They'll never go after him. He's worth too much money to them, and he's way too famous. Now quickly give me the phone.'

Emma did as she was asked and watched in confusion as Frankie punched in a number. Who on earth was this person she was calling? Who was too famous and powerful for even the Bratva to touch?

'Get me Todd,' Frankie said. 'Todd Lands. Tell him it's Frankie and I need his help. Tell him I need it now.'

CHAPTER THIRTY-ONE

In Tenzin Marisco's studio, TV pin-up girl and topless model Monica DuCane straddled a black chair as a make-up artist applied one final brush of powder. Monica's famously ample breasts were poured into a white lace basque, her waist-length, white-blond hair piled into an elaborately curled beehive. She reached up and clawed her long red fingernails over the black codpieces of the two semi-naked male models who stood over her. The assistant tilted the light reflector disk just a fraction to bounce more light on to Monica's sultry pout and Peaches gave the thumbs-up. A second later, Tenzin, LA's most famous glamour photographer, started to shoot, crouching down, circling Monica DuCane with a telephoto lens, calling out a steady stream of superlatives, 'Yeah, baby, that's fabulous, fantastic. Look at me. Wow. Sensational . . .'

'So what happened then?' Ross Heartwood asked. Peaches could hear the shock in his voice. She hadn't meant to tell him so much. She hadn't meant to confide that she'd been on *Pushkin* and had been beaten up by Khordinsky. Nor that Alexei Rodokov had been responsible for getting her away from him.

But this was Ross, her dearest friend. The man she'd trusted her body to – and now her secrets. His phone call had come at a time when Peaches desperately needed to talk. In sharing the facts, she hoped that the pressure of them building inside her would go away.

She turned away from the set and quickly walked over to the back door of the studio. She pushed down the Exit bar and found herself standing in the small concrete yard in the fresh air. She leant back against the brick wall and held her cell phone close to her ear. She closed her eyes, remembering Alexei Rodokov's face.

'I swear to God, Ross, I thought he was going to kill me. But he didn't,' she said in hushed voice. 'He fired into the ground. Then he hissed into my ear. He told me to play dead if I wanted to live. It must have been because he wanted the bodyguard to think he'd done what Khordinsky had ordered him to.'

Peaches adjusted her large shades and baseball hat. She was still nervous as hell. What had happened on *Pushkin* had scared her shitless. She still had bruises on her cheekbone from Khordinsky's beating and her kidneys ached whenever she peed. She'd been checked out by a friend at the hospital, who'd told her that it was a miracle, but she had nothing seriously wrong with her that time and rest wouldn't fix. Even so, every time she thought about it, it made her feel sick.

And yet Alexei Rodokov had spared her.

'Why did he do that?' Ross asked, interrupting her thoughts.

It was a question Peaches had asked herself over and over. Right at the last moment, he hadn't done his master's bidding and Peaches didn't know why. Was he a coward, or was he merciful? She hated owing anyone a nickel, let alone a guy like Alexei Rodokov her life.

'I guess he didn't want it on his conscience. He took off pretty quickly.'

'Hoods don't have consciences,' Ross said. 'People like Khordinsky and Rodokov waste people all the time. Christ, you don't even get initiated into those kind of gang circles unless you've got a string of murders under your belt.'

Peaches knew Ross was right, of course. On paper, at least. On paper, Rodokov had to be a butcher himself to be running with a psychopath like Khordinsky.

But off paper . . . in the flesh . . . well, Alexei Rodokov didn't quite fit the mould. Peaches remembered how he'd looked when she'd first seen him in his office on *Pushkin*: like a businessman – a banker or a broker. Peaches had a nose for these things. She had to, after the life she'd had. She'd come to rely on her knack of summing people up in a blink. Nine times out of ten, her first impressions were her last impressions too. Rodokov hadn't looked like a gangster the first time she'd met him. Hadn't acted like one at the party his boss had thrown for him. And – most crucially – hadn't acted like one when he'd been ordered to blow her away.

The word 'why' multiplied and flocked inside her. But she could find no answer. All she knew was that she was damned lucky to be alive.

'Do you think he told Khordinsky he'd killed you?' Ross asked.

'I hope so,' Peaches said. 'Because if he finds out otherwise . . .'

'Jesus, Peaches,' Ross said. 'You don't think he might come after you, do you? Because if you do – even for a second – then we've got to get you someplace safe.'

'No. I'm sure I'm safe for now,' she said, although the truth was that she felt anything *but* safe. Since meeting Khordinsky, she felt as if she'd been marked out. That she was being watched all the time. Dark sunglasses staring out at her from the crowd at LAX. The black Hummer behind her on the freeway more than once. A Russian accent in a deli on Sunset. A tall man standing too close to her on a bar terrace in Bel-Air. Peaches hoped she was just being paranoid. She told herself that there was no way Rodokov would tell her master that he'd disobeyed his order – not without incurring Khordinsky's wrath himself.

Plus, she reminded herself that her true identity hadn't been compromised. Khordinsky had no idea who she was. She'd managed to find out that the other girls hadn't been questioned. They'd been whisked off the yacht the moment the trouble had started. They'd been paid off and dropped ashore, with all protestations about the whereabouts of Tammy brushed roughly aside. All of them had got home safely, according to Mandy who had called Peaches a couple of days ago looking for more work. And any thought that that girl

Nicki might have been a plant had turned out to be paranoia on Peaches' part. If the authorities had been on to her, they'd surely have made their presence felt by now, wouldn't they?

Even Valentin had gone quiet. She'd wondered at first whether he'd come after her, but either he hadn't heard about what happened on *Pushkin*, or he hadn't told Khordinsky that Peaches had been his contact for the girls.

But not all the loose ends had been so neatly tidied up. Peaches couldn't believe, in retrospect, how stupid her valedictory swipe at Khordinsky had been. How could she have taunted him with Irena's name like that?

So, she'd thought she was going to die. So what? How could she have thought that there wouldn't be repercussions to people other than herself?

The first call Peaches had made after she'd succeeded in getting Angela to wire her some money to a cash shop in Cannes was to Yana, her mother's nurse in the Moscow hotel. She'd told Yana to stay vigilant and tell no one where they were staying. And she'd made her promise that whatever happened, she wouldn't tell anyone Peaches' name.

Perhaps, Peaches thought, she should tell Yana to move with Irena to a different apartment. But Irena was too sick, and Peaches couldn't risk scaring her.

Peaches knew what a brute Khordinsky was. She was terrified he would track Irena down. And if he did, what the hell would he do?

Khordinsky. How easily he could have snubbed her life out. Having raped her first.

Her own father . . .

Peaches wished everything had been different. She'd screwed up and she hated herself for being so sloppy. She hadn't had a proper plan. She'd been so blinded by the need to see Khordinsky in the flesh that she hadn't thought through how to exact her revenge. Instead, stupidly, she'd relied on opportunism. She'd been impulsive, hoping she could rely on her instincts, and it had backfired.

How could she have thought that she would have – *could* have – killed him? Even in self-defence? She wasn't a murderer.

She knew now that whatever her next move was, she had to plan it carefully. She didn't want Khordinsky to die. Oh no. She didn't want him to have such a simple way out. She wanted him to suffer first. To realize what an animal he was.

But how could she get to him? Those bodyguards were everywhere. She knew that supplying call girls to a business-man like Khordinsky was one of the only ways of getting close to him. And now she'd blown the chance.

'Ross, is there something you're not telling me?' Peaches asked, suddenly aware that he'd gone very quiet.

'It's just . . .'

'Just?'

'There's something I've got to tell you – although it breaks all rules of patient confidentiality . . .'

Confidentiality? Peaches' hearing was as finely tuned to gos-sip as anyone else's in LA, but the tone of Ross's voice was all wrong for that. She tentatively asked him, 'What?'

'OK. It's just . . . this is *so* weird,' Ross said. 'You're the third person this week who's connected to Alexei Rodokov and Khordinsky. In fact, the two other women I met even hate Khordinsky as much as you do.'

Peaches didn't reply. She was too shocked. And confused. Who on earth could possibly hate Khordinsky as much as her? And how come Ross had met them? Peaches remembered the surgically enhanced prostitutes working the Moscow hotel. Was it possible Ross had met one of Khordinsky's girlfriends, over here for some type of treatment?

Peaches' mind was whirring faster than a Vegas slot machine because, above and beyond her shock and confusion, she sensed opportunity appearing on the horizon, like a lost ship she'd given up hope of ever seeing again.

Maybe these women would provide her with the 'in' she'd so desperately been searching for.

'Tell me everything,' she told Ross.

'It's too complicated to explain over the phone. I think you should come to New York. Like, as soon as you can. Tonight.'

'You're in New York?'

There were so many reasons not to go. Peaches looked back in through the studio doorway. Monica was being rearranged into another pose. The cancan girls with the nipple tassels were waiting in the background. Peaches would have to go back in and help any second. And on top of the photo shoot there were still a million details to finalize for the party.

But none of it mattered a damn. Not compared with taking another shot at Khordinsky.

'OK,' she said. 'I'll do what I can.'

CHAPTER THIRTY-TWO

Peaches stared out of the tinted window into the neon-daubed New York night as Todd Lands's brand-new chauffeur-driven customized Maybach 62S shimmied through the Manhattan traffic and turned up Fifth Avenue. Everyone noticed it. The tourists stopped and took pictures. Even the cab drivers honked their horns in awe.

Sealed off inside, a soft Mozart concerto played over the sound system and Peaches sat next to Ross, safely cradled in the squashy leather seats and black piano-lacquered interior. Ross leant forward and opened the fridge to refill their silver champagne flutes. Then he pressed a button and a velvet curtain slid back across the thick laminated glass that separated them from the driver, leaving them in their own private bubble.

Peaches sighed, glad to be in New York. Something about the early evening lights and the atmosphere of the place always lifted her soul. It always felt like a city of fresh beginnings to her, rather than a city full of broken dreams, like LA.

And Ross was here. Dear Ross. For the first time since her violent ejection from *Pushkin*, Peaches felt herself – albeit momentarily, she guessed – begin to relax. The champagne probably wasn't hurting either. Her thoughts had been so filled with the terror of what might have happened to her.

But Ross always made her live in the present. He reminded her of what was good about life, about all the possibilities for the future. Just sitting next to him, she felt more like herself than she had done in ages. Like she was in control again. No longer a victim: a boss.

She put her hand over Ross's wrist and squeezed. He leant across and nuzzled her neck. 'You smell divine,' he whispered in her ear.

He'd been so kind to her since he'd picked her up from the airport. He'd hugged her and tenderly touched her bruised face and assured her that it was only superficial. He'd brought ointment for her too: to reduce the swelling and accelerate the healing process. He'd told her she'd be back to looking like a goddess in less than a week. She'd smiled and simultaneously winced in pain, her jaw giving off a dull, low ache.

But at least she had managed a smile. And now she managed another.

'You like it? It's part of the brand range,' she said. 'My favourite. I'm calling it Peaches and Cream.'

Ross grinned back at her. 'I imagine that's exactly the thought that'll pop into the head of any man within a mile of you when they smell it.'

'Oh really?' she said. She looked out of the window again, buoyed up by Ross's compliment. He always made her feel more of a woman than anyone.

Ross still hadn't elaborated on these two women Peaches was about to meet. Said he'd been asked not to by Todd Lands. As in Mr Fucking Hollywood. Todd Lands was the one who was putting them all in touch.

Of course this information made Peaches more intrigued than ever. If these women knew Todd Lands, then most likely they weren't simply call girls like she'd previously assumed. Higher profile than that, Peaches was now guessing. Real pros. Or maybe even actresses, perhaps, even well-known ones.

If so, they wouldn't be the first to have got involved with gangsters or foreign billionaires. Peaches herself had once brokered a liaison between a horny Arab playboy and his favourite Oscar-winning actress, who'd needed a couple of extra million to secure the house of her dreams.

Was that what this was all about? Peaches wondered. A couple of Hollywood A-listers who'd got burnt after selling themselves out to the wrong thug? Well, it'd certainly explain the need for secrecy.

But somehow she doubted it. If Todd Lands was involved, then, judging from his no-sex-before-marriage stance, Peaches wouldn't mind betting these women were high-class hookers.

'I didn't even know you *knew* Todd Lands,' Peaches said. 'Is he a client? Do you do his work?'

'No. Believe it or not, Todd hasn't had anything done. He's one hundred per cent himself.'

Peaches sighed. 'Ross, you're being very mysterious about all of this. Why are we in Todd Lands's car? And why are these women at his apartment?'

'They're friends.'

Peaches laughed. 'Come on. Nobody is friends with Todd Lands. He's the least approachable guy in Hollywood. He's famous for the amount of attorneys he's got working for him—'

'Oh Peaches, listen. Stop. Just ... there's something you should know,' Ross interrupted, cutting her off. He sighed heavily, like he was lifting an enormous weight off his shoulders. Then he shifted in his seat towards her and she saw him take a deep breath. He chewed his lip, as if the words were like pins in his mouth.

Peaches felt her pulse race. She'd never seen Ross look like this. She held her breath, waiting for him to speak. Suddenly, the easy familiarity had disappeared. Something else had taken over. It was as if the rules had all changed. As if he were about to make some kind of confession that would change their relationship for ever.

Ross exhaled, preparing himself.

The suspense was killing Peaches, but still she didn't say anything. Ross looked down, putting his hands over hers. Then he looked directly at her. 'The thing is ...' he paused. 'The thing is that Todd and I ... we're ...'

Peaches stared at him.

And the penny dropped.

Could he possibly mean what she thought he meant?

Her mouth fell open. She searched his eyes. Surely it couldn't be true . . .

But she could see that it was.

There was a long beat. Peaches forced herself to recover. She knew she had to say something.

'Jesus Christ, Ross, you're a dark horse,' she said eventually. She was doing her best to cover her shock and surprise . . . and sense of betrayal too. This was huge. Enormous. It changed everything between them. Everything she knew about him.

Why? That's what she wanted to know. Why hadn't he told her before?

But then she stared into Ross's familiar eyes and she remembered how much they'd been through together. He was her best friend: she owed it to him to be supportive. She could tell from his ashen face what a huge deal this was to him.

'So what? Does everyone else know apart from me?'

'No, of course not. Nobody knows.'

Peaches paused, slightly mollified that he wasn't making a fool out of her. It genuinely *was* a secret. And boy, what a secret! She felt as if they were suddenly in uncharted territory. Everything that they said now was like virgin footsteps on an expanse of fresh snow. She was unsure what all of this meant, and she realized that was because she was finding out the truth for the first time. The unabashed, unashamed truth.

'So how long have you been dating Lands?' she demanded.

She'd teased him innumerable times about his sexuality, but she'd never really believed he was gay and so to hear Ross finally admitting to this whole secret side of his life – with Todd Lands, no less – felt totally weird.

She realized now that deep down inside there was a tiny part of her that had always hankered for Ross's celibacy to be somehow connected to her. Now that her fantasy in all its ridiculousness had surfaced and evaporated, she almost smiled at the absurdity of thinking that Ross might have been saving himself for her.

The truth, as always, was much more realistic. He was in a long-term relationship – with one of the most famous supposedly heterosexual men in the world! It was such a massive piece of information that Peaches could hardly believe it was for real.

'Todd and I have been together for three years.'

Peaches nearly choked on her champagne. 'Three years? But . . . wasn't he engaged to – what's that skinny bitch called? – Amy-Kay something?'

Ross smiled, the tension broken. 'Hmmm. That was a bit of a disaster. But she's disappeared now, thank God.'

No surprise there then, Peaches thought. None of Todd Lands's erstwhile other halves stayed famous for long after their relationships with him had finished: probably because Lands was powerful enough to sever their links with the studios with a single phone call, if he was even half the bastard the press made him out to be.

Though maybe that was all bullshit too. Peaches couldn't imagine someone like Ross dating a jerk. Her head spun with questions.

'So that's why he keeps all those attorneys on his payroll,' she said. 'To keep any rumours at bay.'

'To stamp on them flat,' Ross corrected her, a flash of pride in his eyes. 'They keep a lid on it all. We're very discreet.'

How the hell had they managed to keep it secret? If there'd been even one sniff of that one going around, Peaches would have been on to it immediately. In the circles she moved in, one indiscretion, one comment, one accidental sighting of them together and she'd have known all about it within half an hour.

She shook her head ruefully, thinking about the amount of times she'd flirted with Ross in the past, and the number of other women she'd watched stalk him like hungry cats. But Peaches truly didn't care what Ross's orientation was, as long as he was happy. She could tell from the nervous sparkle in his eyes that he was, and that he was proud, too, to be telling her that Todd Lands was his man.

'Why are you telling me this now?' she asked. 'I mean, you nearly had me convinced that you were happily celibate.'

'Because you've trusted me with your secret, so I owe it to you to trust you with mine. And besides, you're gonna meet him. You're the most intuitive person I've ever met. You saw us together . . . you'd have guessed in an instant.'

Images of Todd Lands flashed into Peaches' head. Todd swinging through the jungle in that trilogy he did in the early nineties, and more recently the sci-fi action hero that had made him internationally recognized. Not to mention the twenty-storey-high billboard for *Blue Zero* they'd just passed in Times Square with a close-up of Todd's face. The very same billboard, she now recalled, that Ross hadn't so much as glanced at as they'd driven past, the sly devil.

'How about I try some of that famous intuition now?' Peaches said.

Ross shrugged.

'The apartment in London. The mystery weekend getaways. Your château in France that you've never invited me to . . . all because of Todd?'

'That's right. The place in London is two houses backing on to each other. Even if the press worked out Todd owned them, they'd never catch us going in the same door.'

Peaches whistled. That was a hell of a lot of subterfuge to keep a relationship going. 'You're faithful then, the two of you?'

'Completely.'

'Not bi?'

'No. We love each other. Always will.'

'So what about all these girlfriends of his? What about his reputation? I even read about a new squeeze of his on the plane. Frankie someone. Not a bad ass on her, unless the photo had been airbrushed.'

'I'll let Todd tell you all about that,' Ross said, rubbing the side of his face. 'But for the record, it's all smoke.'

One hell of a smokescreen too, Peaches thought admiringly. Todd was a global brand, Goddamnit, and a heart-throb all over the world. And here she was sitting next to the man who really *did* have his heart, by the sound of it.

Peaches was no stranger to the concept of people creating illusions to mask the reality of their lives. She knew a thousand stories of happy marriages that were all a sham. But this? Ross and Todd? It was hard to get her head around.

'If you love each other, if you're this serious, then why don't you just come out?' she asked, but even as she asked it, she knew the impossibility of such a question. Todd's box-office success relied on women of all ages finding him attractive enough to fantasize about him. Their adoration would turn quickly to vitriol if they found out that he'd rather be in bed with their husband.

And Ross was just the same. Peaches remembered all the ladies in his waiting room. What would they do if their secret fantasies were quashed by the truth about Ross's sexuality?

She could see now why the two of them had kept it a secret for so long. Peaches knew better than anyone the double standards of Hollywood. No matter how much sleaze was under the surface, to really be successful, to be right at the very top, you had to maintain a veneer of squeaky-clean morality. It sucked, she knew, but she could hardly complain. She'd personally made a fortune out of such hypocrisy.

'It would ruin his career. Or so he thinks,' Ross said. 'But New York's a lot more liberal than LA. And Broadway's a world away from the studio lots. '

'Meaning . . . ?'

'Meaning Todd's about to do a huge Broadway show. We both think a theatre run is a good move. And I'm happy to set up a practice over here. It means we can spend more time together with much less risk of being caught out.'

'Wow,' she said. 'I can't believe it.'

'Yes, well, it feels weird telling you. I'm kind of used to living a double life.'

But there was no time to discuss it further. The chauffeur had stopped the car outside a 1930s neo-Gothic skyscraper next to Central Park.

'We're in the penthouse,' Ross said.

Peaches smiled. 'Tell me something I don't know,' she said, stepping out of the car.

She looked up towards the top of the skyscraper and the stars above. She felt a flutter of nerves.

Suddenly, she felt sure that her destiny was about to change.

CHAPTER THIRTY-THREE

Peaches stared at Todd Lands in the kitchen of the colossal open-plan apartment as he handed her a glass of Hildon mineral water. His face was so familiar, although she'd never met him in person. He was shorter than she'd imagined, but fit. Even fitter in the flesh than he was in his movies.

He was barefoot, his tanned manicured feet poking out of the bottom of trendy designer jeans. The sleeves on his black Armani dress shirt were rolled up and he stood facing her with his hands on his slim waist, like a general, or a monarch. Like Burton as Mark Antony, she thought. Or Brynner as the King of Siam. Like a man most at ease when he was in control.

She could tell as he turned on his most seductive smile that he was playing a well-rehearsed game. He didn't even glance at her bruises, let alone remark on them. This was a man who'd won female hearts on screen and off for over twenty years. He thought he knew where all the female buttons were and how and when to press them too. But he was no match for a pro like Peaches.

Todd Lands might be über-famous, but, hell, he was just an actor. Peaches had seen hundreds rise and fall. Literally.

No, Peaches could see right through his act, and with just

one bob of her eyebrow, she let him know that he wasn't in charge. That they were equals. Whatever went down here today with these two women Peaches had come to meet, Lands was going to have to play it – for want of a better word – straight. Dead straight. Peaches didn't know how much Ross had told him about her connection to Khordinsky, but if Todd was out to play some kind of power game, she needed him to know right away that, as far as Yuri Khordinsky was concerned, Peaches Gold was not going to be jerked around.

Still, she had to concede how smart he was. He was not to be underestimated. She'd never clocked before that he was gay, and someone who could pull off a global hoodwink like that was not to be messed with.

Of course, now that she knew he was gay, it was so damn obvious. Besides, Peaches thought wistfully, nobody this good-looking or eligible was ever straight.

She saw his eyes dart towards Ross's uncertainly. Had Ross told her about them? he was obviously thinking. It was clearly something that hadn't been agreed.

'So ... Peaches Gold,' he said, nodding and smiling. 'I've heard a lot about you.'

'Not as much as I've heard about *you*.' There. If it was confirmation he was after, he'd got it. By the truckload.

Todd Lands's smile stayed fixed for a second, then he turned on Ross, who'd gone a lighter shade of purple.

'You told her?' he demanded.

'I had to,' Ross said defensively. 'She'd have guessed. Anyway, you told Frankie.'

'Only because I was responsible for destroying her whole goddamned life.'

'Yeah? Well, for your information, Peaches' life hasn't exactly been a bed of roses lately either.'

Great, Peaches thought. This is all I need. The Bickersons. She decided it was time to crack the whip. 'OK, OK, don't start, you two,' she said. 'I won't snitch. As Ross is well aware, I know more secrets than a Beverly Hills priest. And I keep my mouth shut. I've got my reputation to consider.'

Ross and Todd glowered at each other, a whole silent conversation in just one look about who was to blame and how it felt to be outed in front of a stranger. Todd's eyes flickered back to Peaches, searching for signs of deceit. Finally, he nodded, seemingly satisfied.

'Now,' Peaches said, 'would one of you two please tell me about this cloak-and-dagger meeting you've set up?'

Todd and Ross looked at each other again, but this time their antipathy seemed to melt. To be replaced by what? Peaches wondered. Apprehension, certainly. But something else, too. Something more extreme. Something that looked to Peaches very like fear.

What could two powerful men like Ross and Todd have to fear here in the sanctuary of their own apartment?

The answer came back fast as a bullet, hitting Peaches right between the eyes. Khordinsky. Yuri Khordinsky. The true alpha dog. The one all other men cowered before.

The one, Peaches knew, that only a true bitch would be able to bring whimpering to his knees.

'They're on the roof,' Todd said.

'Take me to them,' Peaches said. 'Take me now.'

There were roof terraces and there were New York roof terraces. And then there was Todd Lands's New York roof terrace. The whole of the building top had been turned into a glorious English country garden, complete with a manicured lawn and trees and a honeysuckle archway leading to a grass pathway set between rose bushes. It was surrounded by buildings on three sides with the skyline of Manhattan across the park on the fourth. Peaches whistled, looking out at the Chrysler Building lit up in the distance.

She followed Ross and Todd to a seating area where two wrought-iron benches covered with white cushions looked out over the whole of Central Park below. Two women stood up from the benches as Peaches came towards them, a redhead and a blonde.

They weren't high-profile actresses. Peaches didn't recognize either of them. But she recognized a cautiousness about them both. They had to be pros. Just as she'd originally thought. And it made sense that Todd relied on the discretion of women from Peaches' profession. What other kind of women could he be friends with?

The redhead was older, shorter and was wearing tailored

pants and a stylish orange shirt. Plenty of men would still pay for a slice of that pie, Peaches thought. Yep, whoever this woman was, she'd been in the game a long time, from the looks of things. It was obvious from the slash on her face: the sure sign of a gangster's hand. This woman had crossed the wrong bad-ass. It always happened sooner or later.

Had Khordinsky done it? Peaches wondered immediately. Was that what they were here to discuss?

The younger girl, the blonde, was a knockout. Definitely a ten, Peaches thought, marking her instinctively against her criteria for the best jobs she could send her out to. She was wearing tight jeans with a skinny black T-shirt and high wedges, her lustrous blond hair tumbling down her back from beneath a Yankees baseball cap.

'Peaches, this is Lady Emma Harvey,' Ross said, stopping now in front of the two women and introducing the redhead.

'Lady?' Peaches asked. 'Is that your street name?'

'My what?' the redhead asked, confused. Her accent was English. On the plummy side, Peaches thought.

'Your working name, honey,' Peaches said, thinking that they probably had different lingo over the pond. 'Your pimp give it you?'

Emma blushed deeply. 'I . . . I don't know what you mean. I don't have a pimp.'

Ross came to the rescue. 'Er, Peaches, I didn't explain. Emma really *is* a lady. Titled. From England.'

Peaches raised her eyebrows. So Lady Emma Harvey was a real lady then. So what? For one thing, anyone could buy a title these days. That still didn't mean that Peaches' theory about these two being pros was wrong.

And even if she was the real deal, there were probably plenty of hard-up English aristos. Women with expensive taste who'd tangle with the likes of Khordinsky to make a pile. Well, whatever this woman was, and whatever her connection to Khordinsky may be, Peaches wasn't about to be intimidated by her.

She'd met plenty of hard-nosed aristocratic types like Lady Emma before, who thought because of their education, blood-lines and big country houses the world owed them. She'd lost count of the men married to women like Emma who'd crossed her path, most of them fetishists, with a taste for the whip, and racially adventurous. They were desperate to escape the horsy types they'd grown up with. Women like *Lady* Emma Harvey, Peaches concluded, as Emma primly held out her hand for Peaches to shake. Or maybe even to kiss, with a curtsey, Peaches considered, feeling her hackles rise. Either way, she ignored it. She hadn't come all this way to like these women – only to find out if they could be of use.

'And, Emma, this is Peaches Gold,' Ross said. 'I told you about her.'

What? Peaches wondered. *What* had Ross told Lady Emma Harvey about her? Did they know what she did for a living? Or her connection to Khordinsky?

Emma let the hand she'd held up to greet Peaches drop. She smoothed her short red hair behind her ear and Peaches could tell instantly that she was suspicious, even disapproving, of Peaches. Of what she was or how she looked.

She knew that Emma was assessing the bruises on Peaches' own face. Was she wondering, too, whether they'd been caused by the same person? Despite herself, Peaches felt a link between them. They were both damaged women, holding it together. Being strong.

And as Emma held her gaze, Peaches felt ashamed for having refused to shake her hand. But it was too late now and she didn't want to appear soft by apologizing. Not until she'd got to the bottom of what was going on.

'I'm Frankie,' said the younger woman, breaking the awkward silence. Frankie didn't wait for a repeat of what had happened between Peaches and Emma. She stepped forward and smiled widely, pumping Peaches' hand up and down.

'Frankie's my current muse,' Todd said. Frankie laughed and took off her baseball cap and dumped it on Todd's head. That's when Peaches recognized her from the magazine on the plane. A real friend of Todd's then. Someone who'd been hanging out with him all this time. Someone he'd even confided his greatest secret to.

If Peaches had got Frankie wrong, then maybe she'd got Emma wrong too.

Peaches suddenly felt completely thrown. Usually, when she met women, she was the one in control, knowing the outcome she wanted and steering the proceedings her way. But now, as Todd picked up the champagne from the ice bucket on the table and poured more in each glass and a fresh one for Peaches, she saw that she wasn't in charge. Not of these women. Not yet. If anything, she was the outsider.

She watched Frankie sit next to Emma, and she realized that theirs was a closed circle which she instinctively knew she couldn't break. Not without an invitation.

It soon became apparent that Frankie and Todd really *were* great friends, and Emma seemed comfortable in his company, suggesting that he contact Eduard, her designer friend, to restyle the apartment downstairs.

'Bunny, Eduard's wife, thought the world of Julian,' Emma said. Peaches suddenly saw a depth of sorrow that made Emma seem much more vulnerable than she'd thought. 'She sang at his birthday. I could call her, but . . .' She trailed off, and Peaches noticed Frankie squeezing Emma's shoulder. 'I think she's the same as everyone else. They're embarrassed by what happened. They don't know what to say about Julian.'

Peaches was confused. Who the hell was Julian?

Emma shook her head and dabbed her eyes. Then she cleared her throat and steadied herself. 'Sorry,' she apologized to Peaches.

Peaches stared across the park at the twinkling lights and the lights of a plane cutting across the sky. Out of nowhere the image of Harry Rezler at the bar in Moscow popped into her head. She wondered where he was. Who he was with. Sometimes, it seemed like everyone else in the world had someone but her.

'I think it's best we leave the girls to it whilst we order in dinner,' Ross said to Todd. 'Marco at Cipriani's said he could send over some of his wild mushroom ravioli.'

Peaches watched him touch Todd's arm. She was amazed how natural they looked together, at their level of familiarity and easy intimacy. She was jealous too. All this time she'd thought Ross was her best friend but now she could see that she'd only ever been second in his eyes.

This was so Goddamned weird, she thought as she watched them go. She felt as if the scales had fallen from her eyes. At last she was beginning to see the whole truth about her life, about her family . . . and now her friends too.

But she couldn't think about Ross right now, only why he'd brought her here. It was time to get down to business. Toughen up, girl, she told herself, feeling the other two women silently contemplating her.

'So . . . let's cut to the chase,' she said, deciding to take control despite the apprehension she felt. 'First of all, all of this – everything we say tonight – is absolutely confidential. Agreed?'

Emma and Frankie glanced at each other. 'Agreed,' they said.

'Right. Well, all I know about you two is that you have . . . ' She paused, choosing her words carefully. '. . . issues with Khordinsky. And that's why I've flown here to New York. Because I'm on a mission to bring that scumbag to justice.'

'Me too,' said Emma.

'And me,' Frankie said.

Something about the forcefulness of their responses had shocked them all. 'OK,' Peaches said slowly, with an intrigued smile. She sensed that beneath the starlit sky a bond of trust was being born. And for the first time since leaving *Pushkin*, she didn't feel quite so alone.

CHAPTER THIRTY-FOUR

Frankie was reeling. It was only minutes, but it felt like hours since she'd sat down to talk to Peaches and Emma. Already, Frankie and Emma had laid their cards on the table. They'd both told Peaches what Khordinsky had done to them. How he'd set Frankie up with Todd, and how Emma suspected that it was Khordinsky who had engineered the collapse of Platinum Holdings and driven her husband to suicide . . . at the very least.

But now the conversation had taken an even more macabre turn, and Frankie could hardly believe what she was hearing.

'You went to *Pushkin*? That night?' Frankie checked again with Peaches. 'For Alex's birthday?'

She remembered the harbour master arresting her moments before she'd reached *Pushkin* on the stolen tender and that horrible night in the cell. But for a mere twist of fate she'd have met Peaches.

Peaches Gold. The woman sitting here right now.

She was more than a little intimidating. She oozed power and sexuality and a knowingness that Frankie had never seen in anyone before. She was wearing a simple wrap-around black dress and heels, but Frankie could tell she had the kind of body and sexy lustrous hair that most men would find hard to resist. Where Frankie came from, there were names for women like Peaches Gold. And none of them were nice.

But this wasn't back home, Frankie reminded herself. This was a different country and the rules she'd grown up with didn't apply here. She didn't even know if there *were* any rules any more, apart from those made up by people like Khordinsky. Rules that got him whatever he wanted, no matter how horrendous the cost to anyone else.

That was why she was here, she told herself. Because of Khordinsky. Because of everything he'd done to her and Emma. And that was also why she wasn't going to judge Peaches Gold, not before she got to know her. Not until she knew whether they really could, as Ross had suggested to Todd, help each other out.

'Sure I was there. I organized the female entertainment,' Peaches said.

'Female entertainment?'

'You know, hookers. Fun for the boys.'

'Alex was with a hooker?' Frankie asked. She forced herself to beat down the tears she felt rising. The thought of Alex being with someone else – anyone else – made her feel sick. Surely he wouldn't pay for sex, would he? With a stranger?

'Alex?' Peaches said. 'You mean Rodokov?'

'Yes. He's my . . . he and I were . . .'

'Save your blushes, sister. I get the picture. But just for the record, he didn't do anything. In fact, he refused.'

'Refused?' Frankie's voice caught.

'Yeah, honey,' Peaches said, 'Refused. Point blank. Two of my best girls. They'd been paid for too. But he acted like he already had someone else in mind.' Peaches looked her up and down. 'I'm guessing it was you.'

'Oh,' Frankie said. She wanted so desperately to believe that Alex still cared for her, still missed her, still couldn't be with any-one else apart from her. But at the same time, Alex *had* been in the same room as Peaches and a whole load of hookers. Witnessing . . . what? Frankie's mind flew over a dozen scenarios, none of which were probably accurate. The experience she'd shared with him in Marrakech, so intimate and private and pure, didn't stack up with Khordinsky's world at all.

'Was Khordinsky there?' Emma asked. 'At the party?'

'Yes,' Peaches said. 'That's why I went there. To meet him . . .' She looked first at Emma and then at Frankie. Her eyes were hard and determined. '. . . and to kill him.'

Frankie felt the temperature plummet. She sat in silence with Emma as Peaches recalled the events on the night of Alex's birthday. How she'd ensnared Khordinsky so that he was alone with her. How she'd attacked him and how he'd over-powered her. How she'd stabbed him in the neck with her stiletto. How he'd beaten her up and ordered her killed.

And then she told them about how Alex had stopped Khordinsky killing her right at the last moment. How he and his bodyguard had taken her ashore. How Alex had taken out the gun and pointed it at her head.

'He had a gun?' Frankie asked, aghast. She couldn't believe it. Couldn't visualize it. The story Peaches had been telling them had been so vivid, but now it had stopped dead, like a reel of film had just snapped.

Peaches smiled. Not cruelly, Frankie could see. But out of perplexity. 'That surprise you?' Peaches asked.

'But Alex isn't a violent man,' Frankie protested.

'Are you kidding me? He's Khordinsky's number two,' Peaches said. 'What? You think he hasn't got blood on his hands?'

There was something about the way Peaches asked this that left Frankie confused, as if Peaches wasn't just being rhetorical but was unsure herself what kind of a man Alex truly was. It was as if she was challenging Frankie to prove her wrong.

'He's a businessman,' she said without hesitating. 'A gentle-man. He's tough, but he's kind. He could never be cruel. Let alone do what you're saying he would – execute someone on a beach in the dark. In cold blood.'

'Well, obviously not,' Peaches said. 'I'm here, aren't I?'

'So what *did* happen?' Frankie asked.

Peaches started talking again. The movie reel moved on. Alex firing into the sand. Him hissing in Peaches' ear, telling her to play dead. Peaches lying there, listening to the sound of the engine fading into the night. Frozen on the sand. Too terrified to so much as twitch.

Frankie put her hand over her mouth, relief bursting

inside her. 'So he didn't try to kill you? He saved your life?'

'Yes,' Peaches said. 'He tricked the bodyguard into thinking he'd done exactly what Khordinsky had told him to. What I can't figure out is why. Unless what you say is true and that, against all the odds, Rodokov *is* a good guy.'

'Of course it's true,' Frankie said. She looked between Emma and Peaches, desperate for their affirmation. But when she looked at them all she saw was the bruises on their faces: the swollen proof of the violence meted out by Alex's associates and friends.

Frankie took a deep breath, steadying herself. Her head was spinning. No matter what she wanted to believe, Alex had been there on the yacht when Khordinsky had done those terrible things to Peaches. To think that Alex had been a part of that . . . it made her feel breathless. What if her faith in him *was* mistaken? What if the Alex she knew and loved was all just an act? What if, beneath it all, he was Khordinsky's hatchet man?

But he'd saved Peaches. She had to hold on to that. Alex had let Peaches live.

If only he were here. She could ask him herself. She knew she'd be able to look into those eyes and divine the truth.

'But I'm confused,' Emma said. 'Why did you attack Khordinsky in the first place? And why did he want Alex to kill you?'

Frankie forced her concerns about Alex to the back of her mind, in order to listen to Peaches' answer.

'When I met Khordinsky, I saw red. As soon as I looked at him, I thought about everything he'd done and . . .'

'But why?' Emma insisted. 'Why do you hate him so much?'

'Because . . .' Peaches said. She paused. She shook her head, as if to say that she could hardly believe herself what she was about to tell them. 'Because . . . he's my father.'

Frankie assumed she'd misheard.

'Khordinsky's your *what*?' Emma asked. She glanced at Frankie and Frankie could tell she was just as astounded as she was.

Frankie listened in astonished silence as Peaches told them her story, right from the start. Frankie experienced that terrible crushing sensation again, just as when she'd been thrown off *Pushkin* by Richard on the orders of the boss. It was the feeling of her whole world being rocked. Of everything she knew being thrown in the air.

Even her most outlandish assumptions about Peaches Gold hadn't come close to this. She was Khordinsky's *daughter*. But she was American. A Hollywood madam. It couldn't be true.

But as she listened, she discovered that it not only could be, but it was. Why would Peaches make something like this up when, with every sentence, Frankie watched her brow darken with shame and pain?

She recounted her shock at Gorsky contacting her and what he'd told her in the jail. And then she told them about finding Irena in Moscow. She described Irena's burnt-out eyes and about how Khordinsky had stolen Peaches away from Irena when Peaches was three, breaking Irena's heart. And she told them, too, about how she'd been smuggled into America and sold to a paedophile.

Khordinsky had *sold* his own little girl. Deliberately. Into a childhood of horrible abuse.

Peaches spoke clearly. Succinctly. But above all, without emotion. Her voice could have been that of a documentary-maker, summarizing someone else's tragic life, not her own. It was as if she was distancing herself, building a wall between the person she was now and the frightened child she'd once been. She was telling both them and herself that nothing as bad as that would ever happen to her again.

Only her face gave her away.

Frankie felt her whole perception of Peaches shifting. Even if Peaches hadn't truly processed any of this horrendous in-formation, even if she was deep in denial, she'd refused to let her life become derailed. In fact, she'd done the opposite. She'd kept going full speed ahead. Frankie realized that Peaches, rather than being just a hard-nosed hooker, was in fact some-thing else entirely. She was the gutsiest most awesome woman Frankie had ever met.

'I don't think I've ever talked this much . . . to anyone,' Peaches said eventually. Frankie could tell that she felt exposed.

Emma reached forward and touched Peaches' hand and Peaches flinched. She glanced up, her eyes guarded. For a moment, Peaches looked like she regretted having said any-thing at all.

'But I'm telling you this because of what you told me. If we're going to work together, we have to be honest with each other. If we're going to stand a chance of somehow nailing this bastard, we're going to have to stand together as one. No bullshit.'

'No bullshit,' Frankie agreed.

'For what it's worth, I think you're incredible, Peaches,' Emma said. 'I'm amazed you've survived at all.'

'And so brave to have tackled Khordinsky like that,' Frankie added. 'If I'd found out what you did, I don't know what I'd have done. But I know I'd never have had the guts to go for him head-on like you did.'

'Yeah, well, either I'm very brave or very stupid. I'm not sure which,' Peaches said. 'But it makes no difference. I failed.'

'You got close, though,' Emma said. 'Close enough to confront him. Closer than either of us have managed so far.'

'And if you managed it once, maybe you we can do it again,' Frankie said.

'But not to physically attack him,' Emma said. 'I need you to know that, Peaches. Right from the start. I'm not a killer and I don't want to become one.'

'Even though you think he's responsible for your husband's death?' Peaches asked.

'Even then.'

'I believe in fighting fire with fire,' Peaches said.

'You've already tried that,' Emma reminded her. 'And you were the one who got burnt.'

'I did it because I had no other choice,' Peaches said. 'I wasn't even sure I'd go through with it until I saw him. But then I knew it was the only way to really hurt him.'

'What about going after him with a lawyer?' Frankie suggested. 'Let him know you're his daughter. With info like that, you could really make him pay – financially. Which is probably as good a way to hurt him as any.'

Peaches shook her head. 'It's not about money. I can always get money for myself. No, the thing is, I looked into his eyes and I know what he's capable of doing. He did it to my mother. I know how evil he is. When you look into someone's eyes and you see they aren't human like you are, then there's no point in trying to reason with them.'

'I met a man like that once. Another Russian. Dimitry Sergeyokov. He came to Julian's party. He stared at me like I was nothing. Just a piece of meat he could devour,' Emma said.

'Who did you say?' Peaches asked, sitting forward.

'There was this guy in charge of Julian's deal, Dimitry Sergeyokov,' Emma explained. 'He's the one who stole all of Julian's money.'

'I met him,' Peaches said. 'He works for Khordinsky. I was with someone who told me he was disappearing for a while.'

Emma gasped. There was a moment of silence as this new information sunk in.

'See,' Emma told Frankie. Her eyes were bright with triumph, but Frankie could see the tears welling up. 'Didn't I tell you that Khordinsky was behind the Platinum collapse all along?' Emma turned to Peaches. 'Cosmo,' she said, 'my son. He's out there now, trying to find out what really happened to our money. Trying to find Sergeyokov. Oh shit.' She buried her head in her hands. 'It really is Khordinsky he's up against. And Cosmo's all I have left.'

'It's going to be all right,' Frankie said, trying to sound strong for her.

'How do you know?' Emma asked.

'Because we're going to make it all right.'

'How?'

Frankie could hear the desperation in Emma's voice, but she had no answer. Not yet. But what she did know now, thanks to Peaches, was that if Khordinsky was behind the collapse of Platinum Holdings, then Khordinsky was almost certainly also behind Frankie's own abduction in Tortola.

'Look what happened before,' Emma said, swiping angrily at her tears.

'What?' Peaches asked. 'What happened before?'

Frankie took a deep breath. She told Peaches about breaking into Detroy's office to find the files on Platinum Reach and how she'd been abducted and photographed. And how Emma's face had been slashed.

Of course Frankie had speculated as much already. Who but Khordinsky would be sick enough to have had her abducted? Who but Khordinsky would be clever enough to have had photographs of her taken like that? Killing her would have been too risky. Alex might have decided to go looking for her if she'd simply disappeared. The photos were much smarter: insurance to turn Alex against her for ever. And who but Khordinsky would have thugs willing to do that for him?

But now she and Emma had the proof. Khordinsky really had been pulling the strings all along.

Her greatest fear was that Alex might be lost already. Because if Khordinsky had already shown Alex those photos . . .

'They probably used Rohypnol,' Peaches said. 'You been checked out?' she asked. 'Had tests?'

Frankie nodded. 'They didn't . . . I mean, I was lucky. There was no indication of penetration . . . They just posed me . . . to make it look like . . .'

She knew she would have to be strong. What she'd been through was nothing compared to how Peaches had suffered, but she couldn't stop thinking about it. She'd racked her brains over and over. She may have been defenceless and hardly conscious, but the photos sure as hell didn't look like it. It made her feel as if a part of her had been stolen. A part she was desperate to get back.

She became aware of Peaches gazing at her. Her eyes were no longer hard, but searching.

'Hey, Frankie, I understand,' Peaches said.

'Do you?' she asked.

'Just because I work in the industry I do doesn't mean that I approve of people taking advantage of a girl. Quite the opposite, in fact. No, honey, take it from me, what those bastards did was unforgivable. And we're going to get them, OK?'

Frankie nodded.

'But how?' Emma asked again. 'It's all very well knowing all of this, but who's going to believe us? Khordinsky's impossible to get close to. And we've got no hard proof. We need documents. Accounts. We came to a dead end in Tortola but we need a solid trail leading to Khordinsky. Evidence that would stand up in court.'

'Well, maybe we don't have all that, but everyone has an Achilles heel,' Peaches said. 'We've just got to find his. You got any ideas?'

And suddenly Frankie remembered that day Alex had kissed her in his study. 'Well, maybe . . . ' she said. 'Maybe. It's a long shot. I don't know if it will work . . . '

'Shoot,' Peaches said. 'We need every idea we can get.'

After an hour, the three women hadn't stopped talking as they hatched out a plan.

'I just want to make it clear again,' Emma said. 'I don't want any of us to attack him head on again. It's too risky. I don't want to kill him. I want something more painful than that.'

'OK. I want him to lose everything, then,' Peaches said. 'The whole shebang. Everything that he holds dear. All his money. I want him ruined.'

'And I want Alex away from him for ever,' Frankie said. 'And for Alex to know that it was Khordinsky who drove us apart.'

'And I want Cosmo home safely,' Emma said. 'And then for everyone to know what Khordinsky did to Julian. Total public humiliation. You think we can do it?'

'You bet,' Peaches said, smiling. 'Between the three of us, we're going to bring that son-of-a-bitch down. For good.'

CHAPTER THIRTY-FIVE

It wasn't until Peaches' driver, Paul, had picked Frankie and Peaches up in a limousine at LAX airport that Frankie realized that agreeing to go back once more to LA, but this time with Peaches, to work on the first step of their plan may be even more of an eye-opener than she'd bargained for.

'Peaches, if you don't mind me asking, how do people – I mean your clients – actually find you?' she asked as they left the airport and joined the slow-moving lanes of traffic on the freeway. Peaches had already outlined the basics of her business to Frankie and Emma: the services she provided; the kind of girls who worked for her; the kind of men she provided them to. And, of course, how much she charged. Hollywood Madam 101.

But there was still a great deal Frankie didn't understand, and she was so curious. So in awe of Peaches' exoticism. She'd never met a madam before and she doubted she ever would again. She wasn't going to miss out on the opportunity to find out all she could. Her natural thirst for knowledge demanded it. But she was annoyed with herself for sounding prim.

Peaches glanced at her, her pen poised above the open black book on the armrest in between them. 'Word of mouth, mostly.

People always find me, if they want me. What you'll see if you hang around with me might shock you, but I haven't invited you into all this so you can pass judgement on me. You got it?'

'Sure, Peaches,' Frankie said, wishing she'd kept her big mouth shut. 'Of course.'

Peaches smiled, softening her tone. 'Don't worry, Frankie. I'll look after you.' She looked at her phone, which was playing a 'Hey! Big Spender' ring tone. 'Oh Lord, look, there's another call. Excuse me, hon. I'm afraid there's a stack waiting.'

Frankie craned her neck to stare at the palm trees and billboards and the bright LA day outside. Despite everything that had happened, she couldn't help feeling a frisson of excitement at being here. She couldn't believe how far she'd come since cleaning toilets on *Pushkin*. She'd wanted so desperately for something exciting to happen. She'd wanted to get out and see the world. And now she was in Los Angeles. With Peaches Gold, no less.

After everything they'd told each other in Todd's apartment, the lines of communication now seemed wide open. Peaches had been as good as her word: no bullshit. No topics of conversation had so far appeared to be off limits. Nothing was taboo. Already Frankie had discussed more aspects of Peaches and Emma's lives with them than she'd done with other friends she'd known for years. It was as if the speed with which they'd been thrown together and progressed their plans had, in turn, accelerated their friendship. It was exactly as Peaches had predicted: they were becoming a team. Fast.

It had been tough saying goodbye to Emma at JFK. Emma was taking the plane for London via Switzerland, where she was going to retrieve all the documents in Julian's safety deposit box in the bank. Hugo and Victoria were going to meet her. Hugo had had word from Cosmo and Emma was anxious to hear what had happened. As Frankie had hugged her, wishing her luck and assuring her that they'd see each other really soon, she'd felt tears welling up. Emma had been her rock for the past few weeks and she was scared about being apart from her.

But Peaches had had no time for sentimentalism. She was far too busy. On the plane, she'd enlisted Frankie's help in choosing the final shots for the lingerie catalogue from the stills that Tenzin Marisco had emailed over. Frankie never imagined she'd have an opinion on nipple tassels, or whether Monica DuCane looked better in the black or the red lace thong, let alone help Peaches compare costings on the best champagne to serve at her secret sex party. But Frankie had as good a head for figures as anyone and it was good to be of use.

She smiled to herself. It was funny how mundane even the glamour industry became when you reduced it to income and expenditure.

But she wanted to impress Peaches, and she knew she could learn a lot from her, too. Frankie had already worked out that one thing was for sure: Peaches Gold was as smart as one of the whips in her catalogue. The lingerie line was a sure-fire hit in the making. She had a great marketing plan and a seductive brand. Frankie reckoned that Peaches was on course for making even more legitimately than she did underground.

She might end up working for Peaches' brand full-time, Frankie speculated. Help her launch the range. Why not? If Alex refused to forgive her, it might be the only fallback position she had. After all, she was unemployed and she couldn't rely on Todd bailing her out for ever.

Enough idle speculation, she told herself. Her future was wide open but the future she wanted most was her and Alex's. Not her and Peaches'. And Peaches' future was far from decided itself. As Frankie listened to her now on the phone, it was clear that she was not going fully legit just yet.

Frankie's mind boggled at the potential identities of the callers on the other end. The genders were easy to guess. If it was a man, Peaches laughed and flirted and sounded as if she had all the time in the world. If it was one of her girls, she sounded matter-of-fact, even maternal. She could switch between the two with such ease, that Frankie couldn't help wondering who the real Peaches was: the madam or the mommy.

She sure had a thriving business, Frankie concluded, even if it was illegal. Now that she was seeing Peaches' operation first hand, Frankie admired her more and more. She had a way of making it all sound so normal – that it was only sex. It was as if she was merely providing her clients with secretaries or cleaners, rather than call girls and dominatrixes. It was all utterly matter of fact and friendly.

What amazed Frankie most was the huge numbers of men prepared to cheat on their wives and girlfriends. But Peaches was unfazed – amused even by Frankie's disapproval when she brought this up.

'Hey, this is just a normal day.'

'But there're so many,' Frankie said.

'Men want sex. Period,' Peaches told her. 'And they'll find a way to get it. It's just the way of the world.'

But Frankie didn't want to believe her. Not all men were unfaithful, surely? Alex hadn't gone with Peaches' girls, Frankie reminded herself. If their plan worked and she got Alex back, he'd be just hers, wouldn't he?

Because the sex they'd had hadn't been just sex. It had meant so much more than that. When he'd been inside her, holding her close, looking into her eyes, Frankie had felt as if he'd been looking into her soul.

But then she thought of the last time she'd seen him in Cannes and the pain in his voice, and Frankie felt fresh doubts creeping through her mind, like shadows from her darkest nightmares.

She forced herself to keep focused. To sweep away those doubts. To hold the faith.

Alex loved her. She knew he did. Even if he didn't think he did now, he had when they'd been together. Before he'd been tricked into thinking she was something she could never be. He couldn't just switch love that powerful on and off like a tap, could he? There must be a part of him that still cared for her.

There had to be. Because when Peaches had said that Khordinsky had to have an Achilles heel, Frankie knew exactly what it was.

Alex. Khordinsky trusted him completely. He was his heir apparent, his protégé, the son he'd never had. The person he trusted to take over his businesses; the respectable face that Khordinsky had nurtured from a boy, to hide behind now. Yes, Frankie knew that Alex was Khordinsky's weak spot, because Frankie believed with all her heart something that Khordinsky had failed to grasp: Alex was essentially good.

Frankie knew from her time in Morocco with him that Alex

was a man whose instinct was to *save* children, not *sell* them. And whatever evil and corrupt path Khordinsky had attempted to lead him down, Alex had not become a creature of corruption like his master. He didn't go with the prostitutes. He hadn't murdered Peaches. He had integrity. And decency.

Which was why Frankie was determined to hack into Forest Holdings using the passwords she'd set up for Alex in his office. If they still worked, and if she got in, she'd look for something – anything – that might prove to Alex that Khordinsky and Sergeyokov had deliberately ruined Julian. Stolen from him. Defrauded him. Driven him to his death. If she could do that – provide Alex with hard evidence of the corruption Khordinsky was responsible for – then Frankie might just be able to get Alex on their side, because she already knew from what he'd told her that Alex believed the business he was fronting for Khordinsky was legitimate. If she could prove to him his master was treating him like a fool, then it might be enough to turn Alex. Faced with the truth, he might just help them to bring Khordinsky down.

But there were a hell of a lot of ifs. And it was seriously dangerous. Frankie knew what could happen to her if Khordinsky found out that she was hacking into his companies and snooping around.

That's why Peaches had called Danny here in LA. He was her assistant Angela's brother and Peaches insisted he was the best. A super-hacker. Completely off radar. As far as most people knew, Danny, a.k.a 'the Worm', was a ghost. He was practically impossible to find, unless you knew exactly where to look for him – which, luckily, Peaches did. If anyone could help Frankie get into Alex's computer system undetected, then it was Danny.

Nevertheless, Frankie felt herself tingling with nerves. She knew that this plan they'd come up with was their best shot and Peaches and Emma were relying on her. But even if Frankie did find the evidence they needed, she knew it may not be enough, because everything hinged on Alex believing in *her* ... not those phoney photographs. Did he have enough faith? she wondered. Did she?

*

Frankie hardly had time to take in Peaches' louche apartment, with its dancing poles and disco balls and Angela's office crammed with sexy underwear samples, because Angela had bad news.

'Oh Peaches,' she said. 'Thank God you're back. Yana. She called . . .'

'Aw shit!' Peaches said. She looked at Angela, and Frankie could see that they knew each other well enough for Peaches to know what the hell Angela was talking about. Peaches threw her bag across the room. Frankie could tell Peaches was close to tears.

'You got to call her. She's terrified,' Angela said. 'She says she didn't tell them anything.'

'What's happened?' Frankie asked.

Peaches looked up sharply. Her eyes bored into Angela's. 'Khordinsky's men? They found Irena?'

Angela nodded. 'They came in the night.'

'What did they do? Tell me!'

'They . . . they slit her throat.'

Frankie felt her heart aching with pity and fear. Peaches let out just one sob. She wiped her nose on the back of her hand.

'This is my fault,' she said. 'I knew this would happen.'

'No,' Frankie said, going to her. She glanced at Angela, knowing that Peaches' trusted secretary would back her up. 'Listen to me. This is Khordinsky's fault.'

'But if I hadn't mentioned Irena's name—'

'You could have said a lot worse. And you could be dead. It's down to your strength that we've still got a chance to get him.'

'There's no way he can trace you here, is there?' Angela asked.

Peaches blew out a deep breath, clearly forcing herself to stay calm. 'I signed the hotel register in a false name.'

'OK,' Frankie said. 'Let's think. Can they trace you through that name?'

'No. Not a chance. If they suspect I'm Irena's daughter, they'll try and find Albert Rockbine.'

Frankie rushed over to Angela's computer. She booted up the search engine and typed in his name. She bit her lip as the news wire report from Louisiana was flagged up.

'You'd better look at this,' she said, turning the screen around to face Angela and Peaches.

Albert Rockbine had been found last night under an interstate bridge. He'd been stabbed to death.

Peaches pressed her lips together. She looked down at the carpet, then she looked up at Frankie. Tears brimmed in her eyes, but her look was grim. 'Frankie, I'm telling you, you better find a way to nail that son of a bitch. And fast.'

'OK, Peaches, I will,' Frankie said. 'I promise.'

Frankie wasn't going to ask Angela about her face, but Angela volunteered the story as she rushed Frankie away in her car to Santa Barbara where they were going to meet Danny. She owed her life to Peaches, she said. Peaches was her guardian angel. One of a kind.

Frankie could tell how shaken Angela was by what had happened to Peaches' mother in Moscow. She felt more determined than ever to crack on with her part of the plan.

Danny, on the other hand, was hung-over and suspicious when Angela took Frankie to see him in his apartment in Santa Barbara. The room was stiflingly hot. Thick black blankets covered the windows, shutting out the bright day outside. The air-conditioning was hardly able to cope with the heat coming from the snaking mass of routers, wiring and computers.

Frankie marvelled at the serious kit he had and the simultaneous programs he was running. A lot of what was on show was commercial, hardware that Frankie had worked with or read about before. But some things she didn't recognize. They didn't even have manufacturer's IDs on them, which meant that they were ex-Government or military, then. Or hybrids which Danny had constructed himself. She could only imagine what kind of software he had running on them, and to what purpose.

Danny had been on his motorbike down to Mexico and back and hadn't had much sleep. He looked terrible: pale and sunburnt at the same time. His dark hair was curly and matted and he looked as if he hadn't washed for days.

And yet he had a glint in his eye as he looked up and down Frankie's legs in her denim mini-skirt and she told him that she might need a couple of days of his time.

'You got a boyfriend?' he asked.

Frankie looked him dead in the eye and answered, 'Yes.'

'And she's not one of Peaches' girls, if that's what you're thinking,' Angela warned him. 'So don't go getting fresh with her, or you'll have me to deal with. You got it?'

Danny smiled ruefully. 'Receiving you loud and clear, sis. No offence intended,' he said to Frankie.

'He doesn't get out much, do you, Danny?' Angela said. 'You could meet someone, you know, if you made the effort.'

Danny ignored her, his attention still on Frankie, and nodded at the computers by way of explanation. 'I spend too much time down here. These babies are the love of my life.'

Frankie smiled. 'Well, I have to admit, you've got some pretty neat kit. Ex-Government, or military, I'm guessing . . .'

Danny smiled at her for the first time, not flirtatiously but more like a kid in school who'd just spotted a kid wearing the same sneakers.

'Sis told me you knew your stuff. So what kind of work you done before?' he asked.

As Frankie and Danny chatted through their techy CVs, Frankie found herself relaxing in his company. He might be shy and a little left-footed when it came to the opposite sex, but now that they were talking as equals, Frankie knew they were going to get along just fine.

Angela fussed around clearing up old crushed soda cans whilst Frankie gave Danny the brief: how she wanted his help to find enough hard evidence to sink a billionaire. Even as she said it, she knew how impossible it sounded.

But Peaches was right. Danny was the guy for the task. Frankie soon got the impression that the bigger the challenge, the happier he was. She sat down on one of the swivel chairs next to him as his fingers rattled over the keyboard.

After just a few minutes, he smiled and winked at her. 'Just as well you've got memorable blue eyes, eh?'

Frankie grinned. 'The passwords? They work?'

'It seems your friend Alexei Rodokov has been too busy or too sentimental to change them.'

Frankie squeezed her lips together, glad to be over the first hurdle. Alex hadn't changed his passwords. Whatever the reason why not, that meant Alex had to type in 'Frankie's blue eyes' every day. The most memorable thing he could think of. Did that mean that he still thought of her every day, just like she thought of him?

Danny quickly set up a host account to monitor the mail activity and before long they'd found the pathway into the Forest Holding's database and mainframe files. Frankie downloaded the company accounts which Danny printed out.

'What now?' he asked. 'This is nothing special. You could ring up the company and get these sent to you.'

'Can we get into Khordinsky's email and private files?' Frankie asked. 'Is that possible from here?'

Danny leant back in his giant swivel chair and put his hands behind his head. Frankie had to stop herself recoiling from the smell emanating from his armpits and the sight of his hairy belly poking out from under his T-shirt.

'OK . . .' He thought for a moment, scratching his head, before outlining his strategy for getting in. 'It'll take a while, though. You up for staying?'

'Sure.'

It was dark before Danny got a result but Frankie hardly noticed the time. Being with Danny was like doing a crash-course Ph.D. in her favourite subject. She'd learnt more about hacking in a few hours with him than she could have in years alone.

Frankie brushed aside the empty bento boxes and Styrofoam coffee cups and leant in closer. 'What is it?'

Danny was frowning. 'This is really odd. He's got a special link set up to encrypted files.'

'Encrypted? How well encrypted? Can we decrypt them?' Frankie asked.

'We can certainly try. We'll have to run some cracking utilities. We might be in for the long haul.'

'I don't care,' Frankie said. She felt too wired with caffeine and anticipation to leave now. They might finally be on to something.

Tommy Liebermann seemed to be in a good mood, despite the lack of sleep he'd claimed to have had, as he welcomed Peaches and Frankie on to the large motor yacht in Santa Barbara harbour. Frankie was on tenterhooks and still buzzing from her own lack of sleep. She felt like a vole that had crept out into the midday sun after the hours she'd spent in Danny's apartment. Everything seemed too bright. Being so absorbed in Forest Holdings for the past forty-eight hours had left her feeling as if she really had just stepped out of a forest. After her confinement, the world seemed impossibly big again and the challenges ahead like a mighty range of mountains, which she hoped she still had the strength to climb.

Peaches had instructed her to send over copies of all the documents she and Danny had downloaded for Tommy to analyse, insisting that Tommy would be able to work out what they meant.

That was why they were here in the bright morning light. To get some answers. Frankie couldn't wait. She certainly hadn't been able to make head nor tail of the contents of Khordinsky's files, once Danny had busted their encryption wide open. Or the sheafs of emails written in Russian. Peaches had enlisted the help of one of her bi-lingual Russian girls, Magda, to translate, seeing as she owed Peaches a favour. By the admiring look on Tommy's face and Magda's confident swagger as she walked around the deck of the yacht in her skimpy aqua-marine bikini, it looked as if she'd been doing Tommy some favours too.

'So what's the score, Tommy?' Peaches asked once they'd settled around the table in the cockpit. 'You got anything good for us?'

'Man oh man, I've seen some tricks in my time, but this is some scam,' Tommy said.

'Go on,' Peaches said.

'I've done some digging around. Pulled in a few favours with some old contacts and a bod up at UCLA to help fill in the bigger picture behind all that gen you found in the files.'

'And . . . ?' Frankie said.

'The Kremlin are all over Khordinsky. The Government want to renationalize his oil and gas companies. They're on a mission to freeze all of his companies' assets in court. But Khordinsky was very smart. When he left Russia, he got a guy called Boris Nazin to get all his money out.'

'Nazin!' Peaches said. 'He was murdered. I saw it on the news when I was in Moscow.'

'Yeah, but before he got the chop, he squealed, and the authorities know that Khordinsky buried his assets in Forest Holdings.'

'That's Alex's main company,' Frankie said.

'It sure is. And that's where it gets nasty. Khordinsky's name isn't on any of the paperwork.' Tommy let the implication hang in the air for a second or two, before filling in the blanks. 'Alex's is.'

Frankie's caffeine-loaded blood pressure hit yet another peak.

'But Khordinsky has been busy dissolving the assets and siphoning off all the funds through a network of companies branching out of Tortola, the main one of which is called, appropriately enough, Matryoshka-Enterprises.'

'Hang on,' Frankie said, studying the sheet of data that Tommy pushed towards her. 'Can I borrow your phone?' she asked Tommy.

She quickly dialled Emma in the UK and explained where she was. 'All those companies in Tortola,' she said. 'What Detroy told you was right. They were all Matryoshka-Enterprises. Khordinsky's private companies: one within another, within another, just like the Matryoshka dolls. And right here' – she looked at the papers Tommy had given her – 'in my hand, is the transfer deed showing the money went from Platinum Reach to Matryoshka-Enterprises.'

'I knew it,' Emma said, her voice catching. 'He stole all that money.'

This was it then, Frankie thought. Exactly what they'd all hoped for. Physical proof that Khordinsky was behind everything. But any triumph she felt was tinged with fear. She thought about the three masked men in Detroy's office, and of the knife as it slashed Emma's face: it might as well have been Khordinsky himself who'd done it.

And she thought of the photographs those brutes had taken of her. It only went to prove that Khordinsky would do anything to protect his interests. But with this information, she felt that they were one step closer to him, as if they'd found a blurry shadow, which was now pulling into focus in their sights.

But Frankie knew from the time she'd spent growing up on

her Uncle Brody's farm that cornered animals were the most dangerous of all.

Tommy was talking again. Frankie told Emma she'd call her back and listened in.

'What happened with Platinum Reach is just small fry. What you've uncovered here, Frankie, is huge. We're talking billions. The whole of Forest Holdings. That's why there're two sets of accounts,' he said. 'The public ones and the actual ones, which were hidden in the encrypted files. And the actual ones show that Forest Holdings is virtually bankrupt.'

'So let me get this straight,' Peaches said. 'When the authorities want the assets back, there won't be any.'

'Exactly. And guess who's going to take the rap for it?' Tommy said.

'Alex,' Frankie said. 'Oh my God.'

'He's your natural ally, ladies. Magda translated a whole bunch of those emails Frankie sent over.' He flicked through the paperwork. '"Alexei, my fall guy",' he quoted. 'He's said it over and over. I tell you, Khordinsky's smart. He's done enough to clear his name and implicate Alex in everything.'

Frankie felt her throat constricting. This was so much worse than she'd thought. Khordinsky had duped Alex all along. Everything Alex had told her that Khordinsky had said about prizing loyalty and honesty above everything else was all just a big smokescreen. Khordinsky didn't have a loyal or honest bone in his body. It was all bullshit.

It was Alex who was loyal and honest: two perfect qualities for Khordinsky to use to his own advantage to keep Alex in the dark. And Khordinsky could pull the plug on Alex any moment, especially if he found out that Peaches and Frankie were on his trail.

'So I guess Alex is going to have to help us whether he likes it or not,' Peaches said, glancing at Frankie. She was clearly thinking exactly the same as Frankie.

'He sure is. Otherwise Mr Rodokov will be in the slammer before he knows it,' Tommy said.

CHAPTER THIRTY-SIX

Emma adjusted the wide brim of her Philip Treacy hat and undid the jacket of the Vera Wang suit Victoria had let her borrow for the day. She was boiling underneath, the sun beating down on the VIP marquee in Windsor Great Park from a cloudless blue sky.

Next to her, Yolanda De Vere Burrows slugged back her fourth glass of Veuve Cliquot, her cheeks starting to match the magenta silk dress she was wearing. She grinned at Emma as they watched the players assemble for the next match.

'I wouldn't mind some horseplay with him!' she said, nudging Emma. 'Nothing like some decent stud muffin to cheer a girl up, don't you think? Those Argies. Phwaarh! Great thighs! Probably hung like thoroughbreds as well.'

Emma knew what Yolanda was trying to do, but Julian being gone did not mean that she would ever consider being Yolanda's partner in her increasingly frequent indiscretions. Little did Yolanda suspect that Emma was scrutinizing the team for an altogether different reason.

'That's the Maverick team. They're on next,' Emma said, looking at her programme, then tucking it under her arm. She'd already read all about the team: how it was a friendly team made up of international players who had an unblemished record at events like this. 'Come on, Yolanda, drink up. Let's go and watch.'

Yolanda let out a cheeky guffaw. 'Steady on, old girl. They're not even up for grabs until the match has finished. Plenty of time to get revved up before then.' Yolanda held out her glass to a passing waiter for a top-up.

But Emma was already striding out of the marquee, past the vast pedestals of flowers, down the red carpet and out into the roped spectators' area next to the pitch.

She held up her binoculars, feeling her heart pounding with adrenalin. Yes, if she wasn't mistaken, that was him . . . Alexei Rodokov. She watched him laughing on the chestnut horse as he and his team-mates circled on the pitch.

He was in a red team shirt and beige jodhpurs and even from a distance Emma could tell how athletic and fit he looked. She rubbed her face, feeling the tender tissue around her scar. The scar caused by Khordinsky's thugs. She knew that for sure now. Was the handsome young man she was observing now really unaware of everything his boss was responsible for?

Whatever the truth was, something about his carefree smile unsettled her. He was a marked man. He may be enjoying himself in the sunshine, but Emma knew what she'd come here to do, and she knew that it was going to be far from easy.

'It's so good of you to bring me, Yolanda,' Emma said, forcing a smile on to her face as Yolanda caught her up.

'Darling, I'm used to being a social pariah. If you want to throw yourself into the lion's den, then be my guest,' Yolanda said. 'I admire your courage.'

Emma knew what she meant. She'd received a few frosty nods of acknowledgement when they'd arrived, but most people had ignored her completely. And now, as she looked over at Lola Reed and smiled, expecting her old friend to come over and give her a hug, Lola deliberately turned her back.

Yolanda saw the snub too. A sly smile laced with *Schadenfreude* crossed her face. Emma prickled, but she wasn't fooled for a second. She knew Yolanda hadn't asked her here out of sympathy or friendship, but because it gave her a better grandstand from which to gloat.

Well, Emma thought, Yolanda wasn't the only one being two-faced today. Little did Yolanda suspect from the way that Emma had buttered her up for a last-minute invitation that Yolanda had been her last resort. All of Emma's usual sources for event tickets had suddenly dried up and no one had been willing to do her a favour.

'Take no notice of that silly cow,' Yolanda said loudly – but not so loudly that Lola Reed might overhear.

Yet Emma couldn't help feeling riled. She knew Lola and her husband Martin well. They'd been pals at so many social occasions, sharing tables at Ascot and picnics at Glyndebourne. They'd even come to the Platinum Ball.

'She's just cross because Martin had to dump their place in Tuscany after Julian's thing fell through and she didn't have a chance to show it off.'

Emma knew how much the castle had meant to Lola. She'd even put her in touch with her Italian contacts and knew that Luigi Montefiore had cut her a deal on the exquisite stucco paint job as a personal favour to Emma. So how dare she treat Emma like this now? What had happened wasn't Emma's fault. And it wasn't Julian's either.

'Martin, along with everyone else, knew the risks,' Emma said, failing to mask the outrage she felt.

'Maybe they'll see that in time.'

'*They?*'

'You know: Lola, Joss, Katia, Rebecca. At the moment all they can talk about is how much they've lost.'

'But I've lost the most out of everyone, don't you think?' Emma said.

Yolanda patted her wrist. 'Of course you have, darling.'

Emma had certainly found out who her friends were, and it was none of those bitches. She'd had more sympathy and support from Frankie and Peaches than from any of the women she'd known for twenty years and had thought were her closest friends. And Emma vowed to herself now that, whatever happened, Lola and the rest of them would never have the satisfaction of hearing how much they'd got to her. Especially from Yolanda.

She could feel Yolanda staring at her, hoping for a reaction – some tears maybe. But Emma forced herself to be strong. She pictured Frankie on her left and Peaches on her right. They might not be here in body, but they were here in spirit, thinking of her now, willing her mission here today to be a success. Think of the risks they'd taken themselves, she told herself: Peaches aboard *Pushkin*; Frankie drugged in Tortola. Emma wouldn't let them down now the time to play her part had arrived.

She raised her binoculars once more, rising above Yolanda's comments. In the vernacular favoured by Peaches Gold, Emma thought, Yolanda and the others could go fuck themselves. She was going to make every one of them eat their words. Every one. They'd never have her respect now, no matter what happened. And once she'd cleared Julian's name and done whatever it took to get Wrentham back, they'd be sorry. Emma knew that she'd come on too great a journey ever to return to the person she'd once been. All the things that concerned those judgemental women: their homes abroad and new season's wardrobes – didn't matter a stuff any more. It was all horse shit.

And if Yolanda thought that Emma was here to show face, to claw back some kind of pitiful social footing with them, then she was very, very much mistaken.

Oh no, she was here to hunt much bigger game than that.

Emma let the conversation pause for a minute and then asked, 'And what of the Khordinskys? Are they coming today?'

Again, Emma saw that sly smug smile flicker over Yolanda's features. 'Not as far as I know. Natalya is busy redecorating Wrentham, so she says.'

Emma felt Yolanda's casual remark like a carefully aimed dart. Once again, she forced herself not to react, but she still felt her voice tremor as she asked, 'So you see her, then?'

'Her, yes, him ... not so much. He's so rarely in the Cotswolds. Either he's in their Chelsea place or he's abroad. But they're very nice. You're lucky they took Wrentham off your hands. It could have gone to somebody awful. I think they've taken over from you rather well.'

What a *bitch*! Emma bit her lip. Yolanda would be sorry when Emma got Wrentham back. She'd never set foot in it again. Emma was going to remove every trace of the Khordinskys for ever, including all the horrible toadies like

Yolanda who'd sucked up to them in the wake of Julian's death. The thought of it buoyed her up.

'Well, she can do what she likes to it,' Emma said.. 'People will still think of it as mine. You know, it's such a shame that you missed the Platinum Ball, Yolanda. People remember a party like that for years and years.' Emma had no doubt that this was going to be reported straight back to Natalya Khordinsky. 'I mean, the Khordinskys might think they've arrived by getting hold of *my* . . . ' She paused deliberately. '. . . I mean, Wrentham. But where're their social credentials? Surely they need to put their money where their mouth is and show everyone that they mean business. But maybe all their money is just hearsay. You never know.'

'Oh no. They're loaded. Everyone knows that,' Yolanda said with a frown, but Emma could tell she was getting somewhere. Yolanda was so transparent. She could almost see the seeds she was planting growing inside Yolanda's mind. 'Well, between you and me, Emma,' she suddenly added, 'I do think that Natalya is keen to get herself established here. You know, introduce Yuri to the right sort of people.'

'I see,' Emma said, pretending to give this serious consideration. 'Well, if *I* were Natalya Khordinsky, I'd get straight on the phone to someone like Damien, who catered the Platinum Ball, and throw a big party. And Damien would definitely be the best person for the job, as he knows Wrentham so well.' She glanced up at Yolanda, pleased to see she was taking in every word. Emma casually put the binoculars to her eyes again. 'But then it would be *so* hard getting hold of him. He *is* the best.'

'But he knows Wrentham, you say? So it wouldn't be a risky job for him,' Yolanda said. 'So he might do it . . . ?'

'Well, I suppose, if Natalya Khordinsky by some miracle *could* get hold of him, she should get Damien to organize an event to launch the Khordinskys into society properly. I happen to know that the English Ambassador to Russia, Hugo McCorquodale's old friend Willy Woolcott, is in town in a couple of weeks. A guest like him would certainly give the Khordinskys credibility.'

'The Ambassador to Russia?'

'Sure. And it would be enough of a draw to get everyone along and make a big show. But I guess Natalya doesn't really know anyone well enough to help her. Or have the competence, or confidence, or' – and here Emma glanced pointedly at Yolanda – 'the social contacts to pull it off. Which, to be honest, does provide me with some comfort. And, between you and me, amusement. I've moved on from Wrentham, but unfortunately for the Khordinskys, so have the social set who used to hang out there with us. You know, the right *sort* of people.' Emma paused, just long enough to let this last comment sink in, and to enjoy the dawning comprehension and resulting flash of anger in Yolanda's eyes as she realized how badly she'd just been insulted.

Yes, Emma thought, satisfied, that party at Wrentham would be announced within the week. She pointed to the pitch. 'Oh look,' she said. 'It's starting.'

Horses thundered past, churning up the perfect turf, wheeling in groups like cavalry in battle formation, or splintering off in ones and twos as play cracked back and forth. But Emma wasn't interested in the flow, or outcome, of the match, only in Alexei Rodokov. Her binoculars stayed on him the whole time. She could tell how aggressive and competitive he was, but she also saw him smiling at his team-mates and working with them. She thought again about what Frankie had told her last night on the phone, all she'd discovered from hacking into Forest Holdings, and felt the burden of what she must do weighing down on her.

There was an almost palpable buzz of excitement as the match finished. The Mavericks had won, trouncing the Guards team in style. As was traditional, all the ladies were invited on to the field to press in the clods of earth with their elegant shoes.

Emma could feel all eyes on her. But she held her head up high. She walked straight over the pitch, stone-walling Lola Reed, and on to the main players' marquee, following the line of horses being led through to the Players' Enclosure.

Rodokov dismounted, but didn't leave his horse's side. Two security men were guarding the gate, checking the security passes of the riders on their way through. They were pros, wearing head-mikes, muscular and lean. Half the royal family were here today: it was hardly surprising that security was tight.

Rodokov held up his pass for inspection, then led his horse through the gates. Emma slowed and turned around. There was no way she was going to be able to bluff her way in after him.

Think, she told herself. What would Peaches or Frankie do? She had to find a way in. They were relying on her. And time was running out.

Emma looked around and noticed a handsome older player leaning over a table in the marquee. His security pass was clipped to the back of his jodhpurs. She watched him look her appreciatively up and down as she approached.

She felt awkward and so damn obvious. But she had to get into the Players' Enclosure and talk to Alexei Rodokov right now. Before he left. This was the only place they knew for certain that he was going to be. And without any access to his diary, this could be the only opportunity for any of them to get to him for months.

You can do this, she told herself, arranging her face into her most flirtatious smile. She'd handled Vincent Detroy, she reminded herself, so an old boy like this should be no problem.

'Hello,' she said, noticing that his shirt was the same colour as the team which had just lost. 'That was jolly bad luck, you know. I think you deserved to win. And if the rest of your team had played half as well as you, you would have, too. I'm Emma, by the way,' she said, holding out her hand. 'Although, I'm absolutely positive we've met before. I couldn't forget a face as handsome and distinguished as yours . . .'

The man positively glowed at this unexpected flattery. 'Lionel Blakeley,' he said, taking her hand. 'May I offer you a glass of champagne?'

Taking her arm, he led her towards the bar. He flinched only slightly when she allowed her hand to come to rest just at the top of his jodhpurs and gently applied pressure. Then he smiled, no doubt thinking that his luck had just changed for the better. The whereabouts of his security pass was, without doubt, the last thing on his mind.

Ten minutes later, after fobbing off Blakeley with some very bogus promises to meet him later, Emma flashed his pass at the guard, pretending she was talking to a trainer on her phone. She kept her thumb over Lionel Blakeley's ID, giving the guard a grateful smile when he waved her through.

Act as if you own the joint, and it was amazing how many people believed that you did. It was a lesson Emma had learnt from the Khordinskys – from the way they'd moved like cuckoos into her former house and life.

Well, Emma was a quick learner. And now she was turning the lesson back on them, to get what was hers by right.

Inside the enclosure, Emma calculated that there must be at least thirty huge horse boxes, with the teams' logos emblazoned on the sides. People were everywhere: riders, trainers, grooms and ground staff.

Emma followed the horses into a paddock beyond the lorries where the stables were. The riders were all chatting excitedly as the grooms threw blankets over the steaming horses. She searched the men's faces, ducking through the crowd to catch a glimpse of the red-shirted riders. Then she saw him.

'Excuse me. Alexei Rodokov?' she asked, approaching the group of players.

Alex turned away from his conversation. He looked confused, as if trying to place her.

It was definitely him: just as Peaches and Frankie had described and yet disarmingly different too. He'd taken off his riding hat and his hair was wet with sweat. He pushed it back from his face. Emma supposed it was impossible to describe someone's charisma and their natural charm, but it radiated out of Alex. He had amazingly long eyelashes, she noticed, which counter-pointed his rugged, handsome face, making him seem friendly and approachable.

Emma could see immediately why Frankie had fallen for him. She could picture them together so easily. For a second, she was tempted to blurt out that she knew Frankie. That he had to reconsider everything he thought he knew about her. That her so-called relationship with Todd was a sham, and those photos – if he'd seen them – were an outrage . . .

But at the same time, Emma felt a maternal protective side kick in too. Was Alex really good enough for her Frankie? Did he deserve someone so wonderful having such faith in him? Emma would have to wait and see.

'Yes?' he said. His mouth was smiling, but his eyes were still assessing, no doubt trying to match a name to a face.

She saved him the effort. 'You don't know me, but we have friends in common. I know this sounds very presumptuous, but would you mind if I had a word with you?'

The smile disappeared, but he kept on staring at her with those wide intelligent eyes. 'If you want.'

'In private,' Emma insisted. 'It's extremely important.'

On hearing this comment, one of his team-mates muttered something to the man standing beside them. A wave of raucous schoolboy laughter rippled through the group but Alexei Rodokov silenced them with a single glance.

'Very well,' he told Emma, 'but it will have to be quick. I have a very busy schedule ahead of me today.'

Alex led her into a nearby stable block. The air was heavy with the steam coming from the horses and the pungent smell of leather saddles and dung. It instantly reminded Emma of the stables at Lechley Park and she thought of Pim and Susie and their desperate situation, how they'd put most of the Park up for sale, dismissed the staff and sold the animals, breaking Susie's heart.

'Is this private enough?' Alex asked.

'My name is Emma Harvey. My husband, Julian, set up a company called Platinum Holdings. You probably read about its demise in the press?' she said, wondering whether she sounded as nervous as she felt.

Alex glanced quickly at his watch. 'I'm sorry, but I don't know what you're talking about.'

Emma tried to read his expression. Was he lying? she wondered. It was impossible to tell.

She felt the gloom of the stables suddenly closing in on her, as if someone had drawn a blind. The weight of optimism and determination that had driven her here seemed to evaporate under Alex's cool stare.

Their whole plan, everything, relied on him, but now that she was face to face with him, she realized what a terrible mistake it could all be. What if Alex turned out to be as corrupt as Khordinsky? She felt the information she had that could affect the young man's life so dramatically burning inside her mind. He was holding a time-bomb and he didn't know it.

But she couldn't tell him. Not yet. That wasn't the plan.

'My husband, Julian Harvey, set up a platinum mine in

Russia,' she said, 'on a development site sold to him by Dimitry Sergeyokov.'

Rodokov's poker face wavered for the first time. She had his attention now.

'Go on.'

'But you see the mine – everything about the project was fraudulent.'

Alex narrowed his eyes. 'I'm really not sure what this has to do with me,' he said. He crossed his muscular arms and glanced back at his team-mates, who'd set off for the main marquee.

Emma took a deep breath. She had to get straight to the point. She couldn't risk him walking away. 'I'm afraid it has a great deal to do with you. You see Julian committed suicide as a result of what happened. Well . . . that's the way they made it look.'

'They? Made it look? What are you saying?'

'I'm saying that I think your boss Khordinsky used Sergeyokov to set up my husband. In order to steal all our money, and move into my house.'

His eyes darkened with warning. 'You should be very careful what else you say. And who you say it to. These are very serious accusations—'

'But what if I could tell you that I've got proof that Khordinsky will frame you for it?'

Alex looked stunned. He stepped towards her. 'Is this some kind of joke?'

Seeing Alex react like this filled Emma with strength. She knew that there must already be a seed of doubt in his mind, or he would have laughed in her face and dismissed her as a crank, or a blackmailer. Or both.

'No,' she told him. 'It's not a joke. I'm serious. Deadly serious.'

He stared at her for a moment. Searching her eyes. Finding only the truth in what she was saying. She could tell he was flustered. 'If you have information, then I demand to see it.'

'I have to know that I can trust you. You really can't tell Khordinsky – or anyone – about any of this.'

'I'll be the judge of that.'

'No. You see, you may be in great danger. And once *you*

know what *we* know about the connection between Forest Holdings and Matryoshka-Enterprises—'

Rodokov's cool composure collapsed entirely now. He gave up all pretence of being in control. He looked suddenly so much younger, Emma couldn't help thinking, as if the clothes he was wearing belonged to somebody else. As if he really didn't belong here at all.

'*We?*' he asked, unable to keep the astonishment from his face. 'Are you the police? Government? What?' He glanced furtively over her shoulder towards the security gates, as if he expected at any second to hear the whoop of a siren and see a police van come bursting through.

'Neither, but I can't tell you any more.' She'd already said way too much. And she'd done what she came here to do. She'd lit a flame of curiosity in Alex Rodokov. A flame that she hoped his self-doubt and instinct for survival would soon fan into an all-consuming fire. 'Not now. Not here.'

'When?'

'Go to LA. This weekend.'

'Los Angeles? You want me to go to Los Angeles? Just because you tell me to?'

Emma opened her handbag and handed him a card. 'There'll be a suite for you at Boulevard 19. When you get there, call this number and someone will tell you where to go. But you have to come alone. It's absolutely essential.'

Alexei Rodokov held the card in his hand. 'Why should I trust you?' he asked, his look dark.

'Because, I'm afraid, you really can't afford not to.'

CHAPTER THIRTY-SEVEN

From the front, the Clover Hill mansion in Bel-Air looked just like it normally did these days: empty whilst being refurbished. Its windows were blacked out; its front lawns with their famous date palm trees were unlit. The sprinklers watered the lawns in the dark. Perhaps it would be possible for a passer-by – in the unlikely event that there would be one – to detect a faint thudding of muffled music, but it would be hard to pinpoint where it was coming from, let alone suspect it was coming from inside the historic mansion itself.

But now, way past midnight, the private road at the back was jammed with a queue of limousines and sports cars. All the headlights were off.

The entrance used by the building contractors had been skilfully disguised so that a black tunnel led from the darkened car pool into the back of the building and then into a lobby where guests' invitations were carefully checked, before each guest was escorted into individual red velvet booths for a series of coded questions.

Once they'd passed all the checks, their coats were taken, their phones, cameras and watches stored and logged, and they were given a moment to adjust their costumes in the giant, flatteringly lit mirrors and don the regulation masks that the invitation had stipulated. Then, escorted by one of the sensationally semi-naked and sequin-covered girls in feather masks, the guests were invited through another black curtain, past a wall of temporary sound-proofing, before finally being ushered through the doorway beyond.

And then, only then, did the full impact of Peaches Gold's Depravity Night party hit home.

The party was in full swing. In every sense. The scene was insane, like a wild Warhol fantasy. Sexy ambient music mixed with a club beat thumped out from the giant sound system, with synched lights illuminating the crowd below. Twenty naked female dancers were doing their most lavish hip-grinding sliding on the poles. Two leather-clad S&M models, suspended above the crowd in a cage, were nonchalantly fucking. At the room's centre, inside a ten-metre-high transparent Perspex cube, a cluster of professional porn stars were hard at it, putting on a live show. A set of double doors led through to the dining room, which had been kitted out with a padded drum in which guests slithered in scented massage oil, a mass of naked bodies.

Upstairs, Peaches leant over the balcony surveying her kingdom, smiling. She pushed aside the skirt of her dramatically high-cut feather skirt and opened the door to the master suite. She felt confident the security was tight enough. She'd taken every precaution. No press. No journos. And, most importantly of all, none of Khordinsky's thugs.

'Going OK?' she asked Melanie. Like all her girls tonight, Melanie was wearing the feathered mask and a sequin harness which exposed her pert breasts and looped around a thong to feather plumage at the back. Christoph Zerelli had designed them especially. They were hot as hell.

'Sure is,' Melanie replied. 'It's a great party, Peaches. It's *all action* back there.'

Peaches peeked inside the long red curtain that had been set up across the master suite. She could see immediately what Melanie meant. Inside, black-and-white 1930s porn movies were being projected on to the walls and ceiling. In the centre of the room was a colossal bed. Next to it was a mirrored table, racked up with lines. Two jeroboams of champagne already lay empty beside it on the thick carpet. On the bed were twenty naked people making out. Others stood. Watching. Stroking. Waiting to be invited in. The air was heavy with scented candles and delirious moans, just audible over the louche French funk.

Peaches had to raise an eyebrow. She could only speculate how many tens of thousands a top paparazzi photographer would throw at her to see what she was seeing right now.

There were at least three Hollywood A-listers on that bed, and Peaches could see that it hadn't taken a certain über-famous newly-wed couple long to break their vow of monogamy. Peaches silently whistled as she watched one of Todd's more notorious female co-stars straddle her husband as he lay on the bed, another girl astride his face. She watched as the actress held open her famous buttocks, inviting in another A-list masked guest. Not so Mrs Humanitarian Charity Worker now, Peaches thought.

Peaches walked back down the main staircase, before stopping for a moment on the half-landing, looking out of the giant square window on to the terrace and pool below. Everyone was having a great time, swimming naked. She could see Eddie Roland in the hot tub with four girls. He was smoking a fat cigar and laughing as he fondled Monica DuCane's breasts.

There must be at least three hundred people here, Peaches thought. Nearly everyone on the guest list. Except one.

Again, she scanned the crowd.

'The chicks with dicks are ready,' Angela said, hurrying over.

Peaches smiled at her and squeezed her shoulder, grateful to her for having helped so much with the organization. And how supportive she'd been in the wake of Irena's murder, organizing a visa for Yana and wiring her money.

Peaches knew that Angela felt extra confident tonight, with her mask covering her face. She was wearing a long sheath dress that showed off her slinky curves. Peaches hoped that she was going to relax a bit and let her hair down. She might even get some action. It would be hard not to in this place.

'Right, OK, I'm on it,' Peaches said, walking down the rest of the stairs, past a girl dressed in a black horse's costume, complete with a mane and a saddle on her back. She was being chased up the stairs by a man with a riding crop. A personal friend of the Queen, so Peaches had been reliably informed.

On the wall behind Peaches, she saw the giant screen projecting the action in the dungeon room downstairs. Betsy, one of Peaches' more curvaceous girls, was clearly enjoying stirring up some crazy S&M shit with those big boy studio execs. Peaches hoped that, with a queue like that, the hot wax didn't run out. She smiled. Good God, that was old Murray Seagram-Cohen, if she wasn't mistaken. Stretched out on the rack. Bet he never expected *that* to happen in his kitchen!

Peaches swept on through the crowd dancing in the main lobby to the drawing room, which she'd kitted out with a hall of mirrors. In every direction, she could see the threesome on the central sofa reflected a thousand times.

Through the drawing room, she went into the small room set up as a dressing room behind the stage area in the hallway. Peaches was virtually unshockable, but she still raised an eyebrow at Loretta, Lily and Livinia, who had all had genital reassignment plastic surgery. In every respect but one, they looked like women. Hot women. Faces, hair, tits, legs – all great. But they still had their dicks. Three great big hard dicks, to be precise. *Tits and tackle. Twice the fun*, their business card had proudly proclaimed. Peaches had no doubt that with the fetishists here tonight, their floorshow would be a hit.

'You girls ready?' Peaches asked. 'The lighting will be just how we discussed. The guys are moving your set on to the stage right now.'

Peaches peeked around the corner of the door into the hall. And then she saw him. She'd had his invitation and mask couriered around to his hotel. But even in his Zorro-like mask, she recognized Alexei Rodokov because of the mole just above his lip and the commanding way he stood, somehow seeming to create space around him without having to try. And because Peaches doubted that you ever could forget the face of someone you once thought was about to shoot you dead.

He stood in the doorway, taking in the cage dancers and the masked party revellers, but there was no sense of enjoyment on what she could see of his face, no sign of a titillated smile.

In fact, if anything, he looked as if he was about to turn to go.

'Good luck,' Peaches told the Ladyboys. 'There's a special guest who just arrived. You carry on, I'll catch up with you later. Enjoy.'

She quickly walked towards Rodokov, glancing up to the landing and nodding to Paul, who was standing guard outside a bedroom door. He hurried down the central stairway. He'd agreed to be her personal security guard for the night. And of all the myriad potential flashpoints Peaches had anticipated, this was by far and away the worst.

'I'm glad you could make it,' Peaches said, walking straight up to Alexei Rodokov. She wondered whether he recognized her at all. She saw his dark eyes beneath his mask, but she couldn't read his expression. 'You came alone?' Peaches remembered Alexei Rodokov's bodyguard all too well.

'Of course I did. How else would I have got in? But what's going on? What's all this about?' His voice was guarded. 'I came for information, not . . . this . . .'

But he'd still come, Peaches thought, smiling to herself. He was here. And now that they'd got him, they were one step closer to achieving their goal. But she couldn't count her chickens yet, she cautioned herself. There was still a long way to go.

'Come with me,' Peaches said. She led him through the party and up the stairs. Paul shadowed them step for step. She watched Alex out of the corner of her eye, feeling suspicion and caution radiating out of him. He glanced out of the window.

'Jesus,' he muttered.

With every step he took, he looked more and more out of place. Probably no bad thing, Peaches thought to herself. Men like Rodokov were used to being in control of their environment and of everyone in them. Throwing him out of his depth like this could only make him weaker and more malleable. Which in turn could only improve their chances of success.

'In here,' Peaches said, stopping by the bedroom door. 'Paul will wait outside the door,' she said. 'If there's any trouble . . .'

'Don't worry,' Paul said to Peaches, whilst eyeballing Rodokov. 'I know what to do if this punk steps out of line.'

Peaches appreciated Paul's support, but she somehow

doubted that Alex would do anything to merit his intervention. No, she already knew that Alexei Rodokov may be many things, but a murderer wasn't one of them.

And now it was time to find out what he was. Or what he wasn't. And what he might become.

CHAPTER THIRTY-EIGHT

Frankie could hear that the party was really hotting up down there. She was surrounded on the other side of all these walls by naked, horny, carefree pleasure-seekers. And yet here she was in a dimly lit bedroom, fully clothed, her heart racing with nerves.

She was sitting on a small sofa with Tommy Liebermann, behind an antique two-metre-high dressing screen, which kept them both concealed from the rest of the room. Their nervous tension was such that they both flinched when the bedroom door finally opened. Frankie felt her toes tingle, as if she'd just climbed up on a roof and was dangling her toes over the edge.

The music was loud for a moment. Then muffled again, as the door closed. Frankie held her breath.

'Hello?'

Alex. He was here! His voice was unmistakable. The plan had worked. Whatever Emma had said had been enough to get him to LA. And Peaches' intriguing note with his mask had then been enough to bring him the rest of the way tonight.

Now it was Frankie's turn.

'Hello?' he called again. 'Is there anyone here?'

Frankie took a deep breath. It took every ounce of her

willpower not to rush out from behind the silk screen to him. But Tommy Liebermann held her back. He stared steadily at her, forcing her to remember the plan. He stepped out from behind the screen and flicked on a switch of the small bedside lamp.

'Who the hell are you?' she heard Alex say to him.

'Actually, I'm someone who's going to save your life,' Tommy said. 'You'd better sit down, son.'

Son? Frankie could only stare at the screen aghast, dreading how Alex might react. Tommy probably thought he was sounding avuncular, but Frankie knew damn well that Alex might equally read it as patronizing and walk straight back out. Or worse.

But Alex said nothing. There was silence – two seconds, three, four – until Frankie couldn't bear it any longer. She crept forward and peered through the hinged gap in the screen into one of the bedroom's wall mirrors, which showed Alex in profile.

Her stomach involuntarily twitched with desire. God, he was gorgeous, Frankie thought, even staring fixedly at Tommy Liebermann as he was doing now, his mask already off, gripped in his hand like a gun.

She clasped her hands in front of her. Alex. Her Alex. Her lover. He was here. Just footsteps away.

For a second, she forgot the seriousness of the situation and all the hard work and planning that had allowed it to come about. All context seemed to disappear. Instead she saw the man of her dreams, standing at the foot of a huge wooden bed, and her whole body ached to rush into his arms. To fall back on the bed. To be naked. To have him holding her close and tight, whispering words of love in her ear.

But then she remembered the reality. He might be physically only a metre away, but they were still emotionally worlds apart. They were estranged. No longer an item. They'd been smashed by Khordinsky. And that's why she had to keep her cool. To wait, to watch, to see if they could ever be together again.

Alex wasn't her lover. Not any more and maybe never again. The truth was she didn't even know whether he was her friend or enemy any more.

Tommy, Peaches and Frankie had decided that it would be best if Tommy confronted Alex first. Alex would be more likely to believe the devastating financial news Tommy had to deliver if it came from a lawyer.

As Tommy started to talk, Frankie saw Alex slowly sit in the low armchair at the foot of the bed. He looked more tense than she'd ever seen him. His eyebrows drew together in a frown as he heard Tommy out.

Frankie stayed still and silent, watching him, as they'd all agreed she should. Only by watching him in secret would she know, and she had to see it for herself. She had to see his reaction. She had to know for sure whether he was working for Khordinsky, or whether, as she suspected, he knew nothing about Khordinsky's plan to double-cross him.

As Tommy started handing him the documents that she and Danny had found, she quickly had her answer. Alex's expression changed from suspicion to bafflement, then to outrage and shame as he compared the two sets of accounts for Forest Holdings. He put his hand over his mouth and Frankie could see the dawning comprehension of what Khordinsky had done. Alex clearly had no idea that he'd stripped all the assets.

'In Tortola, Vincent Detroy—' Tommy said.

'I went there to shut down some dormant companies.'

'Matryoshka-Enterprises? That's what he told you? Bob Veris? Your finance guy? He's in Khordinsky's pocket, along with Detroy. There're emails between them all.' Tommy shuffled through the printed emails and handed some to Alex. 'Those companies weren't dormant at all.'

'But the papers I signed showed they hadn't been used for years.'

'That's what they wanted you to think. But those companies were used for money-laundering for years, including all the money that belonged to Platinum Holdings. And when you signed those papers, your name proves your responsibility for it all. Which means when the fraud squad come calling, it's your name they'll be shouting the loudest.'

And Frankie saw in that moment that the penny had dropped. She could see it in his eyes. In the incredulity on his face.

'I knew nothing. I never suspected...' Alex said. He scanned over another email. 'Jesus Christ. That woman – Emma Harvey – she was telling the truth. Yuri did set up her husband ... and me ...'

'I'm afraid so,' Tommy said. His voice was gentler now. He knew he no longer needed to convince Alex he was telling the truth. 'And you'd better take a look at these.' He handed Alex Khordinsky's emails.

'"My ... my *fall guy*",' Alex said, quoting from the page. His voice was a whisper. The colour had drained from his cheeks.

'I'll leave you now,' Tommy said as Alex read on in silence. 'I'm sure you'll want some time to think about what I've told you.'

'Wait,' Alex said, suddenly registering that Tommy was leaving. He quickly rose. 'Wait, don't go.'

But it was too late. Tommy Liebermann had already slipped out of the bedroom door, which now swung shut with a click.

Alex gripped his forehead and asked aloud. 'Why? Why are you telling me this?'

'Because I want to save you,' Frankie answered.

Alex froze at the sound of her voice and slowly turned to face her as she stepped out from behind the screen into the pool of light.

When their eyes met, she felt her stomach lift; her heart was airborne suddenly, just as it had been when she'd first seen him stepping off the helicopter on *Pushkin*.

But there was to be no embrace, no hoped-for instant reconciliation. Instead, he stared at her in dismay. He looked haunted, disorientated, as if he'd discovered he was stuck in a dream which no longer made any sense. As if he no longer knew what, or who, to believe.

His eyes squeezed shut for a second, seemingly trying to wring her image away. But when he opened them again, he saw that she was still there.

'Frankie,' he said neutrally, unemotionally, finally accepting that she was really present. He looked down at the papers strewn over the divan between them, apparently realizing for the first time that Frankie and the information he'd just been given were connected.

He shook his head, as if breaking a hypnotic spell. She saw

his eyes brighten as his brain began to do the maths. She could almost feel the rush of his speeding mind weighing up the possibilities. Processing them all, in order to come back to himself and reassert his grip on his shaken world.

Inside, she ached to touch him. But if he still had feelings for her, he quickly hid them.

'If you knew all this, why the subterfuge?' he said. 'Why not just tell me? Why bring me all the way to LA? To this ridiculous party?'

'Because we had to meet somewhere in secret. Somewhere Khordinsky wouldn't follow you or think of finding you.'

He let her comment hang in the air. 'But . . . how? How did you get all this information?'

'You kept your password,' she said, and he nodded. He'd worked out that much at least. 'I hacked in to the Forest Holdings database,' she went on. 'With some expert help.'

'Remind me to fire my IT guy,' Alex said with a wry laugh. He put his hand on the back of his neck and swallowed hard.

'We had to get this information to you in person, Alex,' she said, wanting to hold him, to tell him that no matter how he might feel now, this was the best thing that could have happened. She wanted him to know that everything was going to be OK – even though she couldn't be sure of that herself. 'In secret,' she continued. 'You know how clever Khordinsky is. And he doesn't want anyone on his trail. The last time I tried to get information in Tortola—'

He looked up at her. 'You were in Tortola?'

She nodded. 'I went to find you. On my birthday. But instead . . .' She didn't know how much to tell him, or how much he already knew. Had he seen the photos? Was he aware they'd been taken by force? She decided that the truth was the only option. 'Khordinsky's men abducted me.'

Alex suddenly looked like he'd been punctured. 'Who? They did . . . they did what?'

'They drugged me and took those photographs of me. They said they were going to show them to you.'

'What? I don't know what you're talking about. No one has showed me any photos.'

Relief washed over her. She couldn't believe she'd got to him first. She took a deep breath to steady herself, then she quickly told him how she'd gone to Tortola and met Emma, and what Emma had told Frankie about Julian. And how Frankie, in turn, had agreed to help her. She described the storm, how they'd just missed Alex, and how they'd broken into Detroy's office to copy the files. And then she told them about the three masked men. How they'd slashed Emma's face, and taken Frankie. Alex put both hands on his head as he listened, his eyes wide with incredulity.

'Oh Jesus, Frankie. Were you hurt?'

'Horrified more than hurt. Horrified that you'd see the pictures and think—'

Alex rushed forward and gripped her wrists. His eyes bored into hers. 'I had no idea. I can't believe anyone would do something so vile. What were their names? Tell me. I swear I'm going to make those motherfuckers wish they'd never been born.'

'No,' Frankie told him, determinedly staring back into the cold fury in his eyes. 'This isn't about them any more. This is about something much bigger. About Khordinsky. About you and me and what happens now.' Her voice cracked. 'I'm just so relieved,' she said. 'I thought you'd believe what you were seeing, like you did with Todd.'

'But I thought you weren't interested. I thought—'

'But don't you see? Khordinsky was behind all that, too. He made you think I cared about Todd Lands, but it was all lies. That night in Cannes . . . I was tricked. Sonny Wiseman owed Khordinsky money. He set me up. I wasn't interested in Todd. Not for a second. You must know that.'

Alex looked around them. 'So all of this?' he asked. 'Bringing me here . . . telling me – no,' he corrected himself, '*proving* to me how Yuri's being using me for all this time, you went through all that . . . for me?' he asked.

'Oh Alex, *of course* I did,' she said. 'I couldn't give up until you'd found out the truth. And now you have.'

'Oh Frankie, Frankie . . .' he gasped.

She saw that he realized the full extent of his mistake. But however much she longed for his apology, for them to be finally reconciled, there was still so much to tell him.

'How could Yuri do that?' he exclaimed. 'To you. To me. To us . . .'

'But it's not just us. Emma, who you met in the UK, and Peaches. She's the one who brought you into this room. They're in on this too. Listen, Alex, I don't know what you want to do, but you've probably got enough time to get yourself off the hook. But it won't be long before Khordinsky pulls the plug and the authorities catch up with you. And there's no way *they'll* believe you're innocent.'

'Oh God, Frankie. This can't be happening.'

Alex turned away from her. He ran his hand over his hair, he stared again at the documents, then up at Frankie. She saw determination in his face. And something else too . . . something familiar. The look she'd desperately wanted since she'd left him in Marrakech.

She wanted nothing more than to fling herself into his arms. To kiss him. To tell him that he must now realize how she felt. To know once and for all that she'd got him back. But she forced herself to think of Peaches and Emma and the commitment they both needed from him.

'We need your help to take him down, Alex. You're the only way to get to him. He won't suspect that you know any of this.'

She looked at him, waiting for his answer, feeling her heart pounding against her chest.

But suddenly the door burst open. Paul stood there, a look of panic on his face.

'Quick, we gotta go,' he said. 'Now!'

Frankie and Alex looked at each other, then followed him on to the balcony. There were people rushing everywhere, naked, half-naked, screaming, trying to cover themselves up. The lights had been switched on. Armed FBI agents were pouring through the front door and the side entrances. The music ripped to a stop. Footsteps pounded. Someone shrieked in pain. Outside, Frankie could hear people screaming in the pool.

'Nobody move!' a voice boomed out through a megaphone. 'This is a raid.'

'Oh *shit*!' Frankie gasped.

'This way,' Paul said, hurrying them along the balcony, close to the wall. He opened a door directly on to a scaffolding grid and the cold night air. Patrol car lights flicked below. Sirens whooped. A naked woman sprinted across the brightly lit lawn, only to be cornered up against a tree by a baying police dog on a handler's leash.

Frankie looked over her shoulder. She stayed, one foot inside, one foot outside. She felt torn. She could see Peaches standing on the bottom step of the staircase. She'd taken off her mask. A female agent stepped up to her.

'Peaches Gold, I'm arresting you on behalf of the United States Government,' she said, as two of her colleagues spun Peaches around and cuffed her hands behind her back.

Frankie should stay and help. They were in this together. But Paul was outside now, and Alex was too, holding out his hand to her.

'Come,' he said. 'Now!'

'Do it, lady,' Paul said. 'Peaches would want you out of here. Both of you.'

She did what Paul said. She no longer had a choice.

CHAPTER THIRTY-NINE

Tommy Liebermann looked like he hadn't slept for days as he wearily sat down on the metal chair in the interview room. Peaches felt like she hadn't slept for months. She'd been a prisoner since the Feds busted her party and now she had no idea what time of day it was, or what the hell was going on.

They'd given her a nylon tracksuit to change into. Peaches couldn't bear the scratchy synthetic feeling of it on her skin, or the acrid stink of detergent. But worst of all was the grim knowledge that she was already dressed in prison clothes and the people who were keeping her here wanted to make that look permanent.

She had plenty of time-tested remedies for freshening up after being at an all-nighter: ice-packs, her wheat-grass and vitamin smoothies and the rehydrating spa bath at Delancy Heights. But right now they all seemed a world away.

'She's a real piece of work, I'm telling you,' Tommy whispered, nodding at the silhouette of Detective Nancy Pounder, who was chatting to an officer on the other side of the reinforced glass door to the interview room. He pulled at the collar of his shirt and a bead of sweat trickled down his brow. 'I did everything I could, but she ain't letting you out of her sight now that she's got you. She thinks she's got enough to put you away.'

'She hasn't got jack shit,' Peaches said. She sighed and rubbed her face. She'd been anticipating this showdown all night, ever since Pounder had cut off their first interview at five a.m. It had been a sneaky move, but Peaches hadn't fallen for it. Throughout that hour-long grilling, Peaches had said nothing, on account of the fact that her lawyer wasn't present. Tommy had gone home to get a change of clothes. He'd come straight back as soon as he'd found out what they'd done.

Pounder had drilled Peaches with question after question. Who did Peaches supply with girls? Where was she on this date and that?

Dates and names from her black book, Peaches deduced. They'd taken it when they'd arrested her. But most of the names were nicknames. Or in code. And even if Pounder were to chase down all the phone numbers, she'd still need one of Peaches' customers to squeal. And who the hell was going to admit to a penchant for call girls?

Other questions had come next. Which girls worked for her? What were their aliases? Where did they live? What was Peaches' cut? Where did she bury the cash? All questions but no answers. Peaches had given nothing away.

But, as Tommy pointed out, once his anger at Pounder's underhand tactics had calmed, Pounder hadn't given away anything either. So far, she hadn't produced one witness or one taped conversation. No evidence, at all, in fact. Zilch.

Which was why Peaches wasn't as worried as she might otherwise have been. The longer she sat here without being officially charged, the weaker Pounder's case began to look.

So Pounder had been tipped off about the party? So what? No doubt some bum with a grudge against Peaches had decided to ditch her in the shit. That still didn't mean Pounder could prove Peaches was behind it. And until she could, Peaches was sticking to her story: she'd just been a paying guest, the same as the other three hundred people. What was Pounder planning on doing? Locking them all up and throwing away the key? With the people in that party and the massed money and power they wielded, Peaches somehow doubted that very much.

Peaches put her hand over Tommy's to comfort him. She knew he'd done everything he could to help her. She knew he'd taken the bust hard, especially after he'd warned Peaches to be careful.

'Keep cool, Tommy,' she told him. 'This is going to be just fine.'

Now Detective Pounder came into the room, her muscular, unmade-up face set in a stern, unforgiving look. But Peaches noticed a flicker of triumph in her eyes as she slapped down a folder on the table.

Peaches was learning to hate this woman more every second. She checked Nancy's hand. Unmarried; no kids. Secret bull-dyke tendencies, Peaches wouldn't mind betting. She was large; her horrible coffee-coloured suit did her no favours; her ill-fitting bra beneath the white shirt made her tits lumpy and unattractive. Her mousy hair was pulled back in a plain bunch and her top lip showed a shadow of a moustache. She was the kind of woman, in other words, who would be likely to feel the most antipathy towards Peaches and her girls.

'My client does not appreciate being held like this,' Tommy Liebermann started.

'Well, she'd better get used to it,' Detective Pounder said, eyeballing Peaches. 'By the time we've finished, Miss Gold – or Stacey-Louise Rockbine – here, will be behind bars for a long time.'

Peaches flinched at the use of her old name. Not just because of the memories attached to it, but because it meant that Pounder did have something on her after all.

She's just sweating you out. Interrogation technique. Hoping to make you crack and admit something, Peaches thought. Well, she could go fuck herself. She was about to discover that Peaches Gold was made of stronger stuff than that.

Still, she had to concede that it was clever that they'd put a woman like Pounder in charge of the investigation. Peaches might have been able to manipulate a man, but she knew she would get nowhere with this bitch.

'Either charge my client or let her go,' Tommy said.

'Well, that's simple, Mr Liebermann, I'm going to get your client here on very serious pandering charges,' Detective Pounder said, still not breaking eye contact with Peaches.

'What?' Peaches glanced over at Tommy.

'You know, procuring prostitutes for other people.'

'What's your proof?' Tommy demanded. Pounder ignored him.

'And that's just for starters. As for that party . . .' She was staring at Peaches as if she were something she'd scraped off her boot.

Hell, Peaches thought, refusing to be intimidated, she hadn't forced people into coming. No one got hurt – apart from the S&M freaks, and they'd queued up for the privilege. But the way she was being treated, anyone would think she was responsible for the crime of the century.

'As a matter of interest, why do I get to you so much?' Peaches interrupted.

'Excuse me?'

'Just your attitude. All this . . .' Peaches said, keeping her tone friendly. She could tell she'd wrong-footed Pounder by making it personal. But what the heck? Peaches thought. She might as well try and rattle her opposite number. Rattled people make mistakes.

Detective Pounder paused. 'You really want to know? OK, I'll tell you. Because if you saw the drug-addled prostitutes that I have, and the way they've wrecked their lives and, more importantly, their kids' lives, you'd get pissed at their pimps too.'

'You're accusing my client of being a pimp?' Tommy chipped in. Again Pounder ignored him.

'Get me out of here, Tommy,' Peaches said. 'She can't prove anything.'

'You want to bet?' Pounder said. 'I know about your office. About what goes on there.'

This was just more bluster, Peaches thought. She made sure someone was in the office to answer the phones all the time, either Angela or Marguerite, or one of the other girls she trusted to help her out occasionally, in return for hanging out by the pool and using the spa.

'My office? I run a legitimate business from there. You gonna bust me for making panties?'

'No, just everything else. We've had your offices bugged for weeks. We're going to bust you for supplying hookers to Loney

Mason, Sheikh Fizal Abdul and Tony Sternberg, to name but a few.'

Peaches almost laughed. Who cared where Pounder had got those names from? If those were the best guys she had, then Peaches was safe. None of them would breathe a word, let alone put in an appearance in court. Mason was probably halfway across the Atlantic already. And the sheikh would squeal diplomatic immunity at the first sight of a Fed's ID.

'Screw you,' Peaches said. She felt Tommy's foot dart out under the table and touch hers.

'What my client means to say,' Tommy said, 'is do you actually have any hard evidence? Witnesses? Or is this just a fishing exercise?'

Detective Pounder sat in the chair opposite Peaches. Then she lifted open the file on the desk and pushed Peaches' black book on to the table. 'What about everyone in here,' she said.

'What about them? That's my address book. Everyone in there is just a friend,' Peaches said. Friends who wouldn't tell Pounder a goddamned thing. Not unless they wanted to wind up in prison themselves.

Peaches smiled. She could almost smell the fresh air waiting for her outside. The first thing she'd do when she got out was go straight for brunch. Followed by a massage and facial.

'Do you want to know how we bugged your office?' Pounder asked, interrupting Peaches' train of thought. 'Do you know who gave us due cause?'

'Assuming you do have due cause, which still has to be established to my satisfaction,' Tommy said.

Peaches looked up and saw that Pounder was now leaning forward across the desk, her hands splayed either side of the folder, like the claws of a cat.

Peaches felt a sudden chill of fear. She didn't like the way Pounder was watching her. Not one bit. She was clearly serious then, about the office being bugged. It didn't look like it was a bluff. Still, she forced herself to stay defiant.

'Surprise me,' she said.

Which is exactly what Pounder did. 'Marguerite Honchas.'

'Never heard of her,' Peaches said automatically. But something in her face must have given her away, because Pounder smiled, looking more like a Cheshire cat than ever.

'Bet you thought you could trust her,' Pounder said. 'After everything you've done for her.'

Peaches didn't answer. She felt her knee begin to tremble and quickly uncrossed her legs. Marguerite? It didn't seem possible. Pounder had to be bluffing. There was no way Marguerite would have betrayed her like this.

'We already knew she was working for you, you see. So when she got picked up on a possession rap, we got right on to her about you. If it's any comfort, it wasn't an easy choice for her. But it was doing hard time or working for us. So guess which one she chose?'

Peaches felt sick. With Marguerite to translate for them, the names and dates in Peaches' black book would soon start to make sense. And if Marguerite was prepared to give evidence herself . . . ? Christ. Peaches suddenly thought of all the recent dates she'd sent her on with the Senator.

And if they linked Peaches and the Senator, all hell would break loose. She wasn't stupid. The Senator would pile everything at Peaches' door. That fat loud-mouthed asshole would make sure she was made an example of before any blame stuck with him.

'It was Marguerite who told us about your party. All the secrecy. All the drugs you'd organized to be there. And how much cash you were gonna be pulling in. *Tax*-free . . .'

Peaches felt a hot flush of anger. After all the money and effort she'd laid out on security, the grass had been on the inside all along, co-ordinating the sting, waiting to give the signal so that the raid would cause maximum embarrassment to Peaches and her guests.

'And she's not the only one,' Pounder continued. 'You see, Miss Gold, it's a bit like dominoes. One rolls over . . . ? It's only a matter of time before the others start toppling too.'

And Peaches had a lot of dominoes. Who else was prepared to talk? Who else had they approached already? What other names were listed in that folder on the desk? Angela. Ella. Suzy too . . . all those girls she'd rescued from the street. And the undergraduates, and the actresses. Would they be loyal to Peaches? Or would they turn snitch, like Marguerite?

Hell, none of them would want to be dragged through a court case, forced to testify against her, asked in public about things they'd done that should only ever be spoken about in private. How the hell would a jury ever understand what they'd all been through? How would they explain away the tips, the lifestyle . . . ? Which one of them *wouldn't* refuse the easy way out?

The room seemed to darken, as if a cloud had just slid across the sun. It was over: the game she'd been playing all these years, the one she'd vowed time and time again to quit, but somehow never had.

She didn't consult Tommy. Didn't need to. She made her decision quick.

It was the only choice she had. The only tiny chink of light she could see. Her only chance.

'I want to make a deal,' she told Pounder, looking up.

Pounder laughed. 'Forget it, sugar. You're in no position to make any sort of deal.'

Peaches leant forward. She took a breath. 'But what if I said I could get you something far bigger than me? Even bigger than a bunch of Hollywood fat cats? What if I could give you something *really* big? International? The kind of catch that'll make your career for good?'

'Peaches, what's going on?' Tommy Liebermann asked.

Peaches shook her head to silence him. She looked Nancy Pounder in the eyes. She could tell she'd more than sparked her interest. It was time to call in the only contact she had in diplomatic circles. 'Get Harry Rezler on the phone,' she said.

'Who?' Pounder and Tommy asked at the same time.

'US Embassy, Moscow.'

Surprisingly, Peaches had never been to Washington before. And now, as she and Tommy were escorted by two Federal Agents into the downtown high-rise and led through the airport-style security with bag and body searches by no-nonsense armed guards, she couldn't help feeling the weight of the situation pressing down on her more and more.

Somehow, in LA, the way she conducted her business had always seemed legitimate, excusable even, considering that the demand far exceeded the supply she was responsible for. She was just filling an economic gap, giving the great American people what they wanted, facilitating democratic freedom of choice and open market capitalism: no more, no less.

But in this grim, grey Government fortress her circumstances suddenly seemed so much worse. She no longer felt like the people's champion, but their enemy. A huge crest hanging above her in the lobby loomed like a giant fly swat. Below it, the marbled floor was polished to a glossy finish with inlaid gold lettering reading *Truth and Justice*.

Whenever Peaches had thought about getting caught she'd always felt a shiver of anticipation along with the fear. She realized now she'd always known that one day, it *would* happen. She would get caught. Her freedom would be on the line. And only then would she face the ultimate challenge. She'd survived some terrible things, she knew, but would she be smart enough to survive this?

Well, she thought, following Tommy and the two agents into the glistening steel-and-mirror elevator, she was about to get her chance to find out.

'You sure about this?' Tommy whispered as the po-faced agents led them down a windowless corridor on the tenth floor. 'I thought you said this Rezler guy was just a consul in the embassy. He must have pulled some pretty big strings for us to be meeting him here.'

Peaches swallowed hard. She didn't tell Tommy, but she was just as surprised as he was. Maybe her gut instinct about Harry Rezler had been right all along. Maybe he *was* more connected than he made out. Maybe he was part of the Government. Hell, for all she knew, he could be CIA.

She certainly didn't expect to see Harry in person, but he was already in the interview room as the guards opened the door and led her and Tommy in. It smelt as if it had recently been refurbished; there was a new-looking speckled grey carpet. A plain wooden table and chairs stood beneath a loudly ticking clock on the wall, next to a window covered with a closed grey slatted blind. The other wall had a large mirror panel on it, probably with a camera recording on the other side, Peaches thought, looking up at the ceiling tiles and their harsh, unflattering lighting.

Harry was sitting on the edge of the table reading a file. A pair of designer tortoiseshell-framed glasses were perched on the end of his nose, making him look more distinguished than she remembered. More intimidating too. He had on a grey suit, but it was well tailored, Peaches noticed. He looked less dishevelled than he had in Moscow and more in control. On the top of his game, in fact.

He looked up as the agents pulled out chairs for Peaches and Tommy. He nodded to the agents and they both left, quietly shutting the door behind them. Still Harry didn't smile. He didn't give any indication of what was going on inside his mind. He contemplated Peaches as he might a stranger who was standing in his way on the sidewalk: as a temporary inconvenience that would soon be brushed aside.

In fact, he was looking at her as if – the ego-crushing realization hit her – *as if she was work*. Peaches felt her stomach flip over. Maybe it was nerves, or maybe it was just that those eyes which had once given her a feeling of safety now seemed to contain no feelings at all.

Peaches had been allowed a shower and Tommy had brought her clothes from home, but she still wished she looked better. Her reflection in the elevator had horrified her. She'd looked five years older than she had done a week ago. She flicked her hair over her shoulder and sat with her hands on her knees.

'Thanks for seeing us, Harry,' she said, trying to smile her most friendly smile.

Harry ignored her. Tommy looked at Peaches, alarmed. 'This is Tommy Liebermann,' Peaches continued, 'my attorney.'

'I know who he is,' Harry Rezler said, not looking up.

'So, um . . .' Peaches paused, trying to stop herself from sounding too nervous. She looked around, waiting for someone else to join them. 'Are we going to see someone official?'

'Official?' Harry asked. He looked at her and her heart jolted.

'You're just with the embassy, right?' Tommy asked. 'We need to see someone who can help us.'

Peaches had assured Tommy that she'd be able to talk Harry into getting them to the right people. She knew how sceptical Tommy was about her plan. Until she'd seen Harry's expression just now, she'd been convinced she was right. Well, anything was worth a try. Anything was a damn sight better than being in the clutches of that bitch Nancy Pounder. And no matter how Harry regarded her now, she still had her trump card to play. She could win him round. She had to believe that.

Be confident, she told herself. Pull this off and it wouldn't only be her own problems she'd be solving, but Frankie and Emma's as well.

Harry Rezler walked to the other side of the desk and sat down. He looked at the file, then he took off his glasses and laid them on top of the paperwork. 'It's OK. I'm official enough. I can deal with this.'

Something in his tone, in the flicker of knowing amusement made the penny drop for Peaches. This office – the embassy job – it was all just a cover. Harry Rezler was way more official than she'd ever guessed. How else would mentioning his name have made this meeting happen so quickly?

He looked at her now, seeing that it was all sinking in, but he didn't offer an explanation or give his real job description. Shocked as Peaches was, she realized what a stroke of luck this was.

'Well, Peaches,' Harry said, 'you've made some pretty big promises to my colleagues back there in LA. And my associates and I had to do some sweet-talking to get you here. So why don't you tell me what this is all about?'

His voice: Peaches remembered it now. It resonated through her like the sound of a soothing cello concerto.

Despite his frosty manner, she took solace from the fact he'd helped her get this far.

'They're cooking up some pretty big charges,' Tommy said.

'They want to take me down.' Peaches looked straight at Harry. Into him. She prayed that their brief encounter in Moscow that night had left an impression on him too. How ironic, she thought, that she'd looked at a thousand men the same way, wanting them to do what she wanted, but this was the only time it had ever really counted. But if Harry felt anything, he didn't show it. Still the neutral look. The work face.

Harry shook his head. 'I've read the file. I've talked to the DA. You don't stand a chance.'

'Don't I?' she asked. She stared at him again. This time he looked straight back at her. She could tell her charm was lost on him. She felt a dart of panic. 'I just thought . . . I mean, you said you'd help me. I thought we were friends.'

Harry raised his eyebrows at her. 'Friends? You sure had me fooled in Moscow. I had no idea you were this sort of—'

'I was being myself in Moscow, Harry,' she interrupted. 'I wasn't working.'

And you're not exactly a lowly embassy consul yourself, she wanted to say, but she didn't. He held her gaze for a moment and she knew that they were both acknowledging how little they'd really known about each other.

But despite all that, their meeting in Moscow *had* mattered and just because they'd both lied about what they did for a living didn't change that, did it? But she could see his scepticism. Why would someone like Harry ever believe that someone like her could have real feelings?

Peaches cautioned herself not to crumble before him. Don't take it personally, she ordered herself. Just because you like him doesn't mean you have a right to expect him to like you too. He's a pro. Deal with him professionally. Give him what he wants. But still, her hands started sweating.

'So what you got?' he asked. 'What's this deal you want to make?'

'Yuri Khordinsky,' she said. 'I have a way to bring him down.'

'Excuse me?' he said. Of course Harry Rezler knew exactly who Khordinsky was.

'You heard.'

'You think you could help us get Khordinsky?' Peaches didn't like the note of sarcasm in his voice. 'Really?'

'Through Alexei Rodokov,' Tommy chipped in.

'Rodokov?' Harry Rezler said, looking at Peaches. 'I see. He's one of your clients, is he?'

For a fleeting second, his mask of neutrality dissolved, giving Peaches a glimpse of something else: his thinly disguised revulsion. And his crushing disappointment in her.

Peaches felt herself automatically go into her defensive mode, but somehow she couldn't stomach any of the usual bullshit that sprang so readily to her mind. Seeing herself through Harry's eyes and his assumptions about her, she felt ashamed of what and who she'd become. Ashamed that her lifestyle and career had moved on from one of necessity into one of choice. Why hadn't she got out sooner, as she'd always vowed she would? Why hadn't she quit when she'd had the chance?

'No, no, not at all,' Peaches said quietly. 'But I know him well enough to know that he could give you and the Kremlin all the information they need on Khordinsky.'

The last time she'd seen Alexei Rodokov was when she'd delivered him into the room with Frankie and Tommy Liebermann. Tommy had said he'd told Rodokov everything they'd agreed he would, but he had no idea how he'd taken the information. Or how he'd reacted to Frankie being there. Peaches hadn't heard from Frankie or Alex since. But then her phone had been confiscated and she hadn't been allowed home.

Now Peaches realized that she was going to have to do something she'd never done before. She was going to have to trust Frankie. Completely. She was going to have to believe that whatever bond she had with Alex, it was stronger than the one Alex thought he had with Khordinsky. Because surely, after what Harry and Frankie had told him, Alex *had* to help them. Didn't he?

Peaches sure hoped so, but Alex was a man, and Peaches knew how men reacted to tough information. What if Alex had gone after Khordinsky himself, because of those photos? Alex might already be dead. Or even Khordinsky. Either way, Peaches would be out of bargaining chips and going straight back into Nancy Pounder's loving embrace.

Or what if Frankie and Alex had got back together and they'd taken off already? What if Frankie had left Peaches to fend for herself? And Emma too? Peaches would be just as screwed that way too.

No, Frankie wouldn't do that to her. Have faith, Peaches told herself, hoping with all her heart that she'd got the kid right. That she'd do the right thing. They were in this together, all the way. They'd agreed.

Harry Rezler laughed, as if it was all a big joke. 'And you think . . . what?'

Peaches took a deep breath. 'What if I told you that I could get Rodokov to turn state?'

Harry Rezler laughed again. Peaches felt the blood rush to her face. *What do you think I am? A fucking comedienne?* She nearly voiced the thought out loud, but managed to bite her lip just in time. Don't lose it, she told herself. Keep talking. Reel him in. Make him believe.

'What if I could?' Peaches said.

'She's telling the truth,' Tommy said. 'I've met Rodokov. He knows that Khordinsky is using him. He knows that he's Khordinsky's fall guy. I've given him proof. Documents. Evidence.'

Harry thought for a moment, his smile fading. 'Do you know what you're dealing with here?' he asked Peaches.

Peaches felt herself stiffen. 'Of course I do.' She knew better than goddamned anyone. Khordinsky had nearly killed her, for Christ's sake. Harry Rezler clearly didn't have the faintest idea. She felt the urge to tell him everything, to confide in him, building up inside her, like a charge. To tell him about Khordinsky being her father and about what he'd done to her and her mother. But most of all she wanted Harry to listen to her like a human being again.

Once again, though, she kept a lid on it. Not now, she told herself. Don't confuse the issue. Keep him focused on how you can help him, not on how much you want him to help you.

She paused and leant across the table, her eyes beseeching Harry's. 'Think about it, Harry. With Alex's help, you could nail Khordinsky for good. Think of how good it would be for international relations. The Kremlin would kiss your feet—'

Harry held up his hand. He'd got the point. And he clearly wasn't going to be drawn on his exact job title and what this would mean to him personally. He frowned. 'But Rodokov . . . ? He and Khordinsky are like this.' Harry held up his fingers twisted around each other. 'The Government has been tracking Khordinsky for years. He's got interests in Europe and in the US, none of them legal. But he's Teflon man. Nothing sticks to him. And someone clever like Rodokov, he could make out he's on your side, but it'll just be yet another scam.'

'That's what *you* think,' Peaches said. 'But we've got a case that will stick.'

'OK,' Harry said, spreading out his hands in surrender. He sighed and Peaches felt a bubble of hope rise inside her as she watched his expression finally soften and his shoulders sag, like a weightlifter who'd finally let the barbell drop, finding the strain of it all too much to sustain. 'Go on.'

'Khordinsky set up an English aristocrat called Julian Harvey with a fake mine in Russia and we've got access to the documents to prove it.'

'Slow down, slow down,' Harry said. 'Julian who?'

Peaches nodded to Tommy. 'Tell him what you told Rodokov,' she said. Quickly, Tommy told Harry Rezler the details of Julian's failed mine. Of his suicide. Of Matryoshka Enterprises in Tortola and the secret asset stripping of Forest Holdings.

In the middle of it all, Harry's eye caught Peaches' for a second. She saw that the neutrality had gone, and the revulsion and disappointment too. In its place was something that Peaches had never expected to see switched on for her again: fascination, curiosity, and the thirst for more.

'I see,' he said eventually. He paused for a long time. 'And you say Rodokov has just found all this out?'

'He's mad as hell,' Tommy said, sneaking a sideways glance at Peaches. He'd sensed the tide had turned.

'And he knows that Khordinsky abducted his girlfriend and had her drugged and had pictures taken of her. Bad pictures,' Peaches said, thinking of Frankie. 'So the point is, he'll help us.' She paused. 'If the deal's right. Right for everyone, I mean.'

'Meaning you too?' Harry said. Peaches felt her confidence grow. She took a deep breath.

'Harry, listen. I want nothing more than to walk away. If you give me this chance that's what I'll do,' she told him, looking straight at him. 'I should have done so a long time ago. I'm done with it. You've got to believe me. It's the truth.'

Harry Rezler sat for a moment. Then he stood up. He walked to the window and twisted the blind. Peaches suddenly saw the bright blue sky outside. She knew that he was weighing up whether to trust her or not. Whether to risk his career on what they'd told him.

He drew himself up before turning back to face Peaches and Tommy. She saw the flash of his badge clipped to his pants.

'There'd have to be first-hand testimony from Khordinsky,' he said. 'Rodokov would have to wear a wire. You think he'd do that?'

Peaches nodded, closing her eyes in silent thanks to whatever God had made Harry see sense. He was going to help her. He was placing his trust in her. He hadn't written her off after all.

'And Rodokov would have to cut his ties with his business for ever. The whole lot would be taken over by the authorities. We'll have to bring the Russians in on this too. He'd come out with practically nothing. That fancy yacht in the Med, his homes around the world. They'd all go. He might have to vanish himself.'

'What do you mean?' Peaches asked.

'He'll be a marked man. You screw someone like Khordinsky, you don't get to gloat about it afterwards.'

'You'd need to guarantee his safety,' Peaches said. 'His girlfriend's too.' Again Peaches found herself reeling at the risk she was taking. She didn't even know if Frankie and Alex were back together.

'I could make sure that they're offered witness protection,' Harry said. 'New identities. Total relocation. They'd have to cut all ties. No one would hear from them again. Including you.'

Peaches thought of Frankie and Alex and everything Frankie had told her. About how their best times had been when they were all alone. Well, if this came off, they'd be doing plenty more of that. 'OK, they could probably live with that.'

Harry nodded. 'Better to live than to die.' There was a beat. He drummed his fingers on the table, then bit his lip. 'OK, so say you did pull it off . . .'

'Yes?' Peaches asked, feeling a rush of hope. Now was the moment of truth.

'What you said just now about wanting to stop your . . . business practices? You'd have to stop for ever. You slide back and you'll be buried,' Harry insisted, a note of finality in his voice. 'I'd see to it personally.'

'I know you would,' Peaches said. 'But you'll never have to. I swear.'

Peaches held her breath, putting her hand on her chest. Harry Rezler believing her suddenly seemed as important to her as her freedom.

'Very well,' he said, holding eye contact with Peaches for

another second before turning to Tommy. 'You've got yourself a deal.'

'You mean I won't go to jail?' Peaches checked.

'No, you won't go to jail.'

'Guaranteed?' Tommy asked.

Harry nodded.

'But, Peaches, I'm telling you, you sure as hell better be right about Rodokov. Or everything we've talked about today . . . it's nothing but smoke . . .'

CHAPTER FORTY

In the library of Wrentham Hall, Yuri Khordinsky slapped Alexei Rodokov on the back before handing him a small shot glass of vodka. Alex smiled back, as they clinked glasses and each downed the clear oily liquid. Both men were dressed immaculately in dinner jackets and polished black Oxford shoes. Beyond the glow of the glass reading lamp on the leather-topped desk, candles flickered on the darkened windowsills, casting shadows over the bookcases. From behind the closed door came the muffled sound of laughter and voices chatting over a string quartet playing a Beatles song medley.

Khordinsky laughed and said something in Russian.

'Ah, ah,' Alex said, chiding him with a smile. 'You're the lord of the manor, Yuri. You've got to speak in English. These people expect it of us. The more practice you get the better.'

Khordinsky lit a match and held it up to his cigar. He puffed, smoke circling his head. 'OK. I appreciate you telling me these things,' he said. 'It is good to know I have someone I can trust around here. I can't say I trust Natalya. She said this was just a small show but there are catering lorries everywhere. I do not like so many people.'

Alex smiled at Khordinsky. 'Don't be too hard on her. Natalya has put on a good party tonight,' he said. 'You have all the guests here you wanted?'

'And more. The Ambassador is putting a brave face on it. He doesn't know whether to believe everything he hears in Russia. Natalya says I must be charming.'

'She's right. Having him here is good for your reputation, Yuri,' Alex said. 'And reputation, as you've told me many times yourself, is at the very heart of what we do.'

'Well, whatever they say in Russia, I must be fitting in here,' Khordinsky said, a note of satisfaction in his voice. 'I've been asked if I want to buy an English football club.'

Alex laughed. 'You going to do it?'

'I thought *you* might. You know . . . front it for me. You'd be better at the exposure. I'd invest the money, obviously.'

'I'd be happy to. It might be fun. And I like being your front man. As I've always said, you put up the money and I'll manage it for you however you want.'

'That's my boy.' Yuri paused a moment. 'You know, I have a young lady here tonight, the daughter of an associate from Dubai. I'd like you to meet her. If you were to form an attachment with her, it would be good for business.'

Alex was silent.

Khordinsky looked at him, one eyebrow raised. 'You still think about that girl? The one who ran off with the movie star?'

Alex frowned. 'Why would I?'

Khordinsky handed Alex an envelope which was lying on the desk. 'I didn't want to show you these before. But it's important for you to know the truth. About who she is. *What* she is . . .'

Alex took the envelope and looked inside. He flicked through the photographs and placed them back in the envelope.

'I see,' he said. His expression gave nothing away and Khordinsky failed to notice the tremor in Alex's voice.

Yuri studied his face closely. 'You made a mistake with her. It's time to move on.'

Alex nodded. 'I know.'

'It's OK. Forget it,' Khordinsky said. 'Come. Let's join the guests.'

They moved towards the door. Suddenly Alex stopped. 'Yuri, I've been meaning to ask you. The man whose house this was – Julian Harvey – did you know him?'

'Why?'

'Questions are being asked about him in Russia by his family. And the police also now, it seems. In connection with the Norilsk site, which I know we used to own. Harvey apparently bought the mining rights for it. He thought there were platinum deposits there. But that can't be true, can it? The land was useless – an old quarry, good for nothing except landfill. That's certainly what it said in the documentation I signed when I sold Dimitry the agenting right to it.'

Yuri put his hand on Alex's shoulder. 'Ancient history. Nothing you need to concern yourself with.'

'But, Yuri, I am concerned. Questions are being asked by the police. They're wanting to talk to me, now that Dimitry has disappeared. And because my name is on the deed of sale.'

Khordinsky squeezed Alex's shoulder. 'Don't fret, my friend. It will soon blow over.'

'I'm sure it will,' Alex said. 'I can put them off, but, Yuri, I still don't like people digging around in our affairs. We must protect ourselves. And we trust each other, right? You can tell me what happened.' Alex leant in close. 'Because I also hear that Harvey is dead now. He was a problem to be got rid of, huh? Just like that whore I killed for you the other day.'

Khordinsky nodded. He paused for a moment. 'Julian Harvey made some stupid investments. He fell for Dimitry's sales pitch. Not the first or the last time these greedy British will get themselves burnt.'

'So Dimitry sold him the rights to the land?'

'Yes. And invested with him, too, on my behalf. Long enough to triple our money.' Khordinsky smiled. 'Only Dimitry was a lot luckier than Harvey. He sold his shares before it came to light that the mine was worthless.'

'A fine stroke of luck, indeed.'

'Quite so. It was also very fortunate timing for me and Natalya.'

'Fortunate?' Alex asked.

Khordinsky smiled, tapping ash into the ashtray. 'Not only did I profit from the way Dimitry structured the deal, but I was able to buy Harvey's house as well. Harvey had put it up as collateral with the bank, you see. As soon as I started looking for a suitable house here in Britain, I knew I had to have this one. So Harvey lost it along with the mine. I was ready and waiting to make an offer the bank couldn't refuse.'

Alex raised his eyebrows. 'Very fortunate.'

'The English have a saying to cover this. Killing two birds with one stone. Yes, that's what Julian Harvey did for me.'

'He was willing to give it up?'

Khordinsky sighed, puffing on his cigar. 'No, of course not. He said he'd fight to get it back. That he'd never let down his investors. Or his stupid wife. Threatened to sue me. All sorts of fighting talk. So he had to be . . . silenced. When I pushed him, it made it easy to make his fall look like a suicide.'

'How? What about a note?'

'Vladimir who does the passports used his handwriting expert. He did a fine job. Come on now. Let's not discuss it any further. I have to show you off to all my guests.'

Inside the surveillance unit in Damien's catering lorry on the driveway outside, Emma let out a sob. She watched the small black-and-white image on the bank of screens as Alex and Khordinsky walked out of the range of the hidden cameras in the library.

'That bastard. That *bastard*!' she gasped. To hear Khordinsky admitting to Julian's murder like that – as if Julian were nothing – made fury course through her.

'You got that?' she asked. One of the secret-service team at the controls lifted up his headphone. 'Yep. All recorded.'

Next to her Harry Rezler held up his radio. 'You heard it, boys,' he said. 'It's a confession. Let's bring him in.'

'No, Harry,' Emma said. She knew that there was a huge team involved, tonight: MI5 and the British police, Harry's team and his Russian counterparts, but this was her show, hers and Peaches' and Frankie's. 'Let us finish this.'

'I wish you wouldn't. It's too dangerous,' Harry Rezler said. 'And you don't need to. We've got this place surrounded. Khordinsky's not going anywhere. You'll get your revenge anyway. You'll get to see him walking out in cuffs.'

'No,' Emma said. 'That's not good enough. That's not what

we agreed. We want to see it happening, when it's happening. I want to be there to look him in the eye and tell him that he's lost.'

'Units in place, sir,' a voice crackled from Harry's radio.

'You promised,' Emma said. She was shaking but, shocked as she was, she had to finish this in person. 'That was the deal you made with Peaches.'

There was a knock on the door of the catering lorry. Harry opened it. One of the MI5 men stood at the door.

'Is Lady Emma in there still?' he asked. 'We have her son here.'

'Cosmo!' Emma gasped, pushing past Harry Rezler.

Cosmo stood behind the catering vans on the driveway. He stubbed a cigarette out in the gravel and pulled his coat closer around him.

'Mum. What the hell's going on?' he asked. 'Uncle Pim told me you were here. What's going on with the cops?'

'Oh my God, oh my God!' Emma cried. 'My Cosmo. You're safe! Oh my darling. Where have you been?"

'In Russia. I've been to the mine. And you're not going to believe this, but I got another geologist. And we're drilling again. They think they've found palladium there. Lots and lots of it.'

CHAPTER FORTY-ONE

Peaches strode through the open front doors of Wrentham Hall arm in arm with Emma and Frankie. It had taken all of their powers of persuasion to get the authorities to agree to wait outside and allow them to confront Khordinsky like this, but it was the final part of their bargain. They were going to deliver the news to Khordinsky that he'd been screwed. Royally. They were the ones who were going to watch him squirm.

Rezler had had to vouch for them to the British, because this was a British bust on British soil. Neither Harry nor the three Russian FSB agents here to observe had any kind of jurisdiction here.

The British had agreed – reluctantly, because it meant placing shooters on the roof and inside, in case Khordinsky or one of his goons made a move on Peaches or one of the girls. But they had had no choice. Alex had refused to cooperate unless Frankie's friends had been permitted to finish what they'd started.

The massive entrance of Wrentham Hall with its domed ceiling and sweeping staircase was full of guests, the hubbub of voices almost drowning out the string quartet which was playing on the balcony. Peaches' eyes flickered towards

Damien, the party organizer she'd met earlier with Emma and Frankie. He'd been amazing, working with Harry and the British team to coordinate tonight. He nodded briefly. He knew what he had to do.

'Great place, Emma,' Peaches said, under her breath. 'Time to get it back off that bastard, don't you think?'

'Just be careful, Peaches,' Emma warned.

Peaches felt Frankie and Emma grip her arm for a moment and she felt a surge of strength. She knew how much it meant to Emma to be here at Wrentham and to have Cosmo back. And she knew, too, how much it meant to Frankie that Alex had so skilfully extracted Khordinsky's confession.

'There he is,' Frankie said. Peaches followed her gaze to where Alex stood in the doorway of a small cloakroom. He was wearing a tuxedo and he looked incredibly handsome, even if his face was creased with anxiety. Peaches had warmed to Alex in the past week, especially when she'd finally had the chance to discuss that night on *Pushkin* with her. He'd told her how sorry he was. How he'd suspected that Dieter was watching him for Khordinsky. How he'd had to make it look as if he was shooting her, even though he'd been horrified by Peaches' injuries. How he'd secretly and anonymously called the coastguard so that she'd get picked up from the remote beach.

Frankie had been right all along. Alex was one of life's good guys. He'd done the right thing then and he was doing the right thing now. Peaches knew how tough the Witness Relocation Programme would be for him. She knew what a huge sacrifice he'd made – and would continue to make, because for the rest of his life he was going to be a marked man. A Bratva target until the day he died.

Alex had spent hours with Harry and his team. Then the British and the Russians too. He'd blown the whistle on every aspect of Khordinsky's businesses and many of his associates.

And now, it seemed, everyone, the Russians and the Americans, wanted a piece of Khordinsky's ass, for murder and fraud, racketeering and money-laundering. The list went on. An almighty diplomatic tug-of-war was already raging as to where Khordinsky would stand trial. Not that it mattered to Peaches. Wherever he ended up, they were going to throw away the key.

Now, Peaches' eyes locked with Alex's. She nodded to him to let him know that the wire had worked and everything had been recorded.

'Go. It's OK,' Peaches told Frankie. 'Tell him thanks from me.' Frankie broke away and rushed into Alex's arms. He kissed Frankie and closed his eyes, holding her head against his chest.

Peaches and Emma marched on into the ballroom. She could tell that they were causing quite a stir, and not just because of the speed and purposefulness of their progress or the tough, no-nonsense business suits they were wearing. Thanks to Emma's skilful manipulation of that dreadful De Vere Burrows woman, and her close liaisons with Damien, nearly every one of Emma's acquaintances and former friends were here tonight.

Even Peaches had to admit it had been quite a hit list of people who'd shut Emma out. Now Peaches could see for herself how embarrassed and confused they were to see Emma back at Wrentham. But good old Emma, Peaches thought, she was tougher than all of them put together. And she was looking fantastic, walking tall, oozing raw charisma, like a politician who'd just been voted back in. As she gripped Peaches' arm, holding her head up high, Peaches knew that every moment of planning had been worth it.

Peaches smiled grimly, amazed as always by how unobservant people were. Peaches couldn't be more aware that the whole operation had galvanized into action around them. Above them, through the glass dome, she could see the black silhouettes of the British armed response police unit fanning out. Every third waiter she passed seemed to have the tell-tale wire of an earpiece curling at their neck.

Beside the library door, Dieter, the bodyguard she recognized from *Pushkin*, was standing eyeing up the female guests, smoking a cigarette. Peaches saw his eyes widen with shock as two sets of gloved hands reached out and jerked him backwards into the library and out of sight. Nobody even noticed.

'Who's this?' Peaches whispered to Emma as a woman in a pale pink evening gown approached them.

'Natalya Khordinsky,' Emma said.

So this was Khordinsky's wife, Peaches thought, staring at

her. She had a sharp but pretty face; her ears and throat glistened with diamond hearts. But Peaches knew they weren't hearts that had been given out of love, but to dominate. She'd seen enough abused women in her life to spot the signs instantly: a dullness to the eyes, a hesitancy in the movements. She carried an aura of fear around her.

Natalya Khordinsky looked flustered and then horrified as she recognized Emma. 'I . . . I—' she began.

'You haven't invited us, we know,' Peaches said, finishing her sentence. 'Don't worry, honey. We ain't sticking around for long.'

'There's Willy,' Emma said. 'The Ambassador.' She broke away from Peaches to stand next to a portly white-haired gentleman in a stiff dinner jacket.

And then Peaches was alone. She realized her legs were shaking as she took the final steps until she was behind Khordinsky.

He and his immediate companions were the only ones who hadn't noticed Peaches' and Emma's entrance. He was talking to a group of people and they were laughing, either genuinely charmed by their host, or more likely because they were sycophants, members of the new Emperor's court. How dare he act so smug and in command? Peaches thought. How dare he have the audacity to behave like an English gentleman when he was rotten through and through? Well, she'd show him. And them. She was going to strip their Emperor of his pretences once and for all.

Khordinksy turned round, as if sensing the change of atmosphere in the room.

The second Peaches looked into his eyes, everything that had happened on *Pushkin* came rushing back. She remembered him naked, his spit landing on her face. She pictured him kicking her in the stomach, his knife poised over her. Ready to kill her.

And she thought of Irena dying in Moscow. Alone. Broken. Murdered.

She felt a rush of adrenalin as she saw a flicker of recognition, then confusion and shock flash in Khordinsky's eyes. He was trying to place her, but couldn't, confounded by her previous disguise and his drunkenness on board *Pushkin*. And the fact that the last time he'd looked at her, he'd kicked her features to a pulp.

'What is the meaning of this?' he demanded. He glanced around him, clearly looking for Dieter.

'Why don't I make it clear for you? And for your guests,' Peaches said. Her words were loud and slow. She forced herself to breathe as, thanks to Damien's signal, the string quartet suddenly fizzled out into silence. The gossipy chit-chat of the guests turned to curious whispers, then complete silence. The air seemed to crackle with tension, like the onset of an electrical storm.

It all comes down to this, Peaches told herself. Do it. Harry would be in the room by now. She was safe. Khordinsky couldn't touch her now.

Natalya Khordinsky pushed past Peaches to her husband's side: loyal to the last, like a beaten lapdog. Pitiful, Peaches thought.

Before either of them spoke, Peaches held up her hand. She saw Emma's triumphant face as she gripped the arm of the Ambassador, making sure that he watched.

'As the Ambassador knows, there will be no party tonight,' Peaches announced. 'I'm here to inform you that your host is the subject of an international criminal investigation. He's wanted on a huge array of charges . . . including murder.'

She heard a shocked rumble as the assembled crowd took in what she'd just said. Then they collapsed back into silence as Khordinsky laughed. A terrifying, cold laugh.

'Good joke,' he said, clapping his hands. 'Now, please, everyone, carry on and enjoy yourselves. This is just a prank.' He turned his back on Peaches. 'Dieter,' he called out across the room. 'Kindly show this madwoman out. And you,' he barked at the musicians, 'keep playing. I never ordered you to stop.'

The musicians glanced nervously at Damien who shook his head.

'Dieter!' Khordinsky shouted again, anger now discolouring his face and voice. 'I thought I told you to—'

'Dieter's not coming,' Peaches interrupted. 'No one can save you now.'

Khordinsky seemed to grow inside his jacket, like a great bear rising up to its full height. Still with his back to Peaches, e dropped his cigar to the floor and ground it into the ntricately patterned tiles with the sharp heel of his shoe.

As he turned back to face her, Peaches wanted to run. Rage radiated from him like heat from a furnace. But she couldn't run. She'd come too far. She couldn't let Irena down now. She'd promised her dying mother that she would get her revenge. Well, this was it. She felt Emma staring at her, willing her to be strong. If she wasn't going to send Khordinsky into the after-life herself, she'd get the next best thing. She'd let him know that it was her who'd turned his life into a living hell. And why.

'You know they have been waiting for you for years, but now we have given them the evidence they needed.'

'Yuri, what's going on?' Natalya Khordinsky asked as Khordinsky's eyes locked with Peaches', like the horns of two bulls. 'What's going on? Make her stop.'

Khordinsky snapped something at her in Russian.

'Who the hell are you?' he hissed at Peaches.

'Don't you recognize me?' Peaches said, trying to keep her voice from shaking with the pent-up fury she felt. 'You should. I was the one you tried to rape on *Pushkin*. Before you nearly beat me to death.'

Khordinsky's eyes roamed the crowd like searchlights, look-ing for Alex. But Alex would probably already be gone, Peaches thought. Far away. Never to be seen again. Safe from Khordinsky for ever.

She saw Natalya Khordinsky gasp and cover her mouth.

'But no, as you can see, Alex didn't kill me like you ordered him to. And you won't find Alex now. You see, I am just *one* of the ways he has betrayed you.'

'Who are you?' Khordinsky demanded of Peaches. Louder this time.

'I am the child of Irena Cheripaska,' Peaches said. 'Your wife.'

Natalya gripped Khordinsky's arm. He threw her off.

'Remember Irena?' Peaches hissed, anger rushing through her now in a torrent. Her fists were clenched. Tears filled her eyes. It was all she could do not to punch him in the face. 'How you burnt out her eyes in a jealous rage? Surely you remember. You had your thugs kill her finally in Moscow. Only a few weeks ago.'

Khordinsky went pale. 'You're . . .'

'Anna. Yes. The one that you told Gorsky to sell. When I was three.'

'No,' Khordinsky said. He didn't move, but she sensed something about him shrink back.

'And, unfortunately, that makes me your child, too,' she continued. '*Daddy.*'

Even now, after everything, for a split second, she wondered whether those words would touch Khordinsky. Whether, in some far-fetched fantasy, he might beg her for her forgiveness. Might throw himself into her arms and embrace her as his lost child.

But Khordinsky clearly wasn't in the business of closure. His shark's eyes stayed blank. 'Lying whore,' he spat.

Peaches felt a steeliness creeping over her. Her first assessment, as always, held true. He didn't give a damn about her. About his own flesh and blood. He hadn't then, and he sure as hell didn't now.

'You want to see the scar on my back?'

'You're lying,' he repeated, but a slick of sweat had broken out on his brow. His eyes looked murderous. 'Irena betrayed me. That child was her lover's. Tomin's.'

'No. I was *your* child. You want the DNA test to prove it?'

Suddenly the PA system burst into life. It was Khordinsky's voice recorded:

'Not only did I profit from the way Dimitry structured the deal, but I was able to buy Harvey's house as well. Harvey had put it up as collateral with the bank, you see. As soon as I started looking for a suitable house here in Britain, I knew I had to have this one. So Harvey lost it along with the mine. I was ready and waiting to make an offer the bank couldn't refuse.'

'Very fortunate.'

'The English have a saying to cover this. Killing two birds with one stone. Yes, that's what Julian Harvey did for me.'

'He was willing to give it up?'

'No, of course not. He said he'd fight to get it back. That he'd never let down his investors. Or his stupid wife. Threatened to sue me. All sorts of fighting talk. So he had to be . . . silenced. When I pushed him, it made it easy to make his fall look like a suicide.'

There was a sudden noise as everyone started talking, gasping, hardly able to believe what they'd just heard. Khordinsky looked around at the crowd staring at him.

Suddenly he moved, grabbing Natalya around the neck. He fumbled for a moment, reaching inside his jacket. Then he pressed his pistol against her temple. At the sight of Khordinsky's gun, everyone started screaming.

'Stay back!' he shouted. 'Stay back or I'll shoot.'

People started running for the exits.

Natalya was whimpering as he dragged her backwards towards the corridor.

Then Alex appeared, sweeping through the retreating crowd as if he was swimming against the tide. 'Yuri. No. Drop the gun. Leave her. It's over.'

'You!' Khordinsky roared. He didn't hesitate. He pointed his gun at Alex and fired.

Peaches watched in horror as Alex fell to the floor.

Then she screamed as Khordinsky turned his gun on her. He grinned wolfishly as he aimed. But then he seemed to trip, stumbling sideways, Natalya with him.

Peaches watched in confusion as a red patch of blood bloomed like a flower on Natalya's pink satin dress. Natalya stared down at it, as if she couldn't believe it.

Then her knees buckled and she slumped to the floor, taking Khordinsky down with her. Her head hit the black and white tiles with a crack. A thin line of blood trickled from her mouth.

'Drop your weapon!' Armed police closed in on Khordinsky.

Khordinsky scrabbled on the floor, desperately looking for an escape route. But he was surrounded. There was no way out.

He dropped his pistol then. It fell on Natalya's body, jogging her elbow before it clattered to the floor. Ignoring her, he slowly sat and raised his hands above his head.

Amongst the screams of his guests and the panic all around him, he sat there like a rock. Cold and inhuman to the last. He said nothing as the police cuffed him, yanking him to his feet.

That's when Peaches caught his eye – only for a fraction of a second, but long enough for him to know that she'd witnessed his fall. That's how she'd remember him: chained like a dog.

She knew then that she'd get nothing more from him. And

needed nothing more. She'd had her revenge. He was dead to her now.

It was to the living she had to turn next.

Peaches rushed to Frankie's side. Her young friend was crouched on the floor, cradling her beautiful Alex in her arms.

His dress shirt was bloodstained and his breath came in short, shallow gasps. He groaned as a spasm of pain rocked him.

'It's all right, baby. It's going to be all right,' Frankie said. 'Will someone please help? Get an ambulance!' she screamed.

Peaches put her arms around Frankie and squeezed her tight as she sobbed. For the first time in her life, she found herself saying a prayer.

Time slowed then. Paramedics rushed in, tending to Alex, lifting him on to a stretcher and carrying him away. Frankie never left his side.

Police had rushed in, trying to control the hysterical crowd.

Peaches stood and stared out of the window at the flashing lights against the night sky. She could see Khordinsky being pushed into the back of a car. She'd wanted to kill him, but as the car door slammed, she understood that the law was the best punishment for him. Khordinsky wasn't above the law. Nobody was. Not even her. She saw that now.

Everything was over for them both. But Khordinsky was off to a dark place, whilst Peaches saw a sliver of freedom opening up before her. So long as Alex lived. So long as his life was not the price for bringing Khordinsky down.

Suddenly Emma was by her side. Peaches saw that Emma's eyes were filled with tears. She too was watching the car carrying Khordinsky speeding off into the night.

'We did it,' she said. 'We did it.'

EIGHT MONTHS LATER

Frankie breathed in cold fresh air and pulled her chunky jumper more closely around her as she stepped out of the front door of the cosy log cabin.

'*Hola*, Gabi!' One of the ranch hands waved to her. She did a double-take, before waving back.

It was still strange getting used to her new identity as Mrs Gabriella Mendola. And even stranger calling Alex, 'Juan' in public. But it was a very, very small price to pay for their freedom. It still amazed her that they'd swapped their old lives so easily for this. But she wouldn't go back, even if she could.

Before she'd arrived here, she'd no idea that Argentina would be so beautiful. Thanks to Harry Rezler they'd really lucked out. After Alex had recovered in a secure British Government hospital, they'd both been relocated through a witness protection programme to a ranch just outside San Carlos de Bariloche in Patagonia. At the time, it had sounded as if they were being sent to the end of the earth, but now, eight months after the fateful events in Wrentham, Frankie felt as if she'd been sent to paradise.

Now that spring was here, the trees were spectacularly bursting into fresh life and the sky was an intoxicating deep blue. She walked down the track to the paddock where Alex was training the new horses.

She climbed up on to the bottom rung of the fence and waved at him. He tipped his gaucho hat and waved back, cantering across the paddock on the large dappled chestnut.

'You OK, Mrs M.?' Alex asked. She laughed and climbed up one more rung and he leant down and kissed her. The horse snorted steam in the cold air.

Frankie smiled. 'Don't worry about me. I don't want you to get too tired,' she said.

The gunshot wound had healed, but although he was mobile enough to ride, he was still in pain by nightfall. Yet Alex loved his job and he'd already set up a riding class for the local kids. In fact, Andrés, the ranch manager, was talking about promoting him. Each night she and Alex practised their Spanish together. Every day they were fitting in more and more.

'I just stopped by to tell you that I'm going into town. I'll see you later,' she said.

He blew her a kiss and winked. 'I love you,' he mouthed, before turning the horse away.

Frankie loved driving the bashed-up jeep that she and Alex had bought. On the ride down into town from the ranch, one side of the road was a forest of fragrant tall pine trees, their shadows flickering across the tarmac. She opened the window, breathing in their incredible smell. A train rattled by on the tracks through the trees and she smiled.

Today was the day she was going to do what she'd been discussing with Alex. She knew it went against all the rules they'd been given, but Frankie needed to do this one last thing. Then she'd be able to rest.

As she began the descent down into town, the view took her breath away. The Lago Nahuel Huapi spread out before her, a stunning expanse of dark blue water, dotted with pine-green islands. The snow-topped peaks of the Andes rose in the distance, mystical and enchanting.

Alex already had plans to save enough to buy a small sailing boat next summer. They might even make the trip all the way across the lake to Chile. Frankie wondered whether he missed *Pushkin* or jetting around the world, but if he did, he never said so. Like Frankie, he seemed to relish the simplicity of their new life together. And now she felt more than ever that they'd always been meant to live this way.

The bell in the old church was chiming midday in the small town as Frankie pulled up outside the general store, which doubled as a post office and café. At this time of year, the town was less crowded with tourists. Frankie loved the way everyone stopped to talk to each other and she smiled now at the kids who were skipping on the pavement.

Inside the store, football was blaring out from the TV bracketed to the pockmarked wall. A little dog nosed its way through the swing door into the kitchen and Frankie called out hello. There was a strong smell of coffee and cigarettes. Behind the swing door, she could hear Señora Delgado shouting at the dog in rapid Spanish.

Frankie smiled and stood by the creaky circular rack of postcards, deliberating for ages before choosing the right one. Then she turned to the dusty rack of magazines, picking up the latest edition of *Hola*! She smiled. Todd Lands was on the cover. Some things never changed.

'Señor Lands, he's handsome, no?' Señora Delgado said. Frankie jumped, realizing she'd been so absorbed she hadn't noticed her shuffling behind the counter. Señora Delgado had taken a liking to Frankie and made a point of speaking in English.

'He sure is,' Frankie agreed.

'My daughter, she has pictures of him all over her walls. He's a good Catholic boy. Maybe one day she marry him, eh? It's a waste for a man like that not to have a wife.' Señora Delgado picked up the small crucifix around her neck and kissed it.

Frankie laughed. If only she knew the truth.

Todd had been photographed at the Oscar ceremony in LA after the triumphant run of his Broadway play and his surprise nomination for his role in *Blue Zero*. Frankie touched his face on the magazine, feeling a pang of regret that she'd never see him again. A new unknown actress was standing next to him on the red carpet in a stunning evening gown and high heels, looking artfully bewildered as she held on to Todd's hand. How long would it be, Frankie wondered, before the press were all gossiping about the latest pretty woman in Todd Lands's life? It would break Señora Delgado's heart.

But if Frankie's brush with glamour had taught her anything, it was that she wouldn't swap it for what she had now: living this simple existence with the man of her dreams in total anonymity. A fresh and wonderful new start.

She went to the counter and paid for the magazine and the small postcard she planned on sending. She wouldn't write anything on it. She'd promised Alex. But when she received it, Emma would know who it was from.

She took her change from Señora Delgado, counting the coins in her hand even though she trusted her implicitly. On their budget, Frankie had to look after every cent. Still, she just about had enough for a chocolate bar. She put it on the counter.

Señora Delgado looked at the chocolate bar and then at Frankie. Her toothy smile was full of joy. 'It's a boy, huh?' she whispered, nodding at Frankie.

Frankie gasped. For a moment, she thought about denying it, but she was already blushing. 'How did you know?' she asked.

Señora Delgado smiled. 'I know,' she said. 'It's written all over your face. So serene. So happy.' She patted Frankie's hand. 'I told Pablo: I think Señora Mendola is having a boy.'

Frankie ran her hands over her stomach, trying to imagine how it would feel in a few weeks when her bump was bigger and she started to show. She smiled back. She didn't mind whether it was a boy, but secretly she hoped her and Alex's baby was a girl. She had a feeling it was. And Frankie knew that her future happiness would grow from the seeds of the past. And when her baby girl was born, Frankie knew exactly what she'd call her: Peaches Emma.

Emma stood in Wrentham Hall, her suitcases and large bags by her feet. She stared through the empty ballroom. Dust motes swirled in the shafts of bright sunlight coming through the dome. Emma stared down at the spot where Natalya Khordinsky had died, seeing only the black and white tiles. No trace of blood. No ghosts.

She'd pictured this moment so many times in her mind and now she closed her eyes, breathing in the smell of the dust. Her dust. Her history.

She smiled. At last, she was home.

Despite Wrentham being one of Khordinsky's seized assets, her team of lawyers had managed to negotiate with the Russian authorities and enabled her to get it back.

Now that the workmen had nearly cleared away all traces of the Khordinskys, she could finally move back in and begin the task of reacquainting herself with her possessions and making it a home once more.

But she knew that even if she could put back every picture in its original position, it would never be the same.

Emma was glad all the press attention had died down. Khordinsky's arrest at Wrentham Hall had made headlines all over the world. And there'd been another flurry of interest after Khordinsky had been found dead in prison: assassinated in the showers by a fellow inmate, who'd already been serving a life sentence. Khordinsky had been stabbed so fast and hard, he'd bled to death before the prison guards had even had time to react to his screams.

The papers could only speculate on who'd ordered the hit from the outside. It could have been any one of a number of Khordinsky's powerful former business associates. Or another crime lord asserting his dominance. Or simply the Bratva protecting their own interests, just in case Khordinsky made a deal.

Emma didn't care. After what he'd done to Julian, he didn't deserve any kind of justice. And his death had saved everyone the trauma of an expensive and lengthy trial. All that mattered was that he was now gone. Nothing but dust himself.

'Hey, Mum, we've got our first piece of mail,' Cosmo said, coming up behind her. 'Look, a postcard. There's no writing on it. Just our address. It must be a mistake.'

Emma took the postcard from him and turned it over and looked at the picture of the beautiful lake in Argentina.

'It's not a mistake,' she said, feeling tears well up in her eyes. She smiled and held the card close to her chest. Emma had made Frankie promise that if she was happy she'd send just one postcard to let Emma know she was OK.

'Oh, and Uncle Pim left this for us,' Cosmo said, holding up a bottle of champagne and two crystal flutes. 'Shall we?' he asked with a grin.

Emma couldn't wait to see Pim. He was a changed man now

that he'd recouped his investment. Thanks to Cosmo's tenacity, the true extent of the reserves of palladium in the Norilsk mine had been revealed. They were immense, enough for everyone to more than double their original investment, apart from Sergeyokov, of course, who'd sold all his shares. But Emma didn't care about the money, only that Pim hadn't lost Lechley Hall and he'd now be able to restore it properly.

After she'd toasted Wrentham in the ballroom with Cosmo, she took her champagne glass into the study and set up her laptop.

Whilst it was booting up, she took a picture from her case and hung it on a vacant hook on the wall. Raising a glass to the picture of Julian, she said, 'Welcome home, my darling.'

She'd had the canvas made from a photograph she'd taken of him when they'd been skiing. Now she stood back to look at him. The tears she'd been expecting didn't fall. The acute pain she'd felt for so long had given way to something else: a dull ache. Of loss? Of longing? Of regret? She wondered which it was.

Yes, she missed him. She missed him all the time. But so much had happened since he'd gone that she felt the time when he'd been here was consigned to the distant past. Locked inside a time vault to which she no longer knew if she had the key.

Her poor Julian. What had gone through his mind the second Khordinsky had pushed him out of the window in that grim Siberian hotel? It was a question she thought of often. She somehow suspected that his last thought would have been of her and Cosmo. Of how their future might become as grim as his own.

She desperately hoped he hadn't died feeling that he'd let them down, because he hadn't. He'd been deceived. And now that she'd punished the deceiver, their future hadn't turned out to be grim at all.

Apart from the one terrible fact that Julian was no longer here to share it with them.

Emma sighed. She'd hoped that it would have been easier knowing that Julian was killed deliberately rather than trying to live with his suicide, but the truth was that neither one was better. There would always be an empty space where he should have been.

She hoped too that she'd be able to move on. In time. She'd try. She knew it's what he would have wanted. But in the meantime, she was determined to keep herself busy and useful. And what better way to start, she thought, than by setting out to make the world a better place.

Emma had visited Norilsk six months ago and witnessed the devastation the mining industry had wreaked across the region. On her return she'd sold her Platinum Holdings shares. She'd be more careful about where she invested her money in the future. Her first step towards independence from Julian's memory was that the business decisions she took from now on would be based on her own set of rules. And absolutely within the letter of the law.

She was using all the money she'd made from the mine to set up an environmental charity. Her first project was going to be in Russia. She was going to plant trees – a whole forest of them – around the mine itself in Norilsk.

And she and Cosmo were going to run the eco-community he'd planned, but here at Wrentham instead of up in Scotland.

Emma propped Frankie's card up on her desk and smiled. Then she opened her emails. There was one from David, a reply to her invitation, saying that he'd be delighted to meet her and Cosmo in a few weeks' time in Switzerland to ski.

Then she opened the Write Message icon. There was only one person she really needed to tell that she was home.

On the other side of the Atlantic, in her beach house, Peaches heard the bleep of an incoming message. The curtains billowed in on the morning breeze, rising up above the packing boxes as she edged around the piled-up furniture to reach her laptop on the table.

Peaches smiled as she read and reread Emma's email. She could tell how happy Emma was. She quickly replied, telling her that she'd be there for the skiing holiday too. Then she looked around her and put her hands on her hips.

Everything was going into storage whilst she went on a long vacation – or a well-earned sabbatical, as Tommy Liebermann had put it – and decided what she was going to do next. But suddenly, the next few months seemed huge and daunting.

Even though her deal with Harry Rezler had meant that the details of the Depravity Night party had stayed private, Peaches had received no thanks from the guests whose asses she'd saved along with her own. All those initially arrested alongside her had been quietly released, much – Peaches had been delighted to discover – to the fury of Detective Pounder.

But Peaches had paid the price too. It seemed that even a brief brush with the law had been way too much for the majority of her former clientele to handle. She'd been stonewalled, blacklisted from everywhere. She couldn't even get a table in Larry's any more. It was as if she'd been completely shut out from the industry she'd helped create.

Everything the British social élite had done to Emma after Julian's death, Hollywood's own aristocracy had now done to Peaches. And while there was no denying that the rejection sucked on a personal level, on a deeper level it had taught her how tenuous and ultimately temporary her position as pleasure-provider to the rich and famous had always been.

She might have been Queen Bee for a while, but LA was a ravenous beast with an insatiable appetite. It didn't do sentiment, and had rampaged on without her in the blink of an eye.

It was kind of funny in one way at least, she supposed. She'd struggled to make Harry Rezler believe she'd give up the game as part of her deal. Well, in actual fact, the game had already given her up and revoked her right to play.

Only Murray Seagram-Cohen had remembered Peaches. She'd been touched to learn he'd left her his signet ring in his will. The clunky gold ring was useless to her, but at least his arrogant family were upset about it. And Peaches had a soft spot for Murray. Always would.

No, she'd done with this town now, which was why she was leaving. She'd already sold Delancy Heights, the condo in Mexico and her controlling interest in the lingerie business to Tommy Liebermann. And if Peaches ever felt a pang of longing for the cut and thrust of her old life, she consoled herself with the thought of how lucky she was. She was free, wearing a silk dressing gown and cashmere-lined slippers looking at the Californian beach, when she could be wearing Day-Glo dungarees in a penitentiary exercise yard.

Yet now, as she walked out on to the porch with her cup of coffee and looked at the fresh day and the clean, wave-washed beach, she sighed. She wondered, as she often did, whether she'd miss this place. Having given up her old life, she couldn't help comparing herself to a reformed junkie. Sure, she didn't want to go back to the errors of her old ways, but she had yet to find the new life that would replace it, which was why she so desperately needed a change of scene. Without one, she'd never shake the feeling that there must be some kind of reward waiting out there for her for being this good.

She'd feel better when she was on the airplane tonight, she told herself. A new place would be sure to cheer her up.

Just then, something caught her eye. She shaded her eyes against the glare of the sun. A man was walking along the beach towards her, his shadow stretched out before him on the sand, as if he was reaching out to touch her.

'Jesus Christ,' she said. It couldn't be . . .

But it was. Harry Rezler was walking up to her house.

She hadn't seen him for months, not since she'd left England. But she'd thought about him plenty. Too much. Always wondering whether she should get in touch and thank him: for cutting her a deal; for getting Emma back her house; for enabling Frankie and Alex to disappear. And for helping them all to bring Khordinsky down.

But she'd always stopped herself. She hadn't been able to forget his face, and the way he'd treated her with professional courtesy, even after Khordinsky's arrest, when she'd found herself hankering for something more.

Had he still been angry with her? she'd wondered. For who she'd turned out to be? Or because he'd known it would be him who'd take the rap for allowing Peaches to confront Khordinsky, as a result of which Natalya Khordinsky and Alex had been shot? Peaches had never got the chance to ask. Harry had already left when she'd gone to say goodbye. The British had been in charge. It was they who'd debriefed her before finally letting her go.

Then back in the States, it had been colleagues of Harry's who'd taken over. She hadn't seen nor heard from Harry again.

But now, here he was, walking back into her life.

He stopped at the bottom of the wooden steps leading down

from her porch to the beach. He didn't smile. Didn't speak. Gave no clue as to why he was here.

'Hey,' he said, as if he was just passing by and this was something he did every day.

She'd thought about him so often, but now that he was standing here, she had no idea what else to say to him. She tried to read him, but she couldn't see his eyes through the lenses of his shades.

There was a moment of silence as he continued to stare. She knew that she should take control of the situation: make chit-chat, invite him in for a coffee, behave normally, but Peaches wasn't sure what normal was any more. Only that he was here and he shouldn't be. And she wanted to know why.

Was there some part of the investigation that he still had to cover? Surely there couldn't be more questions? Peaches had had enough of answering questions. She needed to move on. She *had* moved on.

But Harry didn't look like he was here in a work capacity. He was wearing jeans and a loose blue shirt. His arms were tanned and he looked five years younger than when she'd last seen him. Now he took off his sunglasses and his eyes were soft.

'You're here,' she said, immediately regretting saying something so obvious.

Harry Rezler shrugged. 'I was in the neighbourhood. I thought I'd stop by.'

She stared at him, wondering whether this was as big a lie as it sounded. A part of her hoped it wasn't, that this really was a social call, that he was here because . . . because he just wanted to know she was OK. But at the same time she knew it was wishful thinking. He couldn't have made the trip all the way from Washington just for pleasure. There had to be more to it than that.

'So . . . you heard about Khordinsky?' he asked.

Peaches nodded, deflated. So he *was* here on business. He wanted to talk about Khordinsky. How silly of her to think that he might be here for another reason. Any other reason. Khordinsky was all they had in common.

'I'm sorry,' Harry said.

Peaches raised her eyebrow. 'He had it coming. Why should I care?'

Harry Rezler sighed heavily. He put his foot on the bottom step. 'I read all the background files, Peaches. About Gorsky . . . Irena . . . Rockbine too. Why didn't you tell me all of that stuff in the first place?'

Peaches felt herself blush. Then stiffen. Why had he checked up on her? Why did it matter to him? 'I didn't need your pity. I was handling it myself. I survived, didn't I?'

'Yeah. You sure did.'

His eyes stayed connected with hers and she suddenly felt confused. A jittery nervous feeling started in her stomach.

She was just work to Harry Rezler, so why was he making her feel like this? Why did him talking to her about her personal life throw her into such a flap?

'So, how's tricks?' she asked, deliberately lightening her tone, trying to move the conversation on. 'Any more bad guys come your way?'

Harry shook his head. 'Khordinsky was the one I was after. The slippery fish I'd wasted four years of my life trying to catch. You know, when you walked into my office that day, you just about saved my career.'

He stared at her and Peaches felt the unfamiliar sensation turn up a notch. She didn't know what to say. This was certainly news to her.

'You never did give me your job title and I never did figure it out,' she said. 'Were you CIA?'

Harry smiled and rubbed his face and she knew that even if he was, he'd never tell her.

'It doesn't matter what I was. I dropped by to tell you that I'm retiring,' he continued.

'Retiring?'

He shrugged. 'Now Khordinsky's done with, they've got no further use for me. Sure, there're still bad guys out there, but I haven't got the energy for them. I'm all done.'

'Me too.'

'You are?' he asked. 'Truly? Only . . . ' His eyes locked on hers in a way that belied the words that followed. 'I . . . wouldn't do anything about it, even if you weren't.'

'I made you a promise, didn't I? I'm all wound up with that. And I can't say I'm sorry. I don't even have a cell phone any more. It's kinda quiet, but I'm getting used to it.'

Something altered in Harry then, right in front of her eyes. His shoulders seemed to relax, as if he'd just let out a long, deep breath. For the first time since he'd got here, he smiled at her properly. Openly. Like someone who'd just spotted an old friend. Or maybe a new one, Peaches thought.

'So what are you going to do?' he asked.

'Travel,' she said, swallowing. That tingling feeling inside her still hadn't gone away. 'See what happens, I guess. I'm leaving. In fact, I'm all packed and ready to go.' She turned to look back inside her house at the packing boxes, but all she saw was her own reflection in the large glass door. She was still in her robe, her hair flying in the breeze. And she saw Harry on the step below her and he suddenly looked as if he was kneeling. Behind him was only sand, sea and sky.

She turned back to face him. He looked on the point of saying something, but instead he put his hands in his pockets.

'Well, good luck, Peaches,' he said.

He turned and began to walk away.

Panic stabbed her like a lance. She knew that if she let him walk out of her life now, she'd never see him again.

'Harry?' she called after him.

He stopped and turned. 'Yeah?'

She stared at him. Was she mad? She shouldn't do this. It could go so badly wrong. Peaches' whole life had been built on risks, but somehow this was a bigger risk than them all.

'Why don't you come too?' she asked.

'Pardon me?'

'Why don't we go together?' she hurried on, before she could change her mind. 'Like a joint retirement trip. I haven't got that many plans, except a bit of skiing in Europe . . .'

Harry looked truly shocked. And then for a terrible moment, as the corners of his mouth started to crinkle, she thought he was going to laugh in her face.

But instead he grinned. He walked towards her, rubbing the side of his face. Abashed. He stopped at the bottom of the steps. 'You *really* want us to go together? You and me?'

Now that the question was out, now that he'd asked it and seemed to be seriously considering it, her answer was simple. Natural and automatic. Something she should have said a long time ago.

'Sure. Why not?'

She could feel her heart hammering. This was such a huge, crazy idea. She hardly knew him. She hadn't even so much as kissed him. And yet here she was, asking him to go around the world with her. She suddenly felt stupidly, girlishly excited. She wanted him to say yes so badly.

Harry laughed. 'Well, you know . . . that may not be such a bad idea . . .'

Relief flowed straight into excitement. 'You think so?' she said, laughing.

She started down the steps, just as he started up. They found themselves face to face. Inches apart.

Harry reached out and touched her face. His hand was so soft. So gentle. She felt herself quiver.

'Hell, Peaches,' he said, 'I guess it might be a lot easier if I was *with* you instead of just *thinking* about you every second of the day.'

Peaches gasped, stunned by his admission. Thrilled by it. She stared at him, her heart racing. She'd always had all the answers on the tip of her tongue when it came to men. She'd always known what to say. But for the first time in her life, she was tongue-tied.

And as she looked into his eyes, all the deliciously normal things she'd never done suddenly became a possibility and she felt so awed by the prospect, she wanted to cry.

Harry laughed. 'Say something.'

'OK,' she said, biting her lip, her smile bursting out of her. 'Well, Harry Rezler, how about we start off our trip by going to get some breakfast?'

'OK,' he said.

As he took her hand, she felt as if she were floating on a cloud. And she realized that she'd never felt this feeling before. This feeling of absolute peace.

ACKNOWLEDGEMENTS

Thanks to my wonderful agent, Vivienne Schuster, and to Carol Jackson at Curtis Brown. Also my editor Linda Evans, Larry Finlay, Bill Scott-Kerr, Alison Barrow, Katrina Whone and the fabulous team at Transworld.

For expertise on banking, yachting, hacking and international matters, many thanks to Katy and Kev Whelan, Rupert and Toni Savage, Jacob Potts, Laurel Lefkow, Yann Tricard, Becky Spier. Also thanks to Dawn Howarth. And most especially to Emlyn Rees, to whom this book is dedicated.

087
647
2506
Joe Mumi
Ball